The Stone Mystery

Also By Martin Singer

The Gravity Gone Series

Desperate Measures

The Chesterville Mystery's

Beyond the Bridge

Gravity Gone
The Stone Mystery

Martin Singer

SLEEP WRITER
PUBLISHING

Sleep Writer Publishing

Published in 2026 by Sleep Writer Publishing

Third Edition

This book is a work of fiction. Names, characters, places, and incidents either are the product of the author's imagination or are used fictitiously. Any resemblance to actual persons, living or dead, event or locales is entirely coincidental.

ISBN 978-1-7349937-8-3 Paperback

ISBN 978-1-7349937-9-0 Digital

Library of Congress Control Number: 2026907614

Cover design by: Rebecca Covers

Proofread by Sandra Starkey

Printed in the United States of America

PROLOGUE

September 5, 1977
Laubner Labs, Palo Alto, California, 8:15 a.m.

The air thrummed with anticipation as Doctor Del Jacobson stood in the control room, his heart pounding in rhythm with the hum of equipment. Today was the moment they had all been waiting for: the first test of the Magnetic Mirror fusion reaction chamber, MGFC1, a project that had consumed nineteen long months and over one hundred million dollars.

He glanced at the technicians around him, their faces a mix of excitement and anxiety. This test was more than just a firing; it was their collective ambition, wrapped in steel and magnets. He could almost feel the weight of Edward Lexington's legacy pressing down upon him—the brilliant mind who had envisioned this design but would never witness its completion.

"Are we ready, Mr. Yung?" His voice steadied, but he could hear the slight tremor beneath it.

"Yes, sir," Don Yung replied, his own confidence palpable.

"Turn on the cooling system and bring it up to full velocity." The room filled with a dull hum, a sound that signaled the beginning of a new era—or perhaps its end.

"Cooling system at full flow," Yung reported.

"Good. Now slowly bring the magnet up to fifty percent. Let's keep it from overheating this time." Jacobson's skepticism hung in the air. He had seen too many projects falter to let hope blind him.

The machinery creaked as it responded to the magnetic forces. Precautions had been strict; they had secured every ferrous object nearby, aware of the potential dangers lurking in their ambitious endeavor.

“Temperatures around the magnet?” Jacobson asked, trying to keep his focus sharp.

“Twelve degrees above normal for this power level, sir,” Yung answered, his brow furrowing slightly.

“Increase coolant flow by ten liters per minute. We can’t afford to let this run hot,” Jacobson ordered, his anxiety creeping back.

Yung adjusted the controls, and Jacobson hesitated, his instincts screaming at him to be cautious. They had pushed systems to their limits before, and he wasn’t about to let pride lead them into disaster today.

“Everyone clear?” he asked, locking eyes with his team. The nods that followed reassured him only slightly.

“Bring the magnet up to full power—slowly,” he instructed, watching as Yung adjusted the dial. The power levels jumped, and the machine groaned in protest. Jacobson’s heart raced as the temperature readings climbed alarmingly.

“Hold power at eighty percent,” he said, trying to keep his voice steady against the growing tension.

“Pressure in coolant tubes?”

“Eighty PSI.”

“Good. Increase coolant flow another ten liters per minute.” Frustration seeped into his tone as he made a mental note to have engineering look into the cooling issues. “They assured me this would work.”

“Temperature’s coming down, but we’re at ninety-five percent of recommended,” Yung said, unease creeping into his voice.

“Go to ninety percent on the magnet,” Jacobson ordered, his pulse quickening.

“One hundred two percent of temperature limits, sir.”

“Bring her up to full—slowly!” he warned, as the machine shuddered under the pressure.

“Holding steady,” Yung confirmed, but Jacobson felt the tension building, the barely contained energy in the room palpable as they approached the moment of truth.

“Start countdown to firing the DT,” he commanded, bracing himself for the unknown.

As the plasma injection fired into the chamber, a wave of heat washed over him and then—a rumble from the chamber’s rear, deep and ominous.

“What’s that?” Panic flared within him.

“I hear it too,” Yung replied, though they both felt the tension tightening around them.

“Sounds like a freight train. This can’t be good. Begin shutdown!” Jacobson's mind raced, knowing the fusion reaction couldn’t be stopped instantly. They had to proceed with caution to avoid catastrophic failure.

“DT flow off,” Yung confirmed, urgency in his tone.

A louder thump followed, sending a shock through the control room, accompanied by the blaring alarm.

“Failure in primary chamber! Leaking tritium into outer chamber!” Yung shouted, his voice cutting through the chaos.

“Seal the building! Silence the alarm!” Jacobson barked, his heart racing as Yung rushed to comply. The eerie silence that followed was thick with fear.

The phone rang, and Jacobson snatched it up, breathless. “What’s going on?” Doctor Hunt demanded on the other end.

“Major failure—a breach in the inner chamber causing a tritium leak.”

“How bad?”

“Hard to say. Hang on.” He covered the mouthpiece, glancing anxiously at Yung.

“Temperature and magnet status?” he asked.

“Painfully slow.”

Another thump echoed, and Jacobson's gut tightened.

“Inner chamber fell,” Yung said, his face pale.

“Confirmed breach of external wall.”

“Uranium rods temperature?”

“Safe,” Yung replied, but relief was short-lived.

“Helium coolant leak. We need to vent to prevent fire,” Yung added.

“We need to vent,” Jacobson said, urgency flooding his voice.

"Alert environmental. Hope winds are favorable," Hunt said.

"Vents open. Lowering temperature," Yung reported, but the moment felt futile.

"Fire in section three," Yung nearly yelled, fear creeping into his voice.

"Containable?" Jacobson asked, but silence was the only answer.

"Cause?"

"Coolant pressure loss overheated the main pump. Isolated, no explosion risk. Fire suppression active," Yung confirmed.

Jacobson willed himself to stay focused, glancing at the monitors. Thick gas filled the room; the chamber's bottom appeared collapsed.

"Temperatures improving?" he asked, desperation creeping into his voice.

"Still there, Hunt?"

"Yes."

"Facility on phase one lockdown. Stay inside until it's all-clear. Emergency personnel en route. Any uranium tube breach?" Hunt asked.

"No, just tritium release within short-term exposure limits," Jacobson replied, ending the call.

"No second firing for this chamber," he said quietly.

His team exchanged shocked looks, their hopes dashed.

So much for one hundred million dollars and eighteen months' work, he thought bitterly as he looked at the monitors, the reality of their failure beginning to sink in.

The wind blew favorably as the Fusion Center vented its contents. Jacobson could only hope the nearby communities would be safe, but the unease lingered in the air. Laubner Labs, the area's largest employer, had now become synonymous with catastrophe. As reports of tritium release spread, he felt the gravity of their situation settle heavily on his shoulders—this was only the beginning of the fallout.

# # #

As Dave Holland stepped into the chaotic aftermath of the MGFC1 reactor accident, he felt the weight of responsibility settle on his shoulders. They had assigned him and Cory Hapner to lead the investigation, a daunting task requiring them to manage a twenty-person hazmat team. The pressure was intense; they had only six months for removal and a year for the full investigation. The stakes were high.

Three days after the disaster, he and Cory entered the sealed chamber clad in cumbersome protective gear. Fitting into the suits was a challenge, his broad frame straining against the material, while Cory struggled with his own size and that long blond ponytail that seemed to get in the way. Dave's heart raced as he took in the destruction around them. The sight of the cooling system failure and the breach in the chamber from extreme heat sent a chill down his spine.

Then something caught his eye—a faint glow among the scattered debris. Intrigued, he knelt down, brushing the dust aside. What he uncovered sent a thrill through him: a cluster of strange, luminescent stones embedded in the wreckage. Cory joined him, and they exchanged glances filled with curiosity and excitement. Carefully, they began to collect samples, each stone pulsing with an eerie light that hinted at secrets beyond their understanding.

Six months later, they stood surrounded by sixty barrels and three freight containers, preparing for transport to a storage site thirty miles away. The project had exceeded its timeline, and Dave couldn't help but feel the pressure mount. They were both eager to join the Laser Fusion Reactor team at the new Fusion Development Center, especially since Laubner Labs had abandoned the Magnetic Mirror Fusion project due to costs and advances in laser fusion.

The weight of one hundred million taxpayer dollars invested in this endeavor added to his unease. Dave's conclusions leaned heavily toward a design flaw in the reactor, which was disappointing given the respect and admiration he had always felt for Lexington's vision.

Three weeks later, Dave and Cory stood before Steve Johnson, the chief engineering manager. As they presented their report, he felt pressure in his chest. They detailed the inadequate cooling system and the unstable magnet design that had proven prone to quench issues. Listening to Steve plan his presentation to the board, Dave knew that their hard work had to lead to something more than just another failure. He hoped for a chance to move forward, but the shadow of defeat lingered as they awaited their next steps.

CHAPTER ONE

Two car doors slammed in quick succession, the sound cutting through the stillness. Tessa and Ray exchanged a glance, their eyes widening. There was always a story behind a slamming car door, and this time, curiosity outweighed caution. The front door swung open just enough to peek through. The two men approaching the house were impossible to miss: dark suits, short hair sheens, shoes polished to an almost artificial shine. One stood nearly a head above his partner. Ray stepped out, a beat ahead of Tessa, who managed to keep pace.

She found her voice first. "May I help you?" She squared her shoulders, trying to measure her stance against the tall agent, who didn't hesitate.

"We're looking for Tessa Holmes," the tall one said, glancing at both faces, as if expecting her to step forward.

"I'm Tessa," she said, stepping closer to Ray, feeling the heat radiating from his presence. She planted herself beside him, her heart thumping in her chest.

He introduced himself. "Tessa, I'm Agent Sommers. This is Agent Fitz. We're with the FBI." He drew out his badge with a flick, holding it up for her to see. "We have questions to ask regarding your time with..." A pause, a glance at Fitz.

"Chemco," Fitz supplied, crisp and clear.

"Yes, Chemco." Tessa's tummy twisted at the mention of her old job, chaotic memories flickering to life. Why were they here now?

"I really don't have any time for questions," she said, her palms growing clammy. The orange juice she had for breakfast churned within her, threatening to rise. *I need a breath mint if I have to answer anything. Wait—isn't this Ray's house? Don't they need a warrant?*

"Miss Holmes, we're conducting a criminal investigation into a sabotage event at Chemco. We'd appreciate your cooperation now, or we can continue the conversation in

Dallas. Your choice." Sommers's tone was even, but his words felt like a heavy weight pressing down on her.

Ray stepped forward, his body taut. "Whoa, what do you mean, a few days in Dallas? We're getting married the day after tomorrow."

"You must be Ray Holland," Sommers said, and Tessa could feel Ray's tension radiating from him.

"Yeah, and I don't think you have any right to come here," Ray shot back, fists clenching at his sides.

"Mr. Holland, we only need answers from Miss Holmes. If we get them, we're gone, and your day continues uninterrupted." Sommers's gaze shifted back to Tessa. "Up to you."

She nodded, swallowing hard as she felt her throat tighten. "Ray, it's okay." Turning to the agents, she added, "Would you prefer to come inside? We can sit at the table."

"Yes," Sommers answered immediately. Fitz simply nodded.

Ray hesitated, frustration flickering across his face. "I'll set up the chairs," he said, his voice strained. He led the agents through the kitchen, and Tessa's eyes darted to the moving boxes scattered around, a reminder of their disarray.

"I'd offer coffee or tea, but we're barely moved in," she said, half-apologizing as she gestured to the chaos.

"No worries," Sommers replied, his gaze sweeping across the room. She felt exposed under his scrutiny.

The card table wobbled slightly as the agents settled into their folding chairs, which creaked under their weight. Tessa joined them, her heart racing.

Ray hovered nearby, shifting from foot to foot until Sommers made it easy. "Mr. Holland, these questions are for Miss Holmes. I'll need you to step outside."

Ray's jaw tightened. "I can't stay?"

"It's okay, Ray," Tessa murmured, reaching out to touch his arm, grounding herself in the moment. "Let's just get through this."

"Okay, I'll be in the lab." Ray retreated, the screen door rattling behind him.

As soon as Ray left, Fitz glanced at Sommers. "I'll check on him."

"Do that," Sommers said, his attention returning to Tessa.

Fitz stood and exited through the kitchen, leaving Tessa with Sommers, who settled back into his chair, his demeanor unyielding.

Tessa turned back to the agent, her insides churning. "He's just going to the garage."

"Why call it a lab?" Sommers pressed, his tone sharp.

"He's an engineer, Agent Sommers. Electrical engineer, Laubner Labs. He wants his own workspace," she said, her voice steady.

"Really? What sort of projects?"

"Lab stuff." She folded her arms, holding his gaze.

"Lab stuff, is it? And do you consider yourself a partner in this lab work?"

"Of course."

"So it's more than just 'lab stuff,'" he said, his words dry.

She exhaled sharply, frustration bubbling up inside her. "I don't see how any of this connects to Chemco."

Sommers continued pressing, and Tessa felt herself hardening against the probing questions. "Ms. Holmes, Martinez contacted you three days before the Chemco explosion. Why?"

"I'm not sure who you are referring to. Martinez, was he in production?"

"How about Hernandez? Is this name familiar?"

"It says here they mentioned concerns about safety protocols."

"I was the one addressing protocols and procedures. I was the one warning them. Who's this Martinez? Am I being blamed for something I had no direct access to?"

Just then, Fitz returned, his expression serious. He leaned in slightly toward Sommers, murmuring something that Tessa couldn't quite make out. Whatever this was, it wasn't about Chemco anymore.

Sommers closed his notebook, and Tessa felt relief, thinking they might finally be done. "Okay, Miss Holmes, that's it for today."

Everyone rose, chairs scraping against the floor. "Do you have a phone number where we can reach you?" Sommers asked.

Tessa shrugged, anxiety creeping in. "I don't know the number."

Sommers handed her a card. "When you find out, call my office and let us know." He glanced at her, nodding. "Thank you for your time. We'll be in touch."

The agents left the same way they arrived, through the front door and down the porch steps. Tessa watched them go, the Ford Crown Victoria lingering in the driveway before disappearing down the street. Just like that, they were gone.

She hurried to the garage, her nerves finally tumbling loose. Ray was there, knees drawn up, head in hands.

"Ray, what's wrong?"

He shook his head slowly, not meeting her eyes. "Nothing."

She crouched down beside him, her brow furrowing. "Nothing? Then why are you sitting on the floor?"

"I think we're in trouble." His voice barely rose above a whisper.

Tessa felt her heart race, adrenaline flooding her system. "What do you mean?"

"The FBI... They're going to be a royal pain now. They don't even know what GG-1 is, but they're convinced it's some bomb project. They'll be back."

Ray ran a hand through his hair, the motion betraying his unease. "I'm sure Fitz passed my little lab antics right along to Sommers."

"You missed all the fun inside," she said, trying to lighten the mood, but her own smile faltered.

Ray looked up, a hint of a smile before it faded. "How's that?"

"They think I'm involved with the Chemco accident. Names I don't know, messages I never received—they won't stop."

"Did they figure anything out?" he asked, concern etching deep lines across his forehead.

She shook her head. "No. If anything, they made less sense than before. Anyway, I'm starving and we need bedsheets for tonight."

She helped him up. They shut the garage, locked the door, and left the house behind, for now putting the shadow of the FBI out of mind.

CHAPTER TWO

Friday morning, the day before the wedding, Ray awoke reluctantly, squinting at the unfamiliar light pushing its way between stacks of moving boxes. Tessa had arrived late last night after their dinner, and the thought of her tackling the chaos of their new home made his gut twist. He lay there a minute longer, listening to the silence in the empty house, a cold pressure settled behind his ribs at the weight of the day ahead. He remembered he should check on her after hearing her stressed voice—she was already juggling too much.

Reaching for the phone—the new line installed just yesterday—he dialed.

Natalie answered in a breathless rush, her voice a mixture of urgency and concern that caught Ray's attention. "Hello."

"Hi, this is Ray."

"Oh, hi Ray. This is a new number for you," Natalie said, surprised.

"Yes, just had it installed yesterday."

"Tessa said everything is falling into place regarding the house. I think that is wonderful. I wish I could say the same for the big day tomorrow."

"Is there a problem?"

"Oh, just a couple of things. The cake, the dress, thc flowers. Nothing that can't be fixed today. We have all day."

"Oh, okay." He let out a huge breath, his lungs feeling both tight and relieved. "Is Tessa there?"

"Sure, hang on." Tessa came on, sounding at once close and distant.

"Hello."

"Hey, it's Ray."

"Ray, where are you? I don't recognize this number."

"It's the house number. The new one."

"Oh, hey, I need this to give to the FBI. Hang on, let me write it down. Okay, what's up?"

"Oh, I wanted to see how you're doing after yesterday."

"I'm doing as well as can be expected, I guess. Mom is all over the florist, the bakery, and the seamstress. One thing about Mom: she gets it done, but it feels like so much pressure."

"Sounds like it." Ray pressed his palm to his eyes, feeling the heaviness settle on his shoulders. "I'm glad I'm just the groom tomorrow."

"What do you mean, just the groom? You have a bunch of responsibilities. Effective tomorrow, you have me," she laughed, but he could hear the slight tremor in her voice.

"Ah, come on. How hard can you be?"

"You just wait until tomorrow night. I'll show you how hard it can be."

Ray froze, an unexpected heat creeping into his cheeks. He paused.

"Are you still there?" she asked. "Are you afraid now?"

"No, no, all good." Ray scrambled for composure, straightening his posture as he wanted to be strong for her.

"Oh, doorbell." Tessa cut in. "Seamstress is here with the dress. I need to go. Don't forget the rehearsal dinner at five. Be at the church at four."

"Got it."

He hung up. The house around him was quiet, but the thought of Tessa's voice lingered, along with the weight of the day ahead, folding over him like the boxes stacked around their new home.

# # #

Inside the Park Hills Methodist Church, Tessa stepped into the foyer, where the polished wood gleamed under the soft light. She moved further inside, the vast sanctuary looming above her, its emptiness echoing through the air. At the back, a small group was huddled together in the last few rows of pews, their murmurs punctuating the stillness of the space.

Tessa focused on Ray; her eyes flickered toward him immediately, a beam breaking across her face. She moved, elegant in a blue knit dress, but a flicker of doubt clouded her gaze as she recalled her mother's relentless checklists. What if it wasn't enough? As she hurried over, arms wrapping around him, the warmth of his body settled her nerves, a brush of lips against his cheek making her feel momentarily grounded.

"Oops. I think I'm supposed to wait until tomorrow for that," she teased, but her grin trembled slightly.

Ray smiled back. "I think it's okay," he whispered.

A beat later, Pastor Marshall appeared at the head of the aisle, folding himself into the moment in beige khakis and a riot of hibiscus flowers across his shirt. His voice boomed, asking for introductions; hands were shaken, names repeated. He brought forward two members of his staff, their roles quietly detailed. Then came expectations, a rundown, and a call for Ray and Tessa to join him up at the steps of the podium.

Natalie's questions broke the rhythm, but Chuck managed to dial back her interruptions with a look or a hand at her arm. Pastor Marshall ended with one last check for questions; there were none. He dismissed them.

Tessa slid into the passenger seat of Ray's car as they prepared to make the drive to Torenzo's, the local Italian place for dinner.

Ray's hand was steady on the wheel. "Well, that went well, don't you think?"

"I think so. I'm getting nervous now. Not sure why. I had this dream last night; the FBI showed up and interrupted the ceremony. My dad had to stop my mom from making a scene and getting arrested. What a nightmare."

"That would be."

Tessa furrowed her brow as she fidgeted with her bag, fingers tapping against the fabric. "I thought over the questions they asked and came to a possible conclusion."

"What was that?"

"I think someone at Chemco is deliberately trying to frame me. They must have found my reports on safety issues. They never mentioned them, though. It was all about my communication with Martinez and Hernandez. Only once did I receive correspondence from Hernandez. Maybe if they come out again, we hire an attorney."

"I agree."

"I should wait to give them your phone number until after tomorrow. I really don't want any interruptions for the next twenty-four hours," Tessa said, her voice growing firmer as she focused on their plans for the wedding and future.

"I totally agree."

Dinner at Torenzo's dissolved into a haze of toasts and laughter. Afterwards, Ray and Tessa found themselves together again, slipping into the quiet of Ray's car as the parking lot emptied around them.

"Tessa, don't stay out too late," Natalie called from across the way, a mother's voice echoing even at a distance. "You need your rest."

"Yes, Mother," she said, a hint of irony in her tone, her shoulders tensing slightly.

As they pulled out of the garage, Ray asked, "Where are we going?"

"Did you see the Ford Crown Vic?"

"Ford...Crown Vic?" Ray worked the name around in his head.

"Yes, in the parking lot. Dark, four doors, and two well-dressed men inside, dark suits, white shirts, ties. It had to be Sommers and Fitz again. Don't they have anything better to do than stalk us?" Her jaw clenched, irritation simmering beneath the surface.

"What do they want?" Glancing at his mirrors.

Tessa raised her hand and pointed. "Don't know. Turn right up here, pull in the drive-thru."

Ray glanced over, following her line of sight. "Look, there they go. Right on by."

"Well, if they are tailing us, they are terrible at it. This is the way to my—I mean, our house, so maybe it's where they're headed."

"Could be. If these guys ruin this wedding, my mom will take them down."

"Well, let's hope it doesn't happen."

Tessa's eyes narrowed as she stared out at the street rolling by. "I wonder if we should do something unexpected tonight. Throw them off. Like stay in a hotel."

"Well, my tux and the rings are at the house. They would just follow us from there, and if we do something unexpected, then wouldn't we appear guilty of covering something up?"

"Maybe," Tessa conceded, her body tensing slightly. "But I have an idea."

The drive up the long, shaded lane to Ray's recently purchased two-story craftsman style home was silent, both of them scanning the corners. Sure enough, the Ford Crown Vic idled down the block, a shadow with eyes.

"Let's go inside, get your tux, an overnight bag, and the rings."

"It might look obvious what we are doing, don't you think?"

"Just work with me here. I have a plan."

Tessa watched as the black tux bag hung inert in the utility closet, a silent reminder of the day ahead. Ray moved rapidly, snatching it up and gesturing toward the kitchen desk's top drawer where the rings were kept. She felt her heart race as he sprinted up the stairs, urgency clear in his movements. A few moments later, the soft thump of the bag hitting the bottom step broke the silence, and she was already waiting for him at the door, the black tux bag slung over her shoulder, the rings' weight pressing against her pocket.

As Ray grabbed the key from the table, she saw him take a deep breath, barely glancing down the street at the car idling nearby. Tessa hurried to load the bags into the back seat, a glance confirming the Ford's headlights flickering to life. Someone watched.

# # #

At the Holmes' house, Ray cut across the roundabout driveway and stopped right at the front steps. Tessa was out before the engine ticked down, tux over her shoulder, heading for the porch. Natalie opened the door, her face tight with anticipation.

"What's going on?" Natalie asked as they both walked in, arms full.

Tessa's nose wrinkled, and she bit her lip, casting a quick glance at her mother's anxious expression. "We have a little problem."

"Oh no, not cold feet, I hope."

"No, no, nothing like that. We just have a potential Federal problem."

"Feral?" Natalie blinked.

"No, mom, Fe-der-al." Tessa drew out the syllables, her fingers drumming against her arm. She glanced at Ray, the knot twisting in her tummy tightening.

Chuck entered, giving Ray a handshake. "What's going on in here? I heard the word 'problem.'"

"Remember the calls from the FBI?" Tessa said. "They're here."

"Here?" Chuck glanced around. "Where?"

"Outside, down the street. They stopped by the other day and questioned Ray and me about Chemco. Now they are following us around."

"They can't do that," Chuck insisted. "Heck, they just reported on the news they have charged a suspect regarding the explosion at Chemco."

"They did?" Tessa asked, her heart racing. "Who?"

"They haven't said, but it's some executive in the company, is all they reported."

"I wonder who." Tessa rolled the thought over, the weight of her own reports pressing down on her. Would the Chemco execs ever admit she'd caught them, or just keep pretending everything was normal?

"Well, it makes little sense the FBI needs to follow my daughter around. I'm going to go out and put an end to this harassment."

"Dad, wait," Tessa raised her hands, stopping him, urgency lacing her voice. "That will only make things worse. I have a better plan."

Chuck stood rigid. "You have a plan? What plan?"

"First, we need to know who they are following. So, Ray is going back to the car and driving to the store to get some bread."

Chuck stared. "Bread? Why bread?"

"It's not the bread we need. It's the need to see who they're following. He's coming right back, then we'll decide how to proceed. Now, when Ray leaves, we can't all hover around the window and watch. Too obvious," Tessa paused. "Everybody clear?"

Nods all around. Ray stepped out, started the car, and drove west, away from town—a ritual departure. Sure enough, after a heartbeat, the Ford rolled after him.

"They want Ray," Tessa said, anxiety twisting in her gut. "I still don't understand the Chemco connection or why the usually silent Agent Fitz has so much focus on Ray."

"Why would they want Ray now? If they ruin my daughter's wedding, I'm calling the President," Natalie huffed.

"Mom, take it easy. Nobody's ruining the wedding. Well, at least this makes more sense. Since they have a suspect in the Chemco explosion, they won't need to speak to me anymore."

A handful of minutes later, Ray came back, groceries in hand, the bag swinging at his side. He entered a small receiving line in the foyer.

"Well, that was fun," he said, offering a sheepish grin.

"They followed you, Ray," Tessa said, a frown creeping onto her face.

"Yeah, I know. It was kind of obvious. They aren't the best undercover guys around. Now what?"

Tessa panned the room, her mind racing. "I don't think we want to risk anything tonight. Tomorrow needs to go without a hitch. I think Ray should stay here tonight. We stay together. It will be much harder for them to do anything with just the two of us. What did Fitz ask you the other day?"

"It was mostly about what I do at Laubner and what I'm doing at home. Why I need a lab? Stuff like that. I only told him general stuff. He saw the plan for GG-1, but it's just a mechanical drawing for the framework. Heck, I don't even know the outcome once it's built."

Tessa gave a curt nod. "Well, one thing is for sure, GG-1 needs to fall off the radar of the FBI."

Chuck touched Tessa's shoulder. "What is GG-1?"

"Dad, don't ask," Tessa said, quick and sharp. "I think it's something that needs to go underground for now. I can't even imagine them sitting out there in their car all night, either."

Ray raised an interrupting hand. "Maybe there's a second team."

Tessa made a subtle motion for him to drop the hand, furrowing her brow. "It's possible, but we've only seen Sommers and Fitz so far."

Natalie glanced around, her expression shifting. "Well, we should get to bed early for the long day tomorrow."

No one argued. Ray settled for the spare bedroom, and the house went quiet, each good night echoing down the hallway as if to seal them all against whatever waited outside.

CHAPTER THREE

A sharp metallic whining—a bedspring creaking under Ray as he rolled in the unfamiliar bed. He blinked, something twitching along his back as he sat up, taking stock of muffled voices below, birds outside flinging their quick darts of song through the morning hush. Clothes, soft and worn, came out of his bag. He slipped them on, a quickened breath echoing his unease: the FBI may still be out there, parked, watching. He hurried down the stairs, fingers tapping nervously against the banister as he glanced from the front window. The street was empty. No Ford pulled up at the curb, no silent watchers parked across the street. Had they vanished overnight?

The moment short-lived. In no time, everyone converged downstairs; hunger the only topic, the jostle for cupboards and fridge filled the air with clatter and half-awake greetings. Tessa descended the stairs, tugging at the hem of her dress. Ray noticed the way her fingers fidgeted, and he could see the tension in her posture as she stepped into view.

"You look wonderful," he said, warmth in his voice, hoping to ease the tension.

She gave him a sly sidelong glance, though her eyes flickered momentarily. "Isn't there something about not seeing the bride before her wedding on her wedding day?"

He shrugged, trying to relax his own anxiety. "That could be. I think not sleeping in the same bed counts."

"You have a point." She leaned closer, a small grin breaking through, her voice lifting. "I like the staying together part. Especially after today."

He leaned in, lowering his voice. "Anyway, the FBI are gone."

She moved even closer, eyes searching his. "They are? How do you know?" Her fingers twisted nervously.

"There's no car. Nothing. No one watching now."

"Do you think they're gone for good?" Her voice rose, anxious.

"I doubt it," Ray replied, frowning. "I'd expect them back. We stay sharp, stay together—that's the best plan." He squeezed her hand.

Tessa beamed, relief shining in her eyes. "I like the staying together part. Especially after today."

On the stove, pastries warmed from the oven, and the rich smell of hot cereal simmered in a heavy pot wafted through the kitchen. Ray shared the news—the Feds had vanished—and watched as the room fell into a steady rhythm. People began to eat, then quickly packed plastic containers and bags into car trunks, moving with a sense of urgency. By half-past ten, he squeezed into the backseat of one car, watching Natalie direct the setup with brisk efficiency, her voice cutting through the chatter.

Ray stood at the front of the sanctuary, the air thick with anticipation. He watched as nearly seventy guests slipped into radial pews, their low voices creating a soft murmur which rose and fell like a gentle tide. He caught a glimpse of Natalie moving through the crowd, her eyes scanning the room as she counted quietly, likely ensuring everything was set for the day. A glance at the clock signaled the moment—the bells not yet chiming, but he knew the music would begin any second. With a deep breath, he stepped out alongside Pastor Marshall, the contrast of the pastor's black suit and tie nearly lost beneath the flowing white ceremonial robe.

In his light blue tux and black bow tie, Ray's hands fidgeted with the fabric of his jacket, feeling the cool silk against his palms. As the organ began to swell, filling the sanctuary with a melodic rise, the sound reverberated in his chest, amplifying the quickening beat of his heart. He glanced at the guests seated in the pews, their faces a blur of familiarity and unfamiliarity. Some had likely never seen him dressed up in all their lives, and he swallowed hard, feeling the weight of their scrutiny. Taking a deep breath, he tried to absorb it all—family members and friends moving about, the careful escorting of loved ones—each moment a reminder of the significance of what lay ahead.

Then he spotted Jill Johnson entering in a peach dress, her arm linked with Sam Gordon's matching tux. As the wedding march began in earnest, the doors swung open wide to reveal Chuck Holmes, solemn in black, escorting Tessa, veiled in white, every inch the beautiful bride.

Ray's legs twitched with nervous energy as the music swirled around him, amplifying the silence which hung in the air. Pastor Marshall's voice rang out, asking who gave this woman, and Ray held his breath as Chuck answered, "her mother and I." The handoff complete, he and Tessa faced the pastor, feeling his own nerves taut as piano wire. As their vows tumbled out, the words felt almost lost to the pews.

"Now you can kiss your bride," said the pastor, and Tessa lifted her veil. Ray blinked, caught off guard by the joy radiating from her—in this light, her emerald eyes glowed. He kissed her, gentle, but Tessa's hand pulled him closer, the moment stretching, drawing laughter from the guests.

"Mr. and Mrs. Ray Holland," Pastor Marshall announced, and applause filled the sanctuary. In a flash, nerves dissolved, and Ray and Tessa exited, married, a new gravity settling between them.

Downstairs, reception—a blur: the receiving line, hugs and handshakes, old friends and new relatives. Ray felt the moments slide past in quick succession. He froze, taking in Tessa beside him. She was his best friend, had been since Stanford and their first psychology class. He'd never been truly recognized, always the outlier, the bookworm in the background, invisible to most. But now this—all for him, for them. He caught her gaze; she mouthed "what?" He, self-conscious, sipped his wine, leaning in for a brief, hesitant kiss.

After the reception, Ray changed into casual slacks and a dress shirt, glancing at Tessa as she slipped into a champagne pantsuit that made her look effortlessly elegant. Goodbyes; the Subaru decorated for the occasion, cans clattering on the bumper, shaving cream and tissue streamers. Last hugs from family, then they slid into the car. Ray started the engine and eased up to the street, glancing left, then right.

Across 4th Avenue, in plain view, stood Sommers and Fitz by the Ford. Watching, silent. Ray pressed his lips together, checked for traffic, and pulled out.

He nodded toward the rearview. "See? Just like I said. Didn't expect them gone for good."

"Are they following us?" Tessa peered back, hands twisting in her lap.

"No—they're just standing by their car. They know where we live; they're not in any hurry."

Tessa's voice rose. "Do you think they'll stake out the house?"

Ray shrugged. "Maybe. Didn't they mention they're based in Dallas?"

"That's what I thought." Tessa glanced back again, biting her lip. "They'd have to check in soon, right?"

Ray didn't answer; the drive remained quiet.

# # #

They arrived home about forty minutes later, dusk cooling the sky. Tessa paused, scanning the house and property. "Everything looks the way it should."

Tessa grinned. "You sure picked a quiet street. Nothing but empty lots on either side."

He grinned. "I guess I did. Easier to focus around here."

She nudged the moment lighter. "You know, you owe me a real honeymoon one of these days."

He laughed, "This is your honey, sometime later, moon."

She snorted. "You'll pay for that one."

"If GG-1 comes through, I'll make it up to you," Ray promised.

Tessa leaned against him. "Or if Holmes Acrylic Sealant does," she countered, recalling her own master's work, the chemical sealant she'd invented, tested, and patented. It had promise if she could just find a buyer.

Ray nodded, all business. "We kind of need that before I can get GG-1 off the ground."

"Well, enough about honeymoons." Tessa stepped back, eyes bright. "We need to go make this official."

Ray raised a brow. "Wasn't that what the church was for?"

"No, Ray, and I don't mean the paperwork either." She smirked. "Let me put it this way. There's a bottle of champagne in the back seat. In a box with two glasses. Would you get it?"

Ray opened the driver's door, grabbed the wood box. Tessa, in a move which surprised, slid in the opposite back door, then over the bench seat, pressing in close behind him.

"Okay, close the door." Tessa exhaled, her breath warm against his ear.

A smile broke across her face, and her heart raced as she leaned close. "Now, let's go in the house and toast to a grand future. Then we go upstairs to our bedroom."

"Are we not eating dinner?" Ray asked, his eyebrows raised.

"If you get hungry, we can make a sandwich," she said, a playful smirk dancing on her lips. "But I doubt you'll need it."

Inside, they opened the box, popped the cork, and poured two glasses.

"A quick toast to a happy and fulfilling future," she said, her voice light with anticipation.

"Here, here," Ray replied, raising his glass.

They drank, the taste fizzing sharp and new on Tessa's tongue. She took Ray's hand, leading him up the narrow stairwell.

At the top, he faced her. "What about the bottle?"

"We won't need it."

Night fell as they closed the bedroom door, enveloping them in warmth and quiet. The hush and swirl of the house faded away; the world outside disappeared. Moments of laughter and tangled sheets filled the air, the champagne bottle forgotten downstairs. By 2:00 a.m., fatigue settled around them like a blanket, pulling Tessa under until sleep claimed them both.

CHAPTER FOUR

First light beamed through the bedroom window at about 7:00 a.m., illuminating Tessa and Ray as they exchanged glances. Tessa turned to Ray, her voice barely above a whisper. "Did you think it would be like this?"

"Like what?"

"Like last night?"

"Well, to be honest, it was far better than anything I ever imagined it would be."

Her eyes sparkled with a mix of excitement and anxiety. "Really?"

"Oh, yes."

"You know, it only gets better from here," she said, trying to instill confidence in her own voice.

"If true, I'll be the happiest man on earth."

"Deal," she replied, laughter bubbling between them, momentarily dispelling the tension that had built.

They quickly rummaged through boxes for their robes, the urgency of the day dawning on them. Tessa pulled Ray into the living room, her heart racing as she tried to shake off the remnants of sleep.

"So, what's the plan today?" Tessa asked, scanning the unpacked boxes strewn about.

Ray grinned, mischief dancing in his eyes. "We could go back upstairs."

Tessa rolled her eyes, a playful smile breaking through. "That we could, but we have a mountain of unpacking to tackle first."

"We already did a lot of that," he protested lightly, but Tessa was already tugging him toward the living room, determination etched on her features.

There—a pyramid of wrapped wedding gifts stood sentinel by the wall, three tiers high, ribbons glinting in the morning light.

"That looks more like unwrapping than unpacking," Ray said, studying the pile.

"Well, we need to unwrap these gifts, write everything down for thank-you letters, and set aside what we'll return," Tessa explained, her voice steady as she surveyed the gifts. She looked up at him, challenge in her eyes. "Are you up for it?"

"Let's go," he replied, a hint of reluctance creeping into his tone. "But can we eat breakfast first?"

Tessa laughed, the sound lifting the weight in the air. They moved to the kitchen, ate a simple breakfast then quickly clearing plates before settling into the task: four hours of paper and ribbon, stacking kitchen gadgets and towels into "keep" and "return" piles.

"Okay," Tessa said, dusting her hands as she surveyed the results. "Now that's done. What's next?"

"The option to go back upstairs is still open."

"Ray, come on. I'm sure you can think of other things we need to get done."

He glanced around the half-empty space, uncertainty flickering across his face.

"Um, not really."

She gave him a look, hands on her hips. "Oh, stop. It's not that I don't want to, but we need to get organized. Remember, I have to travel this week."

"Oh, right. Minnesota, right?"

"Correct."

"Thursday, back on Friday?"

"Yes, right again."

"Have you received your tickets?" Ray asked, his brow furrowing.

"They said they'd take care of everything. They'll call with the times and airlines once it's all completed."

Ray nodded. "You have all week to prepare, and we both took time off, so we have time to get everything done."

Tessa glanced at the calendar hanging on the wall. "You need to get GG-1 built. This would be a good week to get it going."

Ray hesitated. "We don't have the money yet."

"Remember what I said. Don't worry about the money. I have it covered." Her voice was firm, determination shining through.

"Are you sure?"

"Yes. Totally."

"Well, Steve Seltzer's shop is closed today, so it'll have to be tomorrow."

Tessa nodded. "Look up his address and get the drawings ready."

With that settled, she turned to her laptop, focusing on numbers and charts for her upcoming trip. Ray vanished into the garage, leaving her to manage their tasks.

# # #

Ray called Steve Seltzer's shop first thing Monday morning. Steve answered on the second ring.

"Hello."

"Yes, Steve Seltzer, please."

"This is Steve."

"Steve, this is Ray Holland, Dave's son."

"Oh yes, Dave said you might call. You have a project for me, I hear."

"Yes. May I bring the plans by today?"

"Sure, I have some time. The shop is actually unusually quiet this week. Orders in the machine shop are down a little."

"Sorry to hear it's quiet this week." Ray rubbed the back of his neck, feeling the weight of their finances pressing down on him.

"Oh, no problem. We've survived worse. This is manufacturing. It has its busy times and its quiet times. I look forward to seeing what you have."

"I'll be down this morning," Ray said.

"Okay, thanks, Ray. See you in a little while."

The call ended, leaving silence in its wake.

Tessa made her way down the creaky stairs after getting dressed.

"Who was on the phone?"

"I called Steve Seltzer, the machine shop owner. He has time to look at GG-1 today."

"Great."

"I'll head down there within the hour."

"Will he give you a bid today, do you think?"

"Not sure. He probably needs to get material quotes, which may take some time. They always do at Laubner."

"You know, I was thinking last night. Why did you name this project GG-1?"

"You'll laugh when I tell you."

"I won't, I promise."

"Well, remember when I told you the story about the car accident in front of the house? The spilled water on the circuit board and the luminescent stones from Laubner my father gave me on my desk, and what happened?"

"Yes, I do, very clearly. Some stones were bouncing around and some floating. I didn't believe you at first, but you were very convincing after a while."

"Well, that's where I came up with the idea for GG-1. If the stones can float, I thought of gravity as the force that keeps things on the ground, and in the absence of gravity, everything would be floating around. So, it stuck. 'Gravity gone' is what I came up with. GG for short, and since this is the first experiment with the stones, I felt it should be called GG-1. Now don't tell anybody yet. The last thing we need is for people to think I'm creating a flying machine. It wouldn't be the FBI in our face; it would be the FAA."

"You know, Ray, not to burst your bubble, but if it flies, we'll have much more than the FAA to worry about."

"Actually, I can show you the numbers; things look good for flight of some sort. It's just a question of power, power distribution, and if I can understand the orientation relationship of the stones."

"Well, I can't wait for the first flight," Tessa said, a smile brightening her features.

"Me too."

# # #

Ray arrived at Steve Seltzer's shop a brief time later. As he pulled into the parking lot, he noticed the single-story brick building was smaller than he expected—probably built thirty or forty years earlier. Peeling paint framed the windows. Approaching the door, he recognized it was wood, painted green, with a vintage metal knob. He knocked and walked in. An old oak desk stood to his right, looking as tired as the building, with an attractive young lady seated at it. A couch was against the wall next to the desk, adorned with framed pictures from the shop's history. Little had changed.

"Hi, may I help you?" the young lady asked with a bright grin.

"Yes, my name is Ray Holland, and I'm here to see Mr. Seltzer."

"Oh yes, Mr. Holland, Steve has been expecting you." She rose from her chair, and he felt a rush of warmth at her smile. "May I get you some coffee?"

"No, thank you. I'm fine."

"You can have a seat over here while I find Steve for you," she said, pointing to the couch.

Ray thanked her and sat. She walked through a dark gray metal door that groaned with age. Once opened, noise and a sweet, musty aroma wafted through. The sound echoed like a train passing by, even though there were no trains in this part of town. There were only two other doors in the room: one marked as a restroom and the other leading to what appeared to be an office. A moment later, the door opened, and in walked the attractive young lady and a tall, skinny gentleman in blue jeans and a gray knit shirt. His hair was short, and he wore eye protection, which he removed as he entered.

"Ray, glad to meet you," he said, his voice deeper than one might expect from a man of his size.

"Yes, thank you, Steve. Same likewise." They shook hands.

"This is my daughter, Shelly."

"Nice to meet you, Shelly," Ray said, reaching out to shake her hand gently.

Shelly returned to her place at the desk, a pleasant expression still on her face.

"Shelly handles the phone and walk-in traffic for me most of the time, and she'll help out in the shop when we're busy. Trust me, if you need a tour, she can give one better than I can."

"Oh, Dad," she blushed.

"So, can I give you a tour, or shall we go into my office and have a look at your drawings?"

"I would like a tour at some point, Steve, but maybe later. Can we go over the drawings?"

"Certainly. Let's go to my office."

He opened the door that led to an office as Ray suspected. He found a sizable oak desk centered in the room with what looked like a very comfortable chair. To the right was a metal table with lighting above it, designed to handle large mechanical drawings. To the left was a solid oak bench, with several machined parts scattered on the desk and a couple of shelves.

"So, what do you have for me, Ray?"

Ray pulled out his drawings and laid them out on the table as Steve cleared the way by rolling up the previous drawings. Steve put on some glasses, glancing over the new drawing. "So, this is a one-off? Correct?"

"Yes."

"You know the setup costs will kill you on a single piece order."

"I understand. It's R&D, so there'd be no reason to make more than one at this time."

"I don't want to scare you, but I can already tell you, the setup and tooling will be about five K. Time and materials will be far less, maybe five hundred."

"Wow, you're fast. I mean, you pulled up a number quick."

"Ray, it's actually pretty easy on a single piece order. I could make you one hundred of these, and the setup and tooling would still be five K. An order of one hundred would amortize the cost over all those pieces, and your per-piece cost would be much more reasonable. It's just the nature of how manufacturing works. You understand, don't you, working at Laubner?"

"Well, I don't get into the manufacturing cost analysis at Laubner, but I do understand what you're saying. The price is close to what I expected. How about delivery? What can you do?"

"Are you in a rush?"

“Not really, but I hoped for a reasonable time frame.”

“Well, let’s see. Materials will take a week. I can pre-build some of the tooling, so how’s two weeks sound?”

“Two weeks sounds great. So, do you provide a written estimate?”

“I can. Shelly can mail it to you, you can sign it, mail it back, then I can get started. Then it will take two weeks from then. Or we can get started today with a handshake.”

“A handshake will do.”

“So, fifty-five hundred?” Ray confirmed.

“Yes, plus tax.”

“Of course.” Ray shook Steve’s hand.

“Are you sure you want to skip a tour today?”

“I am. I just got married, bought a house, so I have lots to do.”

“Congratulations on both accords.” Steve opened his office door. “How about when you pick up your order then?”

“Yes, that works for me, Steve. Thanks.” Ray nodded at Shelly, a polite grin crossing his face. “It was nice meeting you.”

“You too,” she answered, smiling.

Ray hand drifted to his neck, the same knot of worry tightening there. With the five thousand five hundred dollars plus tax due in two weeks, he wondered if it was all worth it.

CHAPTER FIVE

Thursday morning shimmered with a certain nervousness. Tessa packed her things, her hands moving promptly but trembling slightly as she double-checked her laptop case. She stole a glance at Ray as he loaded her carry-on bag into the car. His warm smile gave her a flicker of comfort, but the tension in her shoulders remained stubborn. As they drove toward the airport, Tessa felt her voice waver during their small talk, fingers tapping anxiously against her thigh. "What gate am I departing from?" she asked, trying to focus on something simple.

Ray scanned the concourse, his gaze flickering between the signs. "I wrote down Gate nine, American Airlines," he replied, pointing ahead.

With a deep breath, Tessa straightened her laptop case, resolve washing over her. "I'll go over the presentation. I'm nervous. Maybe reviewing it will help."

"Do you want me to stay?" he asked, concern etched on his face.

She shook her head, decisive. "No, you have things to do. Use this time however you want."

"Good point. Okay, call me when you get to Minneapolis."

Tessa nodded, locking her gaze onto Ray's for a moment longer than necessary. "I will," she promised, their kiss brief but filled with unspoken encouragement.

The flight to Minneapolis was smooth, and as Tessa walked off the plane into the bright terminal, she immediately caught sight of a man in a crisp black suit and cap holding a sign which read "Ms. Holmes." She blinked at it. A driver? For her?

She approached, uncertainty creeping in. "Are you looking for Tessa Holmes?"

"Yes, ma'am," the man replied, voice polite but firm.

"I'm Tessa Holmes."

He dipped his head slightly. “Very good. My name is Charles. I’m your driver. May I take your bag for you?”

She handed it over, still a little stunned. “Yes, thank you.”

“Any other bags, ma’am?”

She shook her head. “No, just this.”

“Right this way,” Charles said, already moving with purpose toward the front exit.

Outside, a black limousine idled at the curb. Charles set her bag in the trunk, moving with the smooth confidence of someone accustomed to this job. He circled to open the rear passenger door, gesturing for Tessa to step inside. As she slid onto the smooth black leather seats, a tingle of discomfort flickered through her. Was this really necessary? The luxury felt excessive, almost overwhelming, especially in her jeans and wool jacket. When the frigid air hit her, it was like a slap, a stark contrast to the mild San Jose morning she’d just left behind. She adjusted the collar of her jacket, grateful for its warmth as Charles handed off a tip to the Sky Cap before joining her in the driver’s seat, his silhouette visible through the small glass window.

“We’ll be at your hotel in about thirty minutes,” he said. “Is there anywhere you’d like to stop, ma’am?”

Tessa ran her palm over the buttery leather. “No, just the hotel is fine.”

“I’ll be available all evening if you need to go anywhere. Just ring the desk and they’ll call me.”

She nodded. “Thank you, Charles.”

He seemed satisfied. “Please sit back and relax. There are refreshments in the console to your left. Beer, wine, soda, bourbon, vodka. Glasses are right behind the console. Let me know if you need anything else.”

“Thank you.” Tessa glanced at the array of bottles and glasses, marveling at the unfamiliar luxury. She’d never traveled like this before, nor been treated like royalty. Was this just how Smith and Rhyne did things, or were they trying to sweeten her up before negotiations? It didn’t matter yet. She tried to relax, finding it warmer in the limousine, so she slipped off her jacket. So this was what a limousine ride felt like: soft leather, gentle light for reading, windows dark enough for secrets, and the steady hum of traffic outside.

They reached the Marriott in downtown Minneapolis right on schedule, just as Charles predicted. He climbed out, popped the trunk, and passed her bag to the doorman after opening the limousine door for her. The chilly air bit through her shirt as she stepped out.

"Thank you, Charles," she said, digging into her purse for a tip.

He held up a gloved hand. "No tip is necessary, ma'am. Everything is taken care of for you this week."

"Are you sure?"

He nodded. "Quite sure. My boss was very clear. The clerk will help you inside. Counter is to your left. I'll be here all night if you need anything."

"Thank you again," she said, and hurried up the few steps into the hotel lobby.

Inside, the glass doors whooshed open and the warmth hit her face. The doorman signaled to the front desk. Several clerks stood ready; one immediately waved her over.

"Hello, welcome to Minneapolis Marriott Hotel. How may I help you?"

"I'm Tessa Holmes."

The clerk's eyes lit up. "Yes, Ms. Holmes, we have been expecting you." He snapped his fingers and a bellhop appeared at her elbow, ready to take her carry-on bag.

"Jim here will show you to your room," the clerk continued. "You're in a suite, fourteen-o-two, fourteenth floor, first elevator on the left. Please sign here. Here's your room key."

She signed the card, still flustered by the attention. "Everything is compliments of Smith and Rhyne," he said, lowering his voice as if it were a secret. "Food and drinks can be sent to your room at any time. Or you may dine downstairs in our restaurant or bar."

"Thank you," Tessa managed, her mind still tumbling through the cascade of fuss. Jim led her to the express elevator and up to the fourteenth floor, just two doors from the elevator lobby. He opened the door and set her bag on the bench, then swept open the drapes to reveal the Minneapolis skyline.

The suite seemed too grand for one person: two queen beds, double bathrooms, a Jacuzzi tub, a stocked bar, and a huge table crowned with a fresh bouquet. Tessa tried to take it all in at once.

"If you need anything at all, just dial one-zero-zero on the phone to reach the desk, or nine first for an outbound call. Any questions, Ms. Holmes?"

She shook her head, still overwhelmed. "No, thank you very much."

Jim retreated, closing the door quietly behind him.

Left alone, Tessa dropped onto the edge of the bed, staring at the space around her. This was excessive. Did they treat all their clients like this? Or was it a sign of lofty expectations for the sealant she presented? Her chest tightened. Breathe, let it go, she urged herself. She remembered her promise to call Ray and reached for the phone.

He answered immediately. "Hello?"

"Ray, it's me."

"You made it safely, I gather. How was the flight?"

"Smooth. But it's freezing here, Ray."

He chuckled. "Did you check the forecast?"

"We were busy. I forgot. They picked me up in a limo. I'm in a suite at the Marriott. Fourteenth floor, downtown."

"You're kidding?"

"No, really. It's over the top. Two beds, Jacuzzi, a bar, conference-sized table."

"That is over the top."

"Now I'm really anxious." Tessa's fingers tugged at her hair, frustration brimming just beneath the surface. "I don't think I brought the right clothes," she said, studying her overnight bag with new skepticism.

"Don't be silly. What you packed will be perfect. What did you bring?"

"The navy-blue pantsuit."

"Fine. Trust me, they'll all be in suits and ties. You'll fit right in."

"I could shop for something else," she offered, a hint of doubt creeping in.

"Nonsense. Just wear what you brought."

The exhaustion settled on her bones. "I'm wiped out. I think I'll take a nap, then get dinner. Maybe call you later."

"Okay," Ray said, but she was already hanging up, letting the dial tone hush the room. She stared at the phone in her hand, then up at the clock, suddenly aware of how swiftly everything had shifted.

CHAPTER SIX

At the shrill insistence of the hotel alarm clock, Tessa surfaced from sleep and, for a moment, couldn't remember where she was. Then it hit her—the meeting. The tiny red message light blinked a pulse from the phone on the nightstand. She pressed the message button, and a woman's calm, unfamiliar voice played in her ear. Their meeting was on schedule for 10:00 a.m., and a car would collect her at nine. The message included the address and suite number for Smith and Rhyne's corporate headquarters. Since she'd be driven, the address barely felt relevant, but the suite number might matter, so she scrawled it onto the hotel notepad. The woman rattled off a number to call with questions; then the message ended with an efficient click.

She glanced at the digital clock: 7:35. Enough time for a shower, a quick run through hair and makeup, and breakfast if she didn't stall. The shower helped a little, but her insides still floated somewhere between dread and hopefulness. After dressing, she rode the express elevator down. Her insides sloshed uneasily as the floor numbers flickered past, and when she stepped from the elevator with bag and laptop in hand, the noise, the light, the scent of coffee hit her all at once. The lobby restaurant's sign and smell beckoned, so she slipped inside.

Every table was filled with business types: men and women in crisp, confident clothing, eyes bright or buried in screens. She glanced at them, then at herself. Maybe she should have gone shopping; maybe she should have picked something which screamed "professional." Too late now. The host led her to a table, and she tried to ignore the faint tremble in her hands as she unfolded her napkin. All the while, her insides spun. Relax, she told herself, just relax. She repeated it like a mantra as she forced down breakfast.

By nine, she repacked her things and took a steadying breath before heading for the hotel entrance. This time, the same limousine waited outside, but a new face. The driver opened the door, “Ms. Holmes?”

She nodded. “Yes.”

He offered, “Would you like me to take your briefcase?”

She clung to the handle. “No, I’ll hang onto it.”

“My name is Ben, and I’ll be your driver today.” He held the door open for her, and she slid into the back seat, settling her bag beside her.

Ben shut the door, hustled to the driver’s side, then slid open the little glass divider window. “Will there be any stops, Ms. Holmes, prior to Smith and Rhyne?”

She shook her head. “No, thank you.”

“We’ll be a little early, but the lobby at the Minneapolis CCI Tower is very comfortable. It has most anything you’ll need.”

“Thank you, Ben.” She tried to smile, but felt the cold tighten her face.

He pulled them smoothly into traffic, and within seconds the city’s freezing air forgotten but a memory between the hotel’s warmth and the heated interior of the limousine. She’d seen the weather report at breakfast: mid-twenties. Thank goodness she hadn’t tried to brave a dress or skirt. If she had, she would have needed a long wool coat, which would have been one hassle too many, given she had no plans to return to Minneapolis in the near future.

The limousine wound through the city until they entered the parking garage beneath the Minneapolis CCI Tower. The ramp led straight to a space directly in front of an elevator. A doorman in navy slacks and a long blue coat waited, and he opened the car door before Ben could even make it around. The doorman extended a gloved hand, “Welcome to Minneapolis CCI Tower.”

Ben pointed across the aisle at several wide parking stalls. “Ms. Holmes, I’ll be parked right over there when you’re ready,” he said.

She managed a small “Thank you, Ben,” as she stepped out.

The doorman asked, “Which floor, ma’am?”

“I’m early,” she stammered. “Ben said I could wait in the lobby prior to going up to Smith and Rhyne.”

"Very good," he replied, steady and calm.

He pressed a green illuminated button; the doors opened. "Smith and Rhyne are on the fifty-second floor, when you are ready."

"Thank you," Tessa said, clutching her bag, heart drumming as she followed the doorman's outstretched arm.

The elevator, with its yawning, mirrored interior, was empty except for her. The ride took only seconds; when the doors opened, Tessa stepped out into a lobby so large and bright it seemed to erase the memory of her queasy tummy. Leather seating lined the walls, punctuated by square oak-and-glass tables. On the right, a small cafe buzzed with the low murmur of business—a few merchants, hawking books, magazines, gum, mints, other things, and it struck her, the way they reminded her of airport concourse kiosks, the same purposeful energy. The lobby bustled, everyone moving with intent, everyone dressed to impress: men in charcoal suits and jewel-bright ties, women in pressed slacks and matching jackets. She looked down at her own outfit and relaxed fractionally. Maybe she would be fine.

At 9:45, she slipped back into the elevator and pressed fifty-two. Three young men, sharp in their suits, and a woman with silvering hair and a crisp blazer fell in behind her, the four of them standing in silence, offering only brief grins and polite nods. Nobody said a word. At fifty-two, the elevator chimed, and she stepped out first.

Ahead, the gleaming counter with the Smith and Rhyne logo announced her destination. Behind the counter: a woman in her forties, tailored and poised, already waiting.

She stood, her voice professional and warm. "May I help you?"

"Yes," Tessa replied, matching her composure as best she could. "I'm Tessa Holmes. I'm here for a meeting and presentation."

"Of course, Ms. Holmes, we were expecting you." The woman's eyes sparkled with the cadence of routine. "Jim Smith and Sam Gordon will be meeting with you. Jim should be here any minute."

"Thank you."

"Please take a seat. Would you like coffee or tea?"

"No, thank you."

The waiting area was curated to perfection: twin leather couches, a glass-topped coffee table, splashy modern art on the walls, sunlight diffused just so. She thought of Stanford, of Chemco, the bare concrete and battered benches, nothing like this. In spite of herself, she wondered if those old rumors about the FBI investigation at Chemco had ever settled down, if Ray was tangled in it this very second. Her thoughts slipped to him, but before she could finish the circuit, a man entered; black suit, white shirt, red tie, hair cut military-short, moving with purpose.

"Ms. Holmes?" he asked, measuring her with a flicker in his gaze. *Was it her clothes? Did she not look the part? No way back now.*

"Uh, yes," she replied, pushing her nerves down, steadying herself.

"I'm Jim Smith. Nice to meet you." He took her hand in both of his, holding it a little too long.

"Nice to meet you too." She managed a smile, surprised by the deliberate slowness of his grip.

He leaned in, eyebrows arched, voice dropping. "We're set up in a conference room. Just to double-check—you're presenting alone today?"

"Yes, yes, of course." Her mind went blank for a moment; had she missed some detail, been supposed to bring a team? She followed him, and he led her through bright corridors lined with glass-walled offices and the low murmur of business. Past the cubicles, heads bobbing up to peek as they passed, then a turn and a brisk walk to a door, opening onto a vast conference room: two dozen chairs around a heavy wood table, projector mounted above, whiteboard gleaming on the wall. Everything neat and organized.

"Will you be using the projector?" Jim asked, already halfway to the controls.

"Yes," she said, feeling the gap between their smooth routine and her own clumsy nervousness. *This would be a disaster, wouldn't it?*

Jim was gone and a young man with glasses and a polite, practiced smile slid in. He fired up the projector, held out his hand for her laptop, and in moments, her opening slide glowed on the wall. Clearly, he'd done this a thousand times before. As he left, Jim returned, joined by a taller, younger man in a deep gray suit, thin-rimmed glasses, hair combed back with precision. Jim introduced Sam; they shook hands, exchanged business cards. Jim's card: COO of product development. Sam's: COO of business development.

"We are excited to see what you have for us today," Jim said, his beam just on the edge of too-wide.

"You'll have to bear with me... I'm extremely nervous," Tessa confessed.

"Completely understandable," Sam said. A quick glance passed between them.

Jim offered again, "Coffee, tea, water?"

"No, thank you. Already had too much at the hotel." She wiped her damp palms on her slacks, hoping they didn't notice.

Jim's tone softened. "Please, Ms. Holmes, just relax. Nothing to fear here." She pressed the remote; the screen brightened with her product name: Holmes Acrylic Sealant.

She cleared her throat and launched in. "Gentlemen, I'd like to begin with a brief history." No sooner had she started than Jim interrupted.

"Tessa, can you speak up a little?"

She nodded, embarrassed. "Sorry, the fan is louder than I expected. I'll speak up."

"In my last year of college, I created this acrylic formula as a term project. I wanted something tough, easy to apply, with a wide range of uses. It worked; I received a great grade. But more importantly, my professor planted a seed. He didn't spell out the idea, just nudged me in the right direction."

She clicked the next slide: bullet points, sketches of chemistry flasks, a photo of a parking lot. "I tested it on a parking lot at school. They always had to resurface it, potholes everywhere, but after applying the acrylic, it lasted. Dried quick, looked the same a year later, even after a hammer test.

The only issue is water can't penetrate it, which could be a runoff problem in some situations, especially commercial."

Next slide: chemical formulas, properties, diagrams. "But here's the cool part: the acrylic seeks its own level. Put it on a slope, and it won't run downhill, just sets in place. It even fills surface holes and keeps things flat, as long as the holes aren't too deep."

She took a breath. "So, I think this could maintain roads, even prevent resurfacing altogether."

She glanced at the screen, the patent number glowing at the bottom. "I own the patent for the formula itself, not the applications yet. I'm getting close. At Chemco, I did some research on road maintenance applications when I had downtime, but honestly—I'm not interested in running a business. Which is why I'm here."

Sam leaned forward. "So, Ms. Holmes, you came up with this based solely on your own research?"

"Completely," she responded, meeting his eyes.

Jim, hands folded, voice steady: "Have you presented this to anyone else, or who else knows about this?"

"My professor, and my husband."

"Very good." Sam said, nudging Jim as if to prompt him. From a stack on the table, Tessa handed over a folio. "Here are the spec sheets, which may answer questions you may have."

Both men fell quiet, heads lowered as they studied the sheets. Tessa waited, the silence amplifying her nerves, watching their eyes comb the printed columns and diagrams.

"Ms. Holmes," Sam spoke at last, quiet and certain. "As we stated before—and are convinced now—we are interested in the product." He paused, hands folded together. "I do apologize, but I'd like a word with Jim, and then make a couple calls, before we make you an offer."

"Of course, I understand," Tessa replied, trying not to let the tremor slip into her voice.

"Would you be able to stay here in the office while we conduct these conversations? An hour, perhaps two? I have an office you can use while you wait. Phone and internet access are available."

"Yes, that's fine," she said, feeling her knees complain at the prospect of standing any longer.

Sam and Jim stood simultaneously, the decision made. Sam led Tessa down a short hallway, stopping at an office on the right. He opened the door, revealing a pale wood veneer desk, a business-class phone, a pad and cup heavy with pens.

"I'll close the door for your privacy. If you need anything, Jan is in the first cubicle to your left."

"Thank you, Mr. Gordon."

He closed the door, and the click echoed in the small office. Tessa reached for the phone immediately and dialed Ray, her fingers trembling for reasons she couldn't explain.

"Ray, it's me," she whispered, and was met with his steady voice.

"Tessa. How's it going?"

"We had the meeting. I made the presentation. They're discussing a proposal, asked me to stay for a couple hours to hear it."

"All sounds good," Ray said in a cautious tone. "I'm afraid it might be getting complicated, though."

Tessa's heart chilled. "What do you mean?"

"I just answered a call from Transco—or an agent representing them. I told him you were out of town and unreachable. Persistent guy. He wants you to call him before you accept any offer for Holmes Acrylic Sealant."

A tightness gripped her chest. "Transco? Who are they and how do they know...? Ray, what do I do?" Her voice quavered. "If Smith and Rhyne make me a decent offer, I think I should take it."

"I totally agree," Ray soothed.

"I really don't want to get stuck between two parties fighting over this. One or both could bail." The dread pooling inside her.

"I get it. Here's my thought: if Smith and Rhyne take some time to formulate an offer, get it, then put them on hold while you get advice. I'm sure they'll understand."

"Makes sense." She took a breath, feeling the empty room press in on her. "I wish you were here. I feel so alone and vulnerable."

"I wish I could be there for you, too." His tone lifted. "But I do have some good news."

She clung to it. "What is it?"

"I found a supplier for the batteries for GG-1, including the power adapter unit."

"Great. Who?"

"It's a company in Japan. Sanyen Electronics. They have a San Francisco office—I'm meeting with them Monday to cover the specs."

"How much do they cost?"

"No idea yet, but hopefully less than a thousand. Standard lead time is two to four weeks, depending on the specifics. I'm hoping for two weeks." She could almost hear him flipping through notes. "Oh, here's the number for the Transco agent. Jeff Johnson." He read off the mobile number. "He said you can call anytime."

"Thanks, Ray." Her mind racing ahead. "I'll call you back with updates."

She set the phone down. The silence in the office was palpable. She navigated the desktop computer, searched for Transco. A website appeared: thin, utilitarian, just enough to stake a claim on the web. She logged onto *Business Watch Analytics*, checked Transco's fiscal status. Not as big, nor as diversified as Smith and Rhyne. How could they even come close to matching the offer? Six states, with plans for eight. Long-term contracts with each department of transportation. So maybe a player, but one a giant like Smith and Rhyne could still swallow whole.

A knock at the door. Tessa startled. Jan, the cubicle woman, peeked in.

"Mr. Smith and Mr. Gordon are ready to meet with you again, Ms. Holmes. If you're ready, I can show you to the conference room."

She tucked her notes away and nodded. "I'm ready."

Jan led her to the conference room. Inside, Mr. Smith, Mr. Gordon, and a woman waited. The new woman wore navy slacks and jacket, a white knit blouse, a red scarf knotted neatly at her throat. Her hair was long and brown, eyes dark, presence both professional and striking. They all stood.

"Ms. Holmes, I'd like to introduce Ms. Catanberry," Jim said. "She's from our legal department."

"How do you do?" Catanberry held out her hand; Tessa clasped it, noting the jasmine perfume mingling with the scent of paper and coffee.

Jim gestured to a seat. Tessa sat, folding her hands tightly in her lap.

"Ms. Holmes, Ms. Catanberry is here to draft an agreement if we come to terms."

Tessa nodded: "I understand."

Jim leaned forward. "Ms. Holmes, we are prepared to make you a very generous offer for your product, Holmes Acrylic Sealant. Please understand, this is a product, not a business, and therefore, the price reflects that. If it were an operating business with customers and proven growth, the number would be higher. But in this case, our only option is to buy the full rights."

"I understand," Tessa said.

Jim slid a piece of paper across the table. Her eyes snagged on the legal jargon, then landed on the number.

"Ms. Holmes, we are offering you six hundred thousand dollars for the full rights to your product. Half in cash, half in Smith and Rhyne stock."

Her heart lurched, chest squeezing so tight she thought she might faint; she felt the blood heat her face and couldn't find her voice.

"Take your time, Ms. Holmes," Jim said, noticing. "This offer is only good for today, so you must decide before you leave."

Still she couldn't speak. The room swam. Why couldn't she form a word? She forced herself to breathe, the panic receding by inches.

"Ms. Holmes," Ms. Catanberry said quietly, "I'm sure you'll find everything to your liking in this agreement."

Tessa took another slow breath. "Gentlemen—and Ms. Catanberry," she managed. "I hope you realize this is the first offer I've had for my product. There is another party with significant interest, and I plan to hear their offer."

Jim pounced. "Will you have the offer today? Ours is only good for today."

"I would hope to complete an agreement today," she said, her resolve firming.

Jim's hands pressed flat on the table. "Our offer is more than generous. I wouldn't expect any company to meet or beat it under these conditions."

Tessa met his eyes. "What I'd like to do is fax this agreement to my attorney, and see if the other party can complete an offer today. Can we take another break, and may I use the office again?"

Jim hesitated. "Sure. Jan can get us when you're ready to return."

They all stood. Tessa left the conference room, followed by Jim, Sam, and Ms. Catanberry. She found her way to the office, shut the door behind her, and reached for the phone. She dialed Ray, her fingers steadier this time.

"What's the story?" he asked. "How did you know it was me?"

"No one else has our home number yet," he laughed.

"You won't believe it. They offered six hundred thousand dollars, of which half is stock."

"You must be kidding," Ray said excitedly.

"No, seriously, it's on paper. I wish we had an attorney to fax this too to look it over. I told them it was what I needed to do."

"Did you call the guy from Transco?"

"Not yet," she said. "I will as soon as I get off the phone with you."

"Here, I'll hang up, and you call, then call me right back."

"Okay." Tessa dialed the number. "Jim Johnson here," the voice said.

"Jim, this is Tessa Holmes."

"Ms. Holmes, I'm so glad you called. I understand you are out of town and possibly in the market to sell your interest in an acrylic sealant you created."

"Correct."

"I represent Transco, and they are very interested in purchasing the full rights to it."

"Mr. Johnson, how does Transco even know about my product?"

"Through word of mouth is what I'm told. I don't know of the sources, but they are willing to take a gamble and not miss this opportunity."

"Do you know what they plan to do with it?"

"I imagine they will create a new business division out of it, but I really don't know. They didn't disclose their plan to me. Anyway, have you received an offer from another interested party?"

"Yes."

"What did they offer, if I may ask?"

Silence followed as Tessa grabbed her shaking knees. "I'm sorry, Mr. Johnson, but I don't feel it's necessary for me to disclose to you as an interested party."

"I understand. Well, Transco is offering one point two million dollars for the full rights to your product."

Tessa's heart skipped, and she felt the room spin for a moment. "Excuse me, Mr. Johnson. Would you repeat the number for me?" she asked, the words slipping out almost breathlessly.

"Yes, one point two million dollars. I can fax an agreement, if you could at least give me a verbal okay, which I can record with your permission."

"Mr. Johnson, that is an amazing offer," she managed, her chest tightening as she fought to stay composed.

"It is. So, can I get your verbal okay, and we can proceed?"

The enormity of the offer pressed down on her, making it hard to think. She needed to call Ray. "No, I'm sorry, but I need to consult my partner."

"Partner?" he questioned. "I didn't know you had a partner."

"Well, my husband," she said, trying to keep her tone light despite her racing pulse.

"Oh, makes sense." He seemed to regain some confidence, returning to his pitch. "Can I call you right back?"

"Yes, please do," he insisted.

Tessa hung up and dialed Ray, her fingers trembling as she pressed the buttons. “One point two million,” was the first thing she said when he picked up the phone.

“What! I can’t believe it,” Ray exclaimed.

“In cash,” she added, forcing a smile even as her knees shook beneath her.

“All of it?”

“Yes, all of it.”

“Did you talk to Smith and Rhyne yet?”

Pausing for a moment, she took a deep breath. “Are you kidding? I just ended a call with Jim Johnson.”

“You should see if they will match or beat the offer, even as amazing as it is.”

“I just can’t wrap my head around this. Ray, I wish you were here. This is way over my head.” Tessa’s voice wavered as her eyes glazed.

“Take it easy. We can do this. Let me think,” Ray interrupted. Silence stretched between them.

“Ray, are you still there?”

“Yes, give me a second. Man, I wish we had more time. Okay, here, do this. Go meet with Smith and Rhyne, and have them match or beat it,” Ray suggested. “I don’t think we should walk away from either offer today.”

Tessa reached into her pocket, pulling out a tissue to dab her eyes gently. “Ray, I think I have this. My head stopped spinning. I have their agreement in front of me. I’ll scratch through, change the offer numbers, and adjust them to one point two million dollars, all cash. I’ll also add a condition: my consultation services are available, if needed, at two hundred dollars per hour, including expenses. If they agree, we have a deal. I did some research on Transco, and I don’t see them as a big player here, even with the offer. I like Smith and Rhyne. They treated me really well.”

“Sounds good to me,” Ray replied. “You can do it, Tessa. Call me right back when you know something.”

“I will.” Tessa marked up the contract, her resolve solidifying as she walked out to the hall to find Jan. “I’m ready,” she told her.

"Okay, Ms. Holmes. I'll get everybody to meet you in the conference room."

Tessa made her way to the conference room and sat, her knees trembling slightly under the table. She had skipped lunch, and the clock read 3:00 p.m. The seconds stretched, amplifying the flutter in her tummy. A few moments later, Jim, Sam, and Ms. Catanberry entered and took their seats.

"So, have you come to a decision, Ms. Holmes?" Jim asked, hands folded in front of him, a confident smile on his face.

"I have," she said, passing the signed agreement to Jim. He glanced at the document, then up at her.

"You made some adjustments, I see."

"Yes," she replied, her back straightening as she attempted to project confidence. Jim passed the agreement to Sam, who quickly skimmed it, then handed it to Ms. Catanberry. Tessa noted the way Catanberry's fingers tightened around the paper.

"Ms. Catanberry," Jim said, his voice steady, "would you redraft this agreement for us with these changes, please?"

"Yes, sir," she responded, quietly standing before leaving the room. "Give me about ten minutes."

"Well, Ms. Holmes, you have a deal," Jim said, reaching out to shake Tessa's hand, which she took firmly.

"Congratulations," Sam added, shaking her hand as well.

"Thank you, gentlemen, but I feel I should be the one congratulating you."

"What do you mean?" Jim questioned.

"Well, you have a product with amazing potential, and a lot of possibilities, of which I was unable to explore. I think you will do well with it."

Jim exchanged a glance with Sam before looking back at Tessa. "I hope so."

A moment later, Ms. Catanberry returned with the revised agreement, passing it to both Jim and Sam to sign before offering it to Tessa. She signed quickly, her heart racing.

"Ms. Holmes, Ms. Catanberry will show you to her office, where she can get the information for a wire transfer of the funds and the paperwork necessary for transferring the patent or patents on Holmes Acrylic Sealant. Also, may we have a copy of your presentation as well?" Jim asked.

"Yes, of course."

"By the way, I'm not sure if you will be able to make the flight we scheduled for you, so please check with Jan before you leave. She can extend your stay in the hotel if necessary and find a workable flight for you," Jim added.

"Thank you," Tessa said, relief flooding through her as she nodded.

Tessa walked with Ms. Catanberry to her office and completed the necessary details. It was now 5:00 p.m., and Jan was still there. She found a 10:00 p.m. flight and booked a first-class seat. She didn't want to stay an extra night; no way she'd be able to sleep. The limousine and driver waited for her, ready to take her straight to the airport. With a couple of hours to kill, she planned to treat herself to a meal at the airport, to include two full glasses of wine.

"Oh, no," she recalled as she realized she hadn't called Ray back or Mr. Johnson.

"What's the matter?" the driver asked.

"Oh, I forgot to call my husband."

"Use the phone in the car," he insisted.

"Can I?"

"Of course. Just pick up and dial like normal."

"Hello," Ray answered. "It's me. I'm so sorry I didn't call earlier. It was all going so fast, just like our wedding."

"It's okay. I've been sitting here wondering where we're at on this," she said, biting her lip as she felt a wave of impatience wash over her.

"Well, we have a deal with Smith and Rhyne." Silence followed. "Are you mad?"

"No...no," he insisted. "Maybe just annoyed by not knowing."

Tessa exhaled sharply, the tension in her shoulders creeping up as she crossed her arms. "Good. We should be thankful for how this all turned out. Anyway, they accepted all my changes without question."

"Great. Interesting they didn't negotiate further. Did you call Jim back?"

"Not yet," she replied, a flicker of irritation flashing across her features. "He'll be disappointed."

"I don't want to call him. You're a partner in this. You call him and give him the unwelcome news," she insisted, her voice firm. After a long pause, she added, "Can you?"

"I will. What time is your flight?"

"10:00 p.m. I land at 1:15 a.m. Can you pick me up?"

"Yes."

CHAPTER SEVEN

Tessa stirred awake, the soft sheets tangled around her. She blinked against the morning light filtering through the curtains, her mind slow to catch up with reality. Memories of the previous night were hazy; she didn't even recall falling asleep in the car. A warmth beside her brought her back, and she found Ray propped up on one elbow, watching her.

"Welcome back," he said, his voice low and comforting.

"Thanks. Good to be back," she replied, trying to shake off the lingering fog of sleep.

"Do you remember getting home last night?"

"Vaguely," she admitted, flexing her toes under the sheet to feel the warmth of the bed. The comfort felt almost foreign, but in a safe way.

"Did you undress me?" she asked, half-teasing but also curious.

"I'm afraid so," he replied, a hint of sheepishness in his tone.

She chuckled softly. "You were in no shape to help either. You must have been exhausted."

"I guess I was. Physically and emotionally. But I feel pretty good now," she said, her eyes lighting up as they met his.

She rolled over, straddled him, and kissed him deeply, but beneath her playful grin lay a flicker of doubt. *Would these moments be enough to draw Ray's focus in every circumstance?* She hoped so, but the uncertainty lingered like a shadow. "It's time to show you how much I missed you. And you better be just as enthusiastic in return," she grinned.

Neither of them paused for the next two hours. When Tessa finally came up for air, she sighed. "Okay, who's making coffee?"

"Depends on if I'm allowed to catch my breath."

She grabbed a pillow and smacked him on the side of the head. "It was very nice," she declared. "I needed that."

"You're welcome. Is this something I get to look forward to after every business trip?"

"Deal," she said, with a little too much energy. She walked naked across the room to the bathroom, searching for her robe, not caring about the chill. "Where's my robe?"

"It's out here."

"Why is it out there?"

Ray didn't miss a beat. "I figured you wouldn't want to freeze walking across the room for it, so I left it on the dresser."

She stood framed in the bathroom doorway, hands on her hips, giving him a look. "Wouldn't it have made sense to mention it earlier?"

Ray shrugged, not hiding his amusement. "The view was worth it. So yes, I think I made the right call."

"Oh, I'm going to get you." She crossed over, grabbed her robe, swirled it on, and yanked the bed sheets clear off the bed, exposing Ray fully to the morning light.

"There. Even Steven. Where's your robe?"

"Good question."

"Well, you may want to find it, or you'll be eating breakfast in the buff. Or, you know, get dressed. I'll go make coffee and see which you pick."

"Hmm, I'll have to think about it."

"You do that. Take your time," she said, glancing back with a playful smirk as she walked down the hall.

Later, Ray and Tessa sat at the card table, coffee mugs warming their hands. Ray had settled for khaki shorts and a light blue T-shirt.

"I almost feel human again," she said, staring into the steam curling from her cup.

"I guess we need to talk finances since we are about to become millionaires."

She shook her head, still not quite believing it. "Did you call Jim Johnson back?"

"I did. He was pretty upset. I told him they should have made their best offer first if they were serious. He didn't like it. He wanted to know who you sold to and your contacts there. I told him you would have to provide those to him."

"If he's a good agent, I won't need to call him and give him any information. He'll find it out for himself. I have no interest in listening to him whine." She shrugged, setting her cup down. "Anyway, we need a financial adviser and a tax planner. We're going to take a huge tax hit. They can help."

"When do we see the money?" Ray asked.

"Monday, by the end of the day. I asked them to wire it into our savings account. I don't think we should do much differently until we get some advice."

"I agree. Do you think I could cut back to part-time at Laubner? I could use more time for GG-1, but it's probably smart to keep using Laubner's equipment and staff. Plus, I figure I owe my dad to stick around."

"I haven't decided what I'm doing yet," Tessa said. "You can cut back. If things go south, we're both young—we can always go back to full-time."

"True. When I go in Monday, I'll talk to HR and my dad about cutting back. I'm sure he'll support it, considering the situation."

Tessa took her coffee and stepped to the kitchen window, gazing out. "Okay, we have a plan then."

# # #

Almost before his plate was clean, Ray was in the garage, hunched over diagrams and numbers, working on the electrical calculations for GG-1. He scribbled theories, testing them against what happened years ago. It became obvious he'd need the right equipment to confirm any of it—a load tester, logic analyzer, oscilloscope, programmable power supply. If money wasn't a problem, why not buy it himself? Maybe it was time to set up the garage as the lab he'd always wanted. Maybe on Monday he'd call for quotes.

Tessa poked her head into the garage, bringing him lunch on a plate. "Ray, I saw a note about going to San Francisco Monday to meet with Sanyen Electronics. I thought you were going into Laubner first thing. Did you forget?"

Ray stared up, blank. “Oh, no, I forgot. What time was the meeting?”

“2:00 p.m.”

“Okay, I have plenty of time. I’ll go into work, then leave early for Sanyen.”

“You’re going to meet with your dad and HR too, right?” she asked.

“Yes. Still plenty of time. I can always call Dad tomorrow.”

Suddenly, a shrill ringing echoed from inside the house.

“What’s that?” Ray asked as Tessa dashed toward the kitchen door.

Tessa called out from the house, “It’s for you!” A fleeting thought crossed his mind—he really needed to get a phone out in the garage. He wiped his hands on a rag and headed inside. Tessa held the phone, her expression focused.

He stepped closer, curious. “Who is it?”

“Steve Seltzer.”

He took the phone, his voice bright with anticipation. “Steve, this is Ray.”

“Hi Ray, I hope I’m not disturbing you.”

“No, just in the garage.”

“The reason I called is I’ve completed your project early and wondered if you could come by Monday to pick it up.”

Ray blinked, surprised. “You’re done already?”

“Yes, we rushed it through. Remember, I told you we had time to fill. Things have slowed.”

Ray remembered. “This is quite a surprise. I’ll come get it on Monday.”

“Ray, would it be possible to bring a check also? I don’t usually ask, but things are a little tight.”

“Sure, Steve. Are you in the shop today?”

“Yes.”

“Would it be helpful if I came by today, paid you, and picked it up?”

“Great, if it’s not too much trouble.”

“What’s the total?” Ray asked, pen poised.

“Five thousand six hundred seventy-two dollars and seventeen cents.”

Ray wrote it down. “I’ll be there in about an hour.”

"Thanks, Ray. See you then."

Ray hung up and looked over at Tessa, still stunned. "Steve is done with the GG-1 shell. I can't believe it."

"Really? That's great."

"He needs to be paid right away. Shop's been slow, I guess."

"How much?" Tessa asked.

Ray read off the number.

She pursed her lips. "We have about six thousand in checking, so we're fine, but no big spending sprees this weekend. Without the acrylic sealant money, we'd be in a tough spot."

Ray nodded. "We're lucky. Remember, you were the one telling me to keep going."

"True. I did say that."

"I'll go get GG-1. I can't wait."

"Okay, I'll hold down the fort. You can eat your lunch on the way—it's still in the garage."

He grabbed his lunch, the check Tessa had written and headed out.

When Ray arrived at Seltzer's Shop, the door stood wide open. He walked inside and heard a voice shout from the office, "In here!"

Steve waited behind his desk. "Wow, you made it quick. I didn't even have time to pack your job properly."

Ray glanced at a cardboard box on the table, already filled with packing material. "Oh, don't bother."

"Come have a look." Steve lifted out the largest donut-shaped piece. "I assembled the halves to check the fit. We can take them apart if you want."

"I'd like to see the finish inside," Ray said.

Steve unscrewed a dozen nuts and separated the halves, handing them to Ray. The interior walls were cut with tiny grooves and had the perfect curvature to hold the stones. The polish caught the overhead lights, almost glassy even in the dull shop.

"Did you hand polish these?" Ray asked.

"No, we use a machine. It deburrs and polishes with the right media."

Ray examined the smaller rectangular housing for the electronics and power adapter, then nodded. "Looks good." He handed over the check.

"Thanks, Ray. If you need more, just let me know."

"I will." He packed up the components, shook Steve's hand, and headed home.

# # #

Back at the house, Tessa sat on the bed, gazing out the window as the sunset painted the sky in vibrant shades of orange. The soft light illuminated the rows of books lining the shelf and the closet filled with clothes she had yet to wear. A wave of contemplation washed over her; while Ray had a clear plan for their future, she couldn't help but wonder how things would shift between them as they embraced this new chapter. It was a thrilling prospect, but the thought of their shared dreams sometimes felt daunting, leaving her with a hint of uncertainty. The rumble of his car in the driveway jolted her from her thoughts.

Tessa rose and hurried to the kitchen just as Ray walked in, his face alight with excitement.

"How did it go?" she asked, her voice laced with eagerness.

Ray barely paused, already moving toward the garage. "You have to see this!" His enthusiasm was contagious as he rushed past her, eager to unveil the components of GG-1. She trailed after him, her heart quickening.

"Wow, he does nice work. Those look amazing."

"I can't wait to assemble it with the stones and begin testing. But I need to finish the circuits, and I really hope the power adapter works. I guess I'll be waiting before I can test the full unit."

"See what they say on Monday," she suggested.

He nodded, a grin on his face. "This feels just like Laubner, always waiting for the one missing piece."

Tessa drifted back into the house, casting a glance toward the garage where Ray was already immersed in his work, the pieces of GG-1 spread out in front of him. As she began to empty the rest of the moving boxes, a small sigh escaped her lips. She knew this passion was part of who he was, yet a flicker of worry crossed her mind. Was this what their life would look like—Ray engaged in his projects while she managed the home? She longed for the simple moments they used to share, but as she prepared to organize their new space, she reminded herself they'd navigate this together.

Sunday morning, sunlight angled through the blinds, and Tessa found Ray's side of the bed empty. She went down for breakfast. No Ray. She opened the side door and called, "Ray!"

"Out here," he called back.

She crossed the chilly yard in her robe to the garage. "What are you doing so early?"

"I'm assembling what I can of GG-1. Each stone needs to be oriented before placement. I think it maximizes their power."

She watched him sort, test, and mark each stone, feeling a mix of admiration and frustration. He was brilliant, but his relentless focus on GG-1 felt like a barrier between them—one she feared would widen with each passing day. "Looks tedious. Going to take a while?"

"Why I started early."

"Do you have enough stones?"

"I should. Enough for two, actually."

She watched as he carefully arranged the stones, his focus intense as he marked their positions with a magnet and felt pen. Each piece seemed to require precise attention, and she noted how his fingers moved with practiced ease. Time slipped away, and as she observed him lost in his work, a thought began to form in her mind—was this the kind of dedication that would bring them closer together, or would it create distance between them?

CHAPTER EIGHT

The smell of breakfast startled Ray awake—a vivid aroma sharp enough to sweep away his dreams. Monday again, somehow. He rubbed his eyes and dressed quickly, sensing the urgency in the air. As he walked down the hall, the cool floor against his bare feet led him to find breakfast waiting on the table with Tessa already dressed for work. He paused, bemused by how recently they'd enjoyed a relaxed morning together. Pulling out a chair, he asked, "So, what's on your agenda today?"

Tessa sipped her coffee, her lips barely touching the rim. He noticed the tension in her shoulders as her gaze drifted out the window. "Remember the resume I sent to Stanford three weeks ago? Saturday, I received a letter. They want me to meet with HR about a different teaching position."

"Wait, that's great!" Ray's excitement bubbled over, but he sensed her hesitation. "Why didn't you tell me?"

"I didn't want to bug you while you were busy in the garage."

Ray thought for a moment. "So, do you want what they're offering? We're off to a good start with all the money, but with taxes and the mortgage won't last forever unless we hit it big again. Definitely go, even if it's part-time; it might be worth having your foot in the door."

She buttered some toast and nodded. "How about you? What are you going to tell your dad today?"

Ray let out a breath, collecting his thoughts. "I'll explain our windfall and tell him I want to reduce my hours at Laubner. He'll understand."

"And Laubner? What will they think?" She pointed to the eggs on his plate, a gentle reminder to eat.

He took a bite. "They're short on good researchers and engineers. Cutting back won't push me out; the team will just pick up the slack. You know how government contracts are—they hate delays."

She finished her coffee and reached for her bag. “Call me later and let me know how it goes.”

“I will. You too.”

“And you have the appointment in San Francisco today?”

He nodded, swallowing the last of his breakfast. “Yeah. Power for GG-1. It’s going to be a full day.” He shoved his arms into a jacket and headed out the door.

The drive to Laubner blurred, traffic sliding past almost unnoticed. Once there, Ray went directly to Dave’s office. His father sat behind the monitor, brown hair trimmed and blue eyes alert as he peered over the screen. The sound of keys clicking filled the air as Dave finished typing a quick note. Finally, he looked up, curiosity lighting his expression. “Ray, welcome back. We missed you.”

“Hi, Dad. Good to be back. I need to talk to you about some things. Things have changed this week for Tessa and me.”

Dave gave a surprised look. “Wow, right to it. Usually, this stuff takes weeks.”

“No, not what you’re thinking,” Ray said, a flush rising to his cheeks.

Dave grinned. “Thought I was going to surprise your mother with some big news. Or would you have me keep it a secret?”

Ray shook his head, half-laughing. “Dad. You’re killing me. Tessa sold an acrylic sealant she invented and patented. A company in Minneapolis bought it for one point two million. All cash.”

Silence followed as Dave absorbed it. “Oh my. That’s remarkable. How did this happen?”

Ray shrugged. “Long story. I’ll explain later. Anyway, we want to make some changes.”

“You’re not quitting, are you? Money disappears fast—and before you know it, you’re jobless, your skills get stale. Not good, Ray. Plus, taxes. Do you have any idea how much they’ll take from you?”

“Dad.” He raised a hand. “I’m not quitting. Just cutting back. I want time to work on GG-1 and other personal projects—something I can take credit for myself.”

"You've had your name tied to a lot of your work here."

"That's not what I mean. Tessa found a niche and sold it. We have enough seed money to build our creations. And if it works, it grows from there."

Pride and anxiety wrestled in Dave's expression. "Ray, I'll support you. I just don't want to see you struggle if it falls through. I admire your courage. If I'd tried something daring when your mother and I started out, she would have slapped me and said, 'David Holland, get a good job, work hard, and everything will be fine.' And she was right. Just head to HR and let them know. They'll work with you."

Ray grinned. "Thanks, Dad. Speaking of projects, Steve finished my GG-1 housing."

"That was fast."

"Yeah, apparently he's light on jobs and needed the money."

Dave shook his head, jotting a note on his pad. "A problem with small machine shops. Feast or famine. I'll see if we can send him some work to get him back on track. Wouldn't want to see him run into trouble. Did he do a decent job?"

Ray nodded. "It's incredible. I already started assembling the stones inside."

"Stones?" Dave's brow furrowed.

Ray tilted his head. "I'll explain later. I need to go to San Francisco this afternoon to source a battery and maybe a power adapter."

"What company?"

"Sanyen Electronics."

"Good choice. But if you see Mr. Tanaka, be careful."

Ray hesitated. "Careful?"

"He'll try to dig into your project, order hundreds or thousands of whatever you're building. He will pry. Trust me."

Ray took the advice in stride, finishing up with HR. They offered him a schedule of sixteen to twenty hours a week, which seemed perfect. He left Laubner without saying goodbye to his dad and hit the highway toward San Francisco's industrial edge.

Rolling his conversation with Dad over in his head, Ray wondered if the only thing to worry about at Sanyen was Mr.

Tanaka or if cost would be the bigger issue. He drove, cycling through doubts and possibilities until he finally let go and relaxed into the rhythm of the road.

Sanyen was a broad, single-story building, all glass and clean metal siding painted gray. The sign above the sliding entrance doors simply read: Sanyen Electronics. Inside, Ray found a reception desk just past a second glass doorway.

The receptionist caught his eye, her milky skin glowing in the fluorescent light. Ray took a breath and introduced himself. "Ray Holland, here to meet with someone about a battery and possibly a power adapter for a project."

"Did you have an appointment?"

"Yes."

She checked the computer, nodded once. "Yes, Mr. Holland. You will meet with Mr. Ito. He will be with you in a moment. Please have a seat."

Ray felt a wave of relief wash over him. Not Mr. Tanaka, after all. He waited, glancing at the two sets of vinyl chairs and the glass tables scattered with trade magazines. A sharply dressed man entered the space, looking barely thirty, with dark suit and neatly trimmed stubble.

"Mr. Holland?" The man's accent was crisp and direct.

"Yes."

"My name is Ito. I'm pleased to meet you."

Ray moved to shake hands but saw Ito bowing; he matched the gesture. Then they shook hands, the grip firm.

"Come right this way. I understand you need a special battery."

"Yes."

"We received your specifications. We have recommendations. Very good battery. Long lasting. Lithium-ion type."

They passed rows of high-tech cubicles, where employees barely glanced up, their focus wrapped tight as wire. The conference room was a study in glass and chrome—order and sterility reigned, not a speck of dust in sight. Ito closed the door behind them.

"Will you be placing a large order?" he asked.

Ray shook his head. "No, just one right now."

"Only one?" Ito frowned slightly. "You're lucky we stock this battery. Not special order, or very expensive."

"What a relief. How much is the battery?"

"Two hundred fifty American dollars, plus tax. Now you said you need a power adapter also."

"Yes, I sent those specifications."

"We reviewed. We can make many, very quickly. How many do you want: one hundred, one thousand?" Ito's eyebrows arched.

Ray felt awkward, the weight of the situation pressing down on him. "Just one."

"Only one?" Ito repeated, his voice mixing amusement with disbelief.

"Yes."

"Mr. Holland, it is very expensive to make just one. Maybe you should buy more."

"Mr. Ito, please understand, I'm a researcher and developer. This project only needs one power adapter."

Ito sat back, eyeing Ray thoughtfully. "If your research project goes well, then you'll need many power adapters. You will order from us, yes?"

Ray let out a breath, feeling the pressure lift slightly. "Yes, Mr. Ito, I would order more from you."

Ito's mood lifted. "Good, good. You call me when ready to order many more."

Ray nodded. "How much for the one?"

"This one will take, hmm, one week, hmm, three hundred fifty American dollars."

Ray couldn't help but feel impressed. No wonder Laubner liked Sanyen. He also knew not to negotiate; that would be an insult here. "Very good, Mr. Ito. I agree to the price and delivery."

Ito rose and bowed; Ray did the same, feeling the formalities settling over them. They shook hands again.

"You can have the battery today if you like."

"Great. Cash or credit?"

"Yes," Ito replied, as if both options were equally likely.

Ray hesitated, then fished out his Visa. Ito took it and escorted him to the receptionist, handing her the card.

Ito rattled off in Japanese, "2Tsu no 50-doru no amerikadoru," to the receptionist, who ran the card. Ray double-checked the display, ensuring the charge was right. He signed the receipt, slightly relieved.

"I'll be right back with your battery," Ito said.

Before Ray had tucked his wallet away, Ito returned with a box about the size and heft of a brick, covered in Japanese writing. Ito handed it to Ray with both hands; he matched the gesture, surprised by its weight. They bowed again, shook hands, and Ito guided him toward the doors.

"Thank you, Mr. Holland. Pleased to do business with you."

"Thank you, Mr. Ito," Ray answered, feeling a strange sense of satisfaction as he left.

Traffic through San Francisco was the usual chaos, red taillights stretching for blocks. By the time Ray pulled in at home, it was nearly five. Tessa sat at the table, already eating dinner. She glanced up, a carrot clutched in her hand shielding her mouth as she chewed.

"Sorry," she mumbled, her voice muffled. "I wasn't sure of your plans, so didn't make you anything."

She stood, her grin brightening the room. Ray crossed the space and kissed her forehead.

"It's okay," he said. "I can pull something together from what my mom sent last week."

Tessa relaxed her shoulders, her gaze steady. "How did it go today?"

He recapped everything—the conversation at Laubner, the trip to San Francisco, the battery, and the power adapter coming in a week.

She whistled. "Wow, those guys are fast." She moved in close and kissed him. "Are you sure you don't want me to whip up something for you?"

He slid his hands around her waist, tugging her snug. "No, I can do it. I think I hammered out a good deal today. They're pushy about future orders, but I handled it."

She laughed, the sound light and airy. "Good."

He leaned back, studying her eyes. "How was your day?"

Her look shifted to one of delighted disbelief. "Pleasantly surprising. I went to Stanford—they had me interview with HR, and at the end, they offered me a faculty position in the chemistry building. Full-time if I want it."

"Wow, that was quick. Is that what you want?"

Tessa considered, a thoughtful expression crossing her face. "Well, we agreed I'd teach up to two classes a week for now. Orientation starts next week. Classes resume in three weeks, right after the semester break."

Ray grinned, picturing her in front of a classroom. "That has to feel like a vacation compared to Chemco."

"No contest. Speaking of which—any sign of our two FBI agents?"

"Nope. Quiet. Too quiet."

She raised an eyebrow, concern creeping into her expression. "For some reason... I don't think they're gone for good."

# # #

Ray spent two days at Laubner, helping his team catch up while reassuring them he'd stay in the loop, despite cutting back his hours. Pride and anxiety churned within him as everyone congratulated him and Tessa on their windfall.

Wednesday night, he walked into the kitchen and stopped short. There, beside a huge oak table, was Tessa with her arms raised, a smile lighting up her face.

"Surprise!"

"Where'd it come from?" he asked, curiosity piqued.

"Woodworks. On sale today only."

"And the chairs?" he inquired, noticing the lack of seating.

"I didn't like theirs. We'll get chairs at their weekend sale."

He nodded, examining the table, his heart sinking as he processed the price. "I like it. How much?"

"Twelve hundred dollars—I haggled forty percent off."

He blinked, the price hitting him like a punch to the gut. "Twelve hundred and no chairs? They should've thrown some in." A wave of anxiety washed over him. Was this the point of them losing control of their finances?

"But you love it, right?" Tessa pressed, her eyes searching his for reassurance.

He stroked the smooth grain of the table, feeling the weight of the decision. "It's gorgeous. How'd it get through the door?"

"Three strong guys carried it."

He sighed, the reality settling in. "Okay, just—no more 'savings' surprises."

"Why not?" she asked, a hint of confusion in her voice.

"Dad warned this money would disappear."

"Are you mad?"

"Not mad. I'm used to being poor."

The concern in her expression tugged at him. He could see the tension in her shoulders and the way she studied his face, searching for reassurance.

"Oh. Good. I'm glad you're not mad. Maybe GG-1 could be the next source of income for us?" Her arms relaxed at her sides now, hopeful.

Ray shook his head, half-smiling. "I don't know. So far, its development cost is considerable, and its key component is in limited supply."

"The stones?" she asked.

"Yes. Remember, I only received four buckets full from my dad; the rest were shipped out for disposal. GG-1's already used up about half of what I have. Maybe I'll build a second unit if GG-1 goes sideways. But as far as making any money—it's still unknown. Profit wasn't my goal when I began."

He watched her absorb this, hoping she understood. "Okay, I get it. But honestly, my acrylic formula was the same way. I didn't create it to make a million. It just happened when I finally realized what it could do. Maybe GG-1 will surprise us."

Ray's gaze drifted back to the table, tracing the grain with his fingers. He yearned for success with GG-1 but feared, like their finances, it could slip through his fingers.

"Surprise us? I have no doubt," he said, knowing he carried more questions than answers about what GG-1 would do once it finally functioned.

CHAPTER NINE

The garage pulsed with the hum of fluorescent lights, casting a stark glow over Ray's cluttered workspace. The metallic scent of solder lingered in the air, remnants of a long night spent assembling GG-1. His heart raced at the thought of finally bringing his vision to life. Yet, a nagging thought lingered—was he so absorbed in his work that he was leaving Tessa behind?

Tessa's voice drifted from the kitchen, breaking his focus. "The bank called. They confirmed the transfer from Smith and Rhyne."

Ray stepped into the kitchen, greeted by the inviting scent of coffee. He noticed a hint of hesitation in her tone. Did she worry about the changes ahead?

"We should find a tax adviser to minimize our exposure," he said, lowering his voice, as if the walls might overhear their concerns.

Tessa nodded, her brow creasing in thought. "Absolutely. Let's start looking."

Before either could say more, the low rumble of a car engine echoed up the street and halted in front of their house. They exchanged uneasy glances through the blinds. A black Chevrolet Suburban, new or nearly so, idled at the curb, its tinted windows obscuring the occupants.

"Who could it be?" Tessa whispered, her voice trembling.

"I don't know, but it doesn't look good. Black SUV, dark windows—government written all over it," Ray replied, unease settling. "If it's Fitz and Sommers, they've upgraded."

The doorbell rang, sharp and insistent, and Ray's heart plummeted. He could only imagine how their arrival would disrupt not just his work, but Tessa's calm, too.

"Don't open it," Tessa urged, anxiety creeping into her tone.

"They know we're home. We can't avoid it," Ray replied, bracing himself.

"What do they want? We're not doing anything wrong," she protested, her worry palpable.

The doorbell rang again, demanding their attention.

Ray hesitated, frustration bubbling beneath his calm facade. "Somehow, I know I'll regret this," he muttered, opening the door wide.

"Mr. Holland?" The taller man said, his tone polite yet rehearsed.

"Yes," Ray answered, arms crossed, tension mounting.

"Hi, I'm Agent Sommers, and this is Agent Fitz. We're with the FBI."

Ray wore a baffled expression. "Wait, you two again? I thought you were done with this investigation. What's this about this time?"

Sommers leaned in, expression neutral. "We have a few questions about Chemco—and about Mrs. Holland's involvement."

Ray sensed Tessa's stance tense beside him. She held her breath, and he wanted to reassure her, but the agents' scrutiny made it difficult.

"Involvement? You have to be kidding. The news said your case was closed."

Sommers shook his head. "There are still open questions. Mind if we come in?"

Ray narrowed his eyes. They'd been more intimidating before; now, the agents seemed almost cautious.

He weighed his options, finally sighing. "Fine. Come in."

"Thank you," Sommers said, and Fitz entered without a word.

Tessa remained near the stairs, arms wrapped around her books.

"Would you like to sit down?" she offered, her voice steady despite the tension.

"Not just yet. Mr. Holland, we spoke with Mr. Seltzer at his tool and die shop yesterday. He claims to have machined a bomb casing for you."

Ray let the words hang in the air, disbelief washing over him. "Bomb casing? No. He machined a part, sure, but not a bomb casing."

Sommers continued, “He said you didn’t tell him what it was for, but when we pressed, he did say it could look like a bomb casing.”

Ray sneered. “You guys are amazing. Maybe it’s a donut maker. Or a spaceship. But it’s not a bomb.”

Sommers brushed aside his sarcasm. “Sarcasm can be problematic,” he replied, tone flat. “We’re just here to get the facts.”

“I’m telling you: it’s not a bomb.”

“Let us see the part,” Sommers said, not quite a request.

Ray hesitated but relented. “It’s in the garage. Want me to bring it in?”

“No. Let’s all go.” Sommers stepped closer, motioning toward the back door.

Ray led the way, Tessa following in silence, the weight of apprehension heavy between them.

“I don’t see what this has to do with Chemco or the accident,” she said. “You haven’t asked me anything about it.”

“When we have questions for you, Mrs. Holland, we’ll let you know,” Sommers said, his stride unbroken.

Ray felt pride swell as Tessa stood her ground, but guilt settled within him. Was he pushing her into the line of fire?

Inside the garage, Ray flicked on the lights. GG-1 sat on the workbench.

The agents’ scrutiny felt palpable, and Ray swallowed hard.

“What’s inside?” Sommers squinted.

“Stones,” Ray said flatly.

“Shrapnel?”

“No. Just stones.”

“What kind?”

Ray picked up the bucket of rocks from Laubner, scooped several into his palm, and held them out.

Sommers studied them, then flicked a lighter beneath one. Nothing happened.

“Open the casing,” he said, not quite a request.

Ray's jaw clenched. “If I do, I’ll have hours’ worth of rework. I hope your office is paying for this.”

“It’s necessary,” Sommers replied.

Ray exchanged a look with Tessa, who whispered, "Let's just get it over with."

Ray grabbed a drill with a socket attachment and removed the bolts. He knew what would happen next: inside, the stones would spill everywhere.

"Gentlemen," Ray said, "this is going to be messy."

Sommers nodded. "Proceed."

Ray lifted the top half, and stones poured out in a clattering heap, Tessa helping catch what she could on the workbench.

"Told you. Just stones," Ray said.

Sommers gave the mess a cursory glance. "Why did someone wire one-point-two million dollars to your bank account? Could it be payment for something at Chemco, Mrs. Holland?"

Tessa didn't hesitate. "You're barking up the wrong tree. It's a payment from Smith and Rhyne for a patent. If you'd checked your facts, you'd know. Now, please leave. Our day is ruined."

Sommers didn't argue. "We're done here, Fitz." The agents left, crisp footsteps retreating to the Suburban.

Ray watched them go, disbelief flooding his mind. Not a thank you. Not even a sorry. Just disruption and suspicion.

Frustration bubbled within him. "It'll take hours to put back together."

Tessa moved to his side. "You worked so hard. And for what?"

Ray shook his head. "They act polite, then become demanding. None of it adds up."

"We need to figure it out," Tessa said.

Ray nodded, but his focus shifted to the mess of stones. "Let's gather the rocks."

Tessa began scooping the stones into a tub. "Your alignment marks are still visible on these. You won't need to repeat the orientation, will you?"

Ray grinned, realization dawning. "You're right. It saves time. You load the top half; I'll do the bottom. We should have it reassembled tonight."

CHAPTER TEN

Ray lay beside Tessa, watching her breathe softly, lost in the rhythm of her dreams. Restlessness gnawed at him, and he slipped from the bed, moving quietly down the old stairs into the kitchen. As he set up the coffee, impatience twisted in his gut. He poured the half-brewed coffee, thoughts racing. *I need this to work. If GG-1 flies, I can prove I'm more than just the engineer at Laubner. I can change the world.*

Cradling the cup, he stepped outside, balancing the hot coffee as he fumbled with his keys. The lock was stiff and unfamiliar at this hour. When he opened the garage, a cold, musty air rushed out to greet him. GG-1 sat in pieces, waiting. He set the two assembly plates aside, lining up the work with care. The process mattered.

Time slipped by in silence, the only sounds, his breath and the click of the wrench as he tightened each nut and bolt. He couldn't shake the question looming in his mind. *What if it doesn't work? What will I say to Tessa? What will she think of me?*

Suddenly aware of the late hour, he realized he hadn't eaten. His belly twisted in hunger as he headed back inside.

As he entered the kitchen, Tessa came down the stairs, her hair tousled, eyes still heavy with sleep. The aroma of coffee filled the air, and he couldn't help but admire how the soft morning light illuminated her face.

Her gaze drifted out the window, an edge of worry creeping in. *Orientation at Stanford*—he could see it hanging over her like a storm cloud, bringing both excitement and uncertainty.

"Where's breakfast?" she asked, a teasing smirk tugging at her lips.

"I'm making it now," he replied, trying to keep his tone light.

"Now?" she raised an eyebrow, playful but curious.

"I was in the garage, putting GG-1 back together."

She nodded, moving toward the fridge. "How did it go?"

"It's done. Just need the power adapter; it should come this week."

"Wow, that's great." She set out milk and orange juice, lining everything up meticulously. "What are you making?"

"Eggs and toast," he said, reaching for the pan.

"Sounds good." She clattered out two slices of bread, her movements quickening with anticipation.

"How do you like your eggs?" he asked while cracking them into the pan.

"Over easy."

"Yours will be up in a minute."

They sat at the little table, eating in a comfortable silence, the morning quiet settling around them. Ray sensed the gentle weight of the moment but finally broke it. "Awfully quiet this morning. What's on your mind?"

Tessa pushed her glass gently back and forth. "Nothing, really. Just enjoying the calm before the storm. Thinking about orientation at Stanford. I'm wondering if it's what I really want after all."

Ray frowned, surprised. "Didn't you always want to teach? Wasn't there a teacher who inspired you?"

"Miss Jenson, ninth grade chemistry. She made it come alive for us." Tessa leaned back, a hint of wistfulness in her eyes. "I always thought it was the end goal, but yesterday, helping you in the garage, working on an unknown project—it felt good. I liked it."

He nodded. "Didn't you say you could teach part time? That would give you hours for research. I could use your help with GG-1, honestly. There's still a lot I don't understand."

Her eyes brightened, energy returning. "Tempting. If I teach just one or two classes, I'd have plenty of time to help you." She drummed her fingers on the table, energized now. "I'm excited. I wish it was Monday already. What do you think GG-1 is going to do?"

Ray smiled at her enthusiasm. "I expect GG-1 to levitate. At least hover."

"And if it doesn't?"

He shrugged. "Then it's back to the drawing board. Science is about embracing the failures, too."

Ray noticed a flicker of uncertainty in Tessa's eyes as she asked, "The stones are the key, aren't they?"

"Yes. A couple of years ago, in my bedroom, they floated." He looked at her, remembering. "I believe they'll do it again."

"Why, though? What makes you so sure?"

"They're magnetic, but not like normal magnets. Electricity makes them more active. They interact with the earth's field—trading energy, not just aligning with north like a compass."

"So, GG-1 is basically a magnetic vehicle that responds to the earth's field?"

"The theory, at least. But how, exactly—it's a wildcard. That's why I'm planning to launch at the Laubner test site at Diamond Hills, up north."

She hesitated. "Is it dangerous?"

He weighed it. "I'm being careful. There's a remote control with a five-mile range. If I lose the signal, the power shuts down."

She considered this, then nodded, reassured. "So, how do we get in?"

His voice thinned. "Dad said there might be a guard, but the site's mostly abandoned. Just a locked gate. He has a key."

Tessa rubbed her hands together, a hint of excitement in her demeanor. "Here's hoping for good launch weather."

Ray laughed. "Definitely."

CHAPTER ELEVEN

Since shifting to part-time, Ray found himself overwhelmed with his work on the laser fusion reactor project. Steve, his boss, didn't seem to understand that part-time hours didn't lessen expectations. Emails poured in, a steady stream of requests for updates and reminders of deadlines he struggled to meet. *If I want to prove my worth, I have to make this work.* Frustrated, he bent the rules and brought project journals home, hoping to catch up. He hunched over the papers when a sudden knock at the door startled him upright.

Through the window, he saw a FedEx truck parked out front.

He opened the door to find a young man in a FedEx uniform holding a package.

"Package for Ray Holland."

Ray's face lit up. "I'm Ray."

"Sign here." The clipboard was already out, pen ready.

He scrawled his signature and accepted the box—a little bigger than a paperback. The shipping label read: *Sanyen Electronics*.

"Thanks." He closed the door and headed for a pair of scissors.

After cutting the tape, he pulled out the packing slip. The adapter was wrapped tight in bubble wrap; as he peeled it back, a clean circuit board came into view. Satisfaction flickered within him. They'd shipped it days early. Ready to mount it, he moved out to the garage, voltage meter in hand, and began attaching the adapter to GG-1.

The methodical process of adding trimmers for each output and double-checking calculations calmed him. He'd built a servo as a kill switch—a last-ditch safety if something went wrong. Everything was tuned, each output set to the voltages he'd worked out. Crystals for the radio frequency controls were next, slotted into their designated sockets.

Now ready for final assembly, he considered ventilation. He needed access to the battery and inner components but unbolting with every adjustment wasn't ideal. Sitting at the workbench, an idea struck him: an outdoor electrical receptacle box, designed for weatherproofing and easy access.

Ray headed back inside, grabbed his keys, and locked up. The nearest hardware store sat about twenty minutes away. He hoped to get everything in one stop.

An hour later, he returned home with the receptacle box. He cut away the bottom, clamped it in place, and set up access to the battery and adapter.

Tessa pulled up in the driveway, stepping out and wrinkling her nose. "What smells?"

"Just the new soldering flux," he replied from the garage doorway.

"Soldering?" She raised an eyebrow, glancing at the workbench cluttered with tools.

"Yeah. I had to make adjustments to the circuit board for GG-1."

"You said you'd finish after the adapter arrived."

"I did. The adapter came in early, so I optimized everything."

Tessa shook her head, half-amused. "No wasting time, I see."

"Nope. Everything has to be perfect for the next test."

She pressed her fingers to her nose again. "When does the smell go away?"

Ray laughed. "At least I'm not doing this in the house."

"Point taken."

"Give it a couple hours; it'll settle down."

Tessa eyed the garage, as if verifying. "I was thinking barbecue for dinner, but not if it still smells."

Ray blinked. "Barbecue? We don't even own one."

Tessa arched an eyebrow, gesturing toward the car. She popped the trunk. "We do now." Inside, a boxed barbecue awaited assembly. Ray stared for a moment before laughing. "You want this ready by dinner? You know it's propane, right? We'll need fuel."

She was already at the passenger door, pointing to a five-gallon propane tank nestled in the front seat. He raised an eyebrow. "You're not supposed to carry those inside a car..."

Tessa waved him off. "I wasn't about to strap it to the roof. I know fuel safety—I worked at Chemco."

Ray chuckled, surrendering. "Okay, you have it all figured out."

"Tell you what. You assemble the barbecue, and I'll make salad, thaw the steaks, and prep the bread. Oh, and there's wine. And cheesecake."

"What's the special occasion?" he asked, impressed.

"I finished orientation early. Two days off."

"Great."

"Well, if we want to eat before midnight, you'd better get started."

With groceries in hand, Tessa disappeared into the house. Ray wrestled the barbecue from the trunk to the carport, opened the box, and laid out the parts. An hour later, the barbecue stood ready for its first use.

He poked his head inside, catching the rich aroma of marinated T-bone steaks wafting from the kitchen. Tessa worked at the counter, tossing a salad. "Barbecue's good to go," he announced.

"Bring them in when they're ready. The table's set."

After a few more minutes, he brought the steaks inside. Tessa had transformed the dining area into a small feast: plates, silverware, a vibrant green salad, a bottle of red wine, and two flickering candles.

"Wow, you were serious about celebrating. Where'd the candles come from?"

"Picked them up on the way home, along with the matches," she said with a smirk.

Ray poured the wine. "A toast to a future with plenty of days off."

"Cheers to part-time work and a full-time wonderful marriage," Tessa countered, raising her glass. They clinked glasses, sipped the wine, and shared the meal—each bite marking a moment in their lives together.

"Save room for cheesecake," Tessa warned, her eyes sparkling.

"I'll do my best," he replied, grinning.

As the plates emptied and the candles burned down, they moved to the porch. A gentle breeze swept away the remains of dinner, ushering in the warm hues of the sunset. Tessa settled into the porch swing while Ray took the chair beside her. "The meal was great," he said. "We should do this more often."

"Barbecue or celebrate?" she asked, tilting her head.

"Both. But how do we top this?"

"The night is young," she beamed, rising to take his hand. "Follow me." This time, Ray followed without hesitation.

CHAPTER TWELVE

After a night spent swimming in barbecue and tangled sheets, Tessa felt a warmth spread through her. Moments like this ignited a craving for connection, pulling her away from impending worries. As she padded into the kitchen, hair tousled, she spotted Ray hunched over the morning paper with coffee in hand. She couldn't help but smile at the sight of him, though a hint of unease stirred in her chest. Even in these small moments, she could see how deeply he was pulled into his projects. Did he realize how his focus sometimes made her feel like a ghost in their own home?

He looked up. "About time, sleepyhead."

"What do you mean? I've been waiting for you to come back to bed."

Ray studied her, narrowing his eyes in mock suspicion. "Nah, you just woke up. I can tell."

"Maybe." She planted her hands on her hips, a playful grin spreading across her face. "Where's my coffee?"

"Coming right up." Ray stood and poured her a cup. "Check this out—in the paper today. They convicted a former FBI guy of spying for a Russian company. Says he funneled secrets for ten years."

Tessa took the coffee, her lips pursed. His interest felt too intense. The news weighed on her, a reminder of the uncertainties hovering outside their lives. Was this what she had to look forward to? A constant reminder of unease?

"Makes you wonder about Fitz and Sommers and their integrity, doesn't it?"

"Yeah, no kidding."

She held the cup against her chin. "Speaking of Russians, do you remember when we met? I told you about the Russian guy who said he knew you?"

Ray smirked. "Best part of that day was you introducing yourself."

Tessa's eyes lit up, the memory vivid. "Yes, but also this. That first day of class, the guy who sat next to me had this weird interest in you. Not just curiosity—it felt like he already knew you. I asked him about it, and it was strange. He said your name was Ray Holland and that your dad worked for Laubner Labs. I asked if you knew him, and he claimed no. Then, when I pressed him on what made you so interesting, he just stared at me, gave me a creepy smirk, muttered something in Russian, stood up, and left. Never saw him again... until yesterday. He came up to me at Stanford, introduced himself—Victor Mishkin. He wants to reconnect, see where you're working and how you're doing."

Ray set down his coffee, a frown crossing his face. "So, here's this guy who knows my dad, knows he's at Laubner, knows my name. But how would he know to ask you about me and at Stanford of all places?"

"Maybe the last name," she shrugged. "I was getting introduced all over campus, especially in the library."

He shook his head, skepticism etched across his features. "Seems like a stretch. There's something else here."

A chill washed over Tessa at the thought of Victor's interest. Why did he want to reconnect? She couldn't shake the sense that something about him ran deeper than he let on.

"His questions seemed normal on the surface, but I still don't trust him." She shivered, setting her coffee down with a clink.

"Exactly what worries me. The ones who seem genuine are usually the ones hiding something."

She laughed, though the sound held an edge of nerves. "Ray, now you sound paranoid."

Ray leaned forward, brows furrowing. "So, what does Victor say he's doing now, and why's he at Stanford?"

"Researcher for some Russian company," she waved a hand dismissively. "Didn't catch the name."

Tessa could see doubt etched across Ray's features as he crossed his arms. "He gets to roam around campus, just being a 'researcher'?"

"How should I know? I didn't grill him on his whole biography," she replied, her voice rising just enough to emphasize her point.

"I'd check with campus security, just to be sure. Let's make a mental note about Victor Mishkin. I'll do some digging, see if I can figure out his connection to me."

Tessa exhaled, feeling the weight of the day. They needed a break from all this. Planning a trip to the beach felt necessary—a chance to recharge together and push aside these lurking worries. "So, what's the plan for today and tomorrow? We actually have some free time, for a change."

Ray perked up. "GG-1 just needs a couple more tweaks, and then we're all set for a test launch. Saturday would be perfect."

Tessa's face lit up. "Let's go to the beach."

"The beach?"

"Yes! I want to walk barefoot in the sand, have lunch on the beach with the man I love, explore—just have some 'us' time."

Ray's brow furrowed as he considered. "If we go today, it'll be a late lunch. Maybe two hours to get there if we pick somewhere close."

"Okay, change of plans," she said, her voice decisive. "We'll do dinner on the beach. Since you have to take care of GG-1, I'll put together the food. We might have to stop to pick up a few things. After dinner, we can watch the sunset. If it's too late to come back, we'll find a hotel for the night."

"This is sounding better and better," Ray replied, a smile breaking across his face.

"It's a date, then."

They loaded Tessa's Subaru Outback with the cooler and zipped up the overnight bag, ensuring they were ready for anything. After securing the house and garage, they hit the road around 1:00 p.m., reaching the deli in about twenty minutes. Inside, Tessa quickly scanned the menu, spotting pre-cooked chicken breasts and French bread in the deli case.

"Let's grab those for dinner," she said, excitement bubbling as she added them to their order.

Once they received their sandwiches and chicken, they slid back into the car, planning to enjoy lunch on the road.

"Next stop, wine," Tessa announced as they steered onto the main road.

"Grocery store, two blocks on the left," Ray replied, already thinking about the Chardonnay.

"Got it." Tessa flipped down the sun visor, squinting at the bright afternoon light.

Ray dashed into the store while Tessa leaned against the car, soaking in the warmth. She unwrapped her deli sandwich, taking a bite and savoring the flavors. Glancing toward the store entrance, impatience flickered as she waited for Ray to emerge.

When the door swung open, she spotted him, a frown shadowing his face as he hurried out, arms loaded with bags.

"No fair," he groaned, approaching her.

"What took you so long?" she asked, grinning through a mouthful of sandwich.

"Long lines," he muttered, shaking his head. Tessa handed him a bottle of water, watching as he took a long drink, his brow relaxing a bit.

"It was getting warm in there. If you want, I can drive while you eat," she suggested.

"Deal," he said, sliding into the passenger seat as she took the wheel, their food nestled between them.

"If you're thirsty, I put a couple cans of Sprite in with the wine," she mentioned, pulling onto the road.

"Smart move." He unwrapped his sandwich. "You know where you're going?"

Tessa laughed lightly. "No clue. That's why I have you along."

They drove for about an hour until the highway opened up to a small parking lot just off the shoulder.

Ray pulled out a map, tracing their route with his finger. "Looks like we park here by the highway and walk down."

"It's fine. The cooler's packed. Not a big deal," she replied, relieved they were getting closer.

They observed twenty or thirty cars scattered in the lot, glistening under the sun.

Ray stretched, scanning the scene. "Guess it won't be deserted. But the beach is long; we'll find a quiet spot."

Tessa felt a thrill of happiness as they grabbed the cooler, tucking the wine and rolls inside. Making their way down the sloping road toward the sand, the sun beat down, warming their legs. She reached for her jacket, anticipating the cooler air by the water.

Before long, beads of sweat formed on her brow. "We should have packed more drinks," she said, glancing at Ray, who seemed focused on his thoughts.

As they approached the beachside shop, she spotted a sign advertising bottled water. Ray hurried inside, and she waited outside, her thirst growing as she watched him juggle four bottles on his way back.

He handed one to her, and she gulped it down eagerly. "Wow, you are thirsty," he remarked with a grin.

"I am. Next time, we bring more," she replied, the cool water refreshing her.

They continued north with the cooler in tow. Families lounged on folding chairs, children darted in and out of the surf, and surfers waited for waves that barely reached knee-high. Despite the number of cars parked above, the sandy stretch felt pleasantly uncrowded.

"Where is everyone?" Tessa asked, curiosity flickering.

"Good question," Ray replied, matching her pace. "Maybe there's something better going on further down?"

Tessa shrugged, a twinge of disappointment creeping in at the emptiness.

She drifted from the path, stopping near a tangle of pale, sunbaked logs at the edge of the beach. She set down the cooler with a little flourish, glancing around at her surroundings. The logs offered a natural bench, smooth and bleached, with the sun at her back, keeping the wind at bay. The clock closed in on three, the heat softening, and every few seconds, the sea's steady rumble gave way to children's shrieks. Somewhere close by, the mouthwatering haze of a barbecue drifted across the sand, making her tummy rumble in anticipation.

They paused, reaching for sunscreen, hats, sunglasses—a small ritual. Tessa nudged Ray's knee. "I hope the wine is colder in the cooler than the air out here."

Ray grinned. "I think so."

"Well, break it out! I'm ready to relax."

He propped open the lid, producing a bottle of Chardonnay and two plastic wineglasses, setting them on the log between them. He opened the wine, the moment of quiet punctuated by a gentle pop, and poured, the pale liquid shimmering in the sunlight.

"A toast," he said.

Tessa tilted her cup to his. "A toast to many family vacations on the beach." The cups bumped together, and she sipped. "Oh, that's good. But... cold would have been better."

"On us for not packing enough ice," Ray replied.

"Next time," she said, feeling a sense of warmth as they shared the moment.

The wind shifted, bringing the ocean's chill. More surfers arrived, drifting down to the waves, while families and couples strolled along the shore. The sun inched lower. Ray topped off their glasses, finishing the first bottle.

"I think we may want to wait on the second one, at least until dinner," Ray suggested.

"Sure. What time is it?"

Ray checked his watch. "4:35."

Tessa leaned forward, eager. "Soon enough. Let's break out dinner."

They unpacked everything at once, laughter bubbling as they spread food across the cooler, now their makeshift table. Tessa layered the chicken over Greek salad, swiftly filling both plates.

"Um, second bottle of wine now," she said.

Ray didn't hesitate. "Coming right up."

He uncorked the second bottle, pouring again. Tessa took a bite of her salad and nodded in approval.

"Not bad," she said. "We should do this more often. It's better than working."

As they ate, they barely paused, the salad and bread disappearing along with the wine. By the end, almost nothing remained.

"Okay, out of food and wine," Ray said, pushing back from the log. "Now what?"

Tessa rolled her eyes. "The dishes."

She popped open the cooler and jammed everything inside, slamming the lid with exaggerated finality. "Done," she said, beaming. "I like this. Now we need to walk off dinner. Unless you want me to get fat and sassy?"

"You mean, more sassy? Might not be possible," he said with a playful grin. Tessa felt a rush of warmth at his words, unable to resist leaning in for an enthusiastic kiss.

They clambered to their feet, still laughing, and for the first few steps, they had to hold on to each other, balancing against the shifting sand. Hand in hand, they wove along the beach, heading north.

"Warm enough?" Ray asked after a while.

"Doing okay so far."

They walked nearly twenty minutes when the sun began to dip, making the light syrupy and golden. A thumping sound grew from somewhere behind the dunes, low at first, then unmistakable.

"What's that noise?" Tessa asked.

Ray looked at the sky. "Helicopter," he said.

The chopper came into view, skimming only forty or fifty feet above the sand, painted bright red. Tessa squinted against the sun, trying to make out the words on the side. "It looks like Ben's Helicopter Tours of Hawaii," she called out, excitement building in her voice. The helicopter hovered, spun a perfect three-sixty, then moved down the beach, just offshore. "It says daily tours, private parties, and charters, hourly rate, and a phone number on the side," she added, shading her eyes with her hand.

"Could you see how many on board?"

"Three, plus the pilot. I wonder how much it costs?"

Ray shrugged. "Probably a bunch."

Tessa pointed as the helicopter dwindled. “We need to do that. Go on a helicopter tour. Looks like fun. Come on, while we’re young.”

Ray laughed. “We can look into it. Did you catch the number?”

“No, just Ben’s Helicopter Tours of Hawaii.”

“We can look it up, but we’re not exactly flying to Hawaii to do a tour,” Ray said.

“We could,” Tessa fired back, grinning.

They found their way back to their spot, settling in to watch the sun slide behind the horizon.

“Too bad we don’t have a camera,” Tessa said. “How else will we remember this?”

Ray shrugged. “Guess we’ll have to file it away for now—in the old memory banks.”

“That’s what I like about you, Ray. Obvious things come easy to you.”

Tessa felt a thrill of excitement at the thought of capturing their adventures. “Exactly what I mean,” she said, cutting him off, eager to move forward with the idea.

As Ray glanced at the fading light, Tessa felt the encroaching dusk and the chill in the air. “Plus, we don’t want to rush,” she added, wanting him to relax and enjoy the evening. “There’s a town just four miles up, Half Moon Bay. If we’re not safe to drive, we could call a cab or find a hotel shuttle, and just stay there.”

Ray scanned the beach idly. “Store’s closed, no phone booths I can see.”

“When we get to the car, we’ll see who’s ready to drive.”

“Okay.”

Quiet followed them as they walked up the trail, weaving a little on the soft sand before transitioning to gravel as they neared the car. The sky darkened, and the moon rose—a bright, impossible half-circle lighting their way up the hill.

Ray paused. “How do you feel?”

Tessa considered. “After the walk, a lot better.” She wanted to create moments together, building their life slowly. In a few months, they could be doing this every weekend.

"How about you?"
Ray didn't hesitate. "You're driving."
She laughed. "Fair enough."

The road to Half Moon Bay felt peaceful as Tessa drove, the headlights illuminating the passing fields. She lost track of time, caught up in the serenity of the drive. Suddenly, the Half Moon Bay Lodge came into view, lights blazing against the darkened sky. Tessa's breath caught at the sight of the hacienda-style arches welcoming them.

As they pulled up to the hotel, Tessa glanced at Ray, excitement bubbling within her. Inside, a welcoming clerk looked up, slightly wind-burned from the ocean breeze. After completing their registration, he confirmed they had a non-smoking room on the main floor with an ocean view for one-ten a night. He directed them to Room 121, down the hall, third door on the left, and informed them about breakfast at six and checkout at eleven. Tessa shouldered their bag, the anticipation buzzing between them as they moved down the corridor.

"Not bad, considering the buzz," she said under her breath, a spark of excitement in her voice.

"Hey, I'm completely normal now," Ray replied with a grin.

"I believe you. Except your eyes don't."

He chuckled. "Give it an hour. I'll be fine."

Tessa shook her head, suppressing a smile. "All this air, walking around. Wears a person out."

When they reached the room, the sight of the bed offered a comforting promise of rest.

"I'm in the shower first," Tessa announced, ducking into the bathroom.

"Okay. Oh, tomorrow we should check for helicopter tour brochures. Ben's, right?"

"Yes, Ben's."

The sound of the water running invited her to relax as she wrapped herself in a towel, the warmth enveloping her. Peeking into the hallway, she spotted Ray, eyes closed for just a moment.

"Hey, sleepyhead, are you going to shower? Or just sleep?" she called softly, a playful note in her voice.

He blinked at her, nodding, and finally pushed himself to his feet. "I'm okay," he replied, though she noticed the lingering fatigue in his posture.

As he made his way to the shower, Tessa watched, a mix of affection and concern swirling inside her. He moved with a careful grace, reminding her of someone crossing a river at night. She shut off the AC, a shiver running through her as she settled back into bed, towel tossed to the floor, leaving the light on in the bathroom. Moments later, Ray stepped out, looking refreshed, almost as new as the sheets.

"Better?" she asked.

"Much. Lights out?"

"Waiting on you."

He dropped the towel and slid under the covers. Tessa switched off the light, and they shared a quiet kiss before saying goodnight.

As the calm settled around them, the distant roar of the ocean faded into the background. Tessa sank into the soft sheets, the day slipping away as sleep beckoned softly, wrapping her in its embrace.

CHAPTER THIRTEEN

Friday arrived with sunlight streaming through the heavy, uneven curtains in Ray and Tessa's room at the Half Moon Bay Lodge. Shouts and pounding feet outside startled him awake. Kids darted up and down the hall, laughter ringing out, followed by a frustrated parent. He eased an arm around Tessa, who lay oblivious, lost in peaceful slumber. No chance for mischief this morning; her sleep was far too deep. Ray had mastered the act of leaving her undisturbed, rolling out of bed, finding his clothes, and slipping into the bathroom to dress.

Once he managed to leave the room, he carefully shut the door and wandered into the lobby, feeling wide awake under the bright light of day. Against a paneled wall, colorful brochures caught his eye—Disneyland, Redwood adventures, Yosemite. His search for anything on helicopter tours yielded nothing about Ben's.

At the guest counter stood a young woman with a tumble of black curls and warm, dark olive skin. Her steady brown eyes met his.

"Can I help you?" she asked.

"I'm looking for a brochure for Ben's Helicopter Tours."

She shook her head, certain already. "I'm not familiar with the name."

"We saw one of their helicopters flying up the beach last night."

"Let me check with my manager. Please excuse me." She disappeared through a door behind the counter.

Ray leaned in at the counter, absently fingering the fake marble. He was puzzled over the image of a helicopter painted with Hawaiian branding buzzing the California coast. The door opened; the same hostess reappeared.

"My manager's calling Half Moon Bay Airport to see if they know about the helicopter tour. By the way, have you had breakfast yet?"

He shook his head. “Not yet. I planned to grab something for us.”

She smiled briskly. “Maybe order in the restaurant and stop back by here? I’ll have your answer.”

Ray nodded, appreciating the suggestion.

The empty restaurant smelled of toast and coffee. A hostess in a starched vest offered him a menu, then took his order: two breakfast specials—pancakes, eggs, bacon, juice, and toast.

Once the order was placed, he returned to the lobby. The brunette clerk hammered at her keyboard. Ray stood nearby, forcing himself to stay quiet, the urge to interrupt crawling up through him. He pushed the thought aside.

“Okay, we tracked it down,” she said, looking up. “There’s a Ben’s Helicopter at Half Moon Bay Airport, about fifteen miles north. They work out of a hangar there, but nobody has much info about tours. The manager found a number for the hangar if you want to call.” She handed him a business card with the phone number scrawled on the back.

Ray slipped the card into his pocket, anticipation rising as he made his way back to the room. Navigating the twisting halls and stained carpet, he let himself in quietly. Tessa still lay soundly asleep. He decided to wait for breakfast, settling into a stiff chair by the door and listening for the telltale squeak of a cart.

Soon enough, it came—wheels shrieking down the corridor. He cracked the door and saw the same hostess wheeling in two plates, steam rising from the covered trays.

“Breakfast is served,” she said, placing the trays on the bedside table.

Ray nudged Tessa awake with a gentle hand and a soft kiss.

She came to with a start. “Oh no, what time is it?”

“Nine.”

She sniffed the air, her eyes brightening. “Smells like breakfast.”

“Two specials. Pick what you like. Eggs over easy, just the way you like them.”

Tessa grinned, pulling up the covers. “I have nothing on, so I guess it’s breakfast in bed.”

Ray chuckled, his smile widening. “I figured it would be your preference. Unless you want to eat at the table... nude.”

She laughed, stretching. “Tough choice. It’s warmer here.”

Propped up by pillows, she drew the blanket tight. “This works.”

He brought over her plate, balancing it in her lap. “Need syrup?”

“I’m fine.”

Ray grabbed a wooden chair, slid it next to the bed, and started eating his own plate. He admired how content she looked, though a flicker of worry twisted in his gut.

“I could get used to this,” she said, her voice brightening the room. “Breakfast in bed, hot off the cart, and the man I love.”

Ray smiled, warmth flooding his chest at her words, but a pang of guilt tugged at him. He wanted her to enjoy this happiness without the weight of burdens overshadowing their time together.

He leaned in for a kiss, smiling. “The front desk gave me a number. Ben’s Helicopter is at Half Moon Bay Airport, about fifteen miles north. They said it doesn’t look like a real tour company, though.”

“Maybe it’s why the name references Hawaii,” Tessa suggested.

“Could be.”

“Have you tried calling yet?”

“No, they tried, but no answer. Maybe after ten.”

“Checkout is at eleven, so we have time.”

Ray watched her polish off her breakfast and two coffees, then eyed his empty plate. “Wow, you’ve already cleaned your plate and two coffees.”

“High metabolism,” she said, laughing. “I better get dressed before housecleaning comes.”

Ray shrugged, a smirk playing on his lips. “Housekeepers have probably seen it all. Stories for days.” He watched Tessa slide out of bed, her movements graceful as she danced to the bathroom.

“Don’t say it,” she tossed over her shoulder.

"Say what?" Ray asked, feigning innocence, unable to suppress a grin at her playful mood.

She said nothing, slipping into the bathroom as Ray grinned, ready to seize the day ahead.

At ten, Ray called the number. The phone rang before a man's voice answered.

"Hello?" the man said.

"Hi, is this Ben's Helicopter Tours?"

"Yes and no," the man replied.

Ray hesitated, his thumb tapping the edge of the phone. "Who am I speaking with?"

"My name's Tom Harper. I fly helicopters for different companies. Ben's is currently being tested for a company in Hawaii, but I take private clients up for tours. The owners want feedback."

"Was it you flying over Martin's Beach yesterday?" Ray asked. "Yep."

"How much do you charge?" Ray asked.

"Two hundred per person, minimum two adults."

Ray explained, "We're at Half Moon Bay Lodge this morning. Could we come by, meet you, see the helicopter?"

"Day's wide open. Had a cancellation; just doing paperwork. Come on by."

Ray hung up. Tessa emerged from the bathroom, looking smart in fitted slacks and a pearl-white blouse. Ray looked at his own jeans and t-shirt, suddenly feeling underdressed.

"If I ever want to look half as good as you, we'll need to shop together," he said.

She shrugged, "You look fine. Did you reach Ben's?"

"His name's Tom. He'll meet us today and give us a tour of the hangar."

Ray watched Tessa glance down at her blouse, a hint of uncertainty crossing her face as she said, "Okay, let's pack up and go."

They gathered their things, checked out, and drove up the coast on back roads, arriving at Half Moon Bay Airport around 11:30 a.m.

“Building forty-two B, southeast end,” Ray read from the scrap of paper as they passed through the main gate. A map, just as promised, pointed them to the right of the entrance. They followed the perimeter road to a cluster of metal hangars painted a tired green, with rust streaks running down their corrugated sides. In front of one bay sat the Ben’s Hawaii helicopter, gleaming and out of place. Ray guessed the right door, knocked, and peeked inside.

No answer. He tugged on the door, heavy on its hinges, and stepped inside, Tessa close behind. Inside, a gunmetal gray desk dominated the space, and a man in his mid-fifties, silver hair cropped closely, revealed the wear of years spent in the cockpit. His stubbled jaw spoke of a no-nonsense attitude, and he carried an air of quiet authority.

He looked up, his expression shifting. “Are you Ray?”

“Yes, this is my wife, Tessa,” he said, shifting for the introduction.

The man rose and shook their hands in turn. “Tom Harper. Pleased to meet you both.”

He stood at least six feet tall, all arms and legs, a hint of athleticism still remaining. The hangar felt caught in a mid-century time warp: peeling walls, chipped concrete, and dust clinging to the overhead lights, with faded photos on the wall hinting at a once-bustling history.

Tom grinned. “You’ll have to forgive the mess. I’m no tour guide. This airport’s older than dirt, built during the war and not spruced up much since. Only one chopper in service, the Ben’s unit. She’s a dream to fly—quick, strong, seats six without crowding, and surprisingly quiet inside. This is my last week on her; then I draft my report. Frankly, I don’t see the point since they already painted her up. I think she has a home waiting.”

He sat down, continuing, “You probably want to know how long I’ve been flying.”

Ray felt about to ask, but Tom powered right through. “I’ve been flying choppers since Vietnam. A lot’s changed, but not everything. Up and down, that’s what matters. Key is making sure the down is under control,” he said, laughter in his voice.

Ray glanced around the bare, echoing space, noting the stale air and the tired walls that stubbornly held together. He shifted to see Tessa, her expression unreadable, and felt a flicker of concern.

Tom caught her glance. “Just teasing. Never had a serious accident. Even in Nam, chopper full of holes, I brought her home. Not all pilots managed to do the same. Some luck, I guess. Nowadays it’s safer unless a bird gets you or another plane. These birds have backup systems for everything.” He paused, looking at them. “Not much of a tour guide, like I said. But did you want to go for a ride?”

Tessa’s eyes lit up. “A ride?”

“What you asked, right?” Tom said, with a glint of mischief. “You want to take her up.”

Ray didn’t expect it to be so quick. “We didn’t know it would be today.”

“No better time than now. I’m just sitting here; the chopper’s fueled and checked, charter canceled. You’re good for the money, right?” He stood, waiting, as if this was the way things went out here in sheds and hangars where people acted on impulse.

Ray caught Tessa’s questioning look, her eyes wide and uncertain, but he raised a brow, slow and easy. “No better time than the present, right?” he said, as if this alone should settle things.

“We don’t want to trouble you. We could come back some other time,” Tessa said, casting a hopeful glance at Ray.

Ray shrugged, feeling the excitement bubble between them. “No better time than now.”

Tom didn’t bother answering; he drifted toward a battered metal door off to the side, pulling it open. They followed, hesitating only a moment before stepping out onto the tarmac, toward the helicopter. Tom opened the back door, glancing between them. “Who’s up front with me?”

Ray gestured at Tessa. “You go up front.”

Tessa shook her head, quick. “No, no, not this first time.”

Tom had already reached his large hand out for her to take. She stared at it, at his rough, dry fingers; after a moment, she let him help her climb inside. As she settled into the seat facing forward, the rush of wind filled the cabin. Tom crouched beside her, showing her how to buckle the straps and fit the headset over her hair. "Even though this chopper is quieter than most, it's still easier to communicate with these on," he said. He clicked the door shut and rotated the handle, sealing her inside.

Ray climbed in alone from the other side. Tom repeated the strapping demonstration, adjusting Ray's headset as well.

"Where are we going?" Tom asked as he slid into the pilot's seat.

"Home?" Tessa said, barely above a whisper.

A sudden, boyish grin broke across Ray's face. "How about up and down the coastline for a start?"

"We can do that." Tom nodded, flipping several switches. The engine woke up at once, rotors spinning, blades blurring against the sky. Tom ran through his checks, hands moving quickly and expertly.

"Roger. Clear to takeoff pad 12," Tom spoke into his mic, then shifted his attention to them. "Hey, kids, we're clear to go. Hang on."

The engine whined; they shifted sideways, abrupt, a lurch in the pit of Ray's gut, and suddenly they were off the ground, skimming away in a broad southwest arc.

Tom's voice came out calm, matter-of-fact. "Good thing we have a cloudless day and calm winds. Should be a smooth and scenic flight."

South along the coast they flew, barely a hundred feet above the sand, the blue ocean rushing beneath them, the sharp white line of the surf racing past. Ray glanced over at Tessa, noting her grip on the seat, her knuckles white. He wondered if she felt uneasy about not taking the front seat. He hoped this ride would be a pleasant experience for her. High above the cliffs, homes flickered by—some glittering and angular, others plain and tucked into the greenery—each one a reminder of the world he worked to build with GG-1.

"How fast can this thing fly?" Ray asked, curiosity sparking.

"Up to one seventy, then things can begin to fall off," Tom answered, a dry chuckle behind his words.

Tessa glanced at him, alarmed. “Things fall off?”

Ray shook his head. “He’s joking.”

Tom grinned. “Here, we’ll drop down to fifty feet, and I’ll turn it up so you can feel the speed.” He tipped the helicopter forward, so far it seemed they might slide right out the doors; the ocean rose up, dizzying. At level, straight above the water, he opened up the throttle. The world dissolved into motion, blue-grey streaks racing past as they surged forward.

“There’s one-fifty. How’s it feel?”

“Too fast,” Tessa managed.

Tom pulled back, the nose lifting up, sky filling the windows, and they were pressed deep into their seats. “I hope you didn’t all eat just before we left,” he joked.

“There’s Martin’s Beach,” Tom pointed. “Didn’t you say it’s where you saw me yesterday?”

Ray nodded. “We had a picnic there and walked the beach.”

Tom nodded thoughtfully. “I have a couple of friends who live in those homes there. I should introduce you sometime.”

Ray glanced sideways at Tessa; she shrugged, her expression uncertain, the suggestion hanging between them.

Then Tom seemed to remember something. “Here, I almost forgot.” He tipped the helicopter forward again, dropping low and fast over the water, then slowed, hovering, the nose pointing at the distant line of beach.

“Watch this,” he said, bringing the helicopter lower, letting the waves creep close. Spray flew, drumming against the lower hull, until the world beyond the windows blurred into shifting silver. “Now look down,” Tom pointed to the clear panels in the floor. He eased the landing skids into the water, gentle.

“There, touchdown,” he said. “In Nam, we had to fly these things low. Over the water, especially. Better not to get shot down.” He brought them back up slowly, the spray sliding away, the view clearing.

“Best not to stay low too long; saltwater’s murder on these things. I’ll have to clean her out good when we get back. Now, what do you two do for a living?”

“I’m an engineer at Laubner, and Tessa is a professor at Stanford,” Ray said.

"Oh, I know Laubner," Tom replied. "They make all sorts of stuff for the military. Always have."

"A lot less now," Ray offered. "It's mostly energy systems and power research."

Tom snorted, amused. "I know who your best customer still is. The U-S-of-A. You all do the research, the engineering, spend the real money, and then sell the tech to companies who get the benefit, starting out cheap. Which is why tech moves so fast. Heck, this chopper can nearly fly itself now. Back in Nam, we had to fight to keep these things in the air. You know, we didn't lose the war in Nam."

Ray glanced at Tessa, uncertain. "No?"

"Nope. We're still fighting. We never left. It's all hush-hush. You hear about those young people, younger than you two, who just disappear? Folks say they ran away. But the government, they grab them, ship them off to Nam to fight for us. But, you know, they don't watch their own backyard. Mark my words: the U-S-of-A is going to get bit, and good, if they're not careful. All this funny stuff going on, and they forget about us. Protecting us."

Ray watched Tessa's brow furrow, her expression a mix of confusion and concern. "That's a lot to absorb, Tom," she said, her voice steady. "I'm curious, do you share this with all your tour guests?"

Tom hesitated, a little embarrassed. "Yah, I probably do. I get carried away. But if you don't share the truth, how do you make things right?"

"True," Tessa said, glancing at Ray, who just grinned. What can I say?

Suddenly, a red light flashed on the dash, insistent, followed by a shrill beeping. Tom pressed a button, silencing the alarm.

"What is it?" Ray asked, his concern rising.

"No big deal. Just an oil warning. Probably a leak. Sorry, but we have to head back, pronto."

"That's okay," Tessa said, relief evident in her voice. "This has been quite the experience."

Ray nodded, agreeing. Tom radioed for clearance, getting an immediate reroute straight to the hangar due to the warning. The airspace clear, they circled and settled onto the pavement right in front of where they'd started. Tom cut the engines, and the world slowly became quiet, only the ticking of the cooling machine.

"Go ahead and remove your headgear, and just set them on your seats," Tom said, hanging his on the floor. Ray and Tessa undid their buckles and let the straps dangle.

"Hang on," Tom said. "Let the rotors stop completely before we exit. Safer that way."

Tom opened his own door, then circled, opening Ray and Tessa's doors, steadying them as they climbed down.

"Look at that," he said, pointing to a dark streak of oil along the helicopter's side. "There's our leak. This'll keep me busy the rest of the day."

"Sorry," Ray said.

Tom waved him off. "Not your fault. This is why we test them. This is the job. Now I'll have to do a bunch of paperwork for the manufacturer after I fix it."

"Good luck," Ray said, half-laughing, relieved it wasn't his problem.

Tom grinned. "Now let's go inside and get you settled up. Did I mention the cash discount?"

Ray raised a brow. "Cash discount?"

"Twenty-five percent off. So, it came to two hundred each, four hundred, but with the discount, three hundred, if you can pay in cash."

"Oh, let me check," Ray said, pulling out his wallet. "How much do you have?" he asked Tessa.

"I have a hundred," she replied, digging in her purse.

Ray counted his bills. "Another hundred seventy-five. So we're a little short. All we have is two seventy-five."

"Deal," Tom said, quick.

Ray looked at him, surprised. "Really?"

"Yah, your first trip, we cut it a little short. I like you two. You're planning on going up with me again, right?"

Tessa shot a glance at Ray—a look which asked, do we have to? But she faced Tom with a brightened expression. "Yes, of course."

Tom lit up. “Great. Next time we can do the city, or the Golden Gate Bridge, or maybe one of the islands. Picnic again, maybe?”

“Deal,” Tessa said, hardly able to hide her relief at having both feet back on solid ground.

They shook hands, said their goodbyes. On the way to the car, Ray continued to shake his head. “Wow, quite an adventure.”

“No kidding. I like Tom,” Tessa said. “I feel for him, really. Vietnam, coming back, living a normal life? My heart goes out to them. But some of those theories...they’re out there.”

“In outer space,” Ray supplied.

Tessa pressed him, “What, you don’t believe the stories about Vietnam?”

Ray shrugged. “It’s hard to know what’s true in this country. The media’s not reliable—not for the actual truth, anyway. Just the story they think will sell. Ever seen something you knew firsthand, and then read about it in the papers? It’s an eye-opener.”

“Maybe.”

Ray looked at her. “What do you mean, maybe? No ‘maybe’ about it. I’ll find an example and show you.”

“Okay, but can we get going? I’m hungry and thirsty.”

Ray slid behind the wheel. “Let’s go back to the Lodge. I remember a sushi bar.”

Tessa wrinkled her nose. “Not fish tonight. Not after that ride. I’m not sure.”

He considered. “There’s a place called Pasta Moon. Can you do Italian?”

“Sounds better.”

# # #

They found light traffic on the curvy road, the sea flickering through breaks in the trees. Ray remembered how to get there, looking for the signs in Half Moon Bay. As they approached town, the air thickened with the mingled smells of greasy fish and pizza, a dense, almost comforting blend that made him smile. They found limited parking; Ray thought for a moment about giving up, but then a spot opened, and the inviting aroma of roasted garlic and baked bread solidified his decision: they would stay.

Inside, the smells doubled: tomato, cheese, butter, and the sharp bite of fresh basil. They ordered before settling in—the Pasta Moon Lasagna for Ray, Roasted Chicken Salad for Tessa. The hostess brought glasses of water, and together they demolished a basket of flatbread, finishing eight pieces before the entrees arrived.

Tessa grinned. "I'm afraid I can't match this for any dinner I'll ever make."

Ray smirked. "As good as this is, home cooking always wins."

She gave him a look. "Your mom's home cooking, you mean? We'll see how you feel after a few months of mine."

Ray grinned. "I promise I won't complain."

Tessa leaned back, hand on her belly. "Now I can't decide if I'm going to sleep this meal off or run laps around the house when we get home."

Ray eyed the remnants of her plate. "You just had salad."

She pointed to the empty breadbasket. "Did you miss the bread? And I helped with your lasagna."

They lingered until dusk, then Ray paid, leaving a generous tip. As they drove home, the heavy scent of pasta lingered, soon replaced by the fresh ocean breeze. They arrived in under thirty minutes. When Ray parked, Tessa's eyes were closed, head tilted back, lips parted. He left her there while he opened up the house, clearing a path up to the bedroom. Then he returned, lifted her carefully, and carried her up the stairs. The floor creaked, but she didn't stir. Only when he laid her on the pillows did her eyes flutter open.

"What are you doing?" she mumbled.

"We're home. Go back to sleep."

She blinked at him, blank, then nodded. "Oh." Her eyes fluttered closed again. Ray slipped off her shoes and pulled up the covers. She was out.

CHAPTER FOURTEEN

Saturday morning, finally. Tessa padded downstairs, wrapped in her bathrobe, hair loose about her shoulders. The kitchen sat quiet, and she relaxed, noticing the absence of dirty dishes in the sink—a sure sign Ray had already slipped into the garage. She opened the fridge, letting the cool air wash over her, and despite last night's heavy dinner, she cracked eggs and threw bacon in the pan. The eggs sizzled in bacon grease, filling the kitchen with a sharp, lingering scent. Breakfast was on the way.

Finding two plates, she made up their meals and, still in her robe, carried one out into the cool half-light of morning and the darkness of the open garage.

"Ray," she called, her voice echoing off the unfinished walls. "I've got breakfast for you."

"I'm right here. You don't need to shout." His voice floated from somewhere inside, lost among the scattered tools and shadowed corners.

"I couldn't see you," she replied, pausing by the doorway. "It's darker in here than outside. Anyway, here's some breakfast. You were planning on eating today, right?"

He didn't look up from his work. "Yes. I just needed to finish assembling GG-1 for the test flight today—if it does fly."

"When are we leaving?"

"I was thinking about ten."

"Okay, I guess I better wolf down breakfast and get dressed."

As she watched him set down a screwdriver and turn to face her, she felt a flutter of impatience. "Can you look up a camera store between here and the site? We should buy a camera to record today's events. Remember, you said we should get one for when we were at Martin's Beach, right?"

She shrugged, feeling her heart race. "No argument here. I'll check the phone book."

The morning sun brightened outside; Tessa shielded her eyes as she returned to the kitchen. One bite into her eggs made her grimace—the yolk ran too thin, the whites still soft. She tipped them back into the pan, set the bacon aside, and poured a cup of coffee, letting the ceramic warm her hands as she sat at the table. This would likely be the most relaxing moment of the day. After finishing her toast, she glanced at the clock above the door and felt a rush of realization—the morning had already surged ahead.

As she rummaged through the drawers, anxiety tightened her chest. Was she always going to be the one organizing everything? Biting her lip, she thought, *Maybe I'm overthinking this. Is it too much to want him to notice me, to value my opinions a little more?*

# # #

Ray was still in the garage, oblivious to everything except the task before him. He laid the last wire into the power adapter, secured it with a wing nut, found the watertight compartment cover, and twisted it down with two recessed nuts. "Oomph," he exhaled, hefting the final assembly. If it didn't fly, it would make a fine boat anchor, he thought, and set the GG-1 behind the Subaru in the driveway. The fit would be tight, but he'd measured the hatch weeks earlier. The radio controller went next to it—a Fire Sky Taurus, up to sixteen channels but currently set with eight, each one mapped to a section of the GG-1, the rest reserved for future tweaks. He hoped for a five-mile range.

He ran through the checklist once more, brows furrowed, then eyed the dark garage doorway, just to be certain. The faint smell of bacon drifted in behind him. He reached for his own plate and mug, then brought them inside. The dishes in the sink had multiplied. Ray, meticulous, carefully set his plate on top of Tessa's before glancing at the clock: already 9:30.

Upstairs, he found Tessa fussing with her hair in the fogged bathroom mirror, already dressed in tight blue jeans and a thin red cotton blouse, short-sleeved.

"It might be cold in the hills this morning. Better bring something warmer," he suggested.

She didn't stop brushing her hair. "Are you kidding? It's supposed to be eighty in the foothills today."

"According to WCBC 880's report, it would be about four o'clock. Forecast reported a light marine layer on the water and cloudy above, and some fog in the valleys, burning off this afternoon."

She relented. "I'll bring a jacket then. You're going to put on some clean clothes and comb your hair before we leave, right?"

"Of course, it's why I came upstairs."

"I was thinking we could pack a lunch. I could make a couple sandwiches and grab some juice."

"Sounds fine," he said. "Let's keep it simple."

Ray changed into clean blue jeans and a soft gray t-shirt, combed his hair, and brushed his teeth. He stepped into the kitchen, expecting to find Tessa ready.

"Wait a minute." She held up a hand. "You're just wearing a t-shirt."

"I have a jacket!" The words came out almost too eager, the prospect of the test flight making him antsy.

Tessa raised an eyebrow, a teasing smirk on her lips. "If we're giving advice about what to wear, are you trying to cover up some nerves about today?"

He tried to play it cool. "No... no, sorry. It just slipped out." He couldn't shake the stiffness in his neck. What if it doesn't do anything? What if I'm not smart enough to keep us safe?

"Good. So I won't hear anything about what I packed for lunch then."

"Oh no," Ray said, glancing out the front window.

Tessa followed his gaze, her curiosity morphing into something more cautious. "What is it?"

"Our friends are back."

"Who?"

"The FBI," he said, nodding toward the street. There, in plain sight, sat the black Suburban with tinted windows and antennae like quills on a porcupine.

"No secret when they're around," she said, peering through the blinds.

"What do they want now?" Tessa muttered, more to herself than to Ray.

"Not sure, but I don't see them outside the vehicle. Maybe we can give them the slip and sneak out."

"Somehow, I doubt it. What about GG-1?" she asked, her voice low. "They better not make you take it apart again."

"Do you have a big thick blanket we could use to wrap it up?"

"Yeah, in the closet upstairs."

"Go grab it quick. Let's get GG-1 wrapped and in the car."

She dashed for the stairs and returned moments later with a brown fleece blanket, large enough to cover a queen mattress. Ray nodded, approving.

They crept around the side of the house, careful not to be seen from the street. The Suburban hadn't moved. With the garage and driveway hidden behind the house, GG-1 was stored safe from view, at least for now.

Tessa set the thermos and lunch bag in the front seat, then helped Ray swaddle GG-1 in the thick blanket. Together, they lifted the payload, angling it up to squeeze it into the Subaru's cargo hatch. The controller went beneath, tucked up under the covered side.

"Do we have everything?" Ray asked, half in, half out of the car.

"Yes, just lock the back door and garage, and we can go."

He signaled for quiet. "Shut your door gently when you get in."

The car doors closed with barely a click, but the Subaru itself, when started, roared loud enough to stir every bird in the hedges.

"Okay, did you find a camera store?"

"Yes," Tessa said. "There's one in Menlo Park, just off of Santa Cruz in town."

He pinched his chin. "Oh yeah, I know the shop, Mike's Camera. Plan is to go left, so they have to turn around to follow us. If they do, no big deal. We'll go to the camera store, like normal shoppers. When we leave, we may be able to lose them if they're by themselves."

He backed out of the driveway, rolling quietly toward the street. Tension crept in as he nudged Tessa in the passenger seat, her gaze fixed on the rearview mirror.

"Still nothing," she said, tension creeping into her voice. Then, with sudden urgency, she hissed, "Wait, brake lights!"

"Damn." Ray accelerated into a sharp left, then another. "If they're coming, we won't lose them in here. Too rural, and not enough traffic. We can be on the 35 in about three blocks, but it may not help either."

"Let's stick with the plan and not look like we're trying to flee," Tessa said, her voice steady.

"True." Ray's eyes remained on the mirror. "I just really want to lose them."

Traffic thickened as they neared Menlo Park, shielding their escape; by the time they reached Mike's Camera, it seemed impossible to tell if the black Suburban trailed them or not. Ray eased around the block and parked in the shade behind the row of shops. Two teenagers, giggling and loud, climbed into a car two spaces down; otherwise, the lot sat empty.

They walked in through the back door, facing aisles filled with camera straps and batteries. A glass counter loomed ahead, where an olive-skinned man in his thirties was helping another customer. He glanced up. "I'll be with you in a few minutes."

"Thanks," Ray replied.

Under the counter, cameras were lined up like jewelry—Canon, Pentax, Kodak—all instantly recognizable. Ray needed to document today's events, worried they might soon vanish amid the chaos surrounding them.

"Do you have any idea what we're looking for?" Tessa asked, her voice barely above a whisper.

"Well, digital for sure. A model with video capability would be nice, but I'm not up on this stuff," he said, glancing around for help.

Eventually, the salesman finished with the other customer and walked over, polite and direct. "How can I help you?"

"Are you Mike?" Tessa asked.

"No, sorry, my name is Jeff. No relation to Mike, either. What can I do for you?"

"We're looking for a digital camera. Easy to use, takes good pictures, and reasonably priced," Ray said. "Oh, and maybe something with video capability."

Jeff furrowed his brow. "Hmm, a little tougher. The manufacturers are scrambling to capture a bigger market segment, but so far, the type of device you're looking for is still in its infancy. You might need two devices for decent quality."

Ray glanced at Tessa, then back to Jeff. "Maybe we should stick to the camera for now."

"Okay, let me show you one I'd recommend." He reached beneath the counter and brought out a camera that looked like a classic SLR—sturdy yet modern.

"This is a Canon EOS D30, Digital SLR, with a three-point-two mega-pixel CMOS sensor. You can manually set the options or select the auto function—just point and shoot. We sell a lot of these to professional photographers because it has everything they need. The real cost comes from accessories and lenses." Handing the camera to Ray, he added, "See how lightweight it is?"

"Oh wow, you're right, it is light." Ray passed it to Tessa. "Check this out."

"Much lighter than it looks," Tessa agreed, testing its balance.

"Power button is right here," Jeff said, demonstrating. "It's set to auto; just press the button on top. The picture will display on the screen for about ten seconds before it shuts off to save battery. Try it out; I'll be right back."

Tessa snapped pictures—Ray, Jeff, the aisles and shelves, and the glass counter, image after image, the new camera already breaking in.

Jeff returned. "Where were we?" He smoothed a hand over the glass counter. "Oh, the camera comes with a one-hundred-twenty-megabyte CompactFlash card. You'll get a couple hundred photos on there, depending on your settings. It has a built-in flash too. Make sense so far?"

"How much?" Tessa asked, not missing a beat.

"On sale for two ninety-nine this week. You get the fifty-millimeter lens with it—and if you decide today, I'll throw in a couple filters at no charge. Fair enough?"

Ray glanced at Tessa. No words, just a look. She nodded—a clear approval.

"I think this'll work. We'll take it."

"Great." Jeff moved behind the counter, a practiced hand sweeping up the box. "It comes with a case, so you don't need to purchase one. You might want some extra batteries, though. I'll toss in a spare set for you. Good?"

"Great," Ray said, grinning.

At the register, Ray handed over his card. Jeff explained the basics while Tessa kept up a steady stream of questions, determined to get her answers. Once satisfied, they left the shop behind. On their way out, Ray glanced back to check for the black Suburban—but the lot remained clear. They headed to their car.

"So, where's the Laubner site?" Tessa asked as she buckled in.

"Diamond Hills, north of Laubner. Should take us about ninety minutes. Plenty of time to mess with the camera."

Tessa powered it on, her movements quick. "I like the point-and-shoot."

Ray raised his brow. "Don't you want to learn all the tricks of photography?"

Tessa shook her head. "Not really."

"All right. As long as we get good shots of GG-1."

He guided them north along the 92, the scenery shifting as they spanned San Francisco Bay, cutting through Hayward toward 580 east. The drive felt like a blur, miles clicking by beneath them. Just shy of an hour and a half later, North Vasco Road loomed ahead: four bustling lanes rising into the barren sweep of the Diamond Hills.

Five miles of scrub and silence passed until a gravel turnoff appeared on the left—a weathered sign read: "Laubner Site 4B, 2.2 m." Ray swung the Subaru up the road, the crunch of gravel stirring Tessa, who had slipped into a nap.

"Are we there yet?" Tessa yawned.

"Almost. Just a couple more miles."

The gravel road lay bone-dry, untouched by traffic. Around a bend, an iron-bar gate blocked the way, a heavy lock hanging from its post. Ray hopped out, found the key his dad had given him, and popped the padlock free. The gate creaked as he swung it open. By the time he looked up, Tessa sat in the driver's seat, easing the car forward. He stared, caught off-guard. After she cleared the gate, Ray shut it again and locked it behind them, then circled back to the passenger side, sliding into his seat.

"Let's keep heading up the hill. Dad didn't say much about what's up here."

A quarter mile farther, the road curled again. A parking area came into view: five construction trailers, windows barred, each with a single metal door. Across a patch of parched grass stood a warehouse with metal siding and a roof, all business, no windows. One door faced them.

"How about we park up top?" Ray suggested.

They pulled forward, stopping after two hundred feet. The view opened in every direction. Low clouds muffled the Bay in the distance; beyond the horizon, only blue sky. Ray recalled the afternoon forecast called for a high of eighty-five, winds picking up as a cold front and clouds crept in from the west.

"We better get started before the wind picks up," Ray said, eyeing the sky.

"The sooner, the better," Tessa agreed, squinting against the bright sun beating down on them.

They opened the back and hefted GG-1 twenty yards from the car. Ray knelt, opening the sealed compartment, snapping in the battery. LEDs flicked to green.

"Can you get the camera and controller?" he called over his shoulder.

"Want lunch too? Might as well eat before we launch."

"Sure." Ray sealed up the compartment.

Tessa returned, balancing sandwiches and drinks along with the camera and controller. He watched her come, a jumble of nerves tightening in his chest. Had he done enough to ensure their safety?

"I'm nervous," he admitted.

“We should eat first, then.” She set out the sandwiches and drinks, settling into the grass.

“Maybe I should’ve included navigation lights on this thing,” Ray said, laughing, though his voice came out thin. “Assuming it even flies.”

Tessa didn’t flinch. “Be more positive.”

“I would be, if the technical part was clear.”

“Remember the history of flight,” Tessa said. “Inventors failed a lot, and we laugh at their mistakes. But look at us now. Learn from failure and keep moving forward. It matters.”

He nodded. Lunch disappeared quickly. “Camera ready?”

“Yes. Already taking pictures of the site, the view, GG-1, lunch.” She held up the camera.

Ray grinned, noticing her enthusiasm. “You’ve been reading the manual.”

She grinned back and gave him a quick kiss. “Just doing my part.”

“When GG-1 moves, press and hold. I’ll need all the data I can get.”

“I will.”

“Let’s step back, maybe by the car, just in case.”

They moved, step by careful step, not looking away from the device.

Ray powered on the controller. One by one, the receivers flashed their confirmations.

“Okay, here we go.”

He went down the line, powering up each element. “First one’s up.” Tessa began taking a picture.

“Nothing.”

“Number two, full power.”

Still nothing. Another picture.

“Now number three.” Tessa snapped another.

But then: “Wait, look!” She pressed and held, the shutter flickering every half-second. “It moved.”

“What?”

“It rotated.”

“How much?”

“About thirty degrees to the left.” The camera kept up its rhythm.

"Stop for a second. How do you know?"

"Look at the top, where the power adapter sits."

Ray checked, then nodded. "You're right. That's huge." He paused, thinking. "Did you take any pictures from our location?"

"Like what?"

"From different angles. North, south, east, west."

"No, not yet."

"Do it now. Circle GG-1 like a clock face; get backgrounds in each."

"Why?"

"If it rotated, I need to know its position relative to magnetic north."

Tessa considered. "Magnetic north?"

"Yes. I think it may matter for how GG-1 acts. For the stones."

She shrugged. "Okay, I get it."

"I'll wait until you're back behind the car."

Tessa walked the perimeter, kneeling for each shot, making sure the background showed the lay of the land.

"Twelve shots," she reported.

"Ready?" Ray asked. "Number four, powering up."

Tessa had it lined up, clicking away.

"Full power."

"Nothing."

"Number five, here goes." Another shot.

Again, nothing.

Ray frowned. "At least we have something for the day. Last unit, powering up number six."

Tessa's voice cut in, fast: "It's doing something!" Her finger clamped down on the shutter, camera rattling off pictures.

Ray focused on the controller, watching the last green light. Suddenly the air shifted—a rush like wind.

"Ray, it's gone!" Tessa's shout punched him.

"Gone?"

HAPTER FIFTEEN

At the Laubner Test site, Ray and Tessa stood on gravel, staring at the sky where GG-1 had just vanished. Dust hung in the air, blurred by heat, while the sky above bore a single, unraveling white line. The only sound for a long moment was Tessa's camera shutter, steady as a clock, until Ray broke the silence.

"How can it be gone?" he asked, disbelief echoing in his voice.

Tessa pointed, her finger trembling in the bright air. "Look. There's a trail of white."

Ray followed her gaze, shielding his eyes from the sun. "Are you still taking pictures?"

"Yes," she replied, still pressing the shutter button.

"Good. Don't stop till I tell you. Try to get shots that show where we're standing, the angle of the trail—everything."

"It's disappearing, though," she said.

"It's okay. Just keep shooting." His grip on the controller tightened as confusion and excitement swirled within him, making focus difficult.

Ray exhaled, trying to steady himself. "It flies."

"Why so fast?"

He shrugged, feeling the tension in his shoulders. "Not sure. Back to the drawing board. But where is it?"

"Are we going to be in trouble for this?" Tessa pressed, her mouth in a hard line.

"Probably. But it was an accident—an experiment. We didn't know it would do this, and we don't even know where it is now."

Tessa looked at him, waiting for a plan. "What now?"

"Time to go. I need to make some calls to figure this out."

Ray took the controller, tucked it back in the car, and yanked the hatch shut. Tessa hustled to the passenger seat, slamming the door as Ray leaped behind the wheel. The tires spun up dust as they shot down the access road toward the gate.

Ray braked hard, scrambled out, and fished for the gate key. Tessa didn't wait; she leapt over the center console, jammed the car into gear, and rolled through as soon as Ray swung the gate open. She grinned from the driver's seat while he hurried to re-lock the gate, then moved to the driver's door as she rolled down the window.

"I'm driving this time," he said, grasping the wheel.

"Just trying to speed things along. Speaking of speed, you could slow it down," she urged.

Ray reached for the radio. Tessa spun the dial, searching for any mention of GG-1. She settled on KFRC 106.9; the news reported booms and a white streak in the sky, speculation swirling about a meteor. Ray shook his head at the idea, glancing away.

"At least there's no report of a crash or damage. A small victory," he said.

"True. Where to, then?"

"Home. No sign of GG-1, nothing grounded. We'll think it over from there."

As they drove, the radio hummed softly in the background, the news a faint pulse, filling the silence that stretched between them.

CHAPTER SIXTEEN

All the way home, Ray and Tessa kept the radio on, hoping for a whispered update about GG-1, but the news had nothing new to offer—a streak crossing the sky, sonic booms rolling over the city, then silence. When they reached the house, Tessa unlocked the door and stepped in, almost forgetting to hang up her purse. Ray followed close behind, pulling the camera from the bag, intent on reviewing what evidence he might have captured. Hunched over the dining room table, he plugged the device into the laptop, the icons littering the desktop as he launched the viewer program. The counter reported several hundred images.

"This might take a while," Ray muttered.

The phone rang—a piercing, old-fashioned clatter startling them both. Tessa caught her breath, shot Ray a look, then reached for the receiver. "What if it's another complication? The FBI."

"It's your dad," she said, handing Ray the phone.

"Keep scrolling through the shots. Stop when you see GG- 1 last, right before it vanishes," he told her, taking the handset into the living room.

"Dad, what's up?"

"Hey, did you two go out to Diamond Hills today?"

Ray hesitated, eyes flicking toward Tessa hunched over the laptop. *Do I tell my dad the truth?* "Why? What's going on?"

"Listen to this. Travis Air Force Base called. They wanted to know if we were conducting any sort of test flights out at Diamond Hills. There's a reported UFO which streaked over the bay. They tracked it from just northwest of Diamond Hills."

Ray nearly dropped the phone. "What did they say about it?"

"Mach 2. Northwesterly. Then it stopped, thirty miles beyond the Golden Gate Bridge."

"It...stopped?" Ray asked, locking eyes with Tessa, whose face washed in the blue glow of the laptop. *They can't just let it hover there. What if they shoot it down?*

"They say it's hovering below eleven thousand feet, out near the Farallon Islands."

Ray pressed the phone tighter to his ear. "What are they going to do?"

"For the moment, nothing. Too cloudy to spot anything below the ceiling. They're just keeping everyone clear of the area till the weather improves."

A pause, the faint static of the line. "Wow. Well, thanks for the update, Dad. I need to go."

"Ray, wait," Dave insisted, urgency in his voice. "Did you end up at Diamond Hills like you said you would?"

"Yeah, we made it out there."

"How did it go?"

Ray glanced at the ceiling, thinking of the bright streak. "How did it go?" he repeated. "With your GG device?"

"Oh. GG-1. Let's just say...major failure."

"Oh no. What happened?"

"I'm still gathering the pieces, Dad. I'm honestly not sure. Let me call you later?"

"All right. But before you go, did you see anything strange out there?"

Ray shook his head, in reflex. "No. Just like everybody else—a white streak in the sky."

"Okay, you call me when you figure it out. Maybe I can help troubleshoot."

Ray murmured thanks, hung up, and stood in the open doorway, turning back to Tessa.

She didn't say anything. Just waited for him to process, arms folded, chin lifted.

"What did he say?" she finally asked, voice low but sharp with curiosity.

"GG-1 is still flying," Ray said, the truth of it settling in.

"What? Where?"

"Over the Farallon Islands. We need to get out there."

"Get out there? You mean, actually go out to the Farallones?" She glanced at the darkening window, as if the islands were visible from here.

Ray paced, jacket slung over his arm, his mind racing. "Yes. Yes, if I can get within five miles, I can cut the power and bring GG-1 down. Before someone else takes it out."

"They're going to shoot it down?" Tessa asked, eyes wide.

"No, no. They can't even see it. It's buried in cloud at eleven thousand feet."

"So how do you figure we're getting within five miles of the Farallones?"

Ray stopped pacing, fixed Tessa with a look. "Do you have Tom's number?"

"T-Tom?"

"Helicopter Tom," he said, almost impatient. "Harper."

She blinked, remembering. "Tom Harper? You're going to call him?"

"He might fly us out."

"You can't be serious."

Ray didn't answer. Instead, he rummaged through the drawer until Tessa fished Tom's number from her purse and read it aloud. Ray dialed fast.

"Hello?"

"Tom? This is Ray Holland."

"Who?"

"Tom Harper?"

"Yeah, I'm here. Who is this again?"

"Ray Holland. You took Tessa and me up in the Ben's Hawaii chopper."

A beat. "Oh, yeah, right." Tom didn't sound convinced, but Ray pressed on. "Tom, I have a huge favor to ask."

"Go ahead," Tom said. Ray could almost hear him scribbling on a notepad in the background.

"Can you fly us out to the Farallon Islands today?"

Silence. "Today? Not a lot of today left."

Ray pressed the phone to his ear, cupping his hands over the mouthpiece. "I know, but it's urgent."

"More urgent than the paperwork on my desk?" Tom laughed, but there seemed to be a catch in his voice.

"We can pay extra. In cash."

That caught Tom's attention. The mention of cash always piqued interest. Ray could almost picture him leaning back in his chair, tapping his pen against the desk, weighing the request. "Cash, huh? When do you want to leave?" Ray felt a surge of urgency, hoping the offer would be enough to persuade him.

"Now. As soon as possible."

"Fine, I'll see you in a bit," Tom said.

Ray hung up, grabbed his jacket and the remote. "It'll be cold out there. Get something warm," he told Tessa.

She nodded, already heading for the bedroom. Ray hesitated. "What do we have for cash?"

"Just a couple hundred, maybe," Tessa said, rooted by the door.

He shook his head. "We need more. Hit the ATM on the way. What's the limit?"

"Three thousand."

"Let's get it all; hope it's enough."

They jumped into the car, took a quick drive to the Chase Bank, and managed to withdraw the maximum in crisp hundreds, Tessa counting the bills as they pulled out of the lot.

"Are you sure this will work?" she asked.

Ray nodded, determination settling in. "At five miles, I know I can talk to GG-1. If we get close enough, the remote kill will cut its power. I built it for emergencies."

She cast a worried look at the sky, clouds thickening as the evening cooled. "But the ceiling, and the sun's dropping."

"Tom didn't mention a problem. He must have a plan."

Forty-five minutes later, they pulled up to hangar 42B, expecting to see the bright Ben's Hawaii chopper gleaming in the dusk sky, but the apron sat empty.

Ray leaned forward in the seat, wondering about the possibility of GG-1 being shot down. "Where's the helicopter?"

Further down, past the hangar, they saw something else: a US Coast Guard helicopter, painted in high-visibility orange and white, Eurocopter HH-65, medical stripes on the fuselage.

They parked, hustled to the hangar, and found Tom hunched over a calculator, the stale smell of oil clinging to every surface and the flickering fluorescent lights overhead. He looked up, surprised but pleased.

"You made it." He folded the calculator shut. "Farallon Islands, right?"

"Right," Ray said, tension racing through his body.

Tom narrowed his eyes. "You said this was extremely important?"

"It is."

He shrugged. "Not much out on the Farallones. Plus, when I filed the flight plan, the tower said the area's closed. Fifty-mile radius. Cloudy, but that's not the main issue. The closure is."

Tessa stepped forward. "Did they say why?"

"No, just rumors. Something to do with the white streak today. The booms."

Ray took out his wallet, peeling off a thousand dollars in a neat stack. He hoped it would be enough.

Tom's eyebrows shot up. "You're kidding?"

Ray doubled it, fanned out the rest. The question loomed: would this even work?

"Okay," Tom conceded, "now I'm really listening. What's so important out there?"

Ray looked at Tessa. She nodded; no use keeping secrets now.

"Tom, the streak across the sky? We were part of it. My experimental craft is now hovering above the Farallones, out of control. I need to shut it down before the authorities do."

Tom whistled. "So, it's uncontrolled."

Ray nodded. "Could be up there for days."

Tom looked thoughtful. "They'll shoot it down before then."

"Which is what I'm afraid of," Ray said.

"So, we fly out, you kill it, we come back?"

"An extra thousand if we can recover it in one piece," Ray said.

Tom loosened his shoulders, considering. “Will it survive the fall?”

Ray shrugged. “It hit Mach 2. I think so.” Saying the words felt reassuring.

“And if it lands in water?”

Ray winced. “Should float, but probably not for long. Can’t guarantee it’s watertight after a supersonic flight.”

Tessa glanced at Ray, mouthing, “Three thousand?” Ray nodded in return, lips barely moving, “Yes.”

“Deal,” Tom said, almost grinning.

Tessa asked, “What are we flying? The Ben’s chopper’s not out front.”

Tom gestured out the hangar window. “Sent it to LA this morning, for a Hawaii delivery. But we’ve got something better. A Coast Guard Eurocopter. More room; more range. Some toys which might help.”

Ray straightened. “How soon can we leave?”

“Soon as she’s fueled. I’ll call the truck. Meet me at the chopper in five.”

They left Tom to his preparations, the adrenaline now mixing with nerves. At the car, Ray grabbed the remote and an anorak. Tessa zipped her jacket as the fuel truck rumbled up, a man waving to Tom and starting the refuel.

Tom rejoined them with two Coast Guard helmets, giving the fueler a parting wave as the truck rolled off. “Okay, new ride, new rules,” Tom said, voice echoing.

He pointed out the harnesses, emphasized how to handle a ditch in the open water, showing them the flares and floating devices, his hands quick and sure.

“This helicopter’s seen some use,” Tessa said, running her hand over the seat frame, her lips pressed in a thin line.

“Yep. Just refitted with a fresh LTS101-750 engine and new avionics. Most of the upgrades are in the cockpit. Which is why I’m the one who gets to take it out.”

“Which doesn’t sound exactly safe,” Tessa said.

Tom shrugged, unconcerned. “No different than last time. With the night vision goggles wired into the twin GPS control displays, we’re flying in style. This is her maiden run.”

Ray and Tessa exchanged a look, concern flickering between them, but Ray squared his shoulders and nodded. *This was necessary. I need this.*

"Let's go," he said.

Tom instructed Ray to get in front with him, and Tessa to strap into one of the seats in back. She wound up even farther from the cockpit in this helicopter compared to Ben's. Before they put on their helmets, Tessa called to Ray, "How are we going to recover GG-1?"

He hesitated. "I'm not sure yet." *What if I can't figure this out in time?*

"Hey, kids, how much does the thing weigh?" Tom asked over his shoulder.

"Forty pounds," Ray said.

"Okay, good, I have an idea."

Tom stepped into the back, moving with easy confidence, and pulled out the recovery winch line—the kind they used for lowering a basket to stranded swimmers. He showed them the basic controls, raising and lowering, the snap of the latch.

"We could lower a person, or the basket. Either should work," Tom said.

"Who is going to do that?" Tessa asked.

"I will," Ray answered without hesitation.

Tom nodded. "Then you need a flight suit. Better to put it on now than try to fight it in the air. Trust me."

Ray zipped himself into one of the one-piece flight suits strapped against the wall, the fabric stiff but clean.

"Is this really worth it?" Tessa asked, watching him.

His expression, more of a grimace. "Yes, of course. Come on, how hard can this be?"

"For a trained Coast Guardsman, easy. For an electrical engineer, I'm not sure," she said.

He shrugged, determined. "We're going for it."

Tom began running through the operation of the basket, winch, and harnesses. He made them test the controls, the clack of metal audible over the low throb of the starting engines.

"Everybody clear?" Tom asked when he seemed satisfied. Tessa and Ray both gave a thumbs-up. "This could be a quick trip, kids. Once we're up, we'll be to Farallon in ten minutes. Okay, helmets on."

Ray buckled his chin strap, Tessa mimicked him, gaze flickering from window to instrument panel. Tom checked his switches and started the engine. The rotor blades spun with a rising whine as the helicopter came alive.

"What about the closed area?" Ray asked.

Tom hadn't seemed concerned until now. "No problem. This is Coast Guard Helicopter six-zero-one-four, still broadcasts a Coast Guard transponder code to the towers. They'll hail us. We respond we're answering a distress call from VHS. Before anyone gets suspicious, we'll be in and out of the area."

Ray shifted uncertainly. "Can we get in some sort of trouble for impersonating the Coast Guard?"

Tom grinned without turning. "Like I said, we'll be in and out quick. We can fly low and turn off the transponder if we have to. It will really get them going—they might think we went down and then scramble a search party. But it's only if we have to. We're good for now."

Ray glanced back at Tessa, who sat silently in the back, strapping herself in with both hands. He watched her eyes flicker as she processed Tom's words, a moment of uncertainty evident in her posture.

Tom called the tower and checked traffic. "All clear, everybody?"

He received nods, then taxied away from the hangars and onto the strip. Once lined up, Tom pushed the throttle smoothly forward; the HH-65 lifted, angling up into the gray sky. He clicked the intercom, his voice oddly calm in their helmets.

"Cloud ceiling still above eleven thousand, and only about five hundred feet above the water. Perfect for us. There's hardly any wind, one to two-foot seas. San Francisco Tower should see us soon, so I'll give them a heads up."

"San Francisco Tower, this is Coast Guard 6014."

"Coast Guard 6014, this is San Francisco Tower." The answer resonated though the headsets.

"Tower, we are heading three one four, at one thousand."

"6014 three one four at one thousand, roger."

They left the city behind—a checkerboard of houses, then the wrinkled green of fields, all shrinking beneath the chopper. Ray watched as the gray band of cloud rose to meet them, filling the windows. He observed the water vapor curling and streaming along the plexiglass, and below, a ghostly orange flickered through the haze from the setting sun.

"Interesting they haven't mentioned the closed area," Tom said. "They probably figure we're Coast Guard and already know about it."

Ray leaned forward. "Does this helicopter have radar?"

"Sure does."

He nodded, thinking. "Can you see anything over the Farallon Islands yet?"

"Not yet. But we're halfway there."

"How fast are we going?" Ray asked.

"One hundred thirty knots. Like I said, this won't take long."

Ray squinted at the clouds, noticing how they thinned in spots, allowing brief glimpses of sunlight which glinted like gold before disappearing again. He could hear Tom's voice steady through the intercom, grounding him amid the shifting scenery.

"Good news—we'll get there with daylight left. Bad news, maybe we won't see what we're after."

Ray's eyes narrowed as he stared at his device. "I calculate less than two minutes for GG-1 to hit the ground or water." He exhaled once, a controlled breath to clear hesitation.

"Ten miles to go," Tom said, scanning the nav display. "I can see your GG-1. It's the only blip on the screen."

Tom pointed to the tiny white dot, nearly swallowed up by the jagged green and orange outline of Farallon Island on the nav display.

"I'll turn and head right for it. Dropping to five hundred feet, so hopefully ATC doesn't call us up, or anyone else."

They dropped to five hundred feet, the helicopter skimming just above the surface. Ray watched as the waves gleamed beneath the fading daylight, a mix of blue and gray stretching out before them. The vapor on the windows cleared, revealing the island—a splintered emerald rising from the sea.

"Look," Ray said.

"The Farallon Islands," Tom confirmed. "Five miles. Everybody ready?"

Tessa, quiet since takeoff, called out. "Ready." Ray caught her checking her seatbelt and harness twice, like it's routine.

"You are awake," he said, smiling, the tension in his voice breaking.

Ray felt the sudden drag of deceleration, his body pushing against the seat belt. Outside, everything seemed to slow down, as if time itself responded to the helicopter's descent. He squinted at the view, picking out the deep blue of the sea and the white scatter of breaking surf against the rocky shore. The sun hung low behind them, a fading ember pressed against the horizon, casting shadows which danced across the waves.

"I hope it doesn't fall on our head," Tessa said.

"Me too," Ray agreed, trusting in his work.

He could see on the nav display, the blip shown nearly atop them; they knew it remained flying, high above in the clouds, invisible to the naked eye.

"This will be a splashdown," Tom said. "No point landing on the island chain. Pure rock and shoals. Pretty from the air, not where you'd want to land a boat."

Ray switched on his radio control.

"I have it, I have it," he said, watching the LED on the controller flick green.

Without hesitating, he flipped the kill switch. "Powered off."

Tom spun the HH-65 with a practiced hand, rotating them one hundred eighty degrees.

"Let's back off and give it room."

Ray glanced at the display, noting the blip behind them as Tom rotated the helicopter, climbing higher. Twenty seconds had passed. The device continued falling, and he couldn't see it. The nav display pulsed, and then his heart leaped. There it was—a flash cutting through the clouds, a frantic streak, grey and round, trailing vapor in the sky."

"There it is!" Ray shouted, pointing at the apparition, a pale shape against the blue-black ocean below.

"It's going to make a big splash," Tom said. "It's falling at three to five hundred miles per hour."

Ray frowned at the controller. "Wait, wait. I have an idea to slow it down."

Careful, he started toggling the power: on, off, on, off. Each time he flicked it back on, the object seemed to halt in mid-air, check its descent.

Tom shot him a look of disbelief. "Kid, I don't know what you built, but I can't believe it can stop like that."

Ray kept toggling: short bursts of power, longer off times, easing the speed with each cycle.

"It's getting harder to see," Tom said.

"Can we get closer?" Ray asked.

"Yes," Tom replied, tipping the nose of the helicopter and accelerating toward the sea, cutting through the dim glow and descending mist.

CHAPTER SEVENTEEN

Voices crackled over the radio as Ray gripped the RC controller tightly, his heart racing. He watched the display screen intently, guiding GG-1's descent into the night. The device responded to his commands as he fought against the rising tension in his chest.

"Who's on the radio?"

"Sounds like Travis Air Force Base is trying to reach us," Tom said, scanning the dials.

"How do they know we're out here?" Ray asked.

"Radar."

Ray shook off some worry. "I thought we were below radar?"

"Not for them. They can see us, down to five hundred feet. They must have seen your GG-1 fall and can see we're headed for it. If we don't answer, they'll call the Coast Guard and report us as nonresponsive. That'll be trouble. Keep a lookout for your GG-1 while I get rid of Travis."

The call came over again.

Through the crackling headset, the voice from the radio came through flat and clipped, lacking the urgency Ray expected. "Coast Guard 6014, this is Travis Air Force Base, do you read?" The blandness of the call contrasted with the tension in the helicopter, leaving Ray uneasy.

Tom reached for the mic. "Travis, this is CG 6014, we read you."

Ray felt tension rise in the air as the transmission lagged, a moment stretching out before the response came through.

"CG 6014, you are flying in a restricted area due to unknown traffic. You should turn heading one eighty-one and leave at once."

"Travis, we received a distress call on VHF 16 and are in a search pattern," Tom replied.

"CG 6014, did you see anything hit the water directly in front of you within the last few minutes?"

"Negative, Travis ATC, of any object hitting the sea."

"CG 6014, are you in need of assistance in your search?"

"Negative, Travis ATC. No assistance needed. We're doing one more close sweep, then returning to base. No beacon or VHF call for over twenty minutes."

"CG 6014, roger, no assistance needed, continuing sweep. CG 6014, report any debris in the water."

"Travis ATC, roger, will report any sightings."

Tom switched the mic off and let out a long breath.

Ray's heart raced as the implication of their situation sank in.

"Okay, they'll be off our back for a while," Tom said, but Ray couldn't shake the feeling of unease.

"What if we don't recover GG-1?" Ray peered down through the cockpit window. "I think I see GG-1, but it's too dark to be sure."

Tom reached for the night vision switch and snapped it on. "How about now?"

"Oh, wow, much better." Ray toggled the power to GG-1, blinking it against the black ocean.

"Over there, to the right, um, two o'clock! I see something," Tessa called out.

Ray's head jerked to the side.

"How far out?" Tom asked, pivoting the chopper into the new heading.

"See where the water is cresting white near the shore?" Tessa pointed. "Watch."

Ray leaned in, scanning the restless foam near the rocks. Then, with certainty: "Yes," he said, excitement pitching him forward. "That's it."

"Does it float?" Tom asked, glancing over his shoulder. "Otherwise, this will be near impossible."

"Only one way to find out," Ray said, determination flowing through him. *I'm not going to let it sink.*

He stopped toggling power, sending GG-1 plunging toward the water. All eyes tracked it. A white splash marked where it hit, tossing in the rough sea.

"This isn't looking good," Ray said, grim. The object wallowed, barely afloat.

"This doesn't look good," Tom echoed. "It's barely floating. Okay, kids, this might be our only chance. Ray, go back with Tessa, and let's lower the basket like we went over. I think we should try to fish it out."

Ray looked at the basket, uncertain.

"Tom, that won't work. I'll have to go down in the basket to get it."

"Too dangerous," Tom said instantly. "Remember, I'm not a Coast Guard pilot, not with hundreds of cycles in this. I can't let you go. I have a better plan. We'll get as close as we can and catch it like a fish in a net. Strap in your harnesses and lower the basket about ten feet. Ray, lean out and guide the basket. Tessa, you call out directions. Right, left, forward, backward—whatever."

They inched closer to the water, the basket clanking as it lowered. Ray strained to see through the spray splattering against the windows, the noise of the rotor blades vibrating through him. He felt the helicopter dip as Tom adjusted their altitude: twenty feet, then ten, then five above the churning water.

He called out, "Dead ahead."

"I see it," Tessa said. "Left... left... forward... slow... slow..."

Ray dropped the basket until it vanished, then eased it up, eyes focused on the metal rim.

Tessa's voice kept Tom steady: "Slower... right, a little... okay... straight ahead. Oh no, I lost it."

"Where?" Ray's hands flexed on the hoist. Don't lose it now.

"Only about three feet to go."

The helicopter edged closer, the basket dipping lower, when a sudden vibration shot up Ray's arm—a sharp tug, like a fish strike. He hit the hoist button, pulling the basket up.

"Keep moving forward," Ray called urgently to Tom.

"Doing my best."

As the basket surfaced, GG-1 precariously clung to its edge and Ray kept the hoist rising.

"I think we have it," Ray shouted.

The basket swayed wildly in the chopper's downdraft, the metal mesh slapping against the wind-lashed spray. Ray and

Tessa braced against the cabin doorway, the harness cutting into Ray's chest as he leaned out, arms stretched to the limit. Tessa, anchored behind him, steadied the winch controls and called directions, her words barely audible above the twin roar of the rotors and the hammering ocean.

"There—now!" she shouted as the basket dipped again into the whitecapped trough.

Ray felt the cable tighten with a sudden, sharp tug, the sound of water splashing against it echoing in the cabin. He steadied himself, muscles coiled as he leaned out, heart pounding.

The device wobbled unsteadily, the weight surprisingly heavy and slick with seawater. The hoist wined as GG-1 drew closer rising away from the seas grasp. Within his grasp it began to pivot, Ray instinctively reached for it, but it slipped, grazing his thumb as it threatened to tumble back into the depths. Tessa's hand shot out, gripping his forearm tightly to anchor him against the chopper's sudden lurch. Together, they wrestled with the wayward device, their bodies wedged between the helicopter's doorway and the metal rim of the basket. Panic surged in Ray as he felt GG-1 teeter on the edge, his heart racing at the thought of losing it.

"Hold it steady!" Tessa urged, her knee pressing against the device as she adjusted her position in the doorway.

She reached for the release, breathing hard, while Ray fought to keep their prize from slipping away. The basket jerked upwards, nearly catching Ray's elbow, and for a heart-stopping moment, it felt like they were suspended in midair, caught in a precarious dance with the ocean below.

With a final surge of determination, Ray pulled as the basket swung toward the helicopter. They strained to maintain their grip, the device nearly escaping their grasp. But with one last heave, they yanked it inside, rolling backward as the chopper bucked beneath them, forcing GG-1 onto Ray's chest.

Ray collapsed against the cabin floor, breathless and exhilarated, GG-1 warm against him and sputtering gently. Tessa fell beside him, her face splattered with seawater, both of them erupting into half-laughs, half-cries of disbelief, exchanging a look filled with wild triumph—knowing they had snatched something precious back from the depths.

Tom glanced over his shoulder. "Everyone here?"

Ray couldn't read the chaos around him; the frantic energy in the cabin hammered at his chest. He raised GG-1 off his chest. "We have it!"

"Outstanding!" Tom bellowed, grinning widely. "Next stop, Half Moon Bay!" He craned the stick, and the chopper shot skyward, leaving the surf behind.

Ray glanced over, grinning. "I'm liking your idea more and more, Tom. At least this way I stayed somewhat dry."

"And alive," Tom replied.

Ray and Tessa exchanged a breathless high-five and hugged.

"Okay, let's get out of here," Tom said.

After what felt like an eternity, they finally dropped to the tarmac at Half Moon Bay, settling by Hangar 42B.

"I can't thank you enough," Ray said as they unstrapped.

"Happy to help," Tom replied, his grin still wide.

Ray reached into his pocket, pulling out thirty-one hundred dollar bills. "Here's for the ride."

"Cash? You kids are full of surprises," Tom said, taking the bills with a raised brow. "If you ever want to go for another ride, just give me a call."

"We will," Ray said.

Tessa hurried to get the car, urgency palpable as she avoided drawing unwanted eyes to GG-1. Ray helped her back in, lifting the device into the back while glancing around, feeling the weight of scrutiny on them. Tessa thanked Tom again, and Ray nodded, but his mind pressed only half on the exchange, caught up in the lingering tension.

CHAPTER EIGHTEEN

The darkness pressed against the car windows as they headed south on Cabrillo Highway, and Ray could barely make out the shapes of clustered neighborhoods flickering by. As the Half Moon Bay Lodge—a landmark that had become all too familiar—slipped past the passenger side window, relief washed over him. Maybe, at last, the chaos of the day had eased. Tessa broke the heavy silence first.

"Being back on earth now and my tummy's finally settled, do you think the GG-1 project can maybe calm down? If we keep going like this, I probably won't see forty."

Ray tried to lighten the mood. "What do you mean, wasn't that fun?" But he felt her concern lingering in the air.

She shook her head, still watching the passing darkness. "I don't know if I'd call it fun. It's just—it's like chaos and something wonderful all mixed together. I can't explain it." Ray noticed the tremor in her voice, a hint of unease masked by bravado.

"I bet you're hungry," he said, trying to keep it simple.

"Probably right."

"We could go back to Half Moon Bay. The food was good."

Tessa looked down at herself, dubious. "Are you kidding? Looking like this?"

Ray's heart ached at her frustration, and he wanted to reassure her.

"What? You look great," he said, hoping to lift her spirits.

She gave a small huff. "My hair's a mess. Thirty minutes in a helmet, and this is what happens."

"You could just run a comb through it," he suggested, but her glare was enough to silence him.

"Okay, Plan B: how about a drive-thru?"

"That's more like it. Burger, fries, and a shake," she said, almost triumphant, then pointed at him. "If you so much as mention watching what I eat, I'll fire up GG-1."

Ray laughed, though the threat stuck in his gut. He knew exactly how bad it could get.

Ray sobered. "Actually, we should probably pull the batteries from the controller—just in case it fires up accidentally." His instincts nagged at him; he couldn't shake the feeling they were still in danger, even now.

While Ray drove, Tessa twisted in her seat, reaching for the controller. "Ray, there's a dark sedan behind us."

"So? It's only nine. People are still out."

Tessa's gaze remained fixed in the mirror. She shook her head. "No, this feels wrong." Ray noticed the tension in her shoulders tighten; she'd shifted into high alert, and his heart raced in response.

He tried to soothe her, keeping his hands steady on the wheel. "Okay, take it easy."

She studied the sedan, then popped open the back of the controller, removing all the batteries before setting them in the cup holder. "We should cover GG-1." The confidence she projected seemed forced, and Ray admired her resolve.

"Think you can do it while I'm driving? The blanket's right there." Ray pointed.

Tessa nodded, unlatching her seatbelt, and climbed awkwardly over the seat. "He's still there," she called.

"I see him."

"Not a lot of room back here," she grumbled.

"I know. Maybe we should get a truck." She barked out a laugh, and for a moment, the tension lifted. "Good plan, honey," she said, finishing covering GG-1 with the blanket, tucking it in tight. She slipped back into the passenger seat and clicked her seatbelt. "Best I could do."

"Looks good," Ray said, catching sight of headlights ahead. "Looks like civilization. Might find a drive-thru soon."

Approaching a bright intersection, Ray noted the cluster of burger places. Tessa pointed. "In-N-Out."

Ray steered over, a couple of cars idling in line ahead. They slumped down, taking a moment to breathe. The lingering tension in the car hung like a cloud.

Ray broke the lull. "Where's the car you thought was following?"

"He drove by, kept going."

Ray offered a smile. "See, nothing to worry about." But uncertainty gnawed at him.

Tessa's laugh came out sharp. "Nothing to worry about? We just fished a UFO out of the sea after it shut down the Bay Area, and now we're being followed by dark sedans. Sure, nothing to worry about."

"You're just hungry. Food will help." Ray eased forward, ordered, quickly received their food, and parked in the lot.

Tessa tore into her burger, her silence weighing on him. When she finally put the wrapper down, she said, "I swear, the older I get, the smaller these burgers get. Can you get me another one?"

Ray laughed, "Sure." He crossed the lot, stepping inside the bright restaurant.

A teenage girl in a loose blouse stood at the register, chatting with the boy behind the counter.

The guy in line ahead of Ray, wearing jeans and a t-shirt, didn't move; he just stared straight ahead, oblivious to his surroundings. The manager emerged from the back, glanced over, and spoke to Ray.

"Didn't you just go through the drive-thru? Missing a hamburger, right?"

Before Ray could respond, the manager tossed him a wrapped burger from the warmer. "Sorry about that."

Ray thanked him and left, glancing back at the odd guy in line, who hadn't flinched. An unsettling feeling crept over him; something wasn't right.

Ray slid back into the car and handed Tessa her burger.

"Thanks," she said, looking up.

"You wouldn't believe what just happened in there."

"That bad?"

Ray summarized the standstill in line, the strange man, the manager, the girl at the counter, the kid in the back—the best he could.

Tessa shrugged. "I get the flirting and the messed-up orders, but the guy in line? Strange. Anyway, I finished my fries and half my shake, so you can have half this burger." She ripped it in two and passed the rest to him.

Still chewing, Tessa glanced back at the restaurant. She straightened. “Is that the guy?”

Ray watched a man cross the parking lot, bag in hand. “Yes, that’s him.”

“Oh my God, he looks like...”

“Who?”

“Victor. Victor Mishkin from Stanford.”

“Really?”

“Yes.”

“Does he act strange at Stanford?”

“No, not like you said. But I always had a weird feeling around him.”

“How can you tell it’s him?”

“He looked this way, right at us, then away.”

Ray frowned. “What kind of car did he get in?”

“No idea. He must have parked on the far side.”

A pair of taillights broke free behind the lot. Tessa pointed. “Someone just left the back lot.”

“What kind of car?”

“All I saw were the brake lights.”

Ray hesitated. “Should we follow?”

Tessa shook her head. “No, let’s just go home. I’m exhausted and full.” Ray noticed the fatigue etched in her expression, mirroring his own weariness. The fatigue etched on her face, a reflection of the weight of the day that pulled at him too.

Ray started the engine, the low hum filling the silence as they pulled onto the dark highway. He watched Tessa’s silhouette as she peered through the rear window, her expression tense as she scanned the darkness for headlights. When they finally arrived home, their house resembled a black cutout against the stars. Ray parked just shy of the garage door, leaving the headlights burning on the driveway. He stepped out, opened the back, unlocked the garage, and tossed the keys to Tessa.

As Tessa twisted the lock, the kitchen lights flickered on, illuminating the driveway and casting warm light around them. Ray grunted as he heaved GG-1 into the garage, set the controller beside it, locked up, and closed the door. He found the car keys on the counter, went back out, and parked the car to block the garage. The driveway lights stayed on; he locked the rest of the house and finally headed upstairs.

Ray found Tessa already in the bedroom, the soft glow from the lamp highlighting her in a pink nightgown, the blue sheet half-draped over her legs. When he stepped into the room and the door unlatched, she didn't move.

"You didn't wait for me," Ray said.

"Sorry, just tired," she spoke into the darkness.

He shrugged, trying to sound casual. "No, I get it."

She started, "I was just..." then let it trail off, shaking her head.

When he stepped back into the bedroom, Tessa lay already tucked under the covers, her breathing soft and even. Ray walked over to the window, pulling the curtain back to peer out into the night. The chill of the evening air crept through the glass, and a shiver ran down his spine as memories of the day's chaos played in his mind. Outside, the quiet darkness felt heavy, almost oppressive. He let the curtain fall and climbed into bed beside Tessa, pulling her close, grateful for the peace at last.

CHAPTER NINETEEN

Ray woke as daylight's first brush slipped through the bedroom window, spreading softly across the ceiling. The popcorn texture above him resembled a hilly landscape more than a night sky, peaks and valleys catching the pale light. He blinked, letting the strange topography settle in his sight, his mind racing with thoughts of GG-1. Why had it flown to its perch above Farallon Island? What could it be about the specific location, the exact elevation, that mattered to the machine and the stones it carried?

The stones—they had magnetic properties, always orienting themselves to the earth's magnetic field. If each stone aligned into place, then the answer must spiral back to the controlling board, a tangled web of calculations and circuitry he'd spent weeks designing. He closed his eyes, the design diagram sketching itself behind his eyelids. Suddenly, clarity: the power outputs fell into a complex dance. The first two responded to elevation, the next two to location. Speed still played a part, but the last output, the one that had hurled GG-1 away yesterday, was likely tied to it. A familiar weight pressed in on him; the fear of failure gnawed at his gut.

I need a full week to redraw the schematic, maybe more to actually build the board. Two weeks before another round of tests. He exhaled, feeling some of the tension drop away, but a small voice whispered something Tessa would appreciate more than just the pause; it was her emotional support he had been neglecting.

Tessa shifted in the bed beside him.

"You're awake," she murmured, her voice barely audible.

"Yes," he answered.

"How long?"

"Not long. Just thinking through what happened with GG- 1."

"Any ideas?"

"Yeah. I think I can rework the circuit board. Should give me tighter control."

"That was quick." She arched an eyebrow, her tone both impressed and laced with concern.

"I know. Once I focused on what happened—the location, the way the thing stopped—it just sort of lined up. But I'm warning you, the calculations are ugly. It'll probably be a couple weeks before I have anything to test."

"Fine by me. I wouldn't mind a little downtime after yesterday."

Her lighthearted tone didn't quite reach her eyes, and he sensed the worry lurking beneath. The phone shrieked from the nightstand, making both of them jump.

"Who's calling on a Sunday morning?" Ray muttered, snatching the receiver.

"Ray, sorry to ring so early. Did I wake you?"

He covered the mouthpiece. "It's Dad," he mouthed to Tessa.

She slid out of bed toward the bathroom, the light leaving her expression for a moment.

"No, we're up," Ray said.

"I tried last night but couldn't reach you. Just wanted to check in. I feel bad about how GG-1 went and thought maybe I could help."

"I need to redo the controller's circuit board."

"I thought from your tone you'd blown up half your garage."

"It almost looked like it."

"There's more UFO talk out of Diamond Hills. Travis Base keeps calling. They tracked the streak, and now it's officially unidentified. Last radar had it vanish off the coast. No explanations."

At least relief slipped through him— they weren't being blamed for anything worse.

"It made for a good show," Ray said.

"Lots of people saw it. Not going to be easy for them to sweep it away. So, you coming to the office tomorrow?"

"I'll work from home."

"Alright. If you need a hand, say the word. Remember the guys in lab 8A? They'll fab a board for you, solder anything. They live for oddball projects. Just expense it."

"Thanks, Dad."

Ray bounded downstairs, determined to move forward on the next revision. He stopped short at the sight of Tessa reading the paper, a bagel and orange juice lined up beside her coffee. She looked peaceful, but he could sense the tension in her posture.

"What did Dad want?" she asked.

"He was following up on yesterday. Said I can use the lab crew to help with my circuit board. That could speed up the testing process."

"So you'll be in the garage all day?"

"Yep. Need to stay ahead while it's fresh."

She nodded, but a flicker of disappointment crossed her face. "Go for it. I'll hit the Stanford library, then shop for clothes."

By two o'clock, Ray prowled the kitchen, refrigerator open, searching for a snack. He scanned the shelves and sighed when nothing caught his eye; he shut the fridge, drifting to the pantry—then the phone rang.

"Hello?" Ray answered, distracted.

"Ray Holland?"

"Yes." Instinctively, he recognized the voice.

"This is Steve Seltzer."

"Oh, hey Steve. What's up?"

"Business is still slow at the shop, so I've been cleaning up. Remember the mold I made for you?"

"Sure," Ray said, still thinking about food.

"In this business, you always make extra to guarantee a delivery. I have a second unit, built to spec. I was hoping you'd buy it at a discount."

Ray hesitated. "Really?"

"Could you use a twin? I'll let it go for twenty-five hundred. Half price."

Ray considered. "I honestly don't need a second one right now."

“Fifteen hundred,” Steve said, quick.

Ray laughed. “Alright, Steve, you win. I’ll take it for fifteen hundred.”

“Fantastic. Want me to bring it over and grab a check?”

“Absolutely. I’m home all day.”

“One more thing,” Ray offered, “I’ll call Laubner to see if they need any machine work. Maybe send business your way.”

“Thanks, Ray. See you soon.”

Forty minutes later, Steve’s panel truck rolled up. Ray met him in the driveway as Steve used the gate hoist to lower a heavy box, white cardboard sealed tight with tape.

“Nice truck,” Ray commented.

“Saves my back,” Steve replied, grinning.

“Let’s see it.”

Steve popped the tape, peeled off the packing paper, revealing two halves of Ray’s design—a perfect duplicate.

“Looks just like GG-1,” Ray said.

“I could do more if you need it,” Steve offered.

“No need yet. Still chasing the first one.”

Ray had the check ready, handing it over before shaking Steve’s hand.

“I’m sorry it’s been slow. Wish I could do more,” Ray told him.

“You just did. This helps a lot. If you need more, I have a couple rejects I could sell for scrap.”

“I’ll keep you posted. Thanks, Steve.”

Steve closed up his truck and rolled out while Ray carried the box into the garage. Then it hit him—GG-2. Perfect. Instead of tearing down GG-1, he could build the new controller from scratch with a fresh unit. He had enough stones and only needed another battery. Excitement surged through him, along with the weight of responsibility. He shelved the box and returned to wrestling with the circuit board design on his computer.

At five, Tessa’s car pulled into the driveway. She staggered out, balancing a stack of shopping bags in her arms. Ray caught the sound of the engine idling and stepped outside, anticipation rising as he moved to meet her.

"Looks like you made good use of the day," Ray said.

She lifted the bags. "You won't believe how much I saved."

He grinned. "Not so fast. I might have you beat."

"Oh really? How do you save money hiding in the garage all afternoon?"

Ray ducked into the garage, came back with the box, and flipped it open.

"Another GG-1?"

"This is GG-2. Steve called with a spare but couldn't move it, so he slashed the price. Wasn't even looking for a second, but he kind of talked me into it."

"How was nice of you." Tessa's eyes sparkled with excitement, but Ray spotted a flicker of concern beneath.

"No matter what I tried, the department store never let me haggle their discounts," Tessa said, laughing. "But at least I can wear mine. What do you do with a second GG?"

"I want to keep GG-1 intact. I'll use GG-2 for this phase. I have the parts and am building a new controller. All I need is another battery."

She laughed. "So I'll know where to find you, is what you're telling me?"

Ray shrugged. "About right. You told me to go all-in on this, remember?"

"I did." Her voice held a playful lilt. "And I'm not complaining. Just reporting—it's where you'll be. So, did you make dinner?"

"Dinner?" Ray blinked, suddenly aware of the time. "I, uh, lost track of time, honey. Sorry."

"Maybe GG-2 can make dinner," she said, dropping the bags at her feet in the driveway.

Ray grinned. "You really had a good day."

Tessa beamed, hefting the bags again. "Come on. Let's cook together. Like we do."

Ray raised a brow, uncertainty creeping in. The thought of abandoning her again stung, but the pull of GG-2 called to him, a tug-of-war he couldn't escape.

"Wishful thinking," she teased.

Ray put the new GG-2 prototype back in the garage and helped Tessa unload the rest of her bags. He glanced inside, wondering if any of them held food or if they would just become another reminder of the distance he had created between them.

CHAPTER TWENTY

Monday morning, early. With the sun barely up, Ray poured coffee for Tessa and leaned back against the counter, cup in hand. As he watched the steam rise from the mug, his mind wandered to the day ahead—how much he wanted to make progress on GG-2 and impress Tessa with his work.

"So what's on your agenda today?"

"I'm going to Stanford to help in the library again."

Ray raised an eyebrow. "Again? I thought you were focused on your project."

"I was," Tessa replied, a hint of frustration creeping into her tone. "But then I started talking to the staff, and they asked if I could help out. As a staff member, I get paid. It's not as much as teaching, but there's no pressure, and the students really do need help with the library's resources."

He nodded. "Got it."

"Besides, you're going to be neck-deep in the garage for a couple of weeks, so it's not like we'll be going anywhere together anyway."

Ray grinned. "You've got a point."

"I don't start until ten, so I'll have the morning to get things done here or help you if you need anything. I'll probably be there till six most days, so you're in charge of dinner."

"Okay. Just call me if you'll be late, and I'll put something easy together."

"If you need ideas, let me know." She reached over to refill her mug and stepped away, the warmth of her presence lingering.

Ray had GG-1 and GG-2 side by side on the garage bench. GG-2 remained split in two halves, waiting for its stones. He readied the slots in GG-2, aligning each stone to its magnetic field. As he worked, he felt excitement churn with anxiety about whether this version would perform as he hoped.

Tessa appeared in the doorway, wearing navy-blue slacks and a crisp white blouse. She took one look at his workbench and laughed. “Oh, hey. I’ll stop on the way home and check into cell phones. Time to move into the twenty-first century and get cell phones so we can communicate.”

Ray shrugged, attempting to hide his ambivalence. “Okay.”

She leaned in, gave him a quick kiss on the cheek, and squeezed his shoulder. “I’ve been thinking about how handy they’d be when we’re away from a landline.”

Ray paused, then looked up at her. “Call me if you need any help deciding.”

“I will.” She squeezed his arm briefly and disappeared out the door.

Ray listened for her engine, then focused on the open shell of GG-2, grabbing handfuls of glowing stones, orienting them one by one, and pressing each into its slot. Sometimes the monotony dragged on; he found himself drifting back to the design for the new controller, scribbling ideas as they came.

# # #

Tessa glanced around the Stanford library’s web resource area, where wood-veneer cubicles sprawled like a patchwork quilt, each housing a hulking CRT monitor. Scattered students tapped away at keyboards, their concentration palpable. Assigned to monitor the area, Tessa sat at a small desk near the entrance, watching the ebb and flow of bodies. She’d received a couple of hours of training and now sat comfortably, occasionally circling to check if students found what they needed on the library’s newly minted website. But as she observed, anxiety tightened in her chest—was she doing enough for her career? Just before lunch, she noticed the last computer terminal occupied by a girl crying quietly, making her heart ache at the sight.

Tessa approached and eased into the chair, her focus settling on the girl. The girl’s long black hair framed her olive skin, her head bowed, tears streaking down her face. Hispanic, maybe.

“Can I help you?” Tessa asked softly, but the girl kept her head down, shoulders trembling.

She tried again, her voice gentle. “What’s wrong? Is there something I can do for you?” Nothing.

Switching to Spanish, she said, “Puedo ayudarte?”

Still not even a glance. Tessa reached out, gently touching her arm. The girl startled, jerking upright, then finally looked at her, eyes red and streaming.

“What’s wrong?” Tessa asked, placing her hand over her heart, feeling her own concern.

The girl pointed to her ear, then her mouth, shook her head, then launched into a flurry of sign language, hands rolling and darting. It resonated unmistakably now—she was deaf and mute. Tessa’s cheeks burned; she should have seen it right away. Guilt washed over her as she wished she could bridge the gap between them.

She mouthed *sorry* slowly, touched the girl’s shoulder, and motioned she’d be right back.

Tessa hurried to the information desk and found Molly Johnson, the head librarian, in her office behind a half-open oak door. Molly looked up from a massive book, her short auburn hair framing her face.

“Molly, what resources do we have in the library for deaf and mute students?”

Molly’s eyes narrowed in concern. “What specifically do you need?”

“There’s a student crying in the web resource area. Hispanic, young. Deaf and mute, I think. I would talk to her in sign, but I don’t know any.”

Molly straightened, all business. “We have plenty of resources. The last terminal has accessibility features. Let me have Samantha help her. She’s a student volunteer; she knows sign and can move her to the right computer.”

Molly called Samantha over. She approached quickly, her long dark hair framing her black-rimmed glasses. Her tidy blouse and skirt gave her an air of capability.

Tessa asked, “Mind if I come with you and watch how you help?”

Samantha nodded. “Of course.”

They approached the girl together. Samantha tapped her gently on the shoulder. Instantly, the girl’s face lifted.

Samantha's hands flashed through a series of signs, and, just like magic, the girl smiled—a small thing, but it broke through Tessa's tension. Samantha asked for her name.

"This is Sofia Gonzalez," Samantha signed to Tessa.

"Why are you crying?"

Sofia replied in quick motions. Samantha met Tessa's gaze. "She's having trouble with the computer. I told her the other terminal is set up for her with special links."

Samantha encouraged Sofia to stand, guiding her to the accessible terminal. A few students looked up, then pretended to refocus on their screens.

"She can read English well," Samantha explained. "This terminal has sign language links for most of the videos."

Tessa frowned. "I feel so helpless not being able to help her." The weight of her concern hung heavy, and she longed to bridge the divide.

Samantha offered a soft laugh. "I understand. I started learning sign language for the same reason, after a day like this. It takes time, but it's worth it."

Sofia dove into her research almost immediately, her shoulders easing as she focused on the screen. Samantha signed, checking if she needed anything more. Sofia shook her head, a quiet ease in her expression. Samantha replied in sign, letting her know she'd be at the information center if needed, then stepped away.

Tessa hurried to catch up with her. "How long did it take you to learn sign?"

"Three years to get good, two more to get comfortable. I just finished my fifth year."

"Your dedication is inspiring."

Samantha shrugged. "It's like any language. Time and practice. They actually offer it here."

"Thanks for helping Sofia."

Samantha leaned in. "Anytime. If you need more help, find me at the information desk or ask Molly."

Tessa watched Samantha leave, then returned to her desk, her eyes drawn to Sofia as she navigated the computer with newfound confidence. All afternoon, Tessa's mood darkened by her inability to help directly; maybe taking lessons would open new avenues of connection for her.

# # #

Meanwhile, Ray, tired of the slow work on GG-2, decided to call Sanyen Electronics about a battery. He dialed, and the receptionist answered in perfect English before transferring him to a man named Tanaka.

"This is Tanaka. Mr. Ito is unavailable. They told me it was you, so I want to help. Are you ready to place a large order?"

Ray braced himself, his grip tightening on the phone. "No, actually, I need a different battery. Item B4356654 from your catalog."

"Excellent choice!" Tanaka's expression brightened. "One hundred this time?"

Ray hesitated. "No, just one." He remembered the warnings; Tanaka always pushed for big orders.

"Hmmm." Tanaka hesitated. "Mr. Holland, are you not ready to go into production? We are very good at price and delivery, you know."

Ray replied, "Yes, I understand, but I'm not ready yet."

"Mr. Holland, were you not happy with your other purchase?"

"It worked well."

"Excellent. So, your product is ready for production?"

"No, I'm afraid not."

"Mr. Holland, there is no reason to be afraid. Companies buy our batteries in large quantities and go into production and make big profits."

Ray exhaled, feeling frustration building. "All I need is this battery."

Tanaka pressed on. "Testing still? I have a partner company to help test if you like."

"No, no, not necessary."

"Mr. Holland, this company can save you much time and money."

Ray's patience thinned. "Really, all I need is this battery."

Tanaka relented. “Okay, so sorry. I’ll place your order for one battery. Remember, we can help you when you’re ready for production, yes?”

“Thank you, Mr. Tanaka. Good talking to you. I need to go.”

“Thank you, Mr. Holland. We ship right away.”

Ray hung up and blew out a long breath. Could every battery supplier be like this? He doubted it. He made coffee and threw together a sandwich: ham, cheese, and wheat bread. On his way to the garage, balancing coffee in one hand and his sandwich in the other, he stopped short—the kitchen doorway blocked by two dark figures.

“Ray Holland, you remember us, don’t you?” The taller one’s gaze stayed cold. “F . . . B . . . I ring a bell?”

Ray gritted his teeth. “Agent Sommers. And Fitz. Where the hell did you come from?”

“Just in the neighborhood,” Sommers said, looking Ray up and down.

“Ever think about using a phone? Oh wait, it wouldn’t be your style.”

Sommers didn’t miss a beat. “We heard you hadn’t been to work much, so we thought we’d check on you.”

Ray’s jaw clenched as he held his half-eaten sandwich and steaming cup, an urge to disappear behind the counter tugging at him.

“You know where I work?”

Sommers pressed, “Why haven’t you been to Laubner lately?”

Ray glared at him. “It shouldn’t be your concern.”

He looked at Fitz for backup, but Fitz remained silent. Always silent.

Sommers smirked. “He doesn’t need to talk. I do all the talking.”

Ray shook his head. “No kidding.”

“I bring him along for the brute force.”

The mood shifted. Ray remembered the last time these two had shown up; they forced him to open GG-1 and empty all the stones. He wasn’t about to let them do it again, especially not in the kitchen doorway.

"So, what are you really doing here?" Ray asked, keeping his voice steady. "Or should I ask what interest the FBI has in bothering me at home? Maybe I should call your boss and find out why you like interrupting my life."

Sommers stepped closer, unbuttoning his suit jacket. The strap of his shoulder holster glinted, a reminder of the game they played. Fitz never moved.

"Mr. Holland, I assure you, this is official business. Is Mrs. Holland home?"

"No, and I'm glad. You give her nightmares."

Sommers's eyes narrowed. "Where...is...she?"

Ray gave nothing away. "None of your FBI business." An impulse surged to throw hot coffee into Sommers' face, but he held back, pulse quickening as he sensed the danger they represented. He lifted his coffee and sandwich a little higher, using them as a shield. Compassion? Not a chance; these two were bulldozers.

"Why aren't you working at Laubner?" Sommers asked again.

"Working from home," Ray said. "I have projects here."

"Do you take Laubner work home?"

"No. It's not allowed."

Sommers nodded. "Right answer. You know, we're your best customer. Practically your only customer. We wouldn't want any of our projects wandering into the wrong hands. Are you still working on the stone project?"

Ray thought fast. "Gutters," he blurted out. "House projects. They always slow down the real work."

Fitz leaned in, muttering something to Sommers. Sommers straightened, nodding.

"Mr. Holland—we're going. Something's come up."

With that, Sommers and Fitz stepped away and strode out. Only then did Ray feel a sense of relief wash over him, though the tension lingered in his muscles. He sat, eyes wide, as their sudden departure registered, his heart racing at his own boldness. He bit into his sandwich. The coffee was already cold, but he drank it anyway, too irritated to care.

CHAPTER TWENTY-ONE

As the last of the students trickled out of the library, Tessa finished tidying a cubicle—a scatter of library books, a couple of forgotten paper wrappers, and the usual detritus of late-afternoon study. She sighed, frustrated at the mess. She shook her head, wondering if parents didn't teach their kids manners anymore. Even as a recent hire, frustration simmered beneath her surface; she often felt like the guardian of the library's decorum.

She began shelving books onto a rolling cart, ready to return them to their proper homes. Lost in her routine, she didn't register the gentle tug on her hand until fingers closed around it. Startled, she turned and found herself looking down at Sophia's solemn face.

Sophia held her gaze, intense, then pointed toward the Resource Center desk. At first, Tessa didn't understand why she needed an escort. But Sophia tugged gently, and Tessa allowed her to lead the way. As they walked, Tessa felt a mix of protectiveness and admiration for Sophia; it reminded her of the responsibility she had to support others, especially in moments of vulnerability. They arrived at the desk, where Molly stood overseeing the last of the homework crowd.

Sophia looked up, waited for Molly's attention, then began to sign urgently. Molly nodded and stepped behind the desk to get Samantha.

Tessa glanced between them, acutely aware she missed something, realizing for the first time that Molly knew sign language too. A twinge of envy flickered within her; she wished she could communicate as fluidly. When Samantha appeared, Sophia's face tensed with worry. Samantha started to sign, asking what was wrong, but Sophia cut her off with quick, insistent gestures.

"Sophia says there is a strange man watching you in the library," Samantha translated.

"A strange man? What strange man?" Tessa asked, frowning.

A chill gripped her as memories of past encounters surfaced, stirring discomfort.

Samantha relayed the question in sign, Sophia responding without hesitation. "She says, tall blond man, short hair, gray suit, no tie, blue eyes."

"Staring at me?" Tessa asked, her voice a mixture of disbelief and concern.

Samantha looked to Sophia for confirmation. Sophia nodded.

"She says yes. It made her uncomfortable watching him watch you. Sophia wants you to be careful."

Tessa let the words sink in, then smiled and crouched to Sophia's level. "Tell Sophia I like her too, and I'll be careful."

She opened her arms for a hug, which Sophia accepted.

"Should I call security?" Samantha asked, glancing over Tessa's shoulder as if expecting the mystery man to materialize.

"Not yet. I'll check on the Web Resource Center to see if he's still there. I'll be fine. It's the library. What bad could happen here?"

Her voice wavered slightly, betraying her lingering doubts. A quiet library had always felt like a safe haven, but now uncertainty settled in, making her skin prickle.

"Alright," Samantha agreed, "but I'll have Molly check on you in a few of minutes, just in case."

Tessa nodded and set off towards the Web Resource Center. Sophia lingered with Samantha, hands still moving in animated conversation as Tessa walked away. Tessa scanned the aisles, her eyes alert for a gray suit or a flash of blond hair. Nothing. Maybe the man had already left. She exhaled, almost laughed at her own nerves, and drifted back toward the cubicles, trying to shake it off. Her heart raced as anxiety wrapped around her, a tremor flutters in her hands before she tucks them away.

Then she saw him.

Last cubicle. Gray suit. He sat with his back to the room and slowly rotated in his chair as if expecting her.

"Tessa Holland, we meet again."

Shock ran through her. Victor Mishkin. A cold wave of recognition washed over her, a mix of fear and anger. She pressed her hand against her chest to steady her breathing.

"What are you doing here?"

"Doing my research," he said, the phrase oddly clipped, almost mocking. "Where is your husband today?"

"My husband?" The question caught her off guard.

"You are still married, yes?"

"Yes—I'm still married." She paused. "He's not here, if that's what you mean."

"I know, I know," he persisted. "Why is he not at work?"

Tessa could feel her hands trembling. Her pulse quickened; the sensation of being cornered ignited her fight-or-flight instincts.

"Mr. Mishkin," she said, her voice steady despite the turmoil.

"Call me Victor."

"Victor, I don't understand why you're so concerned about my husband's whereabouts, and I'm not comfortable with the questions."

He raised his hands, a mock gesture of apology. "Sorry. I'll start over. My interest is in what happens at Laubner. I know Ray is very smart, and I know big things are coming."

"Mr.—Victor, everything at Laubner is highly classified. Even if you were to speak with him, he couldn't share details with you. It's not permitted."

A sharp pain pierced the base of her skull. She shook her head, willing herself not to show her fear, but her knees started to wobble. The physical reaction mirrored her internal turmoil, a swirl of anxiety and anger fighting for dominance.

"Tessa, I call you Tessa, yes?" Mishkin leaned in, his gaze penetrating, the corners of his mouth lifting in a slight, unsettling smile. "I am a man of secrets. I am trusted with secrets." He paused, smiling slightly. "I have partners who pay—or, how do you say, buy new ideas. I think Ray has ideas worth selling."

She needed to sit but reminded herself to stand her ground. "Victor, Ray has been working only part-time lately. He wouldn't have anything to share with you from Laubner."

"So he works on his own projects?" Mishkin's eyes narrowed.

An icy grip of fear settled inside her, and she felt a wave of dizziness wash over her, causing her vision to grey at the edges. Panic washed over her; the implication of his interest terrified her. What could he want with Ray's work? Just then, Molly appeared, her timing impeccable, picking up on the silent distress etched on Tessa's face.

"Tessa, could you come to the Resource Center for a moment?" Molly said smoothly, stepping in.

"Yes, excuse me, Mr. Mishkin."

As Molly guided Tessa toward the Resource Center, a chill skittered down her spine, the weight of Victor's gaze heavy on her shoulders.

"That's him?" Molly kept her voice low as they walked.

"Yes, thank you. He made me uncomfortable."

"You sure you're okay? You look pale."

"I'm fine. Just shaken by his questions."

"Who is he, anyway?"

"Victor Mishkin. Supposedly doing research on campus. He seems to know my husband Ray, but Ray's never met him."

"I'm calling security," Molly said, her tone firm. "We need to see who he is."

At the Resource Center, Samantha stood waiting, as if sensing the escalation.

"Call security," Molly instructed her.

Samantha's head snapped up. "What happened?"

"The man in the gray suit harassed Tessa," Molly explained.

"Harassed?" Samantha echoed, turning to Tessa for confirmation.

"He asked personal questions about my husband," Tessa admitted, her heart pounding as the realization of being targeted sank in. "It was unnerving."

"Who is this guy, a student?" Samantha asked.

"He claims he's doing research," Molly volunteered.

Samantha picked up the phone and dialed, her voice steady. “This is Samantha from the Campus Library. We have a man in a gray suit asking inappropriate questions to a female staff member. We need someone to check him out. Yes, Web Center, inside the library. Thank you.” She set the phone back in its cradle. “They’re on their way.”

Tessa glanced at the clock, feeling each minute drag as she waited in the Resource Center. The tick of the second hand echoed in the silence, magnifying her impatience. When she thought she couldn’t wait any longer, the door swung open, and two uniformed security officers strode in, causing her to sit up and take notice.

“Where are we headed?” The taller officer took charge.

“Web,” Molly said, pointing.

They walked as a group toward the Web Center; students there watched openly as the officers entered.

“Where’s the guy?” asked the lead officer.

“He’s gone,” Tessa scanned the booths, heart pounding. “I don’t see him.”

“Can you describe him?” the officer pressed, and his partner opened a notebook.

“Blond, short hair, gray suit, nice shoes. Maybe in his thirties. Five nine, maybe five ten,” Tessa said, her voice steady, despite the tension building inside her.

The taller officer relayed the description into his radio. A student stood across the Web Center, nodding toward the south exit. “He left about four minutes ago.”

“We’ll locate him,” the officer assured them, and both officers hurried to the exit.

“Tessa, you should take the rest of the day off. Go home,” Molly urged.

“I’ll walk you to your car,” Samantha offered.

“I’ll be fine,” Tessa started to protest, but a gentle tug on her arm interrupted her.

Sophia again. She signed emphatically.

“She says she wants to walk you to your car too,” Samantha interpreted.

Tessa couldn't help but smile at their concern. "Okay, okay," she said, glancing at both of them, noting their identical looks of satisfaction.

The ordeal wasn't over, but at least she wouldn't be alone.

CHAPTER TWENTY-TWO

Tessa pulled into the driveway a little after 4:30 p.m., the familiar thrum of her engine announcing her return well before she appeared in the garage doorway. As she parked, relief washed over her, though a cold ripple moved across her skin. Home usually felt like a safe haven.

Ray, who had already heard her arrive, stepped out onto the welcome mat, ready to greet her. But before he could reach the door, there she was, frozen in the garage's shadow, her brow furrowing in worry.

"Wow, short day," Ray said, lifting his eyebrows.

"No kidding, you won't believe what happened."

"Well, we had some drama here as well."

Tessa's shoulders sagged. "Victor?" she whispered, her heart racing at the thought of that unsettling encounter.

"Victor? No, our FBI friends were here again."

Tessa's shoulders eased at the news, a brief wash of relief crossing her face. "Good."

But was it? The FBI's presence still crawled under her skin, a warning she couldn't ignore.

"Good?"

Tessa noted Ray's tone—it felt slightly off. "Yeah, good. We could use the protection."

He paused, searching her face with a pained gaze. "Maybe we should start from the beginning."

They moved inside, settling at the kitchen table. Ray poured her a mug of coffee from the pot he'd brewed earlier. He eyed the cup, apologetic. "It's probably a bit strong."

"It's okay."

"Okay, from the beginning. You first."

Tessa told her story, hands trembling around the mug as she described Victor's unexpected visit at Stanford, his questions about Laubner and all the projects there. Each word felt like a confession, revealing her vulnerability. She listened as Ray outlined the FBI visit, noting the awkwardness of the conversation and the cold sandwich neglected on the table. They traded details but found no link, no thread connecting their day's separate puzzles. What they could agree on were precautions. Cell phones. The lack of them had become an obvious vulnerability, and they resolved to fix it—the ability to call for help, to hold the other's voice in their ear, wherever they were.

Silence enveloped them for several minutes, the weight of their circumstances pressing down on Tessa like a heavy blanket. Tension coiled inside her. When Ray reached out and took her gently by the forearm, drawing her close, a rush of warmth flooded her at the contact—a fleeting reminder of what normal intimacy felt like amid their chaos. They hugged, and she pressed her face into his chest, lips finding his in a lingering kiss. In this moment, she wished they could stay embraced forever. Eventually, they let go. He nodded.

"I'll be back shortly." With his wallet in hand, he strode out of the kitchen, locking the door behind him. As he rolled his shoulders back and headed to the garage, Tessa watched him pause on the driveway, scanning the street for unfamiliar shapes, strange cars—anything that might set his nerves on edge. Nothing. Her heart raced, imagining worst-case scenarios as shadows of their lives crept closer. He climbed into the Subaru and drove off to buy cell phones.

# # #

Ray came back at last, nearly three hours later, cradling a small shopping bag with two brand-new Nokia 5510 cell phones, chargers, and a three-hundred-minute monthly call plan—with texting. He couldn't shake the gnawing worry he'd taken too long; it felt like time stretched endlessly as he drove home. The neighborhood lay quiet and still.

Ray let himself in, the house unchanged except for one thing: no Tessa. Panic gripped him as he called out for her, fearing the worst. He hated how easily his mind spiraled into darkness. What if she'd been taken? What if Victor had returned? The thought was almost unbearable.

Upstairs, he found her lying flat on their bed, arms stiff at her sides, as if arranged in some ceremonial pose. For a moment, he watched the rise and fall of her chest, reassured. Very much alive. But life could change in an instant. The pressure built within him—the need to protect her, to keep them both safe. Sitting at the edge of the mattress, he caught her stirring; Tessa's eyes fluttered open.

"Feeling better?" Ray asked, keeping his voice low.

"Yes, and no."

"Yes, and no?"

"Yes, I don't feel ill anymore. And no, our situation hasn't changed," she clarified, gaze steady. Her resilience impressed him, but it reminded him of his shortcomings—he wished he could provide her with more than temporary comfort.

He lifted the bag, grinning. "Our situation has changed. We have cell phones now."

She sat up, hair messy, skepticism written across her face. "I'll feel a lot better when we can figure out what is going on with these people. Cell phones aren't a cure."

He shrugged. "Still, I feel better. I can reach you whenever, wherever, as long as you keep this with you." He handed her one of the Nokia's.

She studied it, rolling it in her palm. "Pretty fancy looking."

"Not top of the line, but plenty of features we'll need. Hundred texts, three hundred minutes, sixty bucks a month."

"Only sixty dollars?"

"Each."

"Ouch. I'm partial to my nineteen ninety-five house phones."

Ray laughed. "Those things are bricks. This is the new age of telecom."

"I know. I'm giving you a hard time." Now she smiled, almost warmed by the prospect. "Show me how to use it?"

His enthusiasm returned. "Now you're talking." He dumped the contents of the bag onto the bed. Ray powered up both phones, showing her how to flip through menus, how to text, how to reach each other instantly.

Ray watched Tessa's fingers move over the buttons, concentration evident as she tried to decipher the patterns.

His mood lifted with her teasing. “So, will these things cook us dinner? Because I don’t feel like making it tonight,” she said, a hint of humor lightening the tension.

“No problem. I picked up Chinese on the way home,” Ray said, a grin on his face.

“Is that what I smell?”

“All your favorites.” Ray’s voice softened, almost teasing. “Some of it needs reheating.”

They made their way downstairs, the aroma intensifying with each step. Paper bags rustled as Ray unwrapped the containers, spicy steam escaping as he popped the lids. Tessa fished plates and utensils from the dish drainer, the clatter of cutlery ringing in the quiet kitchen. They served themselves heaping portions, found most of it still hot, and ate in contented silence until the plates were empty.

“It tasted wonderful,” Tessa said, gratitude shining in her eyes.

“I agree.”

“So, what’s on tomorrow’s agenda?” She gathered the plates, moving slowly from the meal.

Ray tossed the empty cartons. “What I’d like to do is take a road trip.”

“Road trip?” She gave him a sidelong glance, suspicion coloring her voice.

He nodded, tossing the last container. “Yes. I have a theory to test.”

“Is this GG-1 again?”

“No. I assembled enough of GG-2 for a test.”

“Why a road trip?”

“This testing needs to be far away from society.”

Tessa’s brow furrowed as she rinsed the plates and handed them to Ray. “This sounds concerning. Remember what happened last time?”

Ray’s gaze held steady. “Trust me. It will answer a lot of questions if my theory is right.”

She let out a breath. “I’m taking the rest of the week off from Stanford. Creepy stuff with Mishkin around.”

He nodded. “All right then, road trip it is. Let’s get packed. We’ll leave before daylight.”

Tessa snorted. "Guess I'm calling in sick from the road."

The food made them sleepy, and they trudged upstairs.

"Am I packing an overnight bag?" she asked, already digging through a drawer.

"It would be more fun," he said, tugging a soft black nylon bag from the closet.

Her shoulders relaxed a fraction. "Okay, and where are we going?"

He zipped open the bag. "Mojave."

She stared. "The desert?"

"Yes, the desert."

Tessa shook her head, bemused. "Okay, I'll pack light."

CHAPTER TWENTY-THREE

With only the porch light trickling across the Holland driveway, Ray angled GG-2 up into the tailgate of the Subaru. He'd already pried the battery from GG-1; he couldn't wait for Sanyen's delivery, not after last night. The memory of the day before lingered heavily, like a weight on his chest.

Tessa came out next, lugging her bag and a red cooler loaded with cut fruit, snacks, sodas, and PB&J sandwiches. She juggled the cooler's handle, eyeing Ray over the roof of the car. "Looks like we're going camping, only without the tent," she said.

"You could say that. Should we swing by and grab one to make it official?"

She wrinkled her nose and smiled. "Maybe next time. I'll take a hotel shower and fluffy towels over a tent, thanks. Especially if helicopters are involved again." Her teasing reminded him how much he missed the carefree days before the recent turmoil.

Ray laughed. "Fair point." A flicker of guilt crept in—was he dragging her into another possibly dangerous situation?

She shot him a grin, still wrestling the cooler's edge into the back seat, then dusted her hands on her jeans. Ray admired her strength but wished he could ease her burdens.

By five sharp, they were in the Subaru and rolling out. The neighborhood felt quiet and still to Ray, the predawn hush interrupted only by the occasional headlights of early commuters. With no radio playing, the low buzz of the engine filled the car, and he could sense their sleepy silence settling between them as they aimed for the 101.

"This'll take all day, so I figure we crash overnight somewhere near Mojave," Ray said, eyes ahead. His mind raced with thoughts of the project and the risks that lay ahead, but he wanted to keep Tessa's spirits up.

“Fine by me. As long as you hit a few rest stops—I might sleep the next hour. Nudge me for breakfast?”

Ray nodded, “Deal.”

# # #

Ray and Tessa sped eastward down Highway 58, Barstow drawing close on the horizon, the sky behind them slipping toward orange dusk. The view beyond the windshield: a whole lot of nothing, the desert a wash of sun-bleached earth and heat rising from the blacktop.

“Not much out here,” Ray said, his voice casual.

“I can see that.” Tessa’s gaze never left the streaking lines of the highway. He could feel her tension, palpable in the air, mirroring his own unease.

“Let’s stay in Barstow tonight,” he suggested. “We’ll get dinner and rest up. There’s not much between here and Mojave.”

Tessa shot him a playful look, amused. “As I said, I’m game for a soft bed and a warm shower.”

Ray nodded. “So, food first or hotel?”

“Food.” She barely let him finish. Definite.

He grinned. “Mexican or Mexican?”

“What do you mean, Mexican or Mexican?” Her sigh was theatrical.

“It’s all I see.” He gestured at a cluster of roadside signs as they passed.

Tessa frowned. “I saw a sign back there for Burger Bill’s Diner. That doesn’t sound like Mexican, and I want a burger.” She glanced at him, challenging.

“Okay. That’s if we find it.”

“Exit 181, I remember. Plus, there were hotel signs for the same exit. We can get both without getting back on the freeway.”

Ray shot her an impressed look. “Okay, Burger Bill’s it is.”

Tessa’s expression opened, satisfied.

Ten minutes later, they reached exit 181, swept into Barstow proper—a town left over from eighteen hundreds’ mining, now all rail spurs and asphalt. Old and new layered together: railroad lines, neon signs, hotels hunkered under the desert sun. Burger Bill's came up quick, low and square on the left. The sun was low enough to cast long shadows; the air outside held at a dry, insistent ninety degrees.

"I hope they have the AC running," Ray muttered, eyeing the dash thermometer.

They pulled in among a scattering of cars and trucks: flashy Land Cruisers, battered pickups, a few sedans. The moment they stepped out, the desert heat hit hard—a physical wall, like opening an oven door. But Ray and Tessa didn't linger; they walked fast for the entrance, relief washing over them as soon as they stepped inside and felt the temperature drop.

No host—pick your own spot. They slid into a booth by the window, red vinyl, shiny Formica tabletop, view of the street. Tessa looked around and grinned. "I like this. It's like turning back the clock."

"It is," Ray agreed, glancing around at the walls decorated with antique railroad lanterns and faded pictures of steam locomotives, the ambiance reflecting another century.

A server appeared and took their orders—a pair of quarter-pound burgers, all the fixings, ranch-style fries, two Cokes. The food landed minutes later, generous and hot.

Ray eyed the plates. "You sure you can eat all that?"

Tessa raised an eyebrow. "I could ask you the same."

He grinned. "We can't eat like this all the time."

"Maybe we should, after you taste your burger."

Ray took a bite, pausing at the explosion of flavor. He nodded in approval, eyes wide.

"Wow," he said, savoring the taste. "Might have to come back this way."

They ate, the sun dipping lower in the sky.

Tessa wiped her mouth. "So about tomorrow and the GG-2, what's the plan? Are we supposed to duck and cover while it takes off again?"

Ray shook his head. "No, not this time. This test should give me a limit on the force factor capability on the stones." He recognized the concern shadowing her gaze, a reminder of the risks involved.

She cocked her head. “A force factor? Is this why we’re in the desert?”

He nodded. “Absolutely. And nobody gets hurt.”

“Nobody got hurt last time.” He felt a pang of guilt; her words lingered in the air. Was he being reckless?

Ray shrugged. “True, but think about the commotion, and the expense.”

Tessa dabbed ketchup on her last fry as the server approached.

“You folks going to chase those down with some pie à la mode?”

For a moment, neither of them answered.

Tessa flashed a grin. “Apple for me.”

Ray blinked. “Really?”

She shot him a look. “Burger’s tasting this good, imagine the pie.”

He nodded. “Me too, please.”

The pies arrived, steaming and golden. Tessa was right—the crust was buttery, the apples sharp and tangy. Ray savored each bite, contentment flooding through him. Moments like this reminded him of the joy they could still share. Could they navigate the shadows that loomed nearby? Even lost in food, Ray noted the room was still full, voices and laughter unchanged since they’d walked in.

When they finally eased themselves out of the booth and paid (Ray left a generous tip), the outside world had shifted again: heat still rising off the parking lot, the sky now streaked with the last of sunset.

“Wow, still warm,” Ray said, glancing at the Subaru. “Car’s probably an oven.”

“Best Western’s two blocks down,” he added. “We’ll only roast for a minute.”

They checked in with no hassle. Their room was on the ground floor, facing the street, with the muted roar of traffic outside. The parking lot was half-full, semis lined up out back in the dark—routine, anonymous, but oddly comforting.

Ray dropped the bags. “Want to get an early start, so we can turn in soon?”

Tessa barely hesitated. “I get the first shower.”

He waved her on. “I’ll watch the news on this relic of a TV.”

She disappeared into the bathroom; Ray sank onto the bed, remote in hand, the old TV humming. The sounds of the highway drifted through the closed window. The day behind them, the desert ahead.

CHAPTER TWENTY-FOUR

As Special Agent Steve Anderson approached the Holland home, he could see the chaos from half a block away. Flashing lights—blue, red, and yellow—splashed across the houses and trees, turning the quiet suburban street into a scene of confusion. Police cruisers, fire engines, and aid units crowded the curb, their engines rumbling beneath the chatter of radios and the low murmur of onlookers gathering behind hastily strung yellow tape.

Dispatch had been brief: a neighbor walking her dog had found two men down beside a Ford sedan. Local officers arrived first, checked for pulses, and discovered federal credentials. That was when the call went out to the Bureau.

Anderson's shoulders tightened as he stepped out of his vehicle. Two agents dead on a residential street. No warning. No distress call. Just silence—and now this.

A young woman stood near the tape, pale and shaken, staring at the bodies on the pavement. Anderson followed her gaze. Fitz and Sommers lay where they'd fallen, stark splashes of blood marking the asphalt, their weapons glinting in the grass under the floodlights.

This wasn't just another crime scene. This was an attack on the Bureau.

Anderson strode in, radiating confidence, a trait developed through years of experience. At six feet tall, broad shoulders straining against his navy suit, short strawberry-blond hair sticking straight up—he moved through the crowd like a lighthouse amidst a storm. He surveyed the turmoil—a swirl of uniforms, equipment, and engine noise—and without hesitation, began directing everyone into position. This was his domain, and he tolerated little disarray.

He nodded curtly to Agent Jake Pommeroy and gave his first order. "I want a chopper in the air, searching the area. Now."

Pommeroy appeared fresh out of the academy—young and stocky, his suit bunching at the seams. He nodded. “Yes, sir,” and Anderson noted the nerves flitting across his face.

“And get us more lights. This won’t be quick.”

“Yes, sir.” Pommeroy bent over the portable radio, relaying both requests with mechanical precision.

Anderson scowled, glancing toward the Holland house. The sight stirred grim determination within him. How did two trained agents end up dead by their car? This felt personal.

“Where is forensics?” he muttered, not expecting anyone to answer, though Pommeroy drifted a little closer, as if wanting to help. Anderson motioned him over.

“Come with me.” He didn’t wait for acknowledgment, just walked, expecting Pommeroy to fall in step. They paced across the taped-off border and stood over Fitz, lying face up under a layer of plastic sheeting. Anderson grimaced, irritated by the cover-up. “Can’t they see this is a crime scene? My God, what is this—their first day?”

Pommeroy wisely stayed silent.

“Who’s all here?” Anderson asked, his gaze sweeping the area.

“Agents Greg Stevenson, Kyle Johnson, and Tom Murray,” Pommeroy answered quietly.

“Where are they?”

“Setting up the command post now, sir.”

Anderson’s frustration simmered beneath the surface. The weight of responsibility pressed down on him; two agents were gone, and he could not afford mistakes. “Tell them I’ll be over in five, and I want a status update. Everything.”

“Yes.” Pommeroy left, jogging up the sidewalk toward the makeshift tent glowing under floodlights.

Anderson lingered, taking in the Holland place—the porch, the driveway, the windows reflecting the blue and red lights of the police cars. The empty house stood ominously, and Anderson’s mind raced with questions about the Hollands’ fate. Had they escaped? Were they in danger? A kidnapping, maybe—or something worse? Perhaps a warning.

He knelt beside Fitz, peeling back the plastic for a better look. Fitz’s eyes were open, staring at nothing, blood darkening beneath him from three bullet wounds—one in his shoulder, one in his chest, and one in his neck. Judging by the angle, the neck shot was fatal. No chance, Anderson thought. He covered the body and moved to the second: Sommers, face down, exit wounds torn in his back. Anger flickered like a spark in his gut. One shooter, he was sure of it. The gun on the ground matched, the wounds matched, and unless evidence screamed otherwise, Anderson's instincts would rule.

He covered Sommers again and strode up to the tent, where the rest of his team was gathered at a folding table strewn with maps and radios. Stevenson, Johnson, and Murray stood in a row, dark suits and ties catching the tent's harsh white light.

"We'll be here a while," Anderson announced, his voice cutting through their concentration. "If anyone has plans in the next twenty-four hours, cancel them now."

Stevenson and Murray didn't blink, but Johnson looked rattled, eyes darting and skin pale under the halogen bulbs. Anderson noticed the signs of shock—the way Johnson seemed to search for an escape.

"Johnson, what's your problem?"

"Nothing, sir."

Anderson fixed him with a sharper stare. "That's not going to cut it. Last chance, Johnson. What's wrong?"

Johnson swallowed hard, hesitating as Pommeroy slipped back into the tent. "It's Fitz, sir. We trained together. At Quantico."

Anderson's tone softened, just a fraction. "I'm sorry, Johnson. But Fitz is gone. We need to find the man who did this, and we can't make the same mistakes. Are you with us?"

Johnson straightened, nodding more firmly. "Yes, sir."

"Glad to hear it. Don't make me send you home."

"Yes, sir."

Anderson turned his focus to logistics. "Why were Fitz and Summers here?"

"A protection order from LA office," Murray piped in.

"LA? Who in LA?"

"George Palto's name is on the order."

"Palto from International Operations?"

"Yes, sir."

Anderson frowned, processing. This was bigger than they thought. "What's International doing with the Hollands? Did anyone actually read the surveillance order?"

Johnson answered, pulling a file from the pile. "It was a protection detail, sir. A threat tied to the Moscow embassy. The name Victor Mishkin came up. Son of Dmitri Mishkin—a known spy, expelled from the US a while back."

Anderson nodded. "What's our latest on Victor? Johnson, you're up."

"I'll call it in," Johnson replied, already heading for one of the dark sedans lining the curb.

Anderson's gaze landed back on the Holland house. "Has anyone checked the house?"

"Murray and I did," Stevenson said. "Locked up tight. Nothing looks disturbed. Shades drawn, lights off."

"So you haven't been inside yet?"

"No, sir."

Anderson's frustration grew. "We have two dead agents, a shooter on the loose, and missing people we were supposed to protect. Get inside the house now. Search everything."

"Right away, sir." Stevenson clapped Murray on the back, signaling they'd begin at once.

With a sigh, Anderson muttered under his breath, "Victor Mishkin. Where are you, Victor?"

By now, the harsh white light from the floodlights illuminated the scene, making every detail stark and unforgiving, powered by a diesel generator thumping steadily in the background. The forensics team moved carefully, heads bent and gloved hands ensuring they didn't miss a single trace. The coroner's van waited at the curb, stark and impassive amid the chaos. Pommeroy walked back to the command tent where Anderson skimmed the thick surveillance order, flipping through photos of the Hollands and a grainy customs shot of Victor Mishkin.

"Forensics is finished with the bodies," Pommeroy reported. "Can we release them to the coroner?"

"Yes," Anderson replied without looking up.

"Prints from the gun match Mishkin. Lab will confirm in twenty-four hours."

Anderson nodded, already expecting as much. "Issue a statewide APB for Mishkin. He's armed and dangerous, wanted for killing two FBI agents and possibly kidnapping. Tell locals: do not approach, just locate. Circulate the Hollands' photo too. If they aren't kidnap victims, we need to find them first. Check with LA about why Mishkin's interested in the Hollands."

"Yes, sir," Pommeroy said, cell phone already pressed to his ear as he moved away.

Johnson walked back in a little later, his expression tense, but his concentration was fixed. Anderson looked up, expectant.

"Anything?"

"Last sighting of Mishkin was a week ago—a traffic stop in LA. He was in an airport rental that he dropped off three days later."

"Did he rent anything after?"

"No, sir. It was under the alias Karl Romkof, but I checked all agencies at LAX and came up empty. Maybe he left in a cab, or maybe there's another alias."

Anderson leaned in. "So all we know is Mishkin was in LA, and today he was here, killed our men, and either grabbed or went after the Hollands. That's it?"

"Not entirely, sir. I dug up the Hollands' cell records. They own two phones. No calls today, but tracking puts them headed east on the 58 toward Vegas."

"Good work."

"But both phones dropped off as they hit the desert."

Anderson weighed this, tapping the table. "Set up a soft checkpoint on eastbound 58," Anderson ordered. "Coordinate with CHP and Kern County. Visual inspection only — no full stop unless they spot the Hollands' vehicle or Mishkin. And I want a containment net along the corridor. Every exit, every turnout."

"Yes, sir."

"And see if the chopper can land anywhere nearby at dawn. We'll need air support."

"I'll find out," Johnson said. "Anything else?"

"That'll do for now. Excellent work, Johnson."

The agents' expressions barely changed, but Anderson saw it—the slight relief, the sense of progress, even as all around them the lights strobed and the night deepened, and two agents waited, silent, for justice.

CHAPTER TWENTY-FIVE

With the sheets flung back and the sun bright through the sheer, lemonade-colored hotel curtains, Ray and Tessa woke slowly, gazing up at a ceiling painted the hard white of desert light. The air conditioner hummed steadily, holding the room at seventy-two degrees. Ray wore only his boxer shorts; Tessa, a purple satin nightdress with frill trim, stretched beside him atop the king bed, her silhouette visible as she stirred awake.

"What time is it?" she mumbled, blinking at the brightness.

Ray angled his body to eye the clock radio. "6:37. We need to get moving. If the desert heats up fast, I'd like to launch GG-2 before we melt."

"Drive-thru breakfast?" Tessa asked, sounding more alert.

"They have continental. Grab and go, and coffee too."

Ray felt warmth spread across his face at her enthusiasm. "Coffee, definitely."

Tessa stood, letting the nightdress fall away.

Ray gaped, more amused than shocked, then quickly shook it off. "Ah, you dropped something," he teased.

"Oops," she half-laughed, heading for the bathroom. "I'll come back for it."

Chuckling, Ray slipped into his beige cotton twill pants and long-sleeved t-shirt, then his socks and Timberlands. When he finished tying the laces, Tessa reappeared in the doorway, pulling a blouse over her head.

"Boy, when you said we need to get going, you meant it."

He grinned at her. "What were you doing in there?"

Tessa made a face at him. "What you'll be doing in a minute, except you'll have to peel off all those layers first."

Ray couldn't help but feel a rush of warmth at her playful banter. "You have a point," he replied, shaking his head as he headed for the bathroom.

Ray splashed water on his face, the remnants of sleep fading as anticipation bubbled inside him—the excitement of testing GG-2 in the desert.

When he came out of the bathroom, he noticed Tessa had changed into a cotton blouse and cargo pants. He gave her an exaggerated look. "I liked the other outfit better."

"It's a loaded question, Tessa." A grin spread across his face. He tried to keep his tone light, but the seriousness of the day ahead crept into his thoughts.

"I'm not leaving until I do those three things and at least wear sunscreen. You could at least brush your teeth."

Ray grumbled, "Sure, sure, but let's get going. It's probably 80 already."

In minutes, they were out the door, bags in hand, key dropped off at the counter, the lobby clerk not even looking up as they passed. The air outside felt thick and dry, sunlight flooding the lot, though the hotel cast a sharp shadow they sheltered in for a moment.

"It's not so bad out here," Tessa said.

"Car," Ray said, all business now.

He observed her face shift slightly; concern crossed her features.

"Ray, we forgot breakfast."

"Car," Ray said again. "We'll get something on the way."

She rolled her eyes. "It's not too hot."

"Fine, coffee. McDonald's okay?"

"Yes, fine."

They tossed their gear in the Subaru, slid in, and Ray backed out of the slot, pausing at the end of the drive.

"What's wrong?" Tessa said.

"Trying to remember how to get out to the highway," Ray said. "I know where McDonald's is."

She pointed ahead. "McDonald's is right there."

Ray swung the car around, drove the block to McDonald's, and then pulled up to the drive-thru. Two breakfast sandwiches, hash browns, two coffees, orange juice. Tessa cradled the coffee for Ray, balancing his sandwich on the console as he steered back onto the main road. They spotted the sign: Vegas.

"That's what we want," Ray said.

"Vegas?" Tessa asked, teasing.

He hesitated. "Maybe. Desert first."

Tessa opened the McDonald's bag, the scent of fried hash browns filling the tight cabin. She handed Ray his coffee, took a sandwich for herself, tore into it, then sipped her drink, her expression a mix of satisfaction and eagerness.

"How far is it?" she asked.

"Hour and a half to the cutoff, then a quick drive. Good timing before the heat ramps up."

"You mean hot, right? This is the desert."

"It is," Ray said, sipping. "Speaking of hot, this coffee is a scorcher."

Ninety minutes slipped by, then Ray took the cutoff—a turn north onto a quiet two-lane road. Highway 15 ran frantic just parallel, but out here, no one. Sand, stone, Joshua trees, yucca, and cholla stretched as far as the eye could see. Ray slowed at a barely-there sign, battered by wind and years: Copper World Mill – 1.25 miles.

"That's us," he said, pointing.

"An old mill site?"

"Perfect. Out of the way, ringed by mountains. Ideal for today."

Tessa's voice carried a hint of skepticism, but Ray felt confident.

"We'll be fine."

A rough, rutted road led them to the ruins: roofless, windowless shells scattered like bones on the sand. A large excavation opened at the center, remnants of old parking cleared decades ago. Ray circled the site, selecting a spot near the pit.

"How deep?" he asked.

"Fifty, sixty feet," Tessa guessed, peering down.

Ray nodded, assessing the area for safety. "Should work perfectly. I can drive down, we'll set up at the base, then climb out and launch from the rim. Safe all the way."

Tessa shook her head. “I remember the surprise flight last time, when GG-1 went supersonic.”

Ray shrugged. “First launch. I fixed those glitches. Test number two’s going to be different.”

He noticed Tessa’s brow furrow slightly, concern lingering in her eyes. “Your only safety check?”

He paused, then nodded. “I’ll move the car, for sure. No sense risking it way out here.”

She hesitated, but he could tell she wasn’t quite convinced.

A flicker of determination surged in him; he had to make this work.

Tessa pulled her phone from her pocket and glanced at the screen, frowning as she powered it up. “No bars,” she muttered, frustration creeping into her voice. “Well, these won’t do much if we have an emergency.”

Ray looked unconcerned. “We’ll be fine. How’s the battery?”

“Full. I checked at the hotel. Where’s your phone?”

“Car console, powered off.”

Ray put the Subaru in manual all-wheel drive and nosed around to the mouth of the pit. It appeared three hundred feet easy, black rock and sand descending at a ten percent grade, dropping steeply to sixty feet at the far end. Ray eased the car down, rocking and sliding but careful, keeping the wheels true. Ten minutes to crawl to the bottom, where the sun vanished and the shade wrapped around them like a cave.

“How about that, shade? Feels nice down here,” Ray said.

“Creepy, if you ask me.”

“You claustrophobic, Tessa?”

“Maybe. It’s just odd being down here—nothing but sky and the path behind.”

Ray opened the back. Together, they lifted GG-2 and set it gently on the black ground. He opened the hatch, set the battery in, and checked the lights and power. He sealed it, flicked on the controller, and waited for the system to sync.

“We’re good,” he said, his heart racing. “Back in the car.”

They squeezed back in, and Ray drove up the slope, slow as before. Ten minutes later, they reached the top. He cut over behind the largest brick shell and shut down the engine. Stillness now, the dust falling.

"This is a good safe distance," Ray said.

Tessa angled her head to be sure. "It's not even line of sight."

"I don't expect flight today. Don't worry."

"What's the test, then?"

Ray grinned. "Answers a lot of questions; you'll see."

Tessa gave him a skeptical look. "Last time..."

He cut her off. "This is different. Trust me."

They walked to the edge at the deep end. GG-2 waited far below, haloed in shadow.

"Take a step back," Ray said.

"Oh, where's your confidence now?" Tessa teased.

"Just a precaution."

"And no cameras?"

"Nope," he said. "You'll see why. Ready? Five... Four... Three... Two... One..."

CHAPTER TWENTY-SIX

As Special Agent Anderson surveyed the Hollands' residence, a heavy silence enveloped the cool dawn. He had been on the scene since sunrise, his mind churning with the weight of the morning—a solemn reminder of the stakes at hand. Every moment counted. He had sent Agents Pommeroy and Murray to a hotel for some rest, leaving Johnson and Stevenson to process evidence in the white tent. Anderson's chest tightened as he recalled the hours spent releasing Fitz and Sommers' bodies to the coroner; their loss felt profound, an unwelcome weight pressing on him, a reminder he couldn't afford to fail the Bureau here.

Anderson concentrated at one of the plastic tables under the main tent as Johnson approached.

"Sir, we have a hit on the Hollands. Credit card transaction in Barstow at a hotel. Cell phone ping as well."

"Excellent work, Johnson. It could be the Hollands or Mishkin. Call the hotel and see what you can find out. Wake up Pommeroy and Murray and get them headed there, stat." Anderson's voice was steady, but urgency surged within him; every second mattered, and he needed to act decisively.

"Yes, sir."

"Stevenson," Anderson shouted.

"Sir," Stevenson acknowledged immediately, standing at the adjacent table.

"Where's the chopper?"

"Palo Alto Airport, all fueled up and ready to go."

"Good, we're going for a ride. How quick can you get it here?"

"Here?"

"Yes, here."

"Where here, sir? Where is he to land?"

"I don't care if he lands it on the Hollands' roof. We need to move." Anderson's frustration bubbled beneath the surface; the stakes were high, and he couldn't waste time on semantics.

"Yes, sir."

"Oh, and call a team to take down this site and release it to the locals. Have them put a team on the house. And tell them to send their best team."

"Yes, sir."

Johnson came back over to Anderson as he finished with Stevenson.

"It was the Hollands, Mr. and Mrs. No third party was spotted with them," Johnson said.

"Okay, good news and bad. Are they still there?"

"No, they left about twenty minutes ago."

"Which direction?"

"The clerk didn't know."

"Okay, I'm still banking on the fact they're on the 15 headed to Vegas. Where is Mishkin, though? Why don't we have his credit cards?"

"Sorry, sir."

"Don't say you're sorry unless you did something wrong. I know we don't have his credit card numbers, but I wish we did." Frustration gnawed at him; data was vital, and the lack of it made him feel exposed and vulnerable.

"Yes, sir," Johnson responded.

"I was asking, do we have anything on Mishkin's whereabouts?"

"No, sir."

"Make sure the Barstow locals have pictures of Mishkin. We need to find him. How soon on the chopper?"

"He'll be here in ten, sir."

"Grab your gear then and get those calls made."

"Yes, sir."

Anderson put a few sheets of paper in his jacket pocket and heard the faint whop, whop, whop of the approaching helicopter. He allowed himself a moment to breathe, channeling his anger and frustration into focus. Johnson scrambled to make his calls, grabbing a small leather briefcase for the information they had gathered. Minutes later, the helicopter landed in the street by the empty lot. Anderson,

Stevenson, and Johnson stepped in. Anderson sat up front with the pilot while Stevenson and Johnson took the rear. They each buckled in and put on their headsets.

"How long to get to Barstow?" Anderson asked the unrecognizable pilot, his helmet casting a dark shadow over his face.

"We need to stop for fuel. Bakersfield for sure. About four hours total," the pilot answered.

"Ridiculous. My guys on the ground will get there in five," Anderson said, irritation creeping into his voice. He disliked feeling outpaced, especially in a race against time.

"Sir, it will take Pommeroy and Murray at least six," Johnson added.

Anderson shot Johnson a glare, his silence heavy with unspoken frustration.

"We're facing some winds to start, so it would be a tough go to improve on four," the pilot added.

"Okay, let's stop wasting time and get airborne." The pilot's answer was met with a curt nod. Anderson's focus sharpened; he wouldn't let anything distract him now.

Without further comment, the pilot pushed the throttle, lifting off in the dark green Bell 407 helicopter and spinning it toward Bakersfield.

Four hours later, they landed on a football field, the roar of the rotor blades echoing against the empty stands. As Anderson stepped out, he spotted a deputy standing by, waiting. The man's black uniform and baseball cap caught his attention—a sharp contrast against the morning sun. Anderson approached, ready to assess the situation and the officer's readiness for the task ahead.

"Officer Mackenzie, at your service," the officer yelled as he reached out his hand to greet Special Agent Anderson. The rotor blades screamed above their heads.

"Save the formalities. You said Mackenzie, right?" Anderson offered, pointing to expedite their position away from the noise of the chopper.

"Sure," he said.

"How far is the hotel?"

"Ten minutes."

"Good, let's go." Anderson's voice was clipped and efficient. Time slipped away, and he was acutely aware of the hunt intensifying. They slid into the deputy's Ford Explorer.

"Hollands are long gone," Mackenzie offered. "Left hours ago."

"Have any of your officers spotted them in town after they checked out?"

"No, sir. Probably headed to Vegas. That's where most folk go that stop in here."

"How about Mishkin?" Anderson asked, as Johnson held up a picture to show the officer.

"The Russian guy? Na, we hadn't seen him neither. This heat keeps folks inside, so it's not easy to spot anyone during the day. Don't you guys know what he's driving? That would help a bunch," Mackenzie continued.

"No, Officer Mackenzie, we don't know what he's driving," Anderson offered in a frustrated tone. "Tell you what, as soon as we know, we will let you know."

"That would be great. Oh, hey, sorry about your loss of your two officers."

"Officer Mackenzie. We lost two federal agents yesterday. You do know we're FBI, right?"

"Oh, sorry. Yah, they told us in a briefing this morning you were coming," Mackenzie answered as they pulled into the hotel parking lot. "Hey, did you feel the earthquake just a bit ago?"

Anderson looked at Mackenzie with a bold stare. "Last I checked, you don't feel earthquakes while flying."

"Oh yah, that's right. Darndest thing. We haven't had an earthquake here in twenty years. They get them closer to the coast, but not so much here. It was big too, four point eight, they said."

Anderson made little of the news, more focused on the task at hand. The world could shake and shift around him, but right now, the only thing that mattered was finding Mishkin and ensuring the Hollands' safety.

"Johnson, you go talk to the clerk. Stevenson, you're with me. We're going to their room."

"It's room fifteen," Mackenzie offered.

They pulled into a spot right in front of the room and stepped out. The door was wide open; a shorter officer from Barstow stood guard. Anderson stopped, pivoted toward Stevenson, and pressed a hand to his chest to hold him back.

"Stevenson, I need you to speak with Mackenzie and his team and ensure they are effective in their assistance with us. FBI protocol, not the local serve-and-protect stuff," Anderson said in a low tone. The urgency in his voice was unmistakable. He needed everyone on the same page. "And find Mishkin," he growled.

"On it, sir," Stevenson responded in a military-like tone.

Anderson flashed his FBI badge and strode past as the officer stepped aside. The room hadn't been cleaned; it was relatively undisturbed except for used towels on the bathroom floor and an unmade bed. It was clear to Anderson that nothing was here; a sense of futility gnawed at him. They had lost precious time. He exited the room and headed to the lobby to see what Johnson knew. "What do you have?"

"Just about everything we know. Car, plates, description, credit card, and nobody else with them. He also said there was a big piece of metal in the back."

"A big piece of metal?" Anderson asked.

"I also received a call from Murray. The gun used to kill Fitz and Sommers is registered to a guy named Val Kozlov, found dead two weeks ago in LA. The case is listed as a suicide—one bullet to the temple, close range, same caliber. He had a load of weapons in his apartment. Investigators couldn't locate some of his registered guns and found others not registered to him."

"Russian Mob?" Anderson asked. The familiar knot tightened in his gut. He had seen how swiftly these cases escalated, and it never ended well.

"Not sure," Johnson added, shrugging.

"Well, they better reopen the case. If they check ballistics and match the bullet to our gun, it should connect."

"Mishkin killed Kozlov, you think?" Johnson asked.

"I don't think; I know. It's the why we need to work on. See what you can find out about Kozlov and the metal object in the

Hollands' car. Could it be what Mishkin's after?" Anderson offered.

"Sir, I found out last night the Hollands have a significant amount of money in their bank account. Maybe this is what Mishkin is after," Johnson said, his voice tinged with anxiety.

"How much are we talking about?"

"Close to a million."

"You just made this a lot more complicated. The why is getting harder to pin down. Where did the Hollands get all this money?"

Anderson watched Johnson's expression shift, the uncertainty evident on his face as he opened his mouth to respond but fell silent, frustration pooling in the air between them.

"We need more resources on this. Where the hell are Murray and Pommeroy?"

"Two hours out still," Johnson offered.

"Well, call them up and get them up to speed on what we know. Check our checkpoints and any sightings of the Hollands' car. Also, see if they have any video surveillance here at the hotel. I want to see this metal object in the Hollands' car."

Two hours later, Anderson stood outside the hotel, scanning the parking lot as Pommeroy and Murray pulled up in their black Ford, parking beside a deputy's car. As they stepped out, he noted the discomfort etched on their faces; the transition from cool air conditioning to sweltering ninety-five-degree heat was evident. Anderson felt a ping of tension in his chest; the rising heat mirrored the pressure of the long hours ahead. He signaled for them to follow him into a conference room. Two beige plastic tables sat side by side, surrounded by high-backed metal-framed chairs. He took a seat at one of the tables, spreading out black-and-white images of the Hollands' Subaru—one as they pulled in and another as they left. Each image felt vital, and his mind raced as he processed the details. A large geographical map of the area lay on the table, provided by Deputy Mackenzie for their upcoming travels through the desert.

Anderson looked to the two agents, who straightened their wrinkled jackets. “Gentlemen, what do you have for me?”

“Sir, the Hollands received the bulk of their money from a sale of a patent to a company in Minneapolis, Smith and Rhyne. One point two million in cash,” Pommeroy said proudly.

“Okay, so a business transaction for a lot of money. How does it help us?”

“There’s more. Smith and Rhyne sold it to a company called Transco in Texas two weeks later for five million,” Pommeroy added.

“Well, if the Hollands find out, they’ll be upset. Still, how does it help us?”

Silence followed.

“Gentlemen, what do you make of this metal object in the back of the Hollands’ car?”

The group looked over the grainy photo of the car as it exited the hotel.

“Not sure. Never seen anything like it,” Stevenson offered.

“Look outside. What do you see?”

They clustered around the frozen frame, each face intent.

“A sedan. Man behind the wheel,” Pommeroy said.

“Rental, probably,” Murray added, squinting at the grainy view.

Johnson leaned in close. “It’s Mishkin. He’s staring at the Hollands.”

“Bingo,” Anderson murmured, his eyes never leaving the image. “Just caught it myself.”

“How old is this?” Johnson asked, urgency rising in his voice. “We need this on the street ASAP.”

Anderson’s reply came out quiet and measured. “No need for that, gentlemen. Not yet.”

Johnson frowned. “What do you mean?”

Anderson motioned toward the window. “Look across the street.”

He could sense the surprise ripple through his team as they directed their attention to the scene outside. A rush of movement followed; he watched as they bolted for the building’s main entrance. The sudden heat hit them like a wave when they stepped onto the sidewalk. The car remained in the same spot, the sun glaring off its roof. Instinctively, they scattered, seeking cover behind a stoop, the shadow of a white van, and a parking sign. He saw their weapons drawn, hands steady on grips.

From across the intersection, Anderson caught sight of Deputy Mackenzie in his patrol car, looking up from a half-eaten burger as the agents darted into position. Johnson and Pommeroy hugged the van, inching forward, guns drawn but low. Every sense heightened within him; he could feel the tension in the air.

Anderson's voice cracked through the anxious silence. "Stand down!"

Reluctant, still crouched in cover, they glanced back at him.

Anderson gestured. "Look under the front and at the rear wheels. Right now."

A beat. The agents peered: a dark pool of fluid spread beneath the engine block, and the rear wheel was buried deep, the axle nearly kissing the asphalt through a hole in the street.

Anderson called again, sharper: "He's gone, boys!"

Weapons holstered, Pommeroy and Johnson moved in, the heat rising in waves off the pavement. Stevenson, Murray, and Anderson followed, faces set.

"How do you know?" Johnson asked.

Anderson tipped his chin at the crippled car. "This thing's not moving unless it's on a flatbed headed to San Francisco."

They swept the interior: fast food wrappers, cups jammed under seats, nothing alive inside. The car was abandoned.

"Where did he go?" Johnson pressed, eyes scanning up and down the block.

"Westbound," Anderson replied. "Walked five blocks to Avis, rented a Subaru, and took off."

"How are you sure it was him?" Pommeroy asked, skeptical.

Anderson shrugged, the corners of his mouth lifting. "Sometimes it's simple. I spotted the Avis sign at the end of the street, so I called. Asked if anybody rented this morning.

Clerk said yes, only one man. I asked the name; guy hesitated, then said Val Kozlov. Used his own credit card. Still active."

Johnson frowned. "But the Hollands–they're headed to Vegas?"

Anderson shook his head. "Don't think so. Mishkin probably lost them when his rental died. They have at least an hour lead. He's going home–their home. We head back to Palo Alto unless someone has a better idea."

No one spoke. The silence answered for them.

Anderson assigned Pommeroy and Murray to their car, rolling back toward Palo Alto with an APB to every unit: Subaru rental, Mishkin at the wheel, armed and dangerous, double murder suspect. Do not approach. The Hollands' car is still hot — a second APB to locate and protect only.

He faced Johnson. "Get the chopper in the air. We're not losing time."

Deputy Mackenzie offered a lift to the high school field where the FBI bird waited. Anderson waved him off. "We'll drive."

Fifteen minutes later, Anderson, Stevenson, and Johnson boarded the helicopter. Even before takeoff, Anderson requested two more FBI teams at the Hollands' house for coverage. The blades roared overhead, dawning heat shimmering in waves. The four-hour flight east had begun, everyone silent, every thought focused on the chase.

CHAPTER TWENTY-SEVEN

"Three. Two. One." Ray pressed the controller's button, powering up GG-2, which sat poised in the bottom of the dugout like a cannonball in a slingshot. The desert floor trembled beneath GG-2, vibrating as if a train thundered underground. *What if this doesn't work? What if I've miscalculated?* GG-2 pushed down, the compact machine vanishing in a billowing storm of sand and dust. Within seconds, Ray lost sight of it, the world reduced to shaking ground and a rising curtain of grit. The edge of the pit gave way in slabs; dirt and dust poured into the excavation, each collapse booming through the ground like distant thunder.

Tessa shouted over the racket, "What is happening?" The desert's hush was now shattered by caving ground and raw vibration.

Ray kept his eyes on the pit. "Just what I thought," he called back. *I hope this isn't a mistake.*

"Can you make it stop?" Tessa's voice wavered as she ducked low, steadying herself with a hand on the shaking earth.

"Yes," Ray said, squatting beside her, eyes on the controller. *I have to keep control of this to keep us safe.*

She shot him a look. "Don't you think someone will notice this?"

"It's why we came out here—so nobody would."

She shielded her eyes from the grit, unconvinced. "With the way things are shaking, I think the whole world will notice."

Ray squinted through the dust. Air rushed inside the hole, kicking up another geyser of dust, hotter than the ninety-degree air around them. He tasted it, gritty and dry. *This is more than I bargained for.*

"Okay, maybe it's time to stop," he said, flipping a switch with his thumb. Instantly, the vibration cut out, leaving only the low hiss of settling dirt. *Please let this not be a total disaster.*

The pit still crumbled at the edges, a second landslide pouring black gravel into the opening. From inside the haze, a deep whooshing echoed up, as if the pit exhaled.

Tessa's eyes widened. "Now what? Can you get it back?"

"I hope so. No, I'm sure I can." *I have to be able to do this.*

He powered the unit back on, then eased the control stick forward, his hand steady. A faint scraping, gravel-on-metal, filtered up from the shadows. As the dust cleared, the mouth of the hole looked wider than GG-2's frame, an oddity Ray noted for later.

Tessa wiped dust from her cheek. "Can you tell how close it is?"

"Not really."

She crossed her arms, impatience rising. "Can't you hurry it up? It's getting hot out here, and I bet the next noise we hear is a police siren."

Ray just grinned. "Easy. If I rush it, the thing's liable to come flying out, and then you'll have a flag on this spot for miles. Here's what—we'll need the two-by-fours from the back of the car. Bring those."

Tessa shot him a look, then walked to the Subaru. She dug two pieces of lumber from the back and carried them to the pit.

"Set one on each side of the hole," Ray said, already watching the cavity. "When GG-2 surfaces, we balance these over the opening and set GG-2 on them."

Tessa dropped the wood with a thud. "Or you could just fly the thing into the car," she said, dryly.

Ray snorted. "Tessa, it's not perfected."

She eyed him. "So what exactly did this test prove? GG-2 can dig holes to China?"

Ray tilted his head to listen. "It's coming up. Get ready."

Shoulder to shoulder, they approached the pit. GG-2 emerged slowly from the darkness like a lanternfish from the deep, its metal shell dusted with black sand, gleaming as if fresh from the shop. Ray eased it to a stop, hovering a foot above the pit's floor.

"Okay, Tessa. Go ahead."

She moved in, set the two-by-fours across the lip with practiced speed, then stepped clear as black sand slipped back into the opening. Ray pulled the lever; GG-2 dropped down, boards shifting under its weight. He cut the power; GG-2 bounced, then settled on the makeshift platform.

Ray exhaled. "That was close." *Too close.*

Tessa gave him a glance. "What do you mean?"

Ray shook his head. "Never mind. Later."

He set the controller down and joined Tessa at the edge. They both peered into the hole, careful not to get too close.

Tessa broke the silence. "It looks deep."

Ray nodded. "It is. But look at the walls. They're smooth, almost polished. GG-2 did a clean job." *I don't understand how the physics is even possible.*

He brushed the dust from the top of his head. "Let's get GG-2 to the car. We'll carry it like a stretcher. Just don't step in the hole."

They hoisted GG-2, skirting the edge, hauling it up the black gravel ramp. Ray directed Tessa to bring the car around, guiding her to the crest of the pit. Together, they slid GG-2 into the back. Ray pulled a flashlight from the glove box and directed his attention toward the hole.

Tessa frowned. "What are you doing?"

"I want to see how far down it goes."

She eyed the gaping blackness. "Aren't you going to fill it in?"

Ray smirked. "Maybe later," knowing no amount of shoveling would put the ground right—not without a dozer, anyway. *But I can't let this go. There's something here to gain from this.*

Ray crawled the last few feet to the edge, belly to the gravel, and shined the flashlight straight down. It sliced through the darkness. He could see thirty feet, maybe more, the smooth walls vanishing into a pit blacker than midnight. *What secrets does this hole hold?*

After the first few feet, the sides looked glazed, almost glassy.

Tessa's voice floated down. "Let's go!"

"Okay, okay," Ray called.

Backing up, Ray pushed himself to crawl away when the ground suddenly bucked, trembling beneath him like a coyote shaking off water. The gravel under his elbows turned treacherous.

Tessa whirled at the sound, eyes wide. "Ray!" she screamed.

The pit mouth widened, the edge collapsed in a slow-motion avalanche. Ray tried to scramble backward, but each shove pushed more loose sand beneath him. He lunged, clawing at the gritty surface. The hole consumed earth, and Ray with it.

He twisted and rolled in time to see Tessa jerk open the back of the Subaru, grabbing a coil of braided nylon rope. In seconds, she had it untangled, whipped two loops around the trailer hitch, and sprinted for the pit, the rope streaming behind her. Too late, he thought as he lost sight of her.

"Ray!" she shouted. "Grab it!"

In that instant, he understood just how much he depended on her, his only hope. Time dissolved into a single, blistering moment.

# # #

At the edge of the pit, Ray's outstretched hands vanished, engulfed by an avalanche of sand and black gravel. The world shrank to the whip and snap of nylon rope, the single hope Tessa hurled out like a lifeline to a drowning man. Her own hands burned as the rope tore through her palms, but she refused to let go, knuckles whitening against the friction, every muscle in her body locked in desperate resolve.

The rope strained, biting deep into her skin. All at once, the slack vanished, and Ray's weight yanked her forward onto her knees, heels dragged by the sudden burden. She could feel him at the other end, alive and fighting, but the mass of earth above threatened to swallow him whole. For a heartbeat, the only noise—the shriek of the wind, the grinding collapse of dirt, and the distant, muffled shout of Ray's voice, barely audible beneath the thunder of the falling earth.

“I got it!” he bellowed, somewhere inside the coughing darkness.

Above him, the rim of the pit dissolved in fits and starts, chunks sloughing off into the void. Tessa could hardly see, her vision clouded by dust and grit, but she clung to the rope, the only solid thing left in the world. Ray’s voice, hoarse and urgent, reached her again: “Get back! Tie it to the car! Pull me out! Now!” Then another hacking cough, and silence.

Tessa didn’t wait to see if another word followed—she tore off for the Subaru, keeping the belt of nylon taut. In a frenzy, she looped more rope around the trailer hitch, hands shaking so badly the knots came out jagged, ugly, but unbreakable. She yanked at the line, gave it a test pull, then dove into the driver’s seat, chest heaving, hair stuck to her cheeks with sweat and dirt.

The keys were already in the ignition. She cranked the engine; it answered with a coughing roar, then idled like it might die. She stomped the gas, her legs trembling, and the Subaru jerked forward, all-wheel drive fighting for traction on the shifting slope. Out the rear window, she watched for the rope, praying Ray would hold on, and would not disappear forever into the deep, silent dark.

The car’s wheels spun, then grabbed—a surge of momentum shuddered through the vehicle, sending Tessa’s heart slamming against her ribs. She leaned out the window, hair flying, to watch the rope. For a sickening moment, nothing—no movement, no sign of life, only the sound of the engine. But the line began to snake from the pit, inch by inch, the tension strong. The whole car groaned under the strain, the smell of burning clutch filling the air, but the rope kept moving, stubborn and alive.

Somewhere behind her, a new, sharper series of cracks—like the breaking of bone—echoed from the rim of the hole. The collapse accelerated. The slope forming the ramp into the pit rolled like a wave of sand, chewing away at the edge, threatening to pull half the hillside down with it. Tessa pressed harder on the gas, the car slewing sideways, but she didn’t care. She would wreck the engine, destroy the transmission, strip the tires to steel if it meant bringing Ray out.

At the mouth of the pit, a hand—pale and bloodied, with scraped raw knuckles—clawed for daylight. Ray's arm shot skyward, fist closing around the rope with a death grip. In a jerky, convulsive lurch, his whole body emerged as if the earth itself vomited him out. Coated in a black, glittering paste of sand and blood, the skin on his arms and face shredded, but he was moving, crawling, alive.

Tessa didn't let up. She kept the car in gear, wheels spinning, dragging Ray clear of the widening lip. The rope chewed another gouge in the ground, Ray's boots digging furrows as he tried to keep pace with the momentum. Twenty feet, then thirty. When she saw he had cleared the landslide, she slammed the car into park with a violence nearly braking the shifter, then sprinted back to where Ray sprawled in the dust.

The pit behind him had become unrecognizable—a churning maw spitting out debris and thick plumes of grit. The sound had shifted too, no longer a roar but a low, guttural moan, as if the earth itself were angry at being defiled. The light grew harsher, the heat more punishing, but Tessa hardly noticed. She dropped to her knees beside Ray, her hands hovering over him, afraid to touch, afraid of making things worse.

Ray gasped, each breath ragged and wet. Blood trickled from his nose, and a deep gash across his forehead welled up, painting his eyelashes red. His shirt, torn to ribbons, and beneath the tatters, his skin lay a map of cuts and bruises, some already swelling purple. Small, glassy fragments of black stone were embedded in his arms, and a long, raw scrape ran from his left shoulder to his wrist.

He blinked up at Tessa, trying for something like reassurance, but it twisted into a grimace. "Told you," he wheezed, "I could get it back."

She ignored the joke. "Can you move?" She started checking him as best she could, hands trembling as she ran them over his arms and legs, searching for breaks or deeper wounds. He rolled onto his side, spitting grit, then coughed up a glob of red.

"Nothing broken," he managed. "Just beat to shit."

She grabbed his wrist, feeling for a pulse. She pressed a towel, snatched from the car, to his temple, stanching the worst of the bleeding.

Behind them, the pit finally settled down, the collapse slowing to a trickle. The noise faded, swapped by the distant hum of the car's idle. The air was hot enough to scorch, but Tessa felt cold, the sweat on her back turning to ice.

She wiped his face, hands gentle. "You almost died," she whispered.

Ray coughed again. "Wasn't planning on it."

She rocked back on her heels, staring down at the man who, for all his brilliance, remained just flesh and blood and breakable. They sat for a moment, the burning sun unheeded, the silence between them more immense than the hole Ray had nearly vanished into.

Tessa knelt by him. "Ray?"

Ray tried to laugh. "That was a little scary."

"Scary? You'd be gone if not for the rope. Who knows how deep?" She trembled, the adrenaline draining away.

Ray tried for a reassuring look. "Thanks for saving my life. You're promoted to safety officer."

Tessa let out a laugh, but it choked into worry. "Be serious. Where are you hurt?"

"Like a bad sunburn. Everywhere but my legs."

She gingerly rolled him onto his side. His entire back was raked with scrapes and streaked with blood.

"Can you get up?"

Ray nodded, and she helped him to his feet, then half-carried him up the ramp. At the car, she grabbed the first aid kit and a change of shirt.

Ray slumped in the passenger seat while Tessa cut away the remains of his shirt. "You're not going to like this," she warned, "but I need to get you cleaned up." She took a bottle of water and poured it over his wounds. Ray flinched but didn't protest. The water washed rivers of blood and grit down his back, staining the car seat.

Ray managed a grin. "You're going to ruin the upholstery."

Tessa kept her focus. "Better than the alternative. We'll wrap your hands and elbows, then get moving before the car becomes an oven."

She bandaged Ray's hands and elbows carefully, then shut the door. The heat rose, the desert pressed in on them. Tessa hopped in, cranked the air conditioning, and pulled away from the pit, the dark wound in the earth fading in the rearview.

Once on the gravel road, Ray looked wiped out. Tessa stopped the car, handed him the ibuprofen from the glove box, and watched as he gulped two with a slug of water.

Ray leaned back, already looking a little better. "So, where to now?"

She eyed him. "You need a hospital. I'm not arguing."

Ray laughed, softer this time. "Let's get to the highway. Then we'll decide."

She looked at his bandages. "Home isn't the only option. You're in no shape for detours."

He shrugged. "Hotel room or house—it's the same. Anyway, we're eight hours from home."

Tessa pursed her lips. "You have another plan, don't you?"

Ray grinned despite the pain. "We're halfway to Vegas."

Tessa shook her head, her voice warming. "After today, I think we've gambled enough."

She watched as his gaze drifted toward the desert, his expression contemplative, as if searching for answers in the vastness before them.

CHAPTER TWENTY-EIGHT

By 4:14 p.m., Agents Anderson, Stevenson, and Johnson pulled up to the Holland home. Two FBI teams were already on the scene, their presence evident in the black Ford Econoline van with shadowed windows and a light blue Ford LTD parked discreetly along the curb. Anderson observed the gray clouds gathering overhead, a stark contrast to the heat they had just endured. It seemed the air had cooled suddenly, a welcome relief, but the tension in his gut remained; every second counted. Stevenson steered their LTD up the driveway and parked close to the house. Anderson's gaze swept over the other agents, who sprang from their vehicles as soon as they saw the new arrivals.

"Well, at least these two teams are awake," he couldn't help but comment, a hint of sarcasm lacing his voice. He needed his team to be sharp.

"They were alerted to our arrival, sir," Stevenson offered, one hand on the wheel.

"Who called ahead?"

"I did, sir. I didn't want to set them off with a false alarm."

"Next time, don't. I want to see them in action, so I can kick their butt for being slow." He had seen too many cases where hesitation became fatal; every moment mattered.

"Yes, sir."

As the quartet from the first two teams gathered around the LTD, Anderson took a deep breath, bracing himself before stepping out to greet them.

"Report," Anderson ordered, his tone steady as all eyes fixed on him. He assessed their expressions, searching for any signs of uncertainty.

"Sir, all quiet here. A few local vehicles drove by, local PD, and mail service," a tall agent answered.

Anderson gave him a quick once-over. "Name?"

"Special Agent Perkins, sir," he replied, reaching toward his jacket before thinking better of it.

"And what office are you out of?"

"San Francisco, sir."

"You check the house perimeter?"

"Every two hours, sir," Perkins answered, hand dropping to his side.

"Who's your team?"

"Special Agent Susan Connors, Agent Travis Trent, and Agent Gabe Connelly," Perkins said, indicating each in turn.

"This is Agent Stevenson and Johnson."

Quick handshakes and nods passed among the group, a clear sign of camaraderie Anderson appreciated in the tense moment. His gaze landed on Connors, and he caught her eyebrows arching as she took in the situation, a subtle signal something was off.

As he shook her hand, he asked, "Special Agent Connors, have we met before? You look familiar."

"Yes, two years ago. Haplan kidnapping case."

"Right," Anderson paused, the memory sharp and unsettling. The stakes were high. "You shot both kidnappers: Wilson, Mr. and Mrs."

"I did, sir." Connors met his gaze, her sky-blue eyes narrowing to a point.

"Too bad Haplan was dead too; otherwise, it would have been a big feather in your FBI cap."

"I'm sure the fact Miss Haplan was found dead at the scene had nothing to do with me shooting those two," Connors said, her chin lifted and arms folded in a display of contained energy.

"Agent Anderson, am I under investigation again regarding this closed case?"

"It's Special Agent Anderson, and no, you are not."

"Then what is with the history lesson, sir?" Her smile came sharp, more weapon than welcome.

"I need everyone clear. I have two dead agents. I don't want the Hollands harmed in any way. We know the killer, and both he and the Hollands are missing."

"We understand the case and the orders, sir. We were briefed before we left San Francisco," Connors replied, her voice even.

"Good. Here's the update: Victor Mishkin is armed and dangerous, suspected in the deaths of Agent Fitz and Agent Sommers, who watched this location. Mishkin was last seen in Barstow earlier today; we suspect he's returning. The Hollands may be en route to Vegas, but their car hasn't shown up on I-15. Mishkin's rental broke down—we believe he was tailing them. Witnesses spotted him heading west, bringing us back here."

Connors shifted on her feet, bracing against the car. "Do you know why Mishkin wants the Hollands?"

"I hoped you'd tell me since you had the briefing," Anderson countered.

"No, sir. Just surveillance and a protection order on the Hollands, plus a BOLO for Mishkin."

A gust rustled the leaves nearby, and for a moment, the sudden chill in the air drew Anderson's attention, cutting through the chatter. He glanced toward Perkins, who held out a page, eager to share what he'd found.

"Sir, I found out that George Palto from IOD in LA ordered the initial protection order."

"Which matches my understanding, Perkins," Anderson said, taking the sheet. "Would love to talk to Palto, but he's been unreachable."

"Sir, I understand Mr. Holland works for Laubner as an engineer. Laubner contracts for the DOD. Could it be why Mishkin's after the Hollands?"

Anderson scanned the page as he replied, "We thought about it, but Holland's only part time, mostly personal projects these days."

"And the Hollands have a substantial bank account—something about Mrs. Holland selling a patented chemical," Perkins added.

Anderson grinned. "You've been doing your homework."

"Actually, it's all in the briefing I just handed you."

"Interesting. I'll review more. Here's the plan: I want a perimeter, one block in every direction. Park vehicles unobtrusively but ready to roll. Eyes on the street and house at all times. Stevenson and Johnson, you're inside. Mishkin's likely to show in the next twenty-four hours, so no one stands down. Rotate teams for breaks, but stay in your vehicles while posted. Fitz and Sommers died outside theirs, caught off guard. Radios up at all times; if you see something, you say something. Perkins, you're team one, Connors team two, Stevenson team three. No mention of the Hollands or Mishkin over radio in case he's scanning."

"If Mishkin's spotted, we light him up, contain, and pursue if needed. If the Hollands show, we move in and provide protective custody. Questions?"

Connors asked, "What if Mishkin gets to the Hollands before we do?"

"We treat it as a kidnapping and follow protocol," Anderson replied. "Anything else?"

An uneasy silence fell over the group, heads shaking in answer. Anderson felt the tension rise; it was clear they were all grappling with the same unsettling reality. "Alright, let's take positions."

Anderson watched as Perkins and Trent climbed back into the LTD, rolling down the street to the west. Connors and Connelly slid into the van, heading east, their expressions focused and determined. His attention shifted to Stevenson, who circled to the kitchen door at the rear of the house, Johnson following closely behind. Anderson's heart raced as Stevenson gripped the doorknob, testing it; he held his breath, hoping the door would yield without a hitch.

Anderson focused intently on the scene, the briefing notes still clutched loosely in his hand, forgotten for the moment as he concentrated on the unfolding situation.

"Sir, the door's unlocked," Stevenson called softly.

"Good job. That was quick."

"No, sir—the door was open," Stevenson repeated, his voice measured.

Anderson's face sharpened. "Cover, cover, cover," he called, lowering his voice but keeping it urgent.

He grabbed the radio. "Team one, team two, stand by. The house is not secure."

He crouched behind Stevenson and Johnson. All drew their weapons.

"Wasn't this locked when we left?"

"Yes, sir."

"Damn," Anderson said under his breath. His heart raced; the situation felt all wrong. "Stevenson, you lead left. Johnson, cover the stairs. Sweep left, down the hall, room to room."

"Got it." Stevenson and Johnson exchanged looks and nodded.

Stevenson yanked the door open and swung left into the kitchen low and fast. Anderson covered the stairwell, his finger steady on the trigger, instinctively aware of the danger lurking in every shadow. He motioned for Stevenson to move forward through the hall. They moved in formation, clearing the study first—a library of engineering books, a wood desk, mechanical drawings on a drafting table, everything undisturbed. Anderson's mind raced as he took in the scene, reminding himself to stay focused.

"Keep moving," he indicated, leading them next to the living room: nearly bare, untouched. They looped through the dining room, back to the kitchen. Upstairs on the left. The stairwell looked narrow, barren of cover. He signaled he'd go first, glancing up at the closed door at the top of the stairs. He had Stevenson and Johnson lock down the first floor.

Anderson started up, wood creaking beneath him, every step a warning heightening the tension in his gut. A closed door ahead of them at the top of the stairwell. Remaining low at the threshold, he scanned down the narrow hallway to an open bedroom door, a vanity to its right.

Bang! The crack of gunfire. Shattering glass. Wood fragments flew above them Another gunshot. Adrenaline surged through him as Anderson bolted up the last remaining step, throwing himself against the door—it gave way, and he went down low, revolver leveled at a figure in the shadows: a man with a pistol aimed at him.

"FBI! Drop your weapon!" Anderson barked.

The man dropped to his knees but kept the gun pointed. Two quick shots from Anderson, chest level. The man pitched forward, landing on collapsed arms. Another shot rang wild, punching a hole in the wall.

"Hold your fire! Hold your fire!" Stevenson barked into the radio, urgency ringing in his voice. "Agents upstairs! Hold your fire!"

Anderson felt tension spike as Connors' response crackled over the radio. "Incoming from the woods across the street."

He crawled to the body, his heart racing as he checked for a pulse. Nothing. The grim reality settled in, pressure building behind his sternum.

"Stevenson, he's dead," Anderson said, his voice low but firm. "We need to get to the car and grab M4s. There's a shooter across the street. Move, move! Keep cover!"

They hustled down the stairs, instinctively sticking low to avoid exposure. Anderson glanced through the kitchen window, spotting teams one and two taking up firing positions outside, their M4s trained on the woods. He felt a surge of relief; they were ready, but the stakes were higher than ever.

"Connors, status?" Anderson said into the radio.

"Fifty yards south-southwest of the house, last muzzle flash. SWAT on the way, chopper in ten," Connors reported.

"We need cover," Anderson prompted.

"Go ahead," Connors replied. She braced behind a Ford, the shortest of the team at five-four, while the others crouched, guns ready.

"Stevenson, go!" Anderson ordered.

Stevenson bolted to the LTD's trunk. Anderson covered from the front. Johnson moved with him. Stevenson pulled three M4s, slinging them over his shoulder, ducked to the front grille, and handed them out. Each agent holstered their handgun, checked the M4.

"Ready," Stevenson called.

"Here we come!" Anderson radioed.

They ran up and dropped in behind the LTD.

"Chopper, two minutes!" Connors announced over the radio.

The chop of helicopter blades built over the background wail of sirens.

"Does he have a shooter?" Anderson asked.

"Yes, sir," Connors confirmed.

"Who has glasses?"

Anderson's mind raced, recalling the last time he'd underestimated a suspect—a mistake he wouldn't repeat.

Connelly tossed field binoculars to Anderson, who scanned the woods.

"You said fifty yards?" Anderson checked.

"Yes, sir. What happened in there?"

Anderson shook his head. "Whoever this is, they're good. There's a man with a gun upstairs. I put two rounds in him, but I think he was already shot." He paused. The weight of his responsibility pressed down on him. "Can you make that shot, Connors?"

"Yes, sir, I can. Was it Mr. Holland?"

"No, not Holland. Too short, too much hair," Anderson replied.

The helicopter's rotors throbbed overhead, and Anderson squinted against the sun, watching as it orbited, spiraling outward from the road's southern edge.

A voice crackled over the radio. "Connors, this is Cap One. No heat signatures, but we see car tracks on a dirt road, further south of your location. They run all the way to the main road. I think we lost him."

Anderson's pulse quickened at the news. They were close.

"Hold your position. We're moving in. All teams move forward," Connors commanded, and the agents advanced shoulder to shoulder into the trees, their eyes scanning left and right.

"Hold up," Anderson called from the rear, his instincts sharpening as he noted the tension in the air.

His gaze fell to the ground, where two empty shells glinted on the forest floor. He looked back at the Holland house, a silent reminder of what remained at stake.

"He's good," Anderson murmured, more to himself than anyone else.

"Stevenson, flag this place and bag the shells for evidence."

"Yes, sir."

A hand motion from Connors, and the team resumed the advance. Thirty yards ahead, he heard Perkins call out.

"Tire track here!"

Anderson hurried to him, glancing down at the tracks. "Stevenson, tag this and get some tire prints."

"Yes, sir."

He studied the tracks leading toward the main road; they were already fading into the distance. "He's long gone," Anderson muttered to himself, frustration bubbling beneath the surface. "Stevenson, process the site. Trent and Connelly can assist. Then get back to the house and process the upstairs room. Contact the county; get the coroner on the way."

He drew Perkins and Connors aside, noting the urgency in their faces.

"Back to the house. We've been in these woods long enough, and there's a DB to deal with. It's going to be a long day."

Minutes later, the trio came back, entering through the kitchen. Anderson led them up the stairs, his heart racing with dread. The door at the top remained open. But where the body had fallen, nothing remained but a pool of blood.

"Where's the body?" Connors demanded, stepping into the open.

"It was right here. I put two rounds in him, point-blank. He couldn't have gone anywhere," Anderson said, disbelief creeping into his voice.

"Jacket?" Connors asked, and Anderson felt a pinch tightening in his back.

"No, no... maybe? But look at the blood. I shot him," Anderson insisted. His heart raced as he saw the empty spot where the body should have been. The adrenaline surged through him, sharpening his focus. "We never should have left the house. How did I let this happen? Who was this guy?"

Perkins appeared in the hall. "Blood trail this way," he said, pointing down the corridor.

They followed, ending at a small room. A narrow door opened to the back of the house.

"What is this? A fire escape?" Anderson asked.

They peered down to see a wooden ladder bolted to the siding.

"No way the man I shot climbed down this. He dropped like a dead man," Anderson muttered. "There's no way he's alive."

"And yet you still shot him?" Connors' eyebrows rose.

"His gun was still on me. Of course, I shot him."

"There's more blood on the ladder steps," Connors pointed out. "He's still bleeding. Something at the bottom—we should check it."

They retreated, down the stairs and out to the base of the ladder behind the house.

"Looks like something heavy hit the ground," Anderson noted.

"More blood, a lot more," Connors added, gaze tracking the red trail.

"He couldn't have climbed down or walked away. Someone dropped him and carried him off," Anderson concluded. "We can't afford any mistakes; every piece of evidence counts."

"Bold if you ask me," Connors said, glancing back at the house. "With the FBI everywhere? Crazy."

"Anderson, Connors, over here! Tire tracks!" Perkins shouted from behind the garage.

Racing over, they saw more fresh dirt, more blood marking the way.

"Definitely fresh," Anderson agreed.

Connors pointed. "Look, more blood."

Anderson said, "Perkins, call up Stevenson. Get a mold of these tracks too; see if we can match. We need to see this through."

"Yes, sir."

Connors frowned. "If the guy you shot isn't dead, he will be soon, with this much blood loss."

Anderson's jaw tightened. "There's no way he's alive."

Connors asked, "Should we call local hospitals for gunshot victims?"

"Yes, call it in, just in case."

CHAPTER TWENTY-NINE

Tessa swung the Subaru around and drove the five miles back toward the 15, watching the open sky roll past the windshield, not a cloud in sight. The open sky felt deceptive; it should've mirrored her tension, but instead, it seemed indifferent.

Ray shifted against the seat, checking the dash thermometer. "It says ninety out there now."

"Then let's just stay put." Tessa leaned forward, refocusing on the road. "Have you figured out which way we're heading?"

Ray tapped a finger along the console. "I remember a rest stop about a mile back. Clean up there, maybe."

She shook her head. "The way you look, someone's bound to call 911—and there's no food at a rest stop anyway. Look, there's a Shell station across the 15. They probably have everything: food, air conditioning, the works."

Ray conceded. "Okay, okay. Shell is fine."

She guided the car across the 15, pulling into the station lot. After parking in a spot along the side wall, opposite a shaded row of three picnic tables, she noticed an idle California Highway Patrol car gleaming at one of the pumps. Both of them stepped into the heavy dry heat, crossing the pavement and pushing through the swinging glass doors together.

Inside appeared exactly what she'd pictured: the fluorescent flicker, rows of chips, candy, and a makeshift wine rack against the far wall. The chilly air hit her cheeks like a refreshing wave, and she drifted to the open fridge, picking out sandwiches, fruit, and coffee.

"Oh, there's what I need: a cold sandwich, an apple, and coffee." She reached for the first item.

"You're kidding, right? Hot coffee?" Ray's eyebrow arched in disbelief.

"Have you noticed the temperature in here? Feels like seventy-five degrees, easy. Yes, coffee."

Tessa watched the highway patrol officer again, a tall figure just leaving the counter with a cup of his own. He paused in the open doorway, dark eyes fixing on them—and lingered, as if searching for something.

He called out, “You alright?” not moving any closer.

Ray tensed and coughed. “A little sore, but I’ll live.”

Tessa glared at Ray. Didn’t he realize how vulnerable they were? She wished he would just accept help without hesitation.

“There’s a really nice restroom in the back,” the officer said, thumb gesturing over his shoulder. “Go take a look at yourself. At least clean up. I have a first aid kit out in the cruiser, too.”

Ray offered a polite, “Thanks, but I think I’ll be okay. But I should go clean up.”

He walked away, leaving Tessa to order for him.

Back at the counter, the officer remained. “Tessa, did I hear right? Your name is Tessa?”

She hesitated. “Yes.”

“Your husband?”

“Yes, he is.”

“What exactly happened to him?”

She glanced out the window, trying to keep her voice steady. “He fell in a hole out in the desert. We were exploring.”

He grunted. “Tell him to watch his step. And you, too. Out here in the Mojave, you do something dumb, you don’t get home.”

She couldn’t shake the fear of how close they had come to serious harm. What if he hadn’t made it out?

“Understood, sir. Thank you. We’ll be careful.” Her voice trailed off as he drew closer, standing in the checkout line with their tray of food.

He appeared older, with a straight jaw, white teeth, and an aquiline nose—not at all what she expected. He nodded to the woman behind the counter. “Mary, put this on my tab,” gesturing at Tessa’s items.

She tried to refuse. “You really don’t have to. We have money.” Part of her felt grateful, but another part sensed embarrassment; they were in a situation that shouldn't have happened.

He insisted, "Miss Tessa, your husband's hurting and embarrassed. If he doesn't want first aid, at least let me help with lunch."

"Thank you. I told him he should get checked at a hospital."

He nodded. "He should listen to your good advice."

His shoulder radio crackled, static breaking the silence. He paused, then glanced at Tessa. "Gotta go, Miss Tessa. Take care and stay out of those holes."

She watched him go, coffee cup in hand, through the glass doors. She picked up the tray and sat at a small table, waiting for Ray. Every day felt like another test, and with each challenge, she realized how much she depended on Ray—yet also how much he needed her.

Ray appeared a couple of minutes later, hair wet, with less blood and dust but his movements guarded.

A bit of relief softened her expression. "You look better."

"Not sure I feel better. Just cleaner," he replied, dropping into the chair.

"The officer paid for our food."

Ray stared. "He did? Why?"

"He said it was the least he could do if you didn't want first aid. I think he felt sorry for us."

Ray looked out the window. "Where'd he go?"

She pointed. "Pulled over by the driveway now. Probably watching traffic."

Ray took a bite of his sandwich, chewing slowly. Not many people in the place, just a few popping in for gas. The rest area down the highway probably drew most of the crowd.

Tessa excused herself to the restroom, and a few minutes later, she slid into the seat next to Ray. "Eat up. Then we'll figure out where we're going." She handed him his sandwich.

They finished eating and brushed crumbs from the table, making their way to the parking lot. The patrol cruiser idled, the A/C likely running.

Ray frowned. "What's he doing?"

Tessa watched, then shrugged. "Traffic, maybe?"

"I should thank him for lunch."

Tessa laughed. "Don't. You'll have your chance after he pulls you over on the way to Vegas."

Ray lit up. "So we're going to Vegas?"

"Yes, Ray, for the better hospitals."

He grinned. "That's what I love about you, Tessa. Always thinking."

They slid into their Subaru, Tessa tensing as Ray cranked the ignition, just about to back up when blue and red lights flashed behind them, sudden and insistent. Her heart raced; the patrol officer pulled right up, blocking their way. He stepped out, his expression unreadable, and approached the driver's window.

"Are you Ray Holland?" the officer asked.

Ray nodded. "Yes."

"Turn off your vehicle."

Tessa felt a knot tighten in her tummy as Ray complied, shifting into park.

"What's wrong?" he asked, his voice steady but laced with confusion.

"We're glad we found you," the officer replied.

Ray blinked, and Tessa shared his confusion. "We?"

"The whole county. And the FBI."

Tessa's mind skipped: not Sommers and Fitz again, surely. Unless—the earthquake, the hole. Something bigger. "Did we do something wrong?" Tessa's voice interrupted, nervous. The FBI was supposed to protect them, but why did it feel like they were hunted instead?

"No, ma'am. Actually, you may be in danger."

"In danger?" Ray echoed. "How?"

Tessa's gaze darted back at GG-2 in the rear. Ray shook his head, raising a finger to his lips: silence.

The officer continued, "You'll need to talk to the FBI agent in charge. He's waiting at your house."

Ray tried to process. "Why our house?"

"Sorry, I don't have all the details."

Tessa felt stiff and worried, her heart racing. "Ray, we need to go home, now."

He agreed, but her relief was short-lived as the officer shook his head. “Mr. and Mrs. Holland, I have orders to take you to Las Vegas ER first. Given your injuries, it’s non-negotiable. Get your things and come with me.”

Tessa glanced at Ray, seeing the hesitation cloud his expression. “I’m not hurt too badly. We can go straight home.”

“Again,” the officer said firmly, “orders are orders. Let’s go.”

Tessa’s anxiety spiked.

Ray tilted his head, making strong eye contact. “We can’t just leave our car. I have valuable equipment in the back. I can’t hand it off to a tow company.”

The officer shrugged and leaned over, peering into the Subaru. “That thing—” nodding at GG-2, “is it heavy?”

“Not really,” she replied, her voice steadier than she felt.

“Won’t fit in the trunk, but I can stow your bags there. One of you can ride up front, the other with the equipment in back.”

Ray tried again, frustration lacing his voice. “Wouldn’t it be easier if we just followed you in our car?” He paused, glancing at the officer’s name badge. “Officer Mike Bartholmew.”

Tessa’s breath catches, then she forces a steady exhale as the officer replied, “No. Sorry. This is the way it is.”

Ray and Tessa gathered their bags, the urgency of the moment pressing on them. Tessa glanced at the officer as he opened his trunk, watching him help organize their things around a couple of black nylon bags. Together, they hoisted GG-2 into the patrol car’s rear seat.

“Don’t you want to sit up front?” Ray asked as he locked up the Subaru.

Tessa shook her head, feeling the too-familiar tightness across her shoulders. “There’s not much space. I’ll sit in back.”

Once inside, she felt the rigid plastic seat against her back, a scratched partition separating her from Ray and the officer. The officer opened a small window for conversation, and Tessa shifted slightly, trying to find a comfortable position.

“It’s just a short ride,” Ray said, turning toward her, his expression softening.

Tessa nodded, unable to find her voice.

The officer checked the rearview mirror. “Should be about an hour.”

“Will you be taking us all the way to Palo Alto?” Ray asked.

Bartholomew replied, “No, sir. I’m close to the end of my shift. Someone will transfer you in Vegas, maybe a Nevada State Trooper. It’s up to the FBI if they want to come out this far.”

Tessa felt a pang of uncertainty at the mention of the FBI, and her heart raced as the officer’s radio crackled to life. “Two-twenty, fifteen-twelve, do you copy?”

Bartholomew grabbed the mic. “Fifteen-twelve, roger.”

“Ten-twenty?”

“On the Fifteen, MP fifty-eight, eastbound to Vegas. Transporting injured male and female, approximate age twenty-four, to SVH. Relay to Palo Alto, MP found and safe.”

“Roger, fifteen-twelve,” came the voice before the radio hushed.

Tessa held her breath for a moment, hoping the officer’s report would ease their situation. She glanced at Ray, whose expression remained tense as Bartholomew looked in the mirror.

“Did you feel the earthquake today? Out there in the desert?”

“We did,” Ray replied, and Tessa felt her shoulders tense.

“Is this how you fell in the hole?” Bartholomew sounded unconvinced.

Ray met his eyes. “Maybe. I think it had more to do with the hole itself.”

Bartholomew stared at him. “You know, Mr. Holland, if that’s the case, the geology folks might want a word with you.”

Ray just shook his head. “I doubt it.”

Tessa’s gaze drifted outside, watching the desert road blur past in the rising heat. Each mile felt like a faint hum of unrest and unanswered questions, echoing the uncertainty swirling in her mind.

CHAPTER THIRTY

One of the Palo Alto deputies approached Agent Trent, and Anderson's attention sharpened as he observed the folded slip of paper passed between them. Trent read it, then made a beeline for Anderson, who waited in his car at the Hollands' driveway.

"Sir, we just received word from Palo Alto. A CHP officer located the Hollands and is transporting them to a Vegas hospital."

"A Vegas hospital?" Anderson lifted his head, clenching his jaw. "What are the injuries? Who's hurt?"

Trent shook his head. "No details. Just that they're headed to SVH. I believe that's Spring Valley Hospital."

Concern tightened Anderson's brow. Each minute's passing felt like another chance for Mishkin to slip through their fingers. "One CHP. He called for backup, I hope."

"Yes, sir."

"That was a statement, Trent. Tell the rest of the team about the Hollands, but don't mention their names on the radio. Use 'MP' as the sign. Nothing about Vegas or the hospital, either. Give the details in person."

"Yes, sir."

As Trent pivoted to brief Agent Connors, who moved partway up the driveway, Anderson couldn't shake the feeling that they were racing against time. He could see Connors already assessing the situation as she approached, ready to jump into action.

"You could hear us from the end of the driveway?" Anderson looked at her.

"Every word. It's like a cemetery out here," she replied.

Anderson scowled. "Don't say that. We have three dead people here." The loss of Sommers and Fitz weighed heavily on him—a stark reminder of the dangers they faced and the stakes involved.

"Actually, only two," Connors corrected, her face impassive.

He frowned. "Just because we don't have a body doesn't mean he didn't die."

"Oh, I agree; he's probably dead, whoever he is," Connors said. "What's the plan now?"

"Protect the Hollands. Capture Mishkin. Find the dead guy and figure out who's been shooting in this neighborhood."

"Those are the goals. What's the plan?" Connors pressed.

"I need two agents on the Hollands as soon as possible."

"In Vegas?" she clarified.

Anderson nodded. "Call the Vegas office. See if they can spare a team. Give them the specifics."

"Will do." She left for her car.

Anderson's eyes narrowed as he considered the stakes. This wasn't just another case; it was personal. He couldn't let the Hollands become collateral damage. He began pulling in status updates from the rest of the team. Nothing significant to report. Connors returned a minute later.

"Vegas field office only has one agent," she said. "He just got called out to a child abduction case."

Anderson weighed the options. "You and Perkins go to Vegas. Stay with the Hollands until we locate Mishkin."

Connors didn't hide her surprise. "That's a nine-hour drive."

"Get to the airport. Catch the next flight to Vegas. You'll be there in two."

"All right. What's the rest of your plan?"

"I'm still working on it. For now, just keep the Hollands safe."

Connors and Perkins quickly loaded their gear and drove off. As the team dispersed, Anderson observed their expressions, noting the tension among them. He needed to keep morale high to face whatever Mishkin had planned.

At 10:00 p.m., the headlights of a Palo Alto deputy rig rolled up the Holland driveway, washing Anderson's car in blue-white. He glanced at Stevenson beside him, muttering, "Don't these guys know about radios?"

Stevenson grinned. "Doesn't seem like it, sir."

The officer approached Anderson's window. "Agent Anderson?"

"That's me."

"Just relaying word from County. They found a DB three miles from here. Shot in the chest and head. No ID. Scene is secured as a possible homicide."

Anderson nodded, a sense of unease tightening his chest. "Great. Can we follow you?"

"Of course," the officer replied, heading back to his car.

Anderson radioed the others to cover the Holland residence, then pulled out after the deputy. After a few turns, they found themselves in a swirl of county and city police vehicles, red, yellow, and blue lights flashing against the dark. A fire truck loomed nearby, while an ambulance sat silently, the stillness around it unnerving. Off the main road, floodlights illuminated a patch of wild scrub, yellow tape stretching from the asphalt into the chaparral—a stark reminder of the danger they faced.

Anderson and Stevenson identified themselves with a county deputy posted at the edge of the tape.

"He was dragged here from the road," the deputy reported.

Anderson studied the dirt, the half-smear path back to the blacktop. He'd already guessed. Now he had confirmation. The body lay face up, arms flung above the head. Two close-range wounds in the chest, and the head—a grotesque mask, darkened and sticky with dried blood.

"It's definitely our man from the house," Anderson said, kneeling to unzip the jacket. Underneath: a level-three tactical vest, the kind that can stop serious rounds. "I don't see my slugs, but I bet he felt them."

Stevenson squinted at the head wound. "Honestly, sir, I doubt he felt much of anything."

Anderson straightened, looking out at the dark. "I want to know who this guy is and what he was doing at the Hollands."

Before Stevenson could answer, a call resonated from a nearby radio:

"Engine fifty-one, Engine fifty-one, ten twenty-four, fully engulfed vehicle fire, fifteen hundred block, Whiskey Hill Road, proceed code three."

A fireman gave a shout, and the engine's crew scrambled up and away, siren wailing into the night.

Anderson muttered, "Damn."

Stevenson tipped his head. "Sir?"

"It's not a coincidence. The body's only been here a couple of hours. Now there's a car fire just down the road? Someone's definitely covering their tracks. I want ballistics and ID on the dead guy, which can wait. Right now, the fire's more urgent. Let's move."

They jogged back to their car, urgency propelling them as they sped off toward the growing orange glow. Anderson felt the tension rise in his chest; two CHP units were already closing off traffic as they arrived, lights and flares casting long shadows across the pavement. A compact sedan lay fully consumed: yellow flames licking the air, oily black smoke rising.

"Looks like he's destroying evidence as he goes," Anderson observed, frustration tightening his jaw.

Stevenson nodded as they parked off the road. "He's not leaving much behind."

Anderson scanned the bystanders—just a handful of neighbors, their faces washed pale in the firelight. "Recognize anyone?"

"No, sir. I doubt he'd stick around for this."

"Maybe," Anderson mused, narrowing his eyes. "How long does it take a fire to torch a car like this?"

"Ten minutes, tops."

"So, he's on foot, maybe ten minutes away from us right now."

Stevenson considered. "Assuming he's not getting a ride."

"I don't think he is. The darkness is his ally. Where does he go?"

They both looked at the land across the street: a swath of bare ground beyond the burning car.

"Across there," Stevenson said, pointing at the empty lot.

Anderson nodded, feeling the urgency pulse through him. "Let's get around to the far side."

Switching on the car's red-and-blues, they circled the barricades and veered down Whiskey Hill Road. Soon, the fire faded to a dull glow over the fields. At the intersection with Sandy Hill, Anderson swung left and killed the headlights, the adrenaline still coursing through him.

"This is good," Anderson said. They could still see the burned-out car clearly, but now the night pressed in again. The fire trucks worked the flames, sending up a thick hiss of steam and then a cloud of white as water slammed into hot metal.

Stevenson asked, "Now what? He has the advantage out there."

Anderson replied, "Surprise is ours, for a moment. Let your eyes adjust. Watch for movement."

A low snoring sound punctuated the silence. Both agents shifted, scanning.

"What is that?" Anderson wondered aloud. "Where are we?"

Stevenson checked his map with a penlight. "Sandy Hill Horse Park."

Anderson let his gaze drift over gray metal pole barns and scattered area lights beyond the fence. "Those buildings must be the stables. He could be hiding in there."

"Should we check?"

"He'd have cover, but there might be staff. Otherwise, he risks being spotted."

They waited. Thirty minutes felt like an eternity; the fire was now extinguished. Anderson's gaze remained fixed on the scene, scanning for any signs of movement. He noted a tow truck pulling up, the metallic groan of its winch echoing through the stillness as it hooked onto the burned shell of the car.

Then he caught a flicker of headlights among the pole barns. A heavy-duty truck with a horse trailer drove to the bar gate; the driver hopped out, opened the gate, and drove out toward Sandy Hill Road.

"He didn't close the gate," Anderson remarked, a sense of unease creeping into his gut.

Stevenson nodded, his brow furrowing slightly. "That's a bit strange."

"Let's pull him over. We'll ask if he saw anything."

Anderson started the car, pulling into the drive to block the truck's path. As he stepped out, ID in hand, he signaled for the driver to stop, his heart racing with anticipation. Stevenson exited the passenger side, revolver at the ready, mirroring Anderson's tension.

The truck's diesel engine rattled as the driver complied. Anderson's instincts kicked in; he assessed the man—a short, dark-haired Hispanic wearing jeans and a frayed t-shirt.

"FBI," Anderson said, displaying his badge. He watched the man's hands go up, a mix of curiosity and caution tingling in his veins.

"You can relax," Anderson said, trying to keep his tone steady. "Do you work here?"

"Sí," the man nodded. "Juan Chavez, my name."

"You understand English, Juan?"

He nodded, eyes darting nervously. "Some English, yes."

"Did you see the fire across the street?"

"Yes, I saw," Juan said, voice tight.

"Have you seen anyone around who doesn't work at the compound?"

"No. Nobody," he replied, quick and nervous.

"Where are you taking the truck and trailer?"

"Horses," Juan answered, glancing at the trailer. "Need to pick up horses. Arizona."

"At this hour?"

He nodded. "Yes. Arizona. Many miles."

Anderson looked at Stevenson, gestured toward the trailer. "That way?"

Stevenson advanced toward the back of the rig, his hand hovering over the grip of his revolver. Anderson noted the flashlight beam trembling slightly as it cut through the smoky gloom. The air, even thirty yards from the burned-out sedan, felt heavy with the acrid scent of scorched plastic and wet ash. Keeping his own weapon angled discreetly beside his thigh,

Anderson motioned for Juan to sit on the gravel next to the front tire. He watched as the man folded in on himself, shoulders hunched, hands visible and shaking. Juan looked up at Anderson with wary eyes, and a pang of concern washed over him.

"Stay here," Anderson ordered, his voice flat and purposeful. He circled the front of the truck, scanning the distant fence line before following Stevenson toward the rear. Both agents moved in tandem, the tension palpable. The horse trailer—twenty-four feet of sun-bleached aluminum—stood ominously, its La Mesa Livery logo partly obscured by dirt.

Stevenson's free hand tested the trailer's latch and found it unlocked. He shot Anderson a look—caution, then confirmation—before swinging the heavy door open. The hinges emitted a soft metallic whine, revealing a cramped, musty corridor that reeked of animal sweat and disinfectant. In the faint beam of Stevenson's light, the stalls appeared empty. Anderson stepped up onto the ramp behind him, careful not to silhouette himself, and swept the compartment with a deliberate pan of his flashlight.

"Clear," Stevenson whispered, but Anderson could sense the hopefulness in his tone.

Anderson covered him from the outside, steadying the door with his left hand while training his Glock on the half-shadowed interior. Stevenson moved forward, toeing at the straw with the tip of his boot. He ducked into the left stall, checking above and below the divider, pressing his hand against the metal partition to feel for vibrations. Nothing. He examined the hay bales—each one had been disturbed, kicked, shaken, even stabbed with the muzzle of his revolver. Dust motes swirled in the flashlight's cone.

Stevenson continued, scanning the floor for footprints or blood—a stray thread, a spent casing. Anderson followed, assessing the scene through his lens, the urgency of the situation amplifying his focus. He gestured for Stevenson to join him at the back compartment, keeping his gaze moving across the ceiling, the corners, and the low tie-loops along the walls. Anderson's mind raced with possible scenarios:

Mishkin hiding in the rig, already gone, or maybe the driver was a decoy, paid to stall them.

Stevenson reached the back compartment, sectioned off by a flimsy plywood panel. He rapped his knuckles on the wood, getting a hollow response, then pulled the release and swung it open. The flashlight's beam caught a tangle of horse blankets, a battered plastic bucket, and nothing else. Still, he checked behind each bundle and inside the bucket, hands methodical, eyes darting to every shadow.

Satisfied, Stevenson stepped down from the trailer, wiping sweat from his forehead with the back of his wrist. He looked over at Anderson, who stood still, covering the front with his eyes and barrel. They held a silent exchange: nothing here, let's move on.

They regrouped at the truck. Sweat beaded on Juan's forehead, tension written across his face.

"Juan, why so nervous?" Anderson asked.

"You FBI. I don't want trouble. Have family."

"You're certain you didn't see anyone out here tonight?"

"Nothing," Juan said, trembling.

"Okay, you can go," Anderson told him.

Juan scrambled into his seat and started the truck, glancing nervously at Anderson as he waited for him to make a move. Anderson felt a mix of impatience and unease; they needed to hurry, and he couldn't shake the feeling they missed something. As the truck pulled onto Sandy Hill Road, Anderson leaned back in his seat, scanning the area for any signs of trouble.

"I still don't get why he left the gate open," he remarked, the dust settling in the darkness beyond the pole barns, a reminder of the unanswered questions weighing on his mind.

CHAPTER THIRTY-ONE

Officer Bartholomew eased the car to a stop in the ambulance lane in front of Spring Valley Hospital's emergency entrance. Ray took a moment to absorb the sight of the building, its fresh brick-red facade contrasting with the harsh glow of the parking lot lights. The deep black sky overhead felt unwelcoming, a stark reminder of the night's urgency.

As they stepped out, Ray stretched his arms and legs, trying to shake off the tension. It felt surreal, like a late-night pit stop, but nothing was casual about the circumstances.

"You two head in and check yourselves in. I'll be there in a minute," Bartholomew said, leaning in to grab the radio mic from the dash.

Ray watched him press the button, his voice steady as he reported to CHP about their arrival and the transfer of responsibility for the Hollands to Nevada State Troopers. When Bartholomew headed inside, Ray glanced at Tessa, who looked equally anxious.

"You check in?" Bartholomew asked, standing over them.

"Yes," Tessa replied. "Forty minutes, they told us."

"You sure?"

"That's what they said."

Bartholomew glanced around. "Any Nevada State Troopers here yet?"

Tessa shook her head. "Nope. Just a lot of people waiting," she motioned, indicating the scattered figures in the waiting room.

"I'm not sure what happened to the Nevada State Troopers who were supposed to meet us here, but I need to get back to California. You two stay put until they show. They'll sort out your ride home and protection detail. Hospital's as safe as anywhere. Don't leave without them."

"We won't go anywhere," Tessa promised.

Ray piped up, "We need to get our stuff out of your car. Is there somewhere safe we can leave it?"

Bartholomew nodded. "I'll ask the desk, see if there's a secure area," and walked over to the ER counter, the staff member inside looking up as he approached.

When Bartholomew reappeared, he brought news: "They've got a place to store your gear. Security's sending someone."

Minutes later, a thick-set man in a dark jacket and pants, with black shoes, security stripes at the shoulder, and a shiny badge at his chest made his way over. He introduced himself as Security Officer Miles, eyes lingering on Ray.

"What happened to you?" Miles asked.

Ray shrugged. "Long story. Need a room for our gear while we wait for a ride back to California?"

Miles nodded. "We've got a storage room, just down this hall."

Tessa stood, turning to Ray. "Hang back in case they call you. We'll grab everything."

Ray grunted. "Everything?"

"Yes. Everything," she said, insistent.

# # #

Tessa looked back at Ray, biting her lip as the three walked out into the cool night. *I can't let fear take over. We will get through this, for both of us.* At Bartholomew's car, the trunk popped open, and they pulled out the backpacks. Tessa opened the rear door, gesturing to GG-2.

"That too?" Miles asked.

"Yep," Tessa answered.

Miles eyed the device. "What is it?"

"Science project," Tessa replied, her lips flat.

"Heavy?"

"More awkward than heavy."

He considered, then said, "I'll grab a dolly," and disappeared back through the sliding glass doors.

A minute later, he reemerged, this time with another security officer—tall and young, uniform matching. With care, they loaded GG-2 onto the dolly. As they rolled through the

ER lobby, some heads twisted to take notice; whispers followed their passing.

Down the hall: forty feet, then a door labeled “Storage.” Miles sorted through his heavy ring until the right key clicked. The dolly—and GG-2—fit easily. Inside, shelves lined the walls, some stacked with medical supplies, others with boxes labeled “Pharmaceuticals.” The officers set the bags on a shelf and wheeled GG-2 to a gap at the far end.

“Your gear is safe here. Only a couple of us have keys, and there’s a camera in the room,” Miles said. “When you need it, just tell the staff at the desk. They’ll call us.”

Tessa thanked them both, handshakes all around. Bartholomew shook hands with Miles, then led Tessa back into the hallway, the storage door closing and locking behind them. They passed the unmarked wooden doors and entered the bright waiting area where Ray remained planted in his chair, intent on the movement of the room.

Bartholomew gave a final look. “You two take care. Don’t leave without an officer, understand?”

Both nodded. “Understood.”

“Thanks for the ride,” Tessa said, puzzled he left them, whether it was for protection or not.

She almost looked over at Ray to ask, but a staff member called from the side door, “Ray Holland.” Just like that, the world outside faded. *We’re in a hospital now, and all I can think about is Ray’s treatment.*

They both stood and followed the nurse into a hall lined with curtained bays and a few private rooms.

A nurse in blue scrubs waited. She pulled the curtain and handed Ray a gown, requesting he strip to his underwear. Tessa grabbed a bag for his clothes. The nurse ducked out, then reappeared: blood pressure, heart rate, temperature, questions scribbled on a clipboard.

“What happened to you?”

“I fell in a hole. Full of gravel,” Ray answered.

She inspected his arms and legs, noting the patchwork of cleaned-up scrapes and a few stubborn cuts still leaking blood.

“Some of these need dressing,” she said. “When was your last tetanus shot?”

Ray shrugged. “You’d have to ask my mom.”

The nurse nodded, already jotting. “We’ll give you a booster, just in case. The doctor will be in soon. I’ll get your dressing supplies.”

Ray shivered as she left. Tessa smirked. “Afraid of a little poke?” His humor served as a defense mechanism; she wished he’d let her in on how he really felt. Did he realize how much this was affecting her too?

Ray scowled. “Yes. They hurt.”

Tessa gestured at his battered limbs. “I don’t think you’ll even notice this one.”

A moment later, the curtain swung open and a tall man entered: wearing a white coat and dark pants. He checked the chart.

“Ray Holland?”

“Yes.”

He nodded at Tessa. “Your wife?”

“Yes,” Ray repeated.

“Doctor Newton.” He glanced at the chart, then at Ray’s arms and face. “Scrapes from a fall in a hole, today?”

Ray nodded. “Yes.”

“How?”

“I tripped. Mojave Desert, hiking.”

“Any pain?”

Ray grimaced. “Like a bad sunburn.”

The doctor considered. “We can prescribe pain meds, or you can use ibuprofen.”

Tessa cut in: “Ibuprofen is fine.” He’s lucky they aren’t reattaching broken bones or worse, covering his body with a sheet. Her heart ached at the thought.

Ray shot her a look. “Easy for you. You’re not the one torn up.”

“You didn’t even want a doctor earlier,” she shot back. She wished he could see how close this was to ending badly for them.

The nurse reappeared, tray in hand: bandages, a vial of vaccine, a syringe. She set it up on a table next to Ray’s exam bed.

"Let's see those arms," said Doctor Newton. He twisted Ray's wrist side to side, examining scrapes and deeper cuts, then checked his legs, feet, chest, and back. Drops of blood still welled on Ray's arms.

"We'll put antiseptic on the deeper cuts and wrap them. Change the bandages daily, at least for a couple of days. No stitches needed," the doctor said, jotting down notes.

He rolled a steel tray to Ray's side and pointed: "Rest your right arm here." The silence hung heavy as the doctor soaked a gauze with clear fluid and pressed it to the deepest scratches. Ray winced.

"This will sting a little," Newton murmured.

"Already does," Ray muttered.

The cleaning and bandaging—Ray's arms, now neat stripes of white and beige. The doctor taped the last dressing in place when, from somewhere nearby, came a sudden crash, sharp and violent, cutting through the hospital hush.

What was that? Are we safe in a place like this? I need to be ready for anything.

CHAPTER THIRTY-TWO

A cold ripple moved across her skin. "What was that?" Tessa asked, her heart pounding as she glared at the doctor, then directed her gaze toward the sound beyond the curtain.

"Probably someone knocked down a tray in one of the exam rooms. It happens frequently," Doctor Newton replied, though his tone lacked certainty.

Before he could finish, a woman's scream cut through the air, sharp and terrified, followed by a crash—a heavier sound, like a mountain of equipment tumbling across a Formica floor. Tessa's breath hitched. *This wasn't just an accident; something was wrong.*

"Stay here," Doctor Newton said, drawing back the curtain before stepping out of the treatment bay. Tessa exchanged worried glances with Ray, who sat still, nursing his injuries. Then she instinctively followed Newton's path to the door, peering through the crack. Her pulse raced as other curtains opened around her. Heads poked out from behind them, all eyes drawn toward the commotion—a path leading straight to reception.

In the glaring light of the waiting room, a man stood—a big man, a knife gripped tightly in his fist, swaying it left and right like a flag. Panic surged through Tessa as his wild eyes scanned the room, landing on Doctor Newton. An elderly lady sprawled on the tile, a staff nurse kneeling beside her, both surrounded by a widening pool of blood.

"Are you a doctor?" the man roared, his voice echoing with desperation and rage.

A woman shrieked and bolted for the exit. Tessa's heart raced. *What if he came this way? Did anyone know what happened?* She wanted to scream, to run, but she had to stay strong and do what was necessary to protect Ray.

Before Newton could answer, a young security officer charged in, hands raised. “Drop the knife!” he barked. “She’s bleeding. We need to help her.”

The man wheeled to face him, grinning, his teeth bared in a terrifying smile. “What are you going to do about it?”

“Drop the knife,” the officer repeated, his voice louder now but rattled. “Let us help her. Just put it down.”

Doctor Newton held his palms up, steady. “Yes. Drop the knife. Let me help her.”

“Help her?” the man shouted, his frustration palpable. “I’ve been waiting two hours. Why don’t I get some help?”

Tessa felt a creeping sense of dread. What if this man lost control? The emergency room doors whooshed open, and two officers stepped in, their silver-gray shirts, and dark navy pants with gold stripe stark against the fluorescent glare. The first was a towering figure over six feet tall, the second a woman with a squared stance that exuded authority; both wore campaign hats distinct to the state troopers. Tessa's heart raced as she recognized the familiar gold-tone badge and nameplate on their left chest. They froze, assessing the crowd hunched along the seats before fixing their attention on the man with the knife.

The tall trooper advanced, hands out, his voice firm yet calm. “Drop the knife and get on the ground. Now.”

His partner circled toward the fallen nurse, gauging the wound with sharp, focused eyes, then slid behind the man with the knife.

Tessa felt a surge of hope—maybe they could contain this situation, but she couldn’t shake the fear it could spiral out of control in an instant.

Newton stayed in the doorway, blocking access to the treatment area. The security officer, now just an observer, stood by as another officer joined him, skidding to a halt.

“I called 911,” he blurted. “Oh my God, this is bad.”

The trooper’s arm shot out, holding him back. “Move clear!” he ordered to the crowd behind the man with the knife. His partner directed them to safety, urging them into the hallway. They complied, their feet shuffling, except for one elderly woman dozing in her wheelchair.

The security officer dropped low and scrambled to her, shoving her clear of danger. "Now," the trooper urged.

The Nevada trooper slid left, keeping the man's focus. With a sweep of his hand, he motioned those between him and the man to edge back, toward the female trooper. Soon, only the man and the two women on the floor remained in the danger zone.

"Block entry to the area," the woman officer ordered the security guards, then instructed another officer to warn everyone in the treatment rooms to stay put. Officer Miles sprinted for the phone, urgency fueling him. The younger guard waved anyone lingering farther back.

"What's your name?" the officer asked.

"John," the man replied, his voice shaky.

"John, you need to drop the knife, move away from the nurse, and get on the ground. Do you understand?"

"It shouldn't take two hours to get treatment in this hospital. What's wrong with this place?" John shouted, his frustration boiling over.

"John, hurting people isn't how you get help."

"Well, I got their attention, didn't I?" John took a lurching step toward the trooper, shifting his weight, knife still prominently displayed.

The trooper drew his weapon, low and steady, not quite aiming yet. "John, I don't want to use this. But you're leaving me no choice."

Tessa's breath quickened. *Why was this happening here?* They were supposed to be safe. She leaned closer, straining to hear the commotion, but her heart sank as she realized she could do nothing.

"What, you're going to shoot me? All I wanted was some attention."

"I've asked you to drop the knife. I've asked you to get on the ground. You have clearly hurt someone."

Tessa held her breath, the tension in the air thick.

Without warning, the other trooper darted in—a sweep of long white towels snapped over John's knife hand. He pivoted, confusion etched across his face, and the trooper slammed her forearm against his neck, locking him up. She hooked his leg and dropped her weight. John crashed down, pinned by the officers.

Tessa's body tensed as she watched, feeling both hope and fear. Then, a shot rang out. Sharp, final. She instinctively ducked as screams erupted from the waiting room. She darted back to the treatment bay where Ray sat on the exam bed, her face glowing with fear.

Ray directed his focus on her wide eyes. "That was a gunshot."

The nurse working on Ray's arm angled toward the sounds, her face pale. A ripple of panic broke loose. Voices clamored down the corridor.

"Let's go, everybody out!" shouted a nurse, her finger stabbing at the back door.

Tessa's heart raced as a wave of blue-scrubbed staff poured into the hallway. They were all running, eyes darting in fear.

"Tessa, we need to get out of this hospital," Ray said, struggling to pull up his pants.

She hesitated, torn between the instinct to protect him and the chaos unfolding outside. "But the officer said to wait for the State Troopers."

"It's not safe. We don't even know what's going on. Maybe it's us they're after."

"No, it's not about us; there's a man with a knife, and police officers just tackled him. Maybe the situation is under control now."

"Gunfire tells me things aren't under control. Look, the staff are all leaving. We need to get out of here," Ray insisted, slipping on his untied shoes and grabbing the remainder of his belongings in a bag.

They stepped into the hallway, finding an exit sign to their left. A glass window showed darkness; they pushed through and emerged into a pool of parking lot light, pressed up against the building.

"That's the ER entrance," Ray said, pointing left. Tessa nodded, feeling the cold rush of adrenaline.

Ray glanced at the city glow in the distance, a hard band of neon against the night. “Now what? It’s dark out here.”

“Isn’t Vegas the city that never sleeps?” Ray joked, but his voice shook, betraying his nerves.

“Ray, please. This isn’t funny.”

“We’ll blend in. On the Strip, there are always people out at night. During the day, it’s over ninety degrees. Tourists wait for the sun to go down.”

Tessa pointed at the glow. “That’s where we need to go.” She hesitated, her thoughts racing. “What about our stuff? GG-2?”

“We’ll come back after sunrise,” Ray said. “Once this all calms down, we’ll get a cab or rental and come back for it.”

Sirens screamed, drawing closer. Red and blue lights spilled in a parade toward the ER entrance.

“Like I said, after the drama.” They headed toward the city lights, shadows of flashing blue, red, yellow, and white reflecting against the neighborhood homes.

CHAPTER THIRTY-THREE

They walked on, drawn toward the scattered neon of Las Vegas as the sky paled and smeared out the last of the night. Tessa felt weariness crouch in her bones, her tummy gnawing with hunger. No stopping now; if they could just reach the city, maybe they could find rest. She matched Ray's pace, though every block felt like it stretched twice as far as the last. As they reached the intersection of Las Vegas and Mandalay Bay Boulevards, the street came alive: cars darting like insects, headlights flickering; people everywhere, drifting from entrance to entrance or clustered in small knots, always moving. The noise and light pressed in on her, overwhelming her senses. Then she spotted it: the black pyramid of the Luxor Hotel and Casino loomed before them, its shimmering facade catching the first rays of dawn. Tessa's breath caught in her throat, a mix of surprise and wonder. She had only heard stories of the grand Las Vegas attractions, but seeing this iconic landmark in person stirred a sense of awe within her.

"We can't stand out here," Tessa muttered, twisting her mouth at the crowds. "We could melt into this in no time." A restless energy thrummed in her voice; crowds always made her uneasy.

Ray scanned the concrete as they shuffled along. "Not a bench in sight," he observed, and Tessa felt a flicker of frustration. The walkways were clean, wide, and utterly inhospitable to lingering.

Their only option was to go inside. They passed beneath a Sphinx replica, its stony eyes unblinking, before pushing through the glass doors. The corridor inside felt like the entrance to an upscale shopping mall at first, but as they walked deeper, the space transformed—the walls hunched in, stone Sphinxes and obelisks lining the paths, fountains glistening in the fluorescent light. The ceiling soared to a dizzying height. Guest rooms fanned out above them, visible from narrow walkways like a honeycomb standing on end, surveying the atrium below.

“This place must have cost a fortune,” Tessa said, staring up at the vertical cascade of rooms, trying to distract herself from the chaos outside.

Hieroglyphs and carvings crowded every stone along the winding walkways. Every turn revealed another glimpse—a bar thrumming with music, a corridor of shops, water spilling over polished black rock. To their left, Tessa spotted a restaurant. Its sign promised family-style dining and a casual atmosphere, and she pointed. “Ray, there. I can live with that.”

He nodded, and together they crossed to the entrance, only to find a sign posted outside: “Opens at 9:00 a.m.”

A faint buzzing filled her ears. “What time is it?” she asked, squinting at the light.

“7:38,” Ray replied, checking his watch.

Tessa inhaled deeply, the smell of frying bacon and coffee teasing her senses. “But I can smell breakfast.”

Ray shot her a quick, mischievous look. “Trust your nose. I saw a sign for a café—the Pyramid Café. Let’s follow the arrows.”

They kept walking, the aroma of breakfast growing stronger with every step. They passed a bar and a hostess stand; a woman behind the podium looked up and greeted them.

“Table for two?” she asked.

“Yes, please,” Ray said.

The hostess led them down a row of mostly empty booths and tables, offering them a cushioned bench seat.

As they slid in, Tessa’s hands immediately reached for the menu, her tummy rumbling in anticipation. The waitress arrived within moments, all brisk efficiency, and took their order: two breakfast burritos and two coffees. The food landed on their table less than ten minutes later.

Tessa cradled her mug and let out a satisfied sigh. “It feels good to sit down.”

Ray agreed, massaging his lower back. “Farther than I thought.”

Tessa reclined, allowing herself a moment of relief. “Can we take a cab back to the hospital? I don’t think I’m up for another march through the desert. Maybe I’ll just curl up and fall asleep in the taxi.”

Ray gazed intently at her, brow furrowing. “You’re right. We don’t know what’s waiting for us at the hospital. Maybe we should just get a room here, catch some sleep, rent a car, and drive home.”

Her heart sank at the thought. “But aren’t the Nevada troopers supposed to watch out for us? I thought we were supposed to be protected.”

Ray shrugged, frustration creeping into his voice. “I bet they’re buried in paperwork from the mess at the hospital. I don’t think they care about us anymore.”

Tessa swallowed another bite, pushing her plate away. “I’m done. I could sleep for a week.”

They paid and shuffled back into the casino, blinking at the lights and noise. Down a ramp, they found the registration desk, and Ray booked a room for under sixty dollars: two queen beds on the second floor. The disbelief on his face mirrored her own.

“We should grab our things and stay longer,” he muttered.

Tessa yawned, fatigue washing over her. “I’ll decide after a nap.”

They took the elevator up, found their room, and Tessa collapsed on the nearest bed, asleep before her head hit the pillow. The exhaustion of the day settled over her like a warm blanket, and the world around her faded into darkness. The last thing she remembered was the sound of Ray moving around the room, but soon even that faded, leaving her enveloped in peaceful oblivion.

# # #

Back in Palo Alto, Special Agent Steve Anderson paced the floor of the FBI office, tension coiling in his gut. News of the Hollands' disappearance weighed heavily on him; they were supposed to be under protection, a crucial part of the investigation. He had dispatched Agents Connors and Perkins to Las Vegas to ensure their safety, but as time ticked away, jagged worries clawed at his mind.

His phone buzzed, and he answered without hesitation. "Connors, where are you?"

"SVH, Vegas," she replied, her tone clipped.

"Did you find the Hollands?"

"They're not here, sir."

Anderson's frustration surged. "What? Where are they? What happened to their protection?"

Connors quickly explained the chaos they had encountered in the emergency room. A knife incident had disrupted everything, causing mass confusion and evacuation. He clenched his jaw. "So we're back to square one," he fumed.

"They left their belongings here," she continued. "We think they'll return."

Anderson took a deep breath, attempting to stifle his rising anger. "And their cell phones?"

"In the bag with their things," she said.

"Great. The reason we're not tracking their phones. We can't catch a break," he muttered, his voice sour.

"Anderson, anything on Mishkin?" Connors pressed.

He pinched the bridge of his nose, recalling the near-miss from earlier that morning. His voice was steady but strained as he began, "The locals found a body in the woods not far from the Hollands' home. It was our guy from the house. A car fire nearby is suspected to be Mishkin destroying evidence. We stopped a nervous Hispanic man driving a horse trailer, but Mishkin slipped through our fingers."

Anderson paused, frustration gnawing at him. "The locals found that trailer abandoned south of Mountain View. The driver's in a coma at Stanford Hospital, and his family was gagged and tied up in one of the stables at the ranch he left from."

Connors gasped, piecing it together. "So you found your missing man?"

"Yeah, trying to get a positive ID now." His frustration simmered as he continued, "We suspect Mishkin killed him—a gunshot to the head. Not ours; he was dead before we fired."

"Lucky for you," Connors replied, her tone a mix of relief and concern.

"If it counts as luck. Find the Hollands. Check every hotel. Keep me posted."

"Already working on it," Connors replied.

Anderson ended the call, feeling the weight of urgency settle on his shoulders. The clock was ticking, and he needed to ensure the Hollands remained safe. He gathered his team, preparing to head out and chase down every lead they had. The stakes were rising, and he wouldn't let Mishkin slip away again.

CHAPTER THIRTY-FOUR

In the late afternoon, Tessa opened her eyes. The square of ceiling, the chill of the room, the hush of distant noise; on the other bed, Ray still slept, his chest slowly rising and falling. She sat up, looked around, then crossed the small gap to wake him. With a careful touch to his shoulder, his eyes flickered open.

"Oh my gosh, what time is it?"

"I have no idea. I just woke up myself."

Ray blinked hard, rolling onto an elbow. "I think we missed checkout time."

Tessa stretched, relief mingling with anxiety. "I guess we have an excuse to hang out another day. We can go explore." Just the thought of another day together felt like a small victory, but the weight of their situation pressed on her.

Ray flashed her a quick grin, but it slipped away almost immediately. "Don't get me wrong. I'm all about exploring, but I'm concerned about our stuff and GG-2. We should go get it."

"What about those troopers? The second we step inside the ER, they'll take us into protective custody." Tessa's voice tightened with urgency. "Remember, the CHP officer said the whole county was looking for us, including the FBI. We don't even know why, and they're at our home."

Ray sat up, rubbed his eyes. "Take it easy. We've done nothing wrong. The CHP said we're in some kind of danger. It tells me they know nothing about GG-1 or GG-2. Trust me, if they find out what we've experienced so far, things will change, and not for the better."

Tessa felt her heart race at the thought. How could they be in danger without even knowing why? It feels surreal.

Ray continued, "If they're at our house, whoever it is knows where we live. I don't think the Nevada troopers are supposed to take us home. The CHP said the FBI is coming here."

"Here, as in this hotel?" Tessa stood abruptly, throwing a glance at the window, as if expecting to see black vans below.

"No. At least not yet. They'll come to Vegas, to the hospital. Probably already there. But it won't be easy to find us since we haven't left many clues."

Tessa's eyes widened. "Clues? Oh my gosh, our cell phones. They can track us." Panic bubbled up as she thought about how little they understood their situation.

"They're at the hospital, powered off. Credit cards are traceable, but I paid cash. Vegas is a big town. They won't find us unless we help them. At this point, I'm not sure I want to."

She paced to the window, looking out over the city. "We're in some kind of danger, though?"

Ray shrugged, following her gaze. "True, in their opinion. What I am afraid of is their curiosity about GG-2."

Tessa angled back toward him, arms folded. "What makes you think they would be curious?"

"It's what they do. The less they know, the better for us."

"So now what?"

He smiled, but she detected an undercurrent of unease. "We go eat."

Tessa considered, then with a light shrug, "Works for me."

"Oh, and while we're out, I need to buy a calculator," Ray said, his brow furrowing in concentration. Tessa blinked at him, struggling to understand the significance.

"A calculator?"

"Yes. A scientific one. I need to do some calculations on what we experienced with GG-1 and 2. I ran it through my head, but I need to check the numbers."

She pointed at him, a hint of playful annoyance surfacing. "Okay. But we get to eat first." The thought of food felt like a necessary reprieve from their worries.

Ray nodded, and they both brushed at the wrinkles in their clothes, splashing water on their faces to shake off the remnants of the overnight stay. As they headed downstairs, Tessa felt a flicker of hope; perhaps a delicious meal would help distract them from the turmoil that had engulfed their lives.

At the registration desk, Ray paid for their second night in cash, his focus unwavering. Tessa couldn't help but admire his determination.

When the host recommended the Front Stage Deli, Tessa felt a surge of anticipation. "Sounds good," she said, eager for some semblance of normalcy.

They found the deli easily, and once seated, the menus were dropped in front of them. The scent of coffee and grilled food filled the air, her whole body waking to the promise of food. They both ordered coffee, Ray opting for a cheeseburger while Tessa chose a turkey burger, wishing it were possible to forget their troubles, even for a moment.

As the check arrived, Ray lifted his gaze toward the waitress. "Do you know any electronic stores in Vegas?"

Tessa felt a mix of amusement and tension as she watched Ray's concentration. His determination to work on the calculations, even now, was admirable. She couldn't help but appreciate his focus; it remained one of the things she loved about him, even if it made her anxious.

The waitress mentioned Best Buy on the East Side, and Tessa nodded, feeling the urgent need for preparations. They needed a calculator—if only it could help them make sense of their situation.

When they left the deli, Tessa squinted against the sunlight shimmering beyond the window. "How are we going to get to Best Buy in this weather?" The heat pressed down like an unwelcome weight.

"Cab. The town's full of them," Ray's tone stayed steady, and she took comfort in his confidence.

They stepped outside, the heat hitting them like a wall. Tessa saw Ray motion to the attendant, who jogged to the street and flagged down a cab in seconds. As they slid into the hot vinyl, she took a moment to breathe deeply, feeling the tension in her shoulders ease slightly.

"Where to?" the driver asked.

"Best Buy," Ray replied, his expression focused.

As they drove, Tessa watched the city roll past—vibrant lights, bustling tourists, and the sounds of laughter. It all felt surreal against the backdrop of their heightened reality.

"Ten minutes later, Ray emerged from Best Buy with a calculator in hand, the cab still idling nearby."

The driver glanced back at them. "Where to now?"

"Luxor, please," Ray replied, his voice steady. Tessa felt a rush of gratitude for his unwavering determination, a beacon of calm amid the uncertainty surrounding them.

As they journeyed through the bustling streets of Las Vegas, the neon lights and vibrant atmosphere filled Tessa with a sense of anticipation. "How long is it going to take to crunch those numbers?" she asked, glancing at Ray.

"A good two hours. Why?" He met her gaze, and for a moment, she could see the flicker of worry lurking beneath his calm exterior.

She tapped her foot, feeling restless energy. "I want to go shopping, look around." Despite the heaviness of their situation, she longed for a brief escape.

Ray hesitated, his brow furrowing as he read her expression. "Are you sure you want to do that? All by yourself?"

"Come on, you think I need help shopping?" she teased, trying to lighten the mood, though her heart raced with uncertainty.

Ray smirked, but concern still flickered in his eyes. "Just, after the last couple of days..."

Tessa felt a swell of appreciation for his caution. "Go ahead; I'm sure it's safe. Just look at the Luxor—so many people will be around!"

As the cab rolled to a stop in front of the grand entrance, she felt a mix of excitement and trepidation. Tessa leaned forward and pecked Ray on the lips. "See you in a couple of hours," she said, her words laced with anticipation.

Stepping out of the cab, Tessa navigated through the lively crowd spilling into the hotel, feeling the vibrant energy around her. The hotel lobby buzzed with tourists, staff, and vendors, their laughter creating a sharp contrast to the oppressive weight she carried.

As Tessa walked away, she felt a mix of apprehension and hope. Could she truly take a moment to breathe amidst all this chaos?

She walked back in to their hotel room, just an hour later.

Ray looked up, startled. "Wow, you were quick."

She dropped her purse on the bed, her hands empty. "There isn't much shopping besides souvenirs, exhibits, and food." Her brief adventure had provided no tangible comfort, only more questions.

Ray nodded at her unfilled hands. "Explains no bags."

"How's the number crunching going?" she asked, moving closer to him, eager to reconnect.

He held up the calculator, digits glowing. "I have preliminary figures. Some are exciting. Some are scary."

"Scary again?" Tessa felt a tightening in her chest, the fear creeping back in.

"Yes, actually. I need to double-check some things, but... if the FBI stuff doesn't stop us, I'd rather get back home and do more experiments with GG-2 or GG-1. We need to get our stuff."

Tessa's brow creased. "Maybe we should at least find out what the FBI knows. Can they really hold us if we haven't done anything wrong?"

Ray leaned back, his shoulders tense. "I'm not sure. With law enforcement, you have to know your rights. If they overreach and we're not prepared or don't have a lawyer, they can get the drop on us."

"There's something they're not telling us," she said quietly. "If we're in danger, what do they owe us? Why us? We're missing something."

Ray's fingers drummed the table, echoing her unease. "Maybe it's something from our past or something we know. How about the sealant?"

Tessa shook her head sharply. "It's not that. The company that bought the rights, Smith and Rhyne? They sold it to Transco in Texas for four times what I received. I saw it on the news in the lobby."

Ray's brows rose. "Wow."

Tessa's mouth twisted. "No kidding! I should have held out for more money."

Ray grinned, but it faded. "No, I mean wow, because it's an asphalt company. I bet they bought the patent and buried it.

You just pitched it to the wrong crowd. We'll learn from this and do better next time."

"You mean GG?"

"It's the only thing we have now. If it works, we're onto something."

Tessa stared at the wall, taking a moment to collect her thoughts. "Ray, GG-1 already flew. GG-2 dug a crater. Isn't that something?"

"Sure. But if we can dial it down a notch, it might be useful. Right now, GG-1 was a wild missile, and GG-2 was just scary."

She met his gaze, feeling the weight of their situation. "Almost killed you."

Ray nodded, stood, and walked to the window. "Exactly. Scary. But I have an idea."

He reached for the hotel phone and dialed.

"Security, please."

Tessa watched, curiosity piqued. "What are you doing?"

Ray pressed a finger to his lips. "Shhh."

"Security, Oscar Perez."

Ray spoke clearly. "Oscar. This is Ray Holland. We were in the ER last night. One of your security team locked up our stuff for safekeeping."

He listened intently, watching Tessa's expression shift.

"We're stuck at the Luxor Hotel. It might be a while before we come by. If you see the man and lady, let them know for us, would you?"

"Thank you. Goodbye." Ray hung up, a slight grin on his face.

Tessa's arms went up. "Now, what's the plan?"

Ray grinned back at her. "We go get our stuff."

"But you just told them we're stuck at the Luxor."

"Exactly. Oscar will inform the man and woman whom I presume is FBI, and they'll come here. That gives us a window."

"Sommers and Fitz?"

"No. Security said man and woman."

Tessa frowned, a flutter of anxiety creeping back in. "What if they arrive before we leave?"

"They won't. We're gone in five minutes."

She blinked, processing the plan. “Then what? We just walk into the hospital and grab our stuff?”

“That’s the plan.”

They stepped out the door and into the elevator, glancing past the reservation desk and toward the port concierge. Ray pointed.

“Tessa, look. It’s the same cab and driver.”

The driver recognized them, popped out, and ushered them in, his service as crisp as before.

“Where to?”

“Spring Valley Hospital,” Ray replied.

“Should take about fifteen minutes.”

The cab pulled away from the curb.

CHAPTER THIRTY-FIVE

Across town, the cab rolled up in front of Spring Valley Hospital. "Pull up to the ER," Ray directed, watching the familiar entrance slide into view. His chest tightens as he thinks about what lay ahead. "This time, I definitely need you to wait, but pull forward a little out of sight." The driver nodded.

Tessa's voice trembled as she stepped out: "We're going to get in so much trouble, Ray." He offered a faint smirk and held the door for her, wishing he could reassure her more.

"Tessa, just go with me on this. Oscar probably spoke to the two FBI agents within minutes of my call, and they left in a hurry. How do I know? There are no cars parked here that look FBI." The tension in his voice surprised even him; he needed to keep her calm.

Inside, the ER looked restored, as if turmoil had washed through and withdrawn, leaving only faint traces: neat rows of chairs, no blood, every magazine and table back in its place. Yet the air still felt thick with unspoken worries.

Ray leaned in at the reception desk. "Hi, we're the Hollands. Could you call security, please? We are here to pick up the gear they stored for us?"

The woman at the desk barely looked up, her focus on the computer screen. "Someone is on their way," she said flatly.

Ray swept his gaze across the lobby, his heart racing slightly. "I hope they hurry," he whispered to Tessa, feeling the weight of uncertainty.

A few minutes later, a young security officer appeared, crisp in her uniform. "Are you the Hollands?" she asked, and Ray presented his ID, feeling a surge of urgency.

She studied it and nodded. "Thank you, Mr. Holland. Right this way."

She led them through a hallway Ray and Tessa both remembered, stopping at a locked door. She opened it, and there they were: two backpacks, exactly as left, and GG-2, still poised on the dolly. Relief flooded through him, but it came short-lived.

Suddenly, the door swung wider. A man entered, breathless. Oscar Perez. His badge confirmed it.

"Mr. and Mrs. Holland?"

"Yes," Ray answered, recognition flashing in his mind.

Oscar studied them closely. "Didn't you call me from Luxor a few minutes ago? Said you were stuck there."

Ray didn't blink, keeping his composure steady. "We were, but the FBI came and brought us back here for our stuff."

Oscar hesitated—a pause stretching between heartbeats. "Are they here now?"

"Yes, yes, of course," Ray said, lying easily. "How else would we have gotten here?" Anxiety pulsed beneath his skin, the lie feeling slippery.

Oscar chewed his lip, eyeing the hallway. Ray pressed on. "Mr. Perez. We are in a hurry, and they're waiting for us in the car. Would you like me to tell them you delayed us in the retrieval of our gear?"

Oscar shook his head. "No, no, of course not. Teresa, please help the Hollands with their gear."

Ray wheeled the dolly into the corridor, Tessa right behind with both backpacks. He felt a surge of urgency as he moved, eager to leave the hospital and the uncertainty behind. Teresa led, Oscar trailing, locking the storeroom as they left. In the lobby, Ray halted, scanning the space again. Tessa kept moving toward the exit, bags in hand, a determined look on her face.

"Mr. Holland, what's wrong?" Oscar asked, watching Ray pat down his pockets.

Ray feigned confusion, his heart racing. "I think I dropped my wallet. Did you see it?"

The two security officers peered down the hall. "I don't see it," Oscar replied, glancing back at Ray.

Ray put on a look of disappointment, hoping to buy a few moments. "Oh no, it must be in the storeroom."

"I'll go check," Oscar said, already hurrying back. Teresa, loyal, followed.

Ray grinned, glancing out at the waiting cab. He made the push for the doors, dolly rolling smoothly over the threshold. Tessa had the side door of the cab open, ready for GG-2. Ray swung it onto the back seat with her help; Tessa climbed in after, while Ray took shotgun and shut the cab door.

"Go, go, go," Ray ordered, adrenaline surging as the driver glanced back at them.

"Where to?" the driver asked, eyes darting between Ray and the mirror.

"Airport," Ray said, pointing to the road ahead.

"Airport?" Tessa's eyes widened; she shot Ray a look filled with concern.

"Rental," he told her, voice calm but firm. "We're going home."

"The FBI might be there," Tessa cautioned, her voice tinged with worry.

Ray shrugged, pushing down his own anxiety. "Better we meet them there than here. They pick us up now, who knows when we get home. Home is where the answers are."

Tessa nodded, and the cab peeled away, weaving through traffic toward the airport. Upon arrival, Ray told the driver to wait with Tessa and GG-2 while he found a rental agency. At Hertz, he paid cash for a one-day Ford sedan, gambling their Subaru would be waiting at home.

He signed the paperwork in a flurry, then hustled to the curb, paid the cabbie, and loaded GG-2 into the trunk. In the rising heat, Ray and Tessa stood for a moment on opposite sides of the car, a private grin passing between them. Tessa clapped her hands; Ray tapped a staccato rhythm on the hood. Then both slipped into the car.

CHAPTER THIRTY-SIX

Agent Anderson sat in the stuffy, second-floor conference room of the FBI Resident Agency office in Palo Alto, frustration simmering beneath the surface. The Mishkin trail had gone cold, and the morning had dragged into afternoon with nothing but stale coffee and paperwork as company. Stevenson entered, paper in hand, eyes darting with the hint of urgency.

"Sir, I have a positive ID on the deceased from the Holland shooting."

"That was fast," Anderson said, standing and reaching for the report.

"A Jason Bentz," Stevenson replied.

Before Anderson could process the name, a brisk knock rattled the door. Stevenson answered it. Agent Pommeroy leaned in, already braced for confrontation.

"Sorry for the interruption, but I just heard," Pommeroy started.

"Heard what?" Anderson asked.

"The DB."

"Jason Bentz. We just received the report," Anderson replied.

"Yes, Agent Jason Bentz. He's FBI," Pommeroy said.

"What!" Anderson screamed, snatching the report from Stevenson. "Give me that."

"Counterintelligence Division," Pommeroy offered, as Anderson's eyes snapped across the page.

"I shot an FBI agent," Anderson growled, voice low and tight. "What the hell was he doing in the Hollands' house? Oh, I want answers, gentlemen."

"Sir, it gets more complicated," Stevenson said, cautioning with a hand.

"How so?" Anderson demanded.

"He's Agent Sommers' lead. Bentz also reports directly to the Executive Assistant in the National Security Branch," Stevenson said, watching him.

"Agents Murray and Johnson know about this yet?"

"Yes, sir."

"Stevenson, get George Palto on the phone for me," Anderson ordered. "I don't care how long it takes. I need to talk with Palto."

Stevenson slipped from the room, leaving the door to settle in his wake. The silence lasted seven seconds before another knock. Agent Murray this time.

"Sir, Connors called me and is trying to reach you," Murray said.

Anderson patted his jacket with impatience. "Damn, where's my cell phone?"

"You can use mine, sir," Murray said, passing the device over.

Anderson dialed Connors. Second ring.

"Hello," Connors answered.

"It's Anderson. You trying to reach me? Good news, I hope."

"Sorry, sir, but the Hollands are in a rental car, and we believe they're headed home."

Anderson clamped his jaw. "You're sure?"

"I believe so. They left the hotel they were in and booked a rental."

"What makes you think they aren't just driving around Vegas?"

"They asked the rental agent where the nearest drop-off was to their home in Palo Alto."

"Okay, sounds reasonable. We'll be here waiting for them."

"Orders, sir?" Connors asked.

"Get back here. Catch a plane. Meet us at the Hollands' when you get here. Oh, we have an update on the DB. He's with the FBI, Counterintelligence Division."

"Oh no. Sir, that doesn't make sense."

"Get this. He was Sommers' lead."

"Sir, what does this mean?"

"It means we have a lot of work to do. See what you can find out about Jason Bentz on your way here," Anderson ordered.

"Yes, sir."

Stevenson knocked again, this time holding out his cell phone. Anderson swapped for it, returning Murray's with barely a nod.

"George Palto, sir," Stevenson whispered.

Anderson pressed the phone to his ear. "George Palto, Special Agent Steve Anderson here."

"What can I do for you, Mr. Anderson?" Palto's voice came hollow and official.

"Sir, we have been working on a protection order for Ray and Tessa Holland, which you signed two weeks ago. There are no specific details on the reason for the order, and the situation here has resulted in three FBI agents dead. I was hoping you could fill in some holes for us."

"Three FBI agents dead. This is terrible, but Mr. Anderson, I have not executed a protection order for anyone recently. Who are these Hollands, anyway?"

"You never issued a protection order for the Hollands?"

"No. I've never heard of the Hollands."

Anderson's hand tightened on the phone. "Sir, it looks like a fraudulent order was executed within the Bureau with your name on it, I'm afraid. I'll be turning this over to an investigative team to look into."

"Mr. Anderson. Who are the dead agents?" Palto said, dismay creeping through.

"Agent Steve Sommers, Joel Fitz, and Jason Bentz. Bentz is apparently with Counterintelligence Division," Anderson explained.

"Bentz, Jason Bentz, you say?"

"Yes, sir. Do you know him?"

"No, I haven't met him, but the Bureau is looking for him regarding some intelligence that came out of Moscow."

"Intelligence? What kind of intelligence?"

"They were investigating a trip he took to Moscow, where he was reportedly seen meeting with an Aleksander Koslov, a known weapons dealer," Palto said.

"Sir, does the name Mishkin mean anything to you?"

"No, I can't say it does."

"Thank you for clearing up a few things for us, sir. I'll let you go."

"Keep me informed," Palto said, and the line went dead.

Anderson snapped the phone closed and turned to Stevenson. "Get the team assembled in the conference room." He watched Stevenson hurry out, urgency in every step.

Minutes later, six agents sat with taut faces, Anderson at the head of the table, arms folded, gaze sweeping the room.

"Gentlemen, it appears we have been misled by an invalid order from the Bureau. There is no protection order for the Hollands after all. Now the question is, why were Sommers and Fitz assigned this order, and then murdered? In addition, why was an agent from the Counterintelligence Division in the Holland house? Also, what is the connection between Sommers and Bentz? These are the questions we need to get answered. The false order I'll submit to San Francisco to investigate. I feel Hollands are no longer a responsibility of ours at this point. All of our resources stay on this hunt for Mishkin. Let the locals handle Hollands after we meet with them when they get back. Apparently, they are on their way home from Vegas, and should be there by dark. Stevenson and I'll go there to meet them. Connors and Perkins are on their way back. Murray, put a call into the airport, messaging them to come here, instead of Hollands, assisting in our investigation, location and apprehension of Mishkin. Johnson, put a call into the local sheriff's office and have them sit on Hollands' house in case they get there before we do. Any questions?"

No one spoke. Even the wall clock kept quiet.

"Okay, then let's get to it. Stevenson, we will head to Hollands' about 3:00 p.m."

# # #

Tessa and Ray waited in a cramped line at the Los Banos Brown Bear Diner. The place throbbed with voices; high-noon sunlight cast everything into a pale glare through the windows. They stood for ten minutes, then were seated by the glass that framed the highway. Ray ordered the ribs special, while Tessa chose a Caesar salad. The food arrived in a neat, steamy arrangement, but neither was especially hungry.

"So, what's the plan when we get home?" Tessa asked, pushing lettuce across her plate.

"I figure the FBI will be there waiting for us, and we'll need to deal with them. Hopefully, we'll get an explanation for this danger we're in."

"Will they keep us out of the house, do you think?"

"They could," Ray answered after a pause, "but I have a feeling they won't."

"I'm ready for things to get back to some semblance of normal," Tessa said.

"Don't worry. I think things will be back to normal soon. I'll be back at Laubner."

Every moment spent with Tessa felt like a ticking clock. He wanted to shield her from the dangers that were closing in, but how could he when he was the one working on technology that attracted all this interest?

Was this really going to change their lives, or was it just another experiment that could lead to disaster?

Ray's face pinched, then shifted.

"Oh no, Laubner. I need to call my dad. They have probably been trying to reach us at the house, and we haven't been there."

"Do you think they stopped by?" Tessa asked, concern flicking in her voice.

"I doubt it. After we finish eating, I should call."

They finished the meal in steady silence, eyes watchful. Ray flagged a hostess for the bill, left cash and a tip behind, and walked with Tessa out to the rental car. The sun hit them hard, sweat already trickling down their backs before they reached the doors.

No matter what happened, he resolved to keep Tessa safe and make things right. He was done letting fear dictate his actions.

Inside, they cranked the air conditioning and sat for a moment, the chilly air washing away the heat. Ray dug through his backpack for his cell phone, powered it on, and dialed.

"Hello," Ray said when someone answered.

"Dad, it's me, Ray."

"Son. Where are you? We've been worried about you."

"Long story. We went on a road trip and ended up in Vegas."

"Vegas?"

"Like I said, long story."

"Is Tessa with you?"

"Yes, of course."

"Road trip, huh? What prompted that?"

"We took GG-2 to the desert for a test. I told you, didn't I?"

"I remember you saying you would do another test, and I said be sure and stand back."

"I seem to recall. Unfortunately, I didn't stand back far enough and got scraped up a bit."

"Don't get yourself hurt now. Your mother and I were talking just last night about grandchildren. They're in our future, aren't they?"

Ray felt his father's casual mention of grandchildren weigh on him. How could he even think of starting a family when their lives were in such disarray?

"Yes, Dad, don't worry. It will happen one of these days."

"What, are you getting seriously hurt, or is Tessa having a baby?" Dave asked.

"The baby, Dad," Ray said, and as he spoke, Tessa looked over, eyebrows raised.

"Baby?" Tessa whispered.

Ray raised a hand to silence her, eyes warning her off. She glared back, more insistent.

"What baby?" she pressed, voice just above the hum of the A/C.

Ray waved her off, but she batted his hand away this time.

"Hey Dad, I need to go. We're headed home, so can I call you later?"

"Sure, that's fine."

"Okay, I'll call you later. Bye," Ray said, snapping the phone shut.

"Baby, what about a baby?" Tessa demanded.

"My dad was asking about when we'll have a baby."

"Why would he ask about a baby?"

"Apparently, they were talking about it last night. You know, the grandchildren thing."

She leaned back, thought it through. "Okay, I get it. So, we can rest assured this conversation is going to come up again. We might want to work out an appropriate answer for next time."

"What's that supposed to mean?" Ray shot back. "Do you want to have a baby?"

"Of course I want to have a baby—not right now. We just need to discuss our approach to their pressing questions," Tessa finished, voice gentle.

"Okay, I get it. We can do that. Probably later when we have a quiet night or something."

"I agree. We should get going so we don't get home after dark."

They started the engine, the dashboard blinking in the late afternoon glare. The road home waited, quiet and flat as anticipation.

CHAPTER THIRTY-SEVEN

After zigzagging through the last light at El Camino, Ray eased up to the curb before their house, watching the dark four-door sedan parked tight to the bumper of their dusty Subaru. The white Ford Crown Victoria, Santa Clara Sheriff stenciled in navy, sat idling on the street like a pale stone against the curb.

Of course they'd be here, waiting for them. He'd been expecting this. But a pulse hammers at the base of his throat—what answers would they provide?

The afternoon light threw hard blue shadows over the driveway, and as Ray set the gear and shut off the car, two men in agency-grade suits opened their doors in sync and stepped onto the concrete.

He glanced at Tessa, noting her unease. The last thing he wanted was for her to feel scared or threatened. It was his job to keep her safe, and the weight of responsibility loomed larger by the minute.

"This would be the FBI," Ray said, pulling the key from the ignition and inhaling through his teeth.

As the men approached, Ray shifted uneasily in his seat. They stood between the bumpers, hands at their sides. The first spoke. "Ray Holland?"

"I'm Ray. And you are?"

"FBI. Special Agent Anderson, and this is Agent Stevenson," he said, turning to Tessa. "And you must be Tessa Holland?"

Tessa nodded, squinting against the light. "I'm Tessa. What's going on?"

Ray watched Anderson carefully. His tone held a calmness which felt rehearsed, adding to Ray's unease. "Maybe we should go inside and talk," Anderson suggested.

Ray's eyes flicked from the agents to the garage, where the door stood ajar, three fingers of sunlight slicing through the shadow. “Was there a break-in or something?” he asked, his voice tight, already half aware of the answer.

“We should really talk inside,” Anderson repeated, his demeanor unyielding.

Ray didn’t wait. He sidestepped the agents, hurried to the open side door, swung it wide, and flipped the light. The garage echoed back, hollow and empty. Anderson and Stevenson followed; Tessa trailed, her arms tight across her ribs.

Ray’s voice cracked as he scanned the workbench. “It’s gone. GG-1 is gone.” He rounded on the FBI agents. “What did you do with my equipment?”

Panic surged through him as he scanned the empty garage. GG-1 wasn’t just a project; it was a part of him. What had they lost?

Anderson shook his head. “Mr. Holland, there’s been more than one breach at your home. We didn’t move anything. I’ll need you to do an inventory and make a report.”

Ray’s eyes locked on Tessa. “GG-1 is gone.”

Tessa’s hand flew to her mouth, disbelief washing over her. “Who would take it?”

His gaze shifted to the empty shadows of the garage, a chill creeping up his spine. “Not just GG-1. The plans, the controller, the stones—the whole project. We’re cleaned out.”

Tessa’s voice sounded brittle, echoing his fears. “What do we do now?”

Stevenson spoke quietly. “You’ll need to fill out a police report, Mrs. Holland.”

Tessa’s reply came sharp as a tack. “I wasn’t asking you. I meant my husband.”

Ray patted her arm, trying to infuse her with calm. He felt the weight of his responsibility pressing down on him. *I need to keep her steady. If I can just get rid of these agents sooner rather than later, maybe she can relax.* “He’s right. Let’s take care of the report.”

Anderson motioned toward the kitchen door. “Let’s go inside and sit down. There’s a lot to discuss.”

Ray paused at the threshold, fists pressed to his temples, then squared himself and took two long, slow breaths. Tessa's hand at his back steered him through. Inside, the agents took chairs at the kitchen table. The linoleum appeared cool and clean, shining in the silence.

Anderson led with a question: "Mr. and Mrs. Holland, did you have any other federal agents at your home recently?"

Ray remembered the names. "Yes. Sommers and Fitz."

"I'd like to file a complaint," Ray added, the words tumbling out. "They were rude. Not how I'd expect the FBI to act."

"What were they investigating?" Anderson pressed.

Ray shrugged, feeling the tension rise again. "Explosion at Chemco, where Tessa worked. They asked about Tessa, her time at Chemco. Then they became interested in my projects, even hinted I was building a bomb. Which is ridiculous."

Their behavior had been off, out of character for the FBI. He couldn't shake the feeling their questions masked something more sinister.

Stevenson's pen moved across his pad, quick and silent, while Anderson's eyes flicked between them, making Ray feel like they were pieces on a chessboard.

"Did they say anything else?" Anderson asked.

Ray shook his head. "No. Just the usual questions. They left."

Anderson's voice softened. "I apologize if their conduct was inappropriate."

Ray's brow furrowed. "But why are you here instead of them?"

Anderson's answer was blunt: "Both Agent Sommers and Agent Fitz were ambushed and killed in front of your house."

This was no longer just about his work. This was about their lives.

Tessa caught her breath with a gasp. "They're dead?"

Anderson nodded slowly. "Yes."

Ray's voice was thin as paper. "Who would do that? Have you found them?"

Anderson was careful. "We have a suspect, and we are actively searching for him."

"Him?" Ray's knuckles whitened. "One person?"

"Yes, one individual."

Tessa's gaze drifted up the stairwell. Her face tensed. "Wait. Something isn't right."

She stood and took a few steps, nose lifted. "Ray, do you smell that?"

Ray sniffed the air. "Electrical. Like a short."

Anderson kept his voice measured. "We need to fill you in on an incident here."

Tessa braced herself. "More than two agents shot in the street?"

Anderson nodded. "We found your home broken into. While investigating, we discovered an armed intruder upstairs. Someone shot him through a window while we were here. There's more, but the team already processed the scene and took the evidence. A contracted remediation crew is scheduled for tomorrow, and the window gets replaced."

Ray stared upstairs. "Can we go up there?"

"I wouldn't advise it," Anderson said. "Let the post processing team do their work first."

He tapped the tabletop, shifting the conversation. "We need to get back to finding this killer."

Ray's voice was low, urgent. "Are we in danger? What about the protection order?"

Anderson exhaled. "The order was in error. I apologize. Until we apprehend the suspect, we've asked the local sheriff to post an officer at your house. He'll stay until the situation is resolved."

"I don't know if I can even sleep here," Tessa whispered.

Ray leveled his gaze at Anderson. "Do you know who took my work? Do you have a name?"

Anderson deflected. "We have a suspect, but can't release the name at this point."

Ray leaned forward. "Mishkin. Victor Mishkin. Is he the person you're looking for?"

Anderson's reaction was visible. "How do you know that name?"

Ray insisted. "Is it him?"

Anderson's eyes narrowed. "Let's keep to my questions. How do you know Victor Mishkin?"

Ray gestured at Tessa. "He's been harassing my wife. Following her, asking about my research."

Anderson switched targets. "Mrs. Holland, when did you last see Mishkin?"

Tessa counted them off. "Twice at Stanford. Once at a restaurant last week. He wanted to know what Ray was working on, and why he wasn't at work."

Anderson and Stevenson exchanged a look. Stevenson's pen scratched more notes.

"How would he know your husband wasn't working?" Anderson pressed.

Tessa shook her head. "I don't know. He claimed to be doing research at Stanford, but I couldn't verify that. I think he was trespassing."

"These were the only times you saw him?" Anderson asked.

"Yes. And you believe he killed your agents?"

Anderson was deliberate. "We believe so."

Tessa's hands twisted in her lap. "Then we can't stay here, Ray. Please."

Anderson's tone shifted, gentler. "I think Mishkin has what he came for. He's probably on the run. If he wanted to hurt you, he would have. We recommend staying somewhere else. The sheriff will monitor the house. Here's my card. Call me if anything comes up, and let me know when you return."

Ray nodded toward Tessa. "We'll get a hotel, stay in town for a few nights."

Anderson pushed back his chair, signaling the end. "If you see Mishkin, call 911, then call me. Do not confront him. We're closing in, and it's only a matter of time."

Ray surveyed the kitchen, then out the window. "We still have our overnight bags. We can just lock up and go."

Everyone gathered in the driveway, shaking hands, the agents heading for their car. Ray slipped behind the wheel, but as he pulled forward, something caught his eye on the porch—a square box, brown cardboard, slit open.

"What's that?" Ray said, slowing the car.

Tessa peered. “Where?”

“On the porch. An open package.”

Ray was already halfway out of the car; Tessa joined him.

He stopped at the first step and squinted. “It’s the battery for GG-2.”

Tessa frowned. “Why is it open?”

Ray hefted the box, a chill running down his spine. “Maybe the FBI wanted a look, or Mishkin missed it. If he’d gotten the battery, he’d have everything needed for GG-1 to operate in San Francisco Bay.” He shook his head. “Could be very dangerous.”

“Extremely,” Tessa agreed.

Ray tucked the box under his arm. “Time to find a hotel,” he said, and this time, neither of them looked back as they drove away.

CHAPTER THIRTY-EIGHT

Ray eased the car down Alma Street in Palo Alto, scanning the rows of low, sunbaked buildings crowding the curb. Every glance in the rearview mirror felt like a reminder of their precarious situation. The FBI had suggested Mishkin likely obtained what he wanted from the theft of GG-1, yet Ray couldn't shake the feeling the danger wasn't over. Mishkin might still be after answers, and the possibility of him needing help to understand GG-1's true potential gnawed at Ray. Each moment spent out in the open heightened his anxiety, knowing curiosity could lead someone like Mishkin straight to them.

Tessa spotted the sign first—a simple, hand-painted script reading Melo Inn, perched above a two-story stucco with walls the color of soft butter. She pointed, the sunlight catching on her wrist.

"How about that place? Melo Inn. It's what we need, a mellow place to stay," she said.

Ray nodded, liking it before he spoke. "Actually, I like it. We can park right outside our room, so I can move GG-2 inside where it's safe, plus I can work on it."

Tessa peered at the thick traffic rolling past. "It's on a busy street, so maybe it would be safe here."

Ray picked up the key from the front desk, the host barely glancing at them, and led them to a room on the main floor. Inside, they found a double bed, plus a small kitchenette: two electric burners, a fridge humming in the corner, a battered microwave, shiny metal sink, and a black plastic coffeemaker perched on the counter like a roosting bird.

"I'm thinking this will work for a few days," Tessa said, her attention snagging on a four-foot by six-foot wood table and four sturdy matching chairs, the surface scuffed but solid.

Ray eyed the table. "I agree. The table is perfect to set GG-2 on. If anything happened to GG-2, it would be a blow not just to my work but to our future." He felt a strange mix of pride and fear about how much depended on this project.

"And where are we going to eat?"

"On the bed, the floor, or in the car," Ray replied, quick and a little sharp.

"The bed it is then," she said, almost a tease, and they laughed together, a sudden relief after the road.

"Did I hear the host mention a laundry room we can use?" Tessa asked, looking around.

Here they were, living out of bags and worrying about dirty clothes. Just a week ago, they had been planning their future together in their new home. What had gone wrong?

"He mentioned it, and I saw a sign just to the right of the soda machine down the walkway."

"Great. I'm going to wash up a few items since we've been living in these clothes for days, and it's showing."

He couldn't let this situation defeat them. They would find a way to make it through.

"You mean smells?" Ray shot her a sideways grin.

She bristled but kept smiling. "Are you implying I stink? Remember, you've been in these same clothes as well, and you were in a hole fighting for your life."

"Well, that being true, all those clothes are trashed. What I have on is all I have. If you wash these, I'll be sitting here in nothing."

Tessa met his gaze, serious for just a second, then a laugh broke through. "I don't see a problem."

"I'll freeze."

"You must be joking. If you haven't looked outside, it's still over seventy-five degrees."

Ray shrugged. Tessa had a plan. "Tell you what, why don't we unload the car, you hop in the shower, and I'll do your laundry with mine? You can wear a towel until it's done. If you get cold, you can crawl into bed."

"These clothes are definitely ripe," he said, stabbing his finger toward the door.

They shuffled outside to the car, each trip bringing in another backpack and the inert weight of GG-2 along with its controller. Ray went straight to the shower, letting the hot water hammer his shoulders, relishing the warmth that chased away the exhaustion clinging to him.

When he finished showering and stepped into the room, he spotted Tessa returning, arms loaded with clean, warm clothes.

"You were right. It's not cold, especially once I lowered the A/C."

Tessa lifted the laundry basket to the dresser. "Well, I have your clothes here, unless you want to stay like that. Just hope we don't have a fire drill or some other emergency that puts us on the street," she laughed.

Ray barely looked up while punching numbers on his calculator. "Well, if word gets out about GG-2's capabilities, they might break down the door."

That caught her. "What do you mean?" She started folding shirts without thinking.

Ray stood the calculator on the table like a trophy. "Remember the hole we created?"

"Yes. How could I forget?" Her voice went flat.

"I was able to complete a rough estimate of its force factor."

"Force factor?"

"Newton's really. You know, like the law of gravity."

Tessa sat on the edge of the bed, following his hands as he spoke.

He tried to explain without confusing her. "There are basically three types of force: gravitational, magnetic, and nuclear. We can focus on gravity since it's easy to observe and the simplest to measure. We measure gravity, for example, by a force quantity, which has both direction and magnitude. The magnitude is measured in units called newtons. So, when an object like GG-2 is in motion, we can quantify the energy as the momentum of GG-2: the product of its mass and its velocity."

"Okay, I'm confused."

Ray paused, pulling the threads together. "Maybe this is better—you know Newton's law: every particle attracts every other particle in the universe with a force directly proportional to their masses, and inversely proportional to the square of the distance between them."

She gave a helpless gesture. "Now you've totally lost me."

He let out a short laugh. "Twenty million newtons of force were executed by GG-2 in the making of the hole."

She whistled. "You know if I had studied physics instead of chemistry, it would mean more, but twenty million's a big number, so I'm impressed . . . and scared at the same time."

He nodded. "Which is the point—a lot of force. Not only did GG-2 execute that force, but it wasn't damaged or destroyed. Somehow, it executes this force around the object it's contained in. This may also explain why GG-1 didn't meltdown after flying at Mach 2."

It thrilled him to think about GG-2's potential, but what if it drew the wrong kind of attention? The stakes were higher than ever.

Tessa tilted her head. "Okay, would I be wrong in saying this is a significant discovery?"

Ray weighed the implications, then shook his head. "Yes and no, I'm afraid. All the stones and GG-1 are gone, and so is any further development of this project."

"Maybe you could call your dad and get more stones from Laubner," Tessa suggested.

"My dad said they were to eventually be disposed of out of state. I'll have to ask."

"If there are still more, then problem solved, right?"

"In the short term. But this is a limited supply, and at some point, more stones would need to be produced if something like GG-1 were to go into production."

She frowned, considering. "Well, would that be doable?"

Ray raked a hand through his hair. "I'm not sure. It's not even clear to me how they were created. Apparently, an accident several years ago at Laubner, and they found the stones in the debris. My dad was part of the team which dismantled the site and put together all the reports of the event."

"So, it's an element. Simple enough. It should be doable to recreate it. We just need to research what occurred and what elements were present," Tessa said, her voice steady.

Ray looked at her, respect clear in his tone. "Coming from a chemist who created a sealant worth millions, you exert an abundance of confidence in our ability to do this. Once again, I'll have to ask my dad to see if we can get the reports on the accident. Hey, did you call Anderson to let him know where we are yet?"

Ray rifled through the clean pile of fresh clothes as Tessa dialed Agent Anderson. He could hear her side of the conversation—brief and to the point, just the way she preferred it.

After a few moments, she hung up.

He finished buttoning his shirt then asked, "So, was Anderson glad we checked in?"

Tessa looked at him with a small grin. "He thanked me. Seemed eager to get off the call."

Ray's brow furrowed. "Did he have any updates on Mishkin?"

"No."

He exhaled, frustrated. "I'm going to call my dad and see if we can get together tomorrow and go over our situation and get some of these questions answered. Dad might get a kick out of seeing GG-2."

Ray picked up the rotary phone, the dial whirring under his finger. His mother answered.

"Mom, it's me Ray."

"Oh, hi Ray, so good to hear your voice. You and Tessa doing okay? Seems like we haven't spoken in weeks."

"Mom, it hasn't been that long. Hey, is Dad around?"

"He just went to bed. Something I can do for you?"

"We wanted to come by. I have some questions about work-related things."

Her voice warmed. "Well, why don't you and Tessa come over for dinner tomorrow night, and you can get all your questions answered, and while you do, Tessa and I can talk lady talk."

His voice warmed as he pictured her in the kitchen. "Okay, Mom, see you and Dad about five-ish?"

"Five o'clock it is. See you then."

They each said goodbye and hung up.

"My guess, we are having dinner with your parents' tomorrow night, based on the conversation," Tessa said, folding the last shirt.

"Correct."

"We should bring something," she added.

"There won't be room on the table for anything, if I know my mom."

"How about a bottle of wine?"

Ray agreed. "Sounds doable."

Later, Ray settled at the table, bent over formulas and calculations late into the night, the room lit by yellow lamplight while Tessa watched TV stretched out on the bed. He needed to understand what had gone wrong, to take control back. The weight of uncertainty hung over him like a storm cloud. Eventually, silence crept in, and they called it a night, the hum of the old air conditioner melding with the soft click of numbers in Ray's calculator and the promise of answers tomorrow.

CHAPTER THIRTY-NINE

The next sunrise found Tessa blinking against the soft yellow glow of the Melo Inn's walls, the color still strange enough to remind her this wasn't home. In the corner, Ray had GG-2 pried open across the little table, hunched over the center console, coffee at his elbow, hands deep in the guts of the device.

"You're up early and back at it." Tessa stretched, rubbing at her eyes. She felt a mix of admiration and concern as she watched him work. She wanted him to succeed, but she couldn't shake the worry about his obsession with the project.

Ray didn't look up. "Well, I wanted to get GG-2 converted to flight mode, instead of digging holes. When we get it back home, I'm sure I'll have a fix for the speed and direction figured out."

She shook her head, letting a touch of humor surface. "Impressive. Now, we won't be falling into holes or ducking for cover."

"Or taking helicopter flights for emergency recovery operations," Ray laughed.

Tessa peered at the mess of parts, then met Ray's sleep-rumpled gaze. "So, what's the plan for today?" She tried to keep her tone light, even as anxiety stirred in her chest.

"Dinner with my dad and mom, of course. Picking up a bottle of wine."

Ray's face dimmed a little, tension settling into his shoulders. She knew he felt the weight of their situation, and it made her chest tighten with concern for them both.

Tessa cut him off. "A change of clothes, maybe?"

"We have clothes at home; we could just go get some there," Ray shot back.

She caught his gaze, her voice firm. "I'm not going upstairs in our home until it's cleaned up by the FBI. If I see a drop of blood on the wall or carpet, I'll never forget it. It's already hard enough knowing someone was shot in our home and probably died there."

Ray nodded, his smile fading as if reflecting her unease. "Shopping, then. How about breakfast first?"

She agreed. They dressed in their freshly laundered clothes, splashed water on their faces, and made their way out, with Tessa double-checking the "Do Not Disturb" sign on the doorknob to guard the half-dismantled GG-2. They slipped into the rental car, the windows fogged slightly from the morning chill, and Ray scanned up and down Alma Street.

"What are you feeling like today?" He pulled out, eyes darting to the curb.

"Traditional. Eggs, bacon, pancakes," she replied.

"I see a House of Pancakes down the street. How about that?"

She nodded, and they drove the two blocks in silence, both hungry but saying little. Inside, the air thick with the sweet scent of syrup and frying batter, a hostess in a light blue blouse appeared instantly and led them to a booth by the window. The place was half full: young families corralling toddlers, old couples sipping coffee. Menus slapped onto the table.

Ray slid into his seat. "Remember, we're having dinner at my parents' tonight, so save some room. My mom will put on a huge spread if I know her."

Tessa barely glanced up. "I'll eat enough so we can skip lunch," her words muffled behind the menu.

"Okay. I just don't want to embarrass..."

"Don't worry about your mom's feelings." Tessa cut him off, matter-of-fact. "I have this covered."

A flicker of anxiety stirred beneath her calm façade as Ray watched her, doubt and admiration mixing in his eyes. She wanted to be the force of nature he believed her to be, but the weight of their circumstances gnawed at her. When the waitress arrived, Tessa ordered Canadian bacon and scrambled eggs, along with buttermilk pancakes and coffee, hoping each bite would anchor them in a moment that felt ordinary. Ray, bemused, ordered a ham and cheese omelet, sliced banana, and coffee as well. Their food arrived twenty minutes later, and they finished it in half the time, grateful for the brief respite from the uncertainty looming over them.

"I think we were hungry," Ray said, pushing back from the table.

Tessa grinned. "Totally satisfied."

He eyed her, then the remains of pancakes. "Do you want to let it settle, or get right to shopping?"

"Shopping. No telling how long this will take." She patted her tummy for emphasis.

The drive to Macy's went quickly. Tessa navigated familiar streets, her mind wandering through their recent whirlwind of events. Once they arrived, she and Ray headed straight for the escalator, excitement bubbling in her chest. As they rose into the women's department, she took in the vibrant array of dresses displayed around her. Within minutes, Tessa spotted a black Ralph Lauren slim fit V-neck hanging on a nearby rack. She snatched it up and held it against her frame, studying her reflection in the nearby mirror. Would it fit? Would Ray like it? Her expression remained unreadable as she looked around for Ray.

"What do you think?" she asked, her voice steady.

Ray shrugged, a small grin playing on his lips. "I think you should try it on."

I'll take this as a yes, she thought, feeling a rush of determination. "Men's department is downstairs."

She observed as Ray moved away, pleased to let him find something for himself while she focused on this moment.

Tessa shifted her attention back to the dresses, searching for the perfect fit. After a few moments of browsing, she finally spotted a fitting room and headed toward it, excitement coursing through her veins.

As she slipped into the dress, Tessa caught a glimpse of herself in the mirror. The fabric slid perfectly down to her knees, and she admired how the pointed pumps finished the look. With a slight shift of her weight, she posed playfully, imagining Ray's reaction.

"Ray, over here!" she called out, her voice ringing clear in the spacious room.

When he faced her, she felt a rush of confidence. This became her moment to shine, and she hoped he'd see how much she wanted to embrace this moment.

"Wow," he said, and Tessa could see the sincerity in his eyes.

"So, you like it?"

Tessa watched as Ray shook his head, a thoughtful expression crossing his face. "Are you kidding? Looks great. I just hope Dad isn't in blue jeans and a t-shirt, and Mom isn't in everyday pants and a blouse when we get there."

She remembered. "Your parents? Last time I saw your parents at the house, they both looked like they were headed to dinner at The Ritz-Carlton."

He laughed. "You're exaggerating."

"I may be, but we won't be overdressed, trust me. This is how much we appreciate them and what they're doing for us. It'll be a pleasant break from all the drama of the last few days."

Ray looked her over, then nodded. "I'm glad you picked long sleeves. Fewer questions about the scratches on your arms. Your face may still require some explanation."

Tessa shrugged. "I was thinking about the truth."

"I don't have a problem with the truth." Ray's voice held steady. "Just be prepared for the mom and dad type of questions."

"Mom, yes, Dad, no. My dad will support all we have done and the results. Mom, she will want to put us in a padded bubble."

She laughed softly. "If she hears about what the FBI did to us, she'll march into FBI headquarters in Washington, DC, and demand answers and an official apology."

Ray's face brightened briefly before sobering again. "Well, this is why we filter the FBI information shared around the dinner table."

Tessa nodded. "I agree."

After checkout, Tessa and Ray headed back to the motel, both dressed for a fancy restaurant instead of a quiet family dinner. They stopped at a wine shop where Tessa picked a bottle of Santa Maria Syrah for sixty dollars, wanting them to look sophisticated rather than cheap. Once back at the motel, she noted Ray's hesitance as he booked them another night, and her chest feels too tight for a full breath. She didn't want to think about the FBI lingering over their home.

Once in their room, they changed, and Tessa helped Ray load GG-2 into the back seat. As she closed the door behind them, she felt the weight of the yellow-walled room fade into the background, the uncertainty of the day lingering but their resolve sharper and steadier.

CHAPTER FORTY

It began with the door swinging open, an invitation that set the evening into motion. Ray and Tessa stepped inside, greeted by the familiar warmth of Dave and Debra's hugs. Dave waved Ray past the kitchen, where the aroma of dinner preparation filled the air, into the living room. They settled onto a well-worn brown leather couch, positioned close enough to catch snippets of laughter and the clinking of utensils. Ray absently traced the scars on his arms, silent reminders of the accident that nearly cost him his life, but kept the full story to himself until dinner.

At the table, he caught Tessa's eyes sweeping over the array of steaming pots and dishes, confirming his earlier claim: more than enough food for twice their number. Soon, all four settled around a dark mahogany table, its surface gleaming under the warm overhead lights. Debra, her face alight with joy, carried in a tray of margaritas, the pale green concoctions wobbling slightly in their glasses as she set them down. She offered the first drink to Tessa, who accepted it with a look matching the moment's warmth.

As the meal commenced, Ray launched into his story. He recounted how the fusion-formed luminescent stones had come to him like a puzzle, their peculiar levitation during his time at Stanford. He described the meticulous assembly of GG-1, the exhilarating launch filled with chaos and hope. Then came the creation of GG-2, the force factor, and the relentless calculations he had documented. Finally, he spoke of the shock that shattered their world: the theft, the disappearance of the device, the plans, the precious stones—all gone, leaving their once semblance of security shattered.

Dave set his fork down, looking straight at Ray. "So, who knows about GG-1?"

Ray shrugged. "Nobody. It's just been Tessa and me at the tests. The authorities suspect someone in the theft."

"They do? Did they tell you who it is?"

"Yes—Victor Mishkin." Tessa shot a sharp look across the table.

Dave leaned forward, bracing for a blow. "Victor Mishkin is the son of Dimitri Mishkin. This was brought to our attention at Laubner during a meeting concerning security." He shook his head. "This could confirm Dimitri's involvement and explain the theft. How would he know anything about a project you are working on at home, though?"

Ray watched as uncertainty flickered across Dave's face. When he spoke again, his voice remained low. "Oh my God. There's been concern over information leaks at Laubner. This seems to confirm it."

"How do you know?" Ray asked.

"It explains Victor's interest in you and your work. He can't possibly have any idea what it is, though. Nobody at Laubner knows anything about what you're working on at home unless you shared it." He looked at the others, eyes bright with worry.

"Victor may just want to get it out of the country and have his father and his associates figure it out. Dimitri was very intelligent and discovered contacts back home willing to pay significant amounts for intellectual property, which he found easy to steal and transfer. He was caught, though. Instead of prison, they shipped him out and revoked his visa. He was only in custody for a month, then a decision at the State Department immediately put him on a plane. I think there's more to the story, but the State Department hushed about the possible loss of military intelligence leaking out of the country."

Ray set his glass down. "I don't think Victor or Dimitri will figure out GG-1," he said, more certain than he felt. "It needs a special battery, and the plans don't detail any of the capabilities of the device. They're only construction plans for the shell. The circuit board plans are the first version, which didn't do anything."

"I hope you are right, because if they get it to work the way you say it functions, then they may get somewhere with the technology and functionality of it," Dave replied, sounding almost tired now.

Ray shook his head. "If they get lucky enough to power it up, it won't be a pretty sight based on its current design and how it functioned for us."

Suddenly, the conversation shifted—a glass slid across the tabletop. Debra broke in, genuine fear in her voice: "I'm getting frightened for you and Tessa. What if this Victor comes back? I can't eat the dessert I made."

Ray and Dave exchanged a glance, the weight of the conversation heavy between them. Ray sensed the dinner had veered into dangerous territory, yet neither of them willed to back down.

Tessa reached out, her hand finding Debra's on the table. "I'll help you serve dessert. Maybe we could open the bottle we brought," she said quietly, steadying the moment with a warm, reassuring look.

Dave looked at Debra, gentle but insistent. "I'm sorry, but this is important. We need to help Ray and Tessa." The women rose, gathering plates and clearing the table.

Debra, still focused on stacking dishes, replied, "I think they should turn this all over to the authorities, and Ray and Tessa should get on with their lives, get things back to normal and start a family." Silence fell, thick and unmoving, until Dave finally spoke.

"Debra, the authorities are working on this. They are looking for Victor. When they find him, this will be all over, and the kids can get back to a normal life."

Ray said nothing, unwilling to challenge his father or give any more fuel to the worry. Tessa squeezed Debra's shoulder. "We will be just fine," she said, her voice pitched to soothe.

Dave sat back, arms crossed. "Maybe it was a random choice."

Ray shook his head. "Well, they stole GG-1, the controller, the plans, and all the remaining stones."

Dave's brow furrowed as he leaned forward. "He didn't steal anything else?"

Ray shifted in his seat, glancing at Tessa and then back at Dave. "Nothing we've noticed."

Dave drummed his fingers on the table. "Sounds too specific to be random."

Ray nodded. "I can recreate everything but the stones. You said you knew about the possibility of more stones?"

"Everything has been shipped to a Washington State disposal site."

"Do you know how many more stones there are?"

"There were several drums recorded, but I don't know how many contained stones."

Ray thought for a moment. "Any chance I could requisition them out of storage?"

Dave shrugged. "Hard to say. It's a lot of paperwork and can take months or even years."

Ray exhaled. "What I was afraid of."

"I can put in a request for you this week," Dave offered, pausing to sip his margarita.

"Great, but what about the event itself that created the stones? Any chance I could get a report on the project and the failure event?"

Dave brightened. "Well, I know the Magnetic Mirror Fusion process is well-documented, considered sensitive but unclassified. With your current security classification at Laubner, you'll have access, but you won't be able to remove anything from the property. I believe the failure event itself is unclassified because the report didn't disclose any classified information."

They left the table and found Tessa and Debra at the kitchen counter. With the bottle they had brought uncorked and a glass of wine in hand, the earlier tension of dinner had given way to laughter and soft melodies drifting through the home.

Debra looked up, her expression slightly unfocused. "Did you two solve the states' electricity crisis?" she said, a warm smile spreading across her face, softened by the wine.

Ray watched as Dave raised an eyebrow and reached for her wineglass. "Okay, I can see someone has had enough for the night."

Tessa caught Ray's eye, then gestured toward the door: time to go. He nodded, feeling a mix of relief and concern.

As Ray stood and hugged Debra, he whispered thanks for the meal, catching the gentle warmth in her face, softened by the wine. Tessa followed, her voice soft as she gave both Debra and Dave hugs before turning toward the front hall.

The air felt thick with unsaid words as Dave spoke again. “Remember what I said.”

Debra blinked, seeming to shake off the moment. “What did you say?”

Dave just shook his head. “Never mind, I’ll tell you later.”

Ray and Tessa stepped to the front door, Dave trailing behind them. He glanced back at Debra, who steadied herself against the wall, trying—though with little success—to join them. As the door closed behind them, Ray felt the weight of the evening’s tension linger.

CHAPTER FORTY-ONE

"That was awkward," Tessa said once they'd rolled out of the Hollands' driveway and slid into the dark hush of the lane.

"Why would you say that?" Ray asked.

She glanced over at him. He seemed oblivious, his eyes fixed on the road.

"Your mom was drinking and crying in the kitchen while you and your dad watched TV. She downed three glasses of wine."

Ray's eyebrows pinched. "She seemed off after dinner."

"She was more than off. She was upset with you."

"With me?"

Tessa turned back to the window. The weight of the evening pressed on her-her mother-in-law's tears, the unspoken fears, the silent plea for grandchildren in every glass of wine. Did they really have to navigate this pressure so soon? She wanted to comfort the woman, but how?

"What did I do?" he asked, his voice tinged with uncertainty.

"She's scared. She doesn't want us to get hurt. She started talking about babies, Ray. She cried."

The thought of babies felt heavy in her chest. Could they even handle this kind of responsibility amid all this chaos? But part of her longed for it, too, to share their love in a new way.

"Babies? Crying about babies? What babies?"

"Our babies," Tessa insisted, her tone sharp and final.

"We don't have any babies," Ray protested, nearly laughing.

"Exactly. She wants to be a grandmother."

Why was it so hard to give her mother-in-law that comfort? Wasn't it a simple wish? But how could Tessa promise something she wasn't ready for herself?

Ray exhaled, exhaustion evident. "I've told her it'll happen when it happens."

"I think she wants something more solid."

As they drove, Tessa felt the distance between their hopes and reality grow. She wanted to take the leap, to embrace the future, but they had to be sure first.

Ray kept silent, hands gripping the wheel. "Well, when you get pregnant, it'll be definitive, right?"

A quiet fell over them, and she contemplated the reality of the moment. Did she want it enough? Was she ready?

A stillness enveloped the car as Tessa turned her gaze to the windshield, fingers picking at the seam of the seat. Then, softly: "Maybe we aren't trying hard enough," she said, her voice taking on a sly edge.

Ray looked over. "What's that supposed to mean?"

She grinned wider, twirling a strand of her dark hair around her finger. "Just wait. When we get home, I'll show you."

Ray's nervous laughter filled the car as he shook his head. "Okay, okay, I get it. But we're getting GG-2 in the house first."

"Deal!" Tessa said, hands pressed into her lap, bouncing in her seat like a kid on too much sugar. Yet, even in her excitement, a small voice whispered: Was this all a distraction from the real fears they faced?

They rounded the corner onto their street. The headlights caught a flash of white: a county patrol car, idling, parked across the road with its engine still running.

"Looks like we still have the interest of local law enforcement," Ray observed, his voice low.

Tessa saw their house, floodlit by the porch lamp, and felt her insides ripple. Those memories—the blood, the death, the hollow ring of violence—all crowded at the threshold, cold hands on her skin. She forced herself to breathe, to shake it off, to focus on the present. Possibility. She made herself speak.

"Let's keep moving forward," she said.

Ray looked over. "What?"

"I just said it's nice to be home," she said, her gaze locked on their front steps.

"I thought you said something about moving," Ray said as he parked the rental car in front of their Subaru.

"Moving forward," Tessa murmured, almost chanting it under her breath, "moving forward, moving forward."

He shot her a look. "What did you say?"

She forced a lightness into her voice, though it didn't quite hold. "Nothing. Just glad we're home."

Under the yellow pool of the porch light, they hauled GG-2 out of the back seat and shuffled it to the front door. Ray fumbled with his keys. The house greeted them with a waft of strong disinfectant—like a locker room at the community pool—as if someone had tried to erase everything that had happened before. The living room glowed as they flicked on all the lights, GG-2 standing sentry by the window facing the street.

"Let's go upstairs together, please," Tessa said, her grip tightening on Ray's arm.

"Sure, sure," Ray replied, moving ahead.

The staircase felt constricting, shadows clinging to the corners. At the landing, Ray flicked on the light, illuminating the hall. In the spare bedroom, they paused. The new window gleamed in its fresh white frame, but the air remained heavy with the smell of cleaning solution and the ghost of latex paint.

"They did a nice job," Ray finally said, looking around.

Tessa tried to muster reassurance, but doubt pressed in anyway.

"You okay?"

"Slowly," she replied, her voice trembling. Ray hesitated, and she sensed the tension in his posture.

"We can go back to the hotel if you want, it's paid for."

"No, I need to do this," she insisted, her heart racing.

Tessa stared at the window, fingers gripping the edge of Ray's sleeve, feeling the weight of memories pressing down on her. "I think I want a hot bath first," she said finally.

Ray nodded, gently guiding her down the hall. He opened the bathroom door, switched on the light, and inspected the corners. She faced him, kissed his cheek, and whispered, "Would you please bring me something to wear when I'm done?"

"Sure," he said, his expression a mix of concern and affection, and she saw a brief confusion tug at his features.

# # #

He left her there, the door closing softly behind him. In the bedroom, he stared at the dresser, suddenly clueless about what she'd want. Their bags were in the car, dirty and waiting to be washed. He pulled open the top drawer: a red cotton fleece nightshirt stared up at him. Then he remembered the full-length ruby red satin nightgown. He hesitated, laughed at himself, and pulled a coin from his pocket. Heads: nightshirt. Tails: nightgown. He flipped; heads. He draped the nightshirt over the handrail at the top of the stairs and headed down, hunting for wine.

As he descended the stairs, thoughts of the evening at his parents' house replayed in his mind. The weight of his mother's tears, the unspoken worries, and the fear of what Victor Mishkin intended loomed large. What if their lives were about to spiral out of control once more?

The kitchen seemed unfamiliar, a map of half-remembered cupboards. Canned vegetables, pasta, more pasta. Above the fridge: jackpot. A 2000 Chardonnay, a wedding gift. He found a corkscrew, popped the bottle, and poured two glasses, balancing them carefully to avoid spills as he made his way back up the stairs. The bathroom door hung unlatched, warm steam drifting out. Tessa lay deep in a tub of bubbles, eyes closed, tendrils of hair curling over the rim.

"Room service." Ray set one glass on the counter, another within her reach.

Warmth rose in her as she cradled the wine and took a generous sip. "Mmm, good. What is it?"

Ray relaxed against the doorframe. "A 2000 Chardonnay. From our wedding."

"Who gave it to us?"

He laughed. "My brother."

Tessa's eyes narrowed. "You don't have a brother."

"I know. The card was signed 'Brother Ron.'"

She giggled. "He's somebody's 'Brother Ron,' just not yours. So who was he?"

"Probably a crasher. Brought us a bottle, signed the card."

Tessa took another sip of the wine, considering. "We should do that sometime."

"What, crash a wedding?" Ray asked, raising an eyebrow.

A sly glint flickered in her eyes. "Yes, but only a big, expensive one."

Ray's mind flickered back to the stakes of their situation. If they were to embrace a future together, they had to be cautious. Every decision felt layered with risk, especially with Mishkin lurking.

He poured more wine into her glass. "We'd get caught."

She shook her head. "No way. Ours was tiny, and we didn't even notice 'Brother Ron.'"

Ray shrugged. "If someone brings a gift, they get a seat."

"Exactly. So, big wedding, big crowd, we blend in. Easy."

Ray mimed surrender. "Deal. Just not tomorrow—we need to return the rental car since we have the Subaru."

Tessa winked. "I wasn't thinking tomorrow. I'll plan it."

Ray grinned and set his glass down. "While you plot our criminal future, I'm going to grab a shower."

He undressed, stepping into the glass shower stall next to the tub. Steam fogged the glass as warm water cascaded over him. With each drop, his thoughts drifted to the precarious situation they found themselves in. The quiet popping of bubbles from the tub behind him echoed like an unspoken warning, heightening his unease as he considered the threat still lurking in the shadows.

Moments later, the door opened, and Tessa stepped in behind him, glistening and radiant despite the weight of their reality.

He looked over, surprised by her presence, a mix of relief and concern flooding through him. "Tub didn't get you clean?"

Ray felt a thrill as Tessa pressed up behind him. "No, silly. I needed to rinse off the bubbles." Her fingers traced his shoulders, a gentle reminder of the wounds he had been trying to forget. The contrast between her smooth skin and the scrapes on his arms felt stark.

As the water ran over her, he watched her eyes close, releasing the tension from earlier. The water shut off, and she reached for a towel to dry herself.

"Where's my sleepwear?" she asked.

"On the hall rail," Ray replied, his voice thick with lingering concern.

Tessa dropped the towel and stepped into the hallway, closing the door behind her. Ray wondered if she was in the nightshirt or putting on a show for the patrol car outside. He dried off carefully, avoiding the scabs on his arms and back, before wrapping himself in a towel. Peeking out, he saw the nightshirt still on the rail, but no sign of Tessa.

"Tessa," he called. Silence. He called again, louder. Nothing. The lights were still on downstairs, and a sense of unease settled in his gut as he hurried into the bedroom.

Tessa lay face-down on the bed, still naked and unmoving. Fear twisted in his gut, and he rushed to her, crawling onto the bed to check. Before he could touch her, Tessa flipped over, wrapping her arms and legs around him, pulling him close.

"What took you so long?" she whispered, her lips brushing against his.

Ray blinked, relief and shock coursing through him. He surfaced for air, dazed by her sudden presence and the warmth of her body.

"I called—you didn't answer. I thought something was wrong," he replied, his heart racing with relief.

Tessa rolled him onto his back, a playful grin on her face. "I've been waiting all afternoon for this."

Ray's mind raced. "You have?"

She pressed her finger gently against his lips, silencing him. "No more talking."

As she slid off him and switched off the lights, the room was enveloped in darkness. "Lose the towel," she said, her voice teasing yet commanding.

CHAPTER FORTY-TWO

Anderson worked the quiet Saturday, hunched at one of the desks in the Palo Alto FBI field office. The hum of computers and distant voices provided a backdrop for the knock at his door. Stevenson entered, manila folder in hand.

Anderson eyed the envelope. "What's this?"

Stevenson set it on the desk. "Updated information on Sommers, Fitz, and Bentz. Some we already knew, and some is new."

"You read it?"

"I skimmed it."

Anderson frowned, pulling the folder open and flipping through the sheets. "FBI doesn't skim over reports, Stevenson."

Stevenson's jaw tensed. "Sorry, sir. Poor word choice."

"What does it say, then?"

Stevenson drew in a breath. "The section on Bentz, in Moscow, now confirms he provided plans and some stolen smart laser guidance components for the new Comanche helicopter program being developed by Laubner Labs."

Anderson squinted. "Laubner Labs—where Holland works."

"Holland and his father. There's more, sir. The report says Bentz had a contact inside Laubner."

Stevenson paused, flipping a page. "And you remember Val Kozlov? The Russian found dead in Los Angeles? There's confirmation Bentz met in Moscow with Val's brother, Aleksandr Kozlov, two months ago. CIA and Foreign Intelligence have a file on Aleksandr: weapons trading, espionage, murder, kidnapping—the works."

Anderson kept scanning documents, lips pressed tight. "So how does this help us with Mishkin?"

Stevenson pressed on. "Before Sommers and Fitz took the assignment guarding Holland, they worked intelligence gathering and surveillance with Bentz in LA at Baker

International, which supplies Laubner. Control systems, including missile guidance."

Anderson thumbed through more pages, his expression clouding. "I don't see why Mishkin would kill Sommers, Fitz, and Bentz. There are links, yes, but what was really going on between them? We need Mishkin to fill the gaps," he said, glancing up.

"What's the latest on finding him?"

Stevenson straightened. "As far as we can tell, the van Mishkin took hasn't shown up at any port of entry. My guess is he's either hiding or working on his escape."

Anderson nodded. "Let's keep local law enforcement updated, especially on the van. Alert Customs and Border Patrol in LA, San Francisco, and San Diego. If Mishkin plans to move Hollands' device out, it won't go by plane. Get me manifests for all Eastern European and Russian registered vessels and crews in port or arriving soon."

Stevenson's eyes held steady. "What's on your mind, sir?"

"I'm looking for Mishkin's way out—a detail that doesn't fit."

"Yes, sir." Stevenson headed to the door but stopped. "One more thing, sir. I'd like to send Johnson and Pommeroy to Baker International. They can investigate the Bentz connection and maybe get a line on the Laubner insider."

"Have them report straight to you," Anderson said, still reading.

"Yes, sir." Stevenson smacked his thigh, a hint of a grin on his face, then left.

# # #

Agents Perkins and Connors arrived at the FBI field office in Palo Alto just after dark. In the conference room, Anderson stood by a table cluttered with manila folders and scribbled notes. The chaos mirrored the investigation itself—disorganized yet infused with urgency. He motioned them forward. "Update me on Bentz."

Connors flipped through her notebook, brow furrowing as she glanced up. "We connected more dots today. I spoke with Special Agent Karl Senge, who used to work with Bentz. After

Bentz met Aleksandr Kozlov in Moscow, he feared for his life. Apparently, Kozlov blamed Bentz for the death of his brother Val. He was the go-between for shell companies in Moscow tied to Baker International, but Senge wouldn't go deeper. Said Bentz was hunting for Victor Mishkin."

Anderson's head popped up. "Bentz knew Mishkin?"

Connors nodded, her expression serious. "According to Senge, yes. After Moscow, Bentz went off-grid, taking Sommers and Fitz with him. That's when they visited Baker International. Shortly after, Sommers and Fitz showed up at Hollands'."

Anderson leaned on the table, the weight of the information pressing down on him. "So, Bentz gave the order. Since he was off the grid, he put it under Palto's name. That tracks. Still doesn't tell us why they were shielding the Hollands from Mishkin—or why Bentz ran the operation alone."

Connors ventured, "Did Bentz feel the Bureau couldn't protect him?" She hesitated, her uncertainty palpable.

Anderson's expression sharpened. He remained silent for several beats, pen tapping lightly against the table. If Bentz was scared, it was Mishkin he feared. And if Kozlov was involved, things were worse than they thought. A gnawing sense of frustration simmered within him—how could they have let things escalate this far? Was the Bureau's protection worth anything?

He shook his head, his voice low. "Sloppy FBI work."

Connors startled at his tone. "Sir?"

"Bentz. No wonder he ended up dead. This is a mess." Frustration bubbled within him, a mix of anger and disappointment. How could they have let this happen? He had trusted Bentz to do his job.

"What should we do?" Connors asked, her voice tentative, almost apologetic.

"We stay close to the Hollands. Keep the locals on them until I can get a full team in place. Meanwhile, you two: pursue Mishkin and dig for any link to the Holland family, coincidence or not. See if Senge will give us more on Mishkin."

Anderson issued orders. Time was slipping away. Every moment counted, and he needed to be decisive. The stakes were higher than ever; he couldn't afford to let Mishkin slip through their fingers.

Connors glanced at Perkins as if she had something more to add but held back. Anderson's mood stayed iron. She stood, and Perkins followed her out.

Behind them, Anderson sat heavily at the table, hands pressed into his brow, staring at the chaotic array of folders and notes. A low groan escaped him, barely audible, as the night deepened. This wasn't just a case anymore—it was a tangle of lives at stake, and the weight of their failures pressed down on him.

###

Hours later, at the Palo Alto field office, Special Agent Steve Anderson paced the floor, tension coiling in his gut as he awaited updates. The clock was ticking, and with every passing minute, the urgency of their investigation grew heavier. He'd dispatched Agents Johnson and Pommeroy to Baker International, hoping to uncover more about the recent murders and Mishkin's connections.

When his phone buzzed, he answered quickly. "Johnson, what's the status?"

"Sir, we just wrapped up at Baker," Johnson said, her tone clipped. "We spoke to Mark Jones and Terry Sanders. They had some interesting comments regarding previous FBI visits—Bentz, Sommers, and Fitz made quite the mess during their last investigation."

Anderson's brow furrowed. "What do you mean by 'mess'?"

"According to Jones, they tore through file cabinets, left files all over the floor, and even barged into their clean room without precaution. It shut down production for days."

"Did they take anything?" Anderson pressed, feeling frustration simmer below the surface.

"Not that they could figure out, but it rattled the staff. Jones filed a complaint but heard nothing back from us."

“And how about the buyer for Laubner?” he asked, shifting gears.

“Turns out, Sanders is just sales. The real buyer is Sarah Bourne. There’s been some tension; she cut him off after a brief engagement. Now she’s trying to ditch the account.”

“Any other contacts?”

“Just Jeff Morgenson, the engineer. He’s supposed to help with specs and issues on the assembly line.”

“That could be useful. Get the numbers for Morgenson and Bourne and check on their last audits. I want to know if anything’s gone missing.”

“On it. But we might have bigger problems,” Johnson added, urgency creeping into her voice. “Stevenson just called. We need to head to Whiskey Hill Road—possible kidnapping.”

“Damn it,” Anderson muttered, feeling the weight of the situation press heavier. “I’m calling Stevenson, keep me posted.”

As he hung up, urgency settled into his bones. He gathered his team, ready to respond to the developing crisis. The stakes were rising, and he couldn’t afford to let Mishkin slip away again.

CHAPTER FORTY-THREE

Ray stirred as the late morning sunlight splashed across the bedroom, casting rectangles of brightness over the rumpled sheets. He blinked awake, disoriented for a moment, then eased as he registered her warmth next to him. She rolled onto her other side and studied him, her expression softening as she leaned closer and pressed a kiss to his lips.

"Are we going to sleep all day?" she asked, voice playful.

"What time is it?" he mumbled, still half-asleep.

"10:40."

Ray took a long breath, stretching as he woke. "Well, if it wasn't for the rental car, I'd say we could just stay in bed all day."

But even as he relished the comfort of the moment, memories of last night flooded back—intimate, heated moments that felt electric, yet shadowed by the looming threat of Victor Mishkin. *What if Mishkin watched them?* The thrill of the night clashed with the weight of their reality.

Tessa's playful suggestion broke through his thoughts. "We could return it and come back, pick up where we left off."

Ray grinned, feeling a flicker of warmth despite the tension. "You mean sleeping?"

She laughed, a sound momentarily pushing his worries aside. "We could do some of that too," she promised, kissing him again.

"You're obviously feeling better."

"I am." Her tone brightened, and he could see the excitement in her eyes. "I decided it was better to look forward than back. When I think about the future, it makes me feel excited."

"Was that what last night was?" Ray asked, his grin softening as he searched her expression for reassurance.

"Oh yeah. Did you like it?"

"Loved it." But the warmth came with a flash of panic when she went silent on the bed, not answering him.

She noticed. “What’s the matter?” The question was gentle, alert.

“Oh, I was just thinking how scared I was, seeing you here not answering me.”

“Sorry—I just wanted to surprise you.” She ran her hand over his hair, soft and slow. “I’ll make it up to you. I’ll go make you a yummy breakfast while you get dressed.”

“You mean brunch,” he said, aiming for a joke to lighten the mood.

“Um, Mr. Holland, you know you can have breakfast anytime.” Tessa rolled her eyes, her playful demeanor helping to ease his tension.

As she slipped off the bed, tying her white robe around her waist, Ray felt the familiar warmth between them but couldn’t shake the worry gnawing at him.

Clattering in the kitchen: pots and pans, the tap of silverware. Ray shook off the last of his sleep and made his way downstairs. Tessa had left for work, and two plates of pancakes waited at the table—sliced oranges, syrup, and butter lined up neatly.

“Sorry, no strawberries or blueberries. I could have run and found some, but, well, you know what I mean, my hair’s a mess.”

“You look great... This looks great, too. Tell you what, we can pick up strawberries and blueberries on the way back after dropping off the car.”

“Whipping cream too,” she said, raising an eyebrow.

“Of course.”

They sat and ate, working through the pancakes, cleaning up every last orange segment. Ray cleared the dishes while Tessa disappeared upstairs, her footsteps light on the wood as she went to dress and freshen up.

While washing the dishes, Ray’s mind flickered back to the theft of GG-1. What if Mishkin had dissected it and come to any conclusions? The implications sent a chill through him. They had to exercise patience and hope the FBI found Mishkin and his device. It still wasn’t time to relax.

When Tessa came down, Ray sat hunched over GG-2 in the living room, fine-tuning a connection.

"Have you decided what's next for GG-2?" she asked, pausing in the doorway, her gaze fixed on him.

Ray felt a small flicker of amusement as he kept working. "Well, it's safe to say its hole-digging days are done. I've reversed the signals controlling its relationship to gravity."

"So it'll go up instead of down?" Her tone remained playful, but he could sense her interest.

"Exactly."

She shifted her weight, adjusting the collar of her white blouse. "I think it's safe for you to go out now. You look good in the t-shirt." She ran a hand through her hair, then grinned. "You might want to run a comb through yours before we go anywhere."

He raked his fingers across his scalp. "You're probably right."

Ray took the stairs two at a time. He could hear Tessa moving around downstairs, the sound of her footsteps fading as she likely stepped outside to check on the Subaru.

"The Subaru still runs," she reported, dropping the announcement in the air as she crossed the threshold.

"Good news. Have you seen the keys to the rental?"

"Check the pocket of your pants from yesterday?"

Ray paused, thinking. Nothing.

"Try the bathroom," she suggested, not missing the rising tension.

An "aha" flashed across his face, and he sprinted up the stairs again, returning moments later, keys in hand.

"Found them," he said triumphantly, waving them overhead. "So, you follow me on the 84. We're going downtown, so if you lose me, remember to turn on Portola, then Sandy Hill Road. The agency's just south of the mall. You have your cell?"

"Yes."

"Okay, just call me if you get lost. It's Avis, remember?"

"I got this," Tessa assured him, her voice edged with playful confidence.

They made their way out the kitchen door. At the last second, Ray caught Tessa around the waist and pulled her close for a hug and kiss. Outside, the County Sheriff car remained parked, unmoved.

“Do you think they’ll follow us?” she asked, worry creeping into her tone.

“I doubt it. They haven’t yet.”

“Do you think the FBI has found Mishkin yet?”

“If they had, I think two things would have happened: one, they’d call us. Two, the Sheriff would be gone.”

“I think you’re right.”

“Anyway, we should go. If we make good time, we can get a late lunch in town. Maybe we’ll miss the rush.”

# # #

Tessa slid into the driver’s seat of the Subaru, Ray into the rental, and started it up. He backed out of the driveway, waiting for Tessa to catch up before pulling onto the main road. He headed south toward the 84.

Tessa fell into line; she watched the rental, her mind drifting, but beneath the surface, unease churned inside her. The events of the previous night hung heavily in her thoughts—warm moments with Ray overshadowed by the threat of Victor Mishkin. What if he still watched them? The thrill of intimacy now felt tainted.

Suddenly, a voice sliced through the silence from the rear seat. “Keep driving. No crazy moves, Mrs. Holland,” the voice rasped—a horror-movie growl, but strangely familiar.

Tessa’s heart stuttered, pulse hammering in her neck and chest. Panic surged through her. This wasn’t happening.

“What the!” she screamed, but the voice cut her off.

“Don’t turn around.”

“Who are you? What do you want?” she demanded, panic rising, hands tense on the wheel.

“Let’s say I have a problem you and your husband can help me with.”

“Victor? Victor Mishkin?” She barely recognized her own voice, shaking.

Something cold touched the hollow of her throat—not enough to break skin, just enough to stop her mid-breath. The metal felt impossibly sharp, as if the slightest swallow would draw it closer. Her pulse hammered against it, each beat a warning. She held still, thoughts narrowing to a single point: don't move.

"Come now, Mrs. Holland—or should I say Tessa?" The voice sounded almost conversational, the German stiletto knife pressing against her skin. "I won't hurt you if I get what I want."

"I'm supposed to be following my husband," she whimpered, voice breaking.

"You will follow him, yes. Not close."

"What do you want?" Her hands slipped on the wheel. Tears blurred her vision, but she kept driving, glancing at passing cars, hoping someone would see. No one did. Desperation clawed at her. What could she do to make someone notice?

"Tessa, slow now, not too much. Let Mr. Holland get more distance."

She eased off the gas. Cars stacked behind her, some honked, some passed with angry looks.

"More distance." Victor remained patient. "Ahead, a corner, you see? You turn fast."

Tessa watched the curve, letting Ray slip further ahead. At the right moment, she made the sharp turn, just as Victor ordered.

"Stop. Now go back the way we came."

"Back the way we came?" Tessa echoed, numb.

"Yes, now fast."

Her heart raced as she let herself look at him. Victor wore a deep brown nylon jacket, hood drawn over his head, his face shadowed except for the hard lines of his nose and jaw. Fear cinched tighter around her, and she forced her eyes back to the road, trying to block out the terror sitting behind her. She spotted a gap, swung the car around, and accelerated, retracing her path away from Ray. Her cell phone lay silent on the seat, the seconds stretching longer; how long before Ray would notice before he'd call? Victor directed her through a sequence of turns, winding them into unfamiliar territory. Still nothing on the phone. Tessa's hands trembled.

Finally, the phone rang.

"Hand me the phone," Victor ordered.

She passed it back without hesitation. He pressed answer, waiting for the connection.

Tessa strained to listen, heart pounding. She could faintly hear Ray's voice. It sounded frantic, almost trembling. "Tessa? Can you hear me?"

"Mr. Holland," Victor said, voice sharp now.

"Who is this?"

"Don't you know?" Victor laughed, low and cold. "I am Victor Mishkin."

Tessa's heart sank as she listened to Ray's voice shake. "Victor? Where is Tessa?"

"She is driving right now. She cannot talk."

"What are you doing? What do you want?" Ray's desperation filled the air, and Tessa's chest lightened. She wanted to scream she was okay, she was still there. But the knife pressed harder, stealing her voice.

"Please, Mr. Holland, one question at a time. Let me be clear. I have your machine. I must see what it will do. Can you help me?"

"Don't hurt Tessa, please," Ray said. The raw fear in his voice twisted like a knife in her gut.

"Oh, Mr. Holland, Tessa will be fine. You help me, yes?"

"Yes, yes, don't hurt Tessa."

"No police. Only you help me, yes?" Victor insisted.

"Of course. No police. Where are you?"

"I will call back. Be ready."

"Don't hang up. Let me talk to Tessa!"

Victor ended the call abruptly, pulling the battery from her phone, leaving Tessa breathless and reeling from the intensity of the moment.

# # #

Ray called back. Busy signal. He stared down at the phone, dumbstruck. What now? He sat in his car in the gas station lot on Sandy Hill Road, the tick of the engine cooling like a clock in a sealed room. He'd lost Tessa miles back. Victor had killed FBI agents. This chilling thought twisted in his gut: If he could kill an agent, what would stop him from doing the same to Tessa? Ray couldn't drag anyone else into this. Not friends, not family. But he didn't have a choice. He picked up the phone and dialed the one number that might keep Tessa alive: FBI Anderson.

"Anderson." The voice was clipped.

"Agent Anderson? This is Ray Holland," Ray's words stumbled out, uneven.

"Mr. Holland, is everything okay?"

"No, no, he has Tessa!" Ray's voice boomed.

"Who has Tessa?"

"Victor Mishkin." He spat the name, as if it should explain everything.

"Mishkin has Tessa. You're saying he kidnapped her?" Anderson's tone shifted.

"Yes!" Ray nearly shouted.

"Hold on, Ray." Anderson urged. Ray could hear boots tapping on the tile.

"Ray, I'm putting you on speaker with my agents," Anderson continued.

"He said no police or he'd hurt her," Ray said, the words bitter as copper.

"Ray, you did the right thing. Where are you?"

Ray glanced at the intersection, already knowing his location. "Sandy Hill Road and Santa Cruz Avenue."

"Good. We're close. Any idea where Mishkin and Tessa are?"

"No. Tessa followed me in our car; I was returning the rental. I lost her. I pulled over. I called her phone and Victor answered."

"We'll trace her phone."

Ray's hands shook. "I tried calling back. Just busy."

"Did Mishkin say what he wanted?" Anderson asked calmly.

"He wants me to show him how the GG-1 works."

"Did you tell him how?"

"No, just that if I didn't, he'd hurt Tessa. He said he would call me back."

"And this device does what?" Anderson pressed.

Ray hesitated, mind racing. He couldn't risk GG-2, not with the feds. "It doesn't do anything right now." The lie slid out clean. "It's a failure. First versions always are."

"Understood," Anderson said. "Stay put. We're coming to get you."

# # #

Perkins looked up from the desk at Agent Anderson. "Hang on, Ray, let me call you right back." He killed the call.

"What is it?" Anderson barked.

"No trace on the Hollands' phone. Looks like it's disabled."

"Last known?"

"Five-thousand block of Whiskey Hill Road."

Anderson's pulse quickened. Time passed. If Mishkin was on the move, every second counted. "Go. Get Stevenson and his team covering exits. Roadblocks, whatever you have to do. BOLO on a white van or the Hollands' car. Hostage protocol."

Anderson's orders came out fast, slicing through the air. This was it—the moment that could change everything. He couldn't let Mishkin slip through their fingers again.

# # #

Ray stared at his phone. The call had dropped in his hand. That's it? Coming to pick him up would only waste time. Maybe calling the FBI was a mistake. He couldn't get GG-1 working without the battery, and Mishkin would call back. That was the play.

A sinking feeling settled in his gut. What if this was the moment everything spiraled out of control? How did he fail to shield Tessa from the danger shadowing them?

He pressed the pedal, rolling back onto Sandy Hill Road toward home. The phone rattled on the seat—the screen: Anderson. Ray powered the phone off, cold.

Twenty minutes later, Ray pulled onto his street. The sheriff's car remained parked there; two officers inside. He ignored them and sprinted through his front door, grabbing the spare battery from the table. He thought about GG-2—a backup—and yanked it out, along with the second controller. If Mishkin wanted a show, Ray would give him one. Anything for Tessa.

He loaded everything into the car, then paused, thinking. The FBI would trace his phone or stake out the house with the local sheriff. He needed to be unpredictable, mobile. He slid into the driver's seat and merged back onto 84, heading for the highway. On 280, he powered the phone up again, letting it breathe just enough for Mishkin's call while driving back and forth to stay ahead of a trace.

He gripped the steering wheel, waiting. Somewhere out there, Tessa waited.

CHAPTER FORTY-FOUR

"Go here," Mishkin said, gesturing with his open hand toward an uneven gravel track that broke off from the main road. A battered white van sat ahead, alone in the hush, with enough space for another car to slide in beside it.

"Park there." He motioned again at the van, insistent.

Tessa steered in, cutting the engine. Her hands trembled as she reached for the keys. The silence enveloped them—a hush so dense it felt like waiting for a verdict.

"Let's go," Mishkin ordered.

Her body refused to move, every muscle taut. Her gaze swept the emptiness around them. Was this the place—the point where things resolved, one way or another? Had Ray figured it out, or was he circling, lost? Not Ray. He would be calculating, searching for a solution—maybe reaching the FBI. They wanted Mishkin; maybe they could help. Or maybe not.

"The van," Mishkin snapped, breaking her trance.

As Tessa slid out of the car, she toyed with the idea of making a run for it, but the world beyond the drive was still and unhelpful. Not a car in sight. No witnesses, no chance. Her cheeks still burned, eyes swollen and raw from crying. If she did reach the roadside, would Ray be there—or would it just be more silence?

Mishkin yanked open the sliding door on the van.

"Sit," he said, jabbing a finger at the heap of clothes and trash mounding the van's floor. She obeyed, unable to avoid the smell or the mess.

He slid the knife into a sheath on his pants, then clambered inside after her. Tessa twisted to look behind her: GG-1 sat wedged next to the rear wheel well, the controller visible, beside buckets loaded with luminescent stones.

"Put your hands behind your back."

She did, sobs returning, hot and unbidden. Mishkin tied her wrists with a thick, soft rope, then reached around, pinning her arms with another loop around her waist. Panic bled out of her in short, desperate gasps.

"Miss Tessa, you must not cry. You do not look good when your husband comes."

He dragged her deeper into the van, cinched another rope around the passenger seat, and tied it to her waist so she faced the back, immobilized.

"Where are we going?" she whispered, her voice almost gone.

"Now, Miss Tessa, you must be silent, or I will put a rag in your mouth. We are going to meet your husband, of course." He stepped over her and shut the side door. The dull slam echoed in the hollow van.

A rattle from the driver's door. Mishkin started the van. She heard a snap as he clicked together her phone and its battery, then a brief electronic tone as he powered it up. He jabbed at the keypad.

Tessa's heart raced as she braced for Ray's voice. "Hello?" came a familiar tone, uncertain, hopeful. She held her breath to hear every word.

"Mr. Holland. Victor here."

"Where's Tessa? Is she okay?"

"Mr. Holland. She is with me, of course. She is fine. You are still going to help me, yes?"

"Yes."

"Good. You know the Hopter Factory, yes?" Victor asked.

"Off the 280, near Felt Lake."

"Yes. I will be there in one hour. You alone, no police."

"Yes. Tessa will be there with you?"

"Yes, of course."

"May I speak to Tessa?"

"Sorry, but no. See you in one hour."

Tessa's breath caught. Ray's voice dissolved into the quiet as if the phone was gone, leaving her heart pounding in the silence. Could this truly be happening? She felt the weight of the moment press down on her.

# # #

Agent Anderson sat in his car at 5500 Whiskey Hill Road, Agent Trent beside him, glancing at the intersection where he knew Perkins and Connors were parked at Highway 84. The tension in the air buzzed as he waited, the familiar sound of his phone ringing snapping him to attention.

"Perkins," he answered, focusing on the task at hand.

"Anything on your end?" Perkins asked.

"No." He could hear the low rumble of unmarked cars borrowed from the field office, a tactic to avoid drawing attention. With a quick glance at the buzzing screen, he noted the call waiting: a new number.

"Perkins, I'll call you back," Anderson said, switching lines. His heart quickened; the new number could mean a lead.

"Sir, Stevenson here. Just received a ping on the Hollands' phone."

"Ray or Tessa's?"

"Both now. Ray's been doing circles between the 84 and the 284; we have Tessa in the Teague Hill reserve."

Anderson looked at the map, piecing together the pattern. His gut churned at the thought of the young Tessa in danger. "Let's get everyone to Teague Hill."

Within twenty minutes, four FBI vehicles converged at the gate to Teague Hill Reserve. A caretaker flagged them through, handing over a map with the roads marked. Anderson's gaze narrowed as he scanned for the spot where Tessa's phone last pinged, his breath coming in clipped, measured bursts. He signaled Johnson and Pommeroy to take up position at the main entrance while positioning Stevenson and Murray as the lead car, assigning Perkins and Connors to cover the next Y in the paths.

Ten minutes later, they reached the end of the short drive, stopping at the Hollands' Subaru. With service revolvers drawn, they approached cautiously. Anderson's pulse jumped when he saw the car sitting empty, keys still in the ignition.

"No cell phone," Anderson snapped, frustration biting at his tone. His mind raced with possibilities. "Look around."

“Sir,” Stevenson pointed. Just off the gravel, fresh parallel tire tracks.

Anderson followed the direction of his finger and squinted. Just off the gravel, fresh parallel tire tracks marked the dirt. A rush of adrenaline surged through him. “A second vehicle,” Anderson said, his mind racing with possibilities. The realization hit him like a punch. “Gotta be the van.”

Stevenson crouched and picked up a metallic glint. “Here’s the phone, sir.”

Anderson flicked the flip phone open and scrolled through the menu. Just the calls to and from Ray’s number.

“Not helpful,” he said, pocketing the phone but then reconsidering. He pulled it out again. “Let’s see if Ray will answer if we call from his wife’s phone.”

He hit redial. It rang out. No answer.

“Stevenson, check the latest ping on Ray Hollands’ phone.”

“Yes, sir.” Stevenson nodded, already reaching for his own phone as Anderson crouched by the car, one hand braced on the roof, the other scanning the driver’s seat, the ground, the void where the van had idled.

“There it is,” he said, low.

“What?” Trent asked.

“Victor had been in the back seat.” Anderson pointed: clear heavy footprints, deeper than Tessa’s, pressed into the gravel. He traced the steps to the sliding door of the van.

“He put her in the van from the side door,” Anderson observed. “Look, see? Her feet pointed out. He probably bound her, then secured her in the van so he could drive wherever he’s headed.”

Stevenson straightened. “Sir, based on Mr. Hollands’ phone movements, it’s likely they’re staging a meet. He’s moving with purpose.”

“I agree. Where would they do it?”

“Has to be isolated,” Stevenson countered. “Mishkin won’t risk Tessa in public.”

Anderson nodded, resolve hardening. “Let’s regroup at the entrance and map out likely sites. He can’t have gotten far. Call local LEO; see if they have K-9 units to search this section.”

"Do you think he ditched her here?" Stevenson asked.

"He wants what Ray knows. It's all that matters now. He's keeping her alive until he gets it. The evidence: rope, restraint, and he's moving her in the van."

They piled back into the Bureau cars—the tension acute, like a static charge—and raced back to the main entrance.

CHAPTER FORTY-FIVE

Ray arrived at the abandoned Hopter Helicopter compound just shy of twenty minutes after his call with Victor. The main gate, bent and flecked with old paint, gaped open onto a cracked drive. Directly ahead, the main factory stood stripped and battered, its windows shattered, metal siding peeled and puckered as if clawed at by war. Ray hadn't known much about Hopter before today, only that it belonged to the brief, desperate era when the world first needed helicopters and most they sold went to the US military. Only one workable design, one wartime hope, and after which the company folded into a larger firm. This airfield and its two narrow runways were left to weeds. The tarmac bore scars of grass and wildflowers breaking through, sixty-one acres enclosed by dry grass and, farther out, dense tangles of elder, cottonwood, and oak. Looking around, Ray could see why Victor picked this place. Private. Secluded. Here, no one would stumble by accident on whatever Victor wanted to do. Ray eased his car into the lot in front of the factory, backing in for a view of the entrance, his nerves keyed up as he waited for Victor's arrival.

True to his word, Victor appeared almost exactly an hour later, driving the white van up the slope and through the main gate with an urgent rattle of loose parts. Ray watched as the van slowed, drawing up in a straight line toward him. He saw only a single silhouette in the cab—no sign of Tessa. The question grew cold in the pit of his chest as the van rolled to a stop just feet away.

Victor killed the engine and stepped out, posture tense, almost military. He fixed Ray with a look and, with a flick of his hand, motioned him out of the car. Caught in his seatbelt, Ray fumbled for a moment, then forced calm and walked forward.

"Where's Tessa? I want to see Tessa!" The demand spilled out before he could check himself.

Victor didn't answer at first, studying Ray with his head tilted slightly, eyes narrow. "One moment, Mr. Holland. You still understand the agreement?"

"Yes. I'll show you what it does, and you will release Tessa."

"Very good. Come," Victor said, moving to the passenger side of the van. Ray trailed after, heat climbing the back of his neck.

Victor slid the door open, his hand disappearing inside, and half-lifted, half-guided Tessa upright onto the pavement. She blinked in the daylight, hair wild, her eyes rimmed swollen and red.

"Tessa! Are you okay?" Ray demanded, his voice rising as he saw the rope burns, the mess on her clothes.

"I'm scared, Ray, really scared," Tessa cried. Even beneath the fear, Ray saw a glimmer of relief in her face at the sound of his voice.

A surge of anger, strange and bright, ran through Ray. An animal urge to turn and swing at Victor, to take him down right now and be done with it. He clenched his teeth, breath tight, but Victor watched him.

"Now, Mr. Holland. Tessa tells me your machine can fly, yes?"

"Yes, it has flown," Ray managed, his words edged with anger.

"So, you show me, yes?"

"Yes."

"Very good," Victor said, already headed to the back of the van. He opened both rear doors with one practiced movement.

Inside the van, Ray saw it all: GG-1, buckets containing the remaining marble-like "fuel," spools of crumpled plans, two battered notebooks, and the RC controller.

"How does it work? You show me," Victor said.

"It needs a battery."

"You have battery?"

"Yes," Ray replied. He walked back to his car, opened the trunk, lifted out the custom battery, pocketed a screwdriver, and returned.

He set the battery down beside the van. “It needs to be installed inside,” he said.

“Do. I will watch.”

“We need to take it out of the van and place it on the ground, away from the van,” Ray added, letting caution show in his voice. He wanted distance between GG-1 and Tessa—and Victor. “Over there,” Ray pointed, picking a spot on the tarmac a good thirty yards away, with a line-of-sight to the van, but not within easy range.

“I help,” Victor said. He bent to lift, and together they carried GG-1 to the spot Ray had chosen, the unit heavier than it looked. Returning to the van, Ray grabbed the battery and controller. He closed the van’s rear doors, separating Tessa from view and, he hoped, from Victor’s line of sight.

Victor shadowed him as he knelt by GG-1, screwdriver already turning. The screws came out one by one, the access plate set aside. The control board sat exposed, bare wires and contacts clear in the morning light.

“You say this makes it fly?” Victor asked, peering into the machine. “How is this possible?”

“The stones are the fuel,” Ray said, keeping his answer short and flat. Victor’s eyes fixed on the device as if it might bite.

Battery in, wires connected, the machine now primed. But Ray knew better than to trust Victor’s word on anything. A “Plan B” already formed in the back of his mind, half-blind and risky, but it would have to work. He checked his watch, then glanced up, tracing the sun’s arc, calibrating north and south, east and west. The van sat at twelve degrees relative; southwest corner of the factory at an even three hundred degrees. Good. Close enough.

“What now?” Victor broke in.

Ray looked up. “Victor, this is the power switch. It turns on the fuel,” he said, pointing clearly.

“Now, this is a very complicated step,” Ray added, measuring each word for effect. “It takes two people to start the engine. One must operate the controller,” he gestured to the RC unit. "And one person needs to flip this switch and press this button at the same time."

He showed the coin battery slot, a ghost button, just an empty cavity—the trick seemed simple, but Victor wouldn't know. Victor moved to kneel by the northwest edge of GG-1, peering into the circuit.

"What about the controller?" Victor asked.

"A bit more complicated," Ray said, picking it up.

He demonstrated the power switch. "This just needs to be powered on first. The right control handles up and down movement; the left controls orientation and speed."

"Can I run the controls?" Victor's eyes lit for a moment.

"Of course," Ray said, barely hiding his relief. "But first, we need to start the motor."

"Show me the control."

Ray stood, walked around GG-1, and handed Victor the controller, showing the "on/off" and basic stick movements. Right stick for height, left for direction and roll. Victor fumbled, nearly dropped the unit, and Ray caught it.

"You are right; this is most complicated," Victor muttered, handing it back. "Maybe you come help me show this."

Ray didn't argue. "Yes, of course," he lied. "Are you ready?"

Victor crouched, both hands inside the narrow opening, ready to flip the switch and press the phony button. Ray circled to the southwest, careful to keep Victor between himself and the machine and took two steps back for safety. Power on the controller. Maximum throttle.

"Okay, Victor, you can power it on when you're ready."

Victor grinned, returned his focus to GG-1, and with a sudden twist, pressed the button and flipped the switch.

GG-1 ignited with a thunderclap, a red cloud bursting out, the machine rocketing toward the factory. In a split second, the nose sheared the building's corner, tearing metal and glass, and the aftershock of the impact collapsed the weakened wall. Ray ducked instinctively, feeling the wash of air and grit. He heard two heavy thuds, then, echoing across the lot: a scream from the van.

"Ray!" Tessa's voice, sharp, terrified.

"I'm okay!" Ray shouted, scanning for movement.

He looked to the ruins. There, against the ruptured building, lay two halves of a body, a staccato spray of red and the tangle of torn fabric. Above, the bent roof truss hung like a snapped bone, open to the sky. Beyond, a white vapor trail of GG-1 arched up and out, already veering toward the sea, a brief comet in the daylight. At his feet, burnt fragments of plastic, shards of the battery casing—the last traces of what he'd just installed.

For a moment, Ray stood silent, his mind racing ahead. Nothing left but to move. He jogged toward the van. As he rounded the rear, he saw Tessa, still bound but intact, eyes wide, ropes tight on her wrists.

"What happened?" she gasped. "Where's Victor?"

"We're safe. Victor is gone," Ray said, working at the knots behind her.

"What do you mean, Victor is gone?"

"He won't be bothering us anymore."

"What? Did you kill him?"

"I'll explain later," Ray muttered, hands shaking as he freed her wrists.

"We need to call the FBI. Victor kidnapped me."

"I have a plan for the FBI," Ray said.

"A plan? We should just call them and explain everything that happened."

"GG-1 is at the bottom of the Pacific Ocean, and I don't want to explain it to them."

"What do you mean? You launched GG-1?"

"Let's just say Victor had something to do with it and leave it. We know nothing at this point."

"Where's Victor?" Tessa asked, rubbing her wrists.

"Let me put it this way: he squatted in front of GG-1 when it launched. Remember when we launched it the first time? Imagine what happened."

"Oh my God, what happened to him?" She tried to look around the van.

Ray stopped her with a hand. "You don't want to look."

Tessa hesitated, then shouldered past him anyway. As she rounded the back of the van, her eyes widened in shock at the aftermath: two torn halves, blood pooling in the dirt, and shredded fabric that spoke of violence. Ray's heart dropped; he knew what she was about to face. Tessa stared, her expression shifting from horror to something softer, almost sorrowful. Ray could see it in her eyes—the flicker of empathy for the man who had just tried to take her life. She reeled back, her face draining of color, but Ray watched as her breath hitched—not just in fear, but in something deeper. A choked gasp escaped her lips.

"Oh God, what have we done?" she murmured, her voice trembling, as if she mourned not just for herself, but for Victor's lost humanity.

He took a step closer, his own gut churning. Tessa gagged, then vomited, bent over by the van's fender, the horror of the scene overwhelming her. But Ray understood. In that moment of crisis, Tessa wasn't just seeing a monster; she grappled with the fragility of life—her life, and even the life of the man who had threatened it.

"How awful," she gasped, wiping her mouth, a flicker of sorrow still haunting her eyes.

"He kidnapped you, stole my experiment, would probably have killed us both. I don't see it as so awful."

Her expression faltered, the weight of his words—and the reality of what had just happened—settling heavily in the air. "What are we going to tell the FBI?" she asked, eyeing the ruined building.

"We're not. We're leaving this for the FBI to clean up."

Tessa looked at him, uncertain. Ray could see the conflict in her gaze—a mix of fear and something deeper, a sadness for the man who had threatened her life.

"Okay, look, I'll call the FBI. Tell them Victor let us go; we left him at the Hopter Factory. They'll come here in minutes and find all of this."

Even as he spoke, sirens flared in the distance.

"Oh, oh," Ray said, a dry note slipping into his tone. "Time to go. Plan B. Hurry, get in the car."

They dashed for the car, ducked inside, doors slamming.

"Plan B?"

Ray held up his phone, thumb on the power button. He switched it on, then tossed it from the window of the van.

"What's that going to do?" Tessa asked, thrown by the gesture as Ray backed the car around.

"I don't have to call the FBI. They're tracking my phone."

They rolled out, up the drive and through the front gate. Two emergency vehicles were already approaching, lights flashing, sirens fading as they slowed. A fire engine led, an aid car behind. The young crew inside scanned the lot, faces keen with anticipation.

"I bet someone called in the explosion of GG-1 hitting the building," Ray said.

"It was pretty loud."

As they passed, none of the firemen gave the car a second look. Out of sight, Ray steered them home. He could still feel Tessa's lingering shock, the way her gaze had softened, as if grappling with the loss of humanity—even for a man like Victor. The fragility of life hung in the air between them, leaving an unsettling weight in his chest.

CHAPTER FORTY-SIX

They clustered about the battered Ford, three agents and a map splayed wide on the hood, colors fading under the overexposed sky as if the truth they hunted would bleach itself away if they waited too long. Anderson, Stevenson, and Trent—all with their ties askew, eyes locked on the paper grid and each other, waiting for a sign. The urgency of the moment weighed heavily on Anderson; lives were at stake. He couldn't let this slip away like so many cases had before. It came as Stevenson's phone broke the static. He answered, voice clipped, the agent's version of a heartbeat.

"Okay, stand by. Sir, the Hollands' phone just lit up again."

Anderson didn't blink. "Where?"

Stevenson paced half a step, phone pressed close. "Hopter Helicopter Factory."

"Hopter? Where's that?" Anderson asked again, not looking up.

"East Palo Alto. Abandoned for years," Stevenson said.

Anderson nodded once; something in that set his jaw. "Must be where Victor met him. Makes sense. Let's go."

But Stevenson raised a finger, already a step ahead. "Sir, Murray picked up a radio call—a report of an explosion in the Hopter area a few minutes ago."

Twenty minutes later, the four FBI vehicles rolled onto Hopter's cracked tarmac, slowing beneath the broken sign and empty windows. Anderson and Trent led, taking it easy up the drive. Mishkin might be watching; better to enter like ghosts. This remained a delicate situation, and he felt a flicker of protectiveness for the Hollands. The radio squawked to life as Anderson's hand grabbed the mic.

"White van, white van, there he is!"

He didn't wait. "Spotted van, right side, side door open. Johnson, Pommeroy, block the entrance. Move in."

The engines gunned; positions taken, guns drawn, doors flung open, feet crunching on gravel. "Victor! FBI! There's no way out!" Anderson's shout carried across the silence. He chopped his hand, signaling to advance. The agents crept to the open side door, but they found the van empty. Sunlight bounced off nothing but dust.

"Clear," Stevenson barked. Anderson's attention snapped to Connors as she moved west of the van, her posture shifting as she hesitated. He saw her expression harden, and a sense of dread gnawed at him. Following her gaze, he caught sight of a blood trail leading across the lot, dark and ominous.

"Anderson!" Her voice split the air. "Two bodies over here. Lots of blood."

"Dammit," Anderson spat. "Is it Holland?"

Connors moved close, every muscle tensed. "Male Caucasian." She blinked down. "Upper torso only. No legs."

She didn't move until Anderson arrived, slipping on blue gloves. He holstered his gun in the grass and rolled the body from the shoulder. The face: Mishkin. Anderson didn't look surprised.

"It's Mishkin," he confirmed, letting the body flop back to the dirt. The other agents drew closer but eased up; a dead Mishkin was less of a threat.

"What happened here? Where are the Hollands?" Anderson's gaze leapt from fragment to fragment.

"Maybe they escaped," Trent said.

"Perkins, call in ME, ATF, locals. Tell them what we have."

Connors lifted something from the dust. "Found a cell phone. Tire tracks too."

"Hollands'?" Anderson asked.

"Could be," Connors said, hovering ten feet away. "Maybe they ran for it—or were released."

Stevenson jogged in, rope in gloved hands. "Pulled this from the van. Probably used on Mrs. Holland."

"Anything else?" Anderson asked.

"Nada—a couple buckets, wrappers. Mishkin must've been camping in here."

"Find Holland," Anderson gritted. "Perkins, see if you can get an APB out on their car."

Stevenson gestured at the streaks across concrete. “Explosion must’ve killed Mishkin—the one Murray heard about?”

Anderson surveyed the mess. “With blood spatter and the body halved, it was one hell of a blast.”

Stevenson pointed at the blown-out fragments leading up to the main building. “Debris there doesn’t fit.”

Twenty minutes later, the local uniforms arrived: police and homicide; their cars flashing, tape unspooling, notepads filling up. ATF arrived soon after. Anderson kept command, welcoming the extra hands; nothing like a spectacle to get every department moving. Two hours later, the ME finished with Mishkin’s remains, zipping and boxing them, ready for autopsy. An ATF agent, heavyset and wearing a windbreaker, caught Anderson’s eye after tagging the body.

“Anderson?”

“That’s me.”

“Agent Constantine, ATF. Preliminary findings are... odd.”

Anderson gave him a look. “Let’s hear it.”

“Bomb squad twelve years, LA. This is an explosion, no doubt: debris, close-range trauma, and impact scars on the building. Puzzles us, though—no blast residue. IMS says nothing in the air. Zero powder. No burns. Instead, battery fragments, a plate, screws—nothing more.”

Anderson’s face barely moved. “What’s the official line, then?”

“We’ll report what we have. But it’s up to the FBI to draw final conclusions.”

Anderson nodded. “Send me your report. We’ll combine it with ours and go from there.”

Constantine nodded back and walked off into the chaos. Stevenson arrived next, stepping in quickly.

“A call just came from the Holland stakeout. They’re home.”

Anderson’s eyes narrowed. “Take Murray. Have the locals keep them in place—we need to hear what happened.”

# # #

Tessa heard the car pull up, tires crunching on gravel. Thirty minutes of freeway noise still rang in her ears, the memory of taillights and traffic jams fresh from their escape. Now two well-dressed men exited a two door sedan after parking beside the Palo Alto cruiser that had kept watch over their house. She smoothed her white knit blouse, her face still pale from the morning's terror, and followed Ray to the door.

Ray opened it, his wariness evident but polite. “Mr. Holland, Special Agent Stevenson, Agent Murray. FBI. May we come in?”

With a nod, Ray led them to the living room. Tessa watched his gestures stay gentle, controlled, but she could see the tension in his shoulders. The adrenaline from the morning still coursed through her own veins.

Stevenson locked onto her immediately. “Victor Mishkin kidnapped you?”

She nodded, the memory sharp as broken glass. “He hid in my car, held a knife to my throat.”

“Then what happened?” Stevenson prompted, pen poised over his notepad.

“He waited, lost Ray on the road, made me double back, took me to his van. Tied me up. Called Ray from my phone. Said if Ray didn't come and teach him how to use the device, he'd kill me.”

Stevenson scratched his pencil against the paper, the sound grating. “Mr. Holland, was this when you called the FBI?”

Ray shifted, his tone defensive but controlled. “Yes.”

“Why not wait for us?”

“Victor said to meet him alone. He'd release Tessa if I helped. I thought it was safer this way.”

Stevenson bored in, his eyes sharp. “Mr. Holland, what does your device do?”

Ray hesitated, piecing together his story. “Both devices were failed prototypes. It started with this stone; it moved like a Mexican jumping bean. I tried to add more, get it to move further." Tessa's glance flickered toward Ray, but Stevenson remained focused on him.

"When you say move, you mean fly?" Stevenson asked, his tone calm but sharp.

"No, not really. Casing's heavy; I just hoped for movement," Ray replied, his gaze steady.

"So, what happened at the meet?"

"I brought the battery, showed Mishkin how to hook it up. Walked him through the buttons. He let us go."

Stevenson's tone shifted, a slight edge creeping in. "Then you powered up your phone and left it at Hopter."

Ray shrugged. "I was in a rush. Surprised he let us go. I wanted to get Tessa out before he changed his mind."

"So you dropped the phone, and it powered back on?" Stevenson pressed, scanning Ray's expression for any hint of deception.

"I guess so. Did you catch Mishkin?"

"Mishkin's dead. We think your device killed him."

Tessa's hand flew to her mouth, her eyes widening. The shock hit her like a physical blow-Mishkin, dead? After everything?

"Your device may have exploded," Stevenson added, letting the weight of the statement linger. "Mishkin might've actually saved your lives. It could have happened to you."

Ray took a breath, weaving his response tight. "You may be right."

Stevenson narrowed his gaze. "So, you didn't see anything while there, or hear an explosion?"

"No," both Hollands said at once. "We left fast."

"Were you aware your device could harm Mishkin?" Stevenson asked, his pen hovering above the page.

"He stole it. I had no idea what it did. It was experimental, no instructions," Ray bristled.

"Did you warn him of risks?"

"I gave him the battery and flipped the switch. First tests were failures. Totally unpredictable."

"Did you tell him what it had done before?"

"No," Ray replied tersely.

"So, it was a tragic accident?"

Ray's tone rose, the edge clear. "He kidnapped my wife, threatened us. He stole dynamite and lit a match. Careless accident by a thief and murderer. You should be glad he's dead."

"Ray," Tessa interjected softly, a warning in her voice.

"Sorry. These questions make it sound like you're blaming us."

Stevenson raised a placating hand. "Mr. Holland, we're not accusing you. Reports go to the DA, but honestly, this will stay under wraps. We're closing loose ends. Are we done?"

"Just one more: Do you have a second device, same as the one which killed Mishkin?" Stevenson asked, his eyes sharp.

Ray tensed, his answer slow. "Yes."

"We may need to check it for safety," Stevenson said, watching Tessa closely.

That struck a match inside her. Tessa jumped in, her voice hard, words chosen like tools. "The second device is inert. Completely different construction. Your scientists at the FBI wouldn't know how it works, just like Mishkin didn't. If it was dangerous, I wouldn't let Ray have it in our house-and if you took it, we'd just build another. You can't stop science, Mr. Stevenson. You don't understand what we do, not at home, not at work. So send your questions up the chain. But if you try anything against us, our integrity, or our property, we'll go public about what happened with the two agents you sent here who failed to protect us."

Stevenson held up both hands, trying to project calm. "We're not taking anything. But you might have more people like Mishkin coming, trying to steal your work. We can help."

Ray's face remained unreadable, a tight line forming around his mouth. "We'll take our chances. Safer here than with you."

Stevenson shook his head, frustration creeping in. "Don't underestimate us."

"Your Bureau is about chasing criminals, not science," Ray shot back, his voice firm.

Tessa slapped her thigh, her fiery determination evident. "Maybe if you dig into Mishkin, you'll find who else is interested."

Stevenson maintained eye contact, sensing the tension in the room. "We're working the case. Laubner's involved, too. If you see anything, tell us-but don't discuss this at work; it could blow the investigation."

The mention of Laubner seemed to stiffen both Ray and Tessa. Tessa felt the weight of their concerns pressing down, knowing security seemed paramount.

Stevenson nodded to Murray, who finished jotting down notes. "All for now. We may be back."

"Call first," Tessa snapped, but the agents didn't respond. They left, Stevenson leading the way as Ray followed them to the door. Tessa remained on the couch, her hands anxiously working her nails, eyes distant.

She watched Stevenson shoot one last glance back at them before stepping outside. The FBI car pulled away, and through the window she caught sight of a police cruiser still stationed across the street.

# # #

"Looks like our friends are staying on," Ray said, shutting the door behind him. In the living room, Tessa slouched on the couch, looking wilted.

"I'm ready for a vacation," she said, her voice heavy.

"Vacation? We haven't been at work in days."

She snorted. "Has this felt like a vacation?"

"Vegas did."

"If only we'd planned it."

He dropped down beside her, squeezing her hand. "What are you thinking?"

Tessa shrugged, her gaze distant. "More time together. Less GG-2. Let it go for a while."

Ray considered her words, the weight of the situation settling in. "GG-2's future is dim. The FBI took the last stones; they're not coming back. GG-1's destroyed. The only way forward is new stones—from Washington State. It could be years before I get more."

Tessa sat up, arms crossed over her belly. "Can you make more?"

Ray shook his head, feeling frustration rise. “The originals were a fluke—a hundred-million-dollar accident. No way I could repeat it.”

She held a sly smile. “You have Laubner Labs and your brain, which counts for a lot.”

He saw her point, a flicker of hope igniting. “Maybe I could use the gear at work to reverse-engineer the stone’s structure and find a cheaper path.”

“See? I told you so.” She grinned wide, her enthusiasm infectious.

He nodded, feeling lighter already. “There’s time.”

“Not as much as you think,” she countered, her tone shifting.

He cocked his head. “How’s that?”

With a gentle hand, she rested on her tummy, slow circles tracing her skin. “Three mouths to feed. We’ll need our jobs.”

His frown deepened. “Three?”

Tessa’s eyes sparkled. “We’re having a baby.”

Ray blinked, startled. “Wait, what? You’re sure?”

She laughed, unguarded now, the sound a balm for his worry. “Let me show you.” She tugged him by the hand, leading him upstairs into whatever new future awaited them.

CHAPTER FORTY-SEVEN

Anderson hunched over a desk in the cramped FBI mobile unit parked amid the sodium glare at the Hopter Helicopter site. The night had dropped its curtain; outside, the generators growled, drowning out the hush that had wrapped the scene hours before. The floodlights painted the yard in harsh white, ghosting every edge and movement. At the trailer door—a sharp rap, and Stevenson and Murray ducked inside, closing out the noise.

"How's it coming?" Stevenson kept his coat on, eyes flickering over the scattered folders.

"I have the first pass from ATF and forensics. We'll get full reports in a few days." Anderson tapped the stack in front of him, not looking up.

"Anything you can tell us yet?" Stevenson asked, planting himself across from Anderson.

Anderson's hand made a slow circle in the air, as if stirring the wreckage of the case. "Still sorting through the mess if that's what you're after. What did you get from the Hollands?"

Murray came forward and handed over a summary. "Holland says Mishkin promised Mrs. Holland's release once he received the device components and operating instructions. They left the premises immediately after; didn't see anything else."

Anderson's fingers drummed once, then stopped. "So what was Mishkin supposed to do with the device? What was it for?"

"Holland claims it was only a prototype—and failed completely."

Anderson's lips drew into a hard line. His mind raced, piecing together the fragments of this chaotic puzzle. "See the problem, Stevenson? We have a dead suspect—a murderer and kidnapper, with no way to question him. And the last two people to see him alive didn't get a look at whatever he tried with the device. This doesn't shed light on today or the weeks before—how did we let it come to this?"

"Sorry, sir."

"Don't be sorry. Get me answers." Anderson slapped the Holland report onto the table, papers fanning out like a deck of cards. "We're on the clock. AD Mark Brown will want this sewn up before the week's over." He scanned the two agents, then waved them down into seats across from him. "Here. Preliminary ATF report." He slid the folder to Stevenson. "And here's the forensic prelim." The pages shifted from hand to hand, the rhythm of review overtaking the hum outside. Murray scribbled quick notes, pencil snapping faintly against his pad.

Anderson didn't wait for them to finish. "I don't even need the coroner's report to know what it'll say: blunt force trauma to the lower torso, snapped at the fifth lumbar; instant death from blood loss and organ rupture. Then a few lines about early-stage lung disease, probably from smoking."

Stevenson flipped the page. "Should we impound Holland's other device for analysis—to figure out what really triggered today's explosion?"

"On what grounds? Holland says the second device is totally different. Mishkin's dead; that's all we're sure of. Why, we don't know. If Brown starts poking holes, we'll be left holding the bag."

Murray interjected. "What about the build-up to the murder? Mishkin killed Sommers, Fitz, and Bentz—and we don't know why yet. Johnson and Pommeroy's report ties Bentz to a Moscow weapons trader. There's also a Laubner sales rep with travel records to Moscow—and a lifestyle that doesn't line up with his salary. Possible payoffs. Two Moscow firms could be fronts for the trading."

Anderson shook his head, a brief flicker of wryness crossing his face. "We're not flying to Moscow, Agent."

"Something else, sir. Baker International, Laubner's supplier. The site where Bentz, Sommers, and Fitz were last together, on a fake protection order. Johnson interviewed the plant manager, who gave false leads about Laubner staff. Now he's missing."

Anderson's attention sharpened. "Missing how?"

"Took off right after the interview; never came back. Days now. Nothing at his home, no sign at work. Ex-wife and kids are in New York but haven't heard from him. Plus, Baker International supplies one of those two Moscow firms we think are connected to arms and intellectual property theft. It all feels too tight to ignore."

Anderson pressed his palms to the table, as if steadying a chopper on a rocky pad. "That logic better pay off quick. We have threads intertwining here—if we don't follow them carefully, we risk losing our grip. To me, this sounds like a heap of speculation—but IOD can chase the international tangle; it's their wheelhouse. We stick to the evidence here."

Stevenson nodded. "I read Connors's report on Bentz and the Senge agent. Bentz was terrified of coming forward; didn't want to involve the FBI. He had a file on Aleksandr Kozlov, knew his methods. Kozlov and Mishkin—the elder Dimitri, not Victor here—competing in espionage and weapons trade. As you know, Dimitri is Victor's father and used to work at Laubner. So: was Victor getting payback for his father, or was Dimitri blocking Kozlov from Laubner's secrets?"

Anderson cut in. "Mishkin wanted into Laubner again. It tracks. Bentz's connections to Kozlov led Mishkin to the Hollands. With word about Ray's device, Victor could've planned to blackmail the Hollands or fence the thing through Moscow. Neither worked out. Bentz knew Kozlov was after him, especially after Mishkin killed his brother and buried the facts. Mishkin knew about the Kozlov–Bentz tie—and when Sommers and Fitz got in his way, he took them out. If Kozlov hears Mishkin's dead, he'll be celebrating—but he still has Dimitri to contend with."

Anderson felt the weight of the investigation pressing down. This had moved beyond the Hollands—it was now a network of espionage that had cost lives. He couldn't let it go unnoticed.

Stevenson looked up. "Will it be enough for AD Brown?"

Anderson's features shifted with a restrained hint of amusement. "I don't see another story that fits. We'll move the Baker, Bentz, Kozlov, and Dimitri Mishkin leads to IOD headquarters in DC. Our focus is today, though the mechanism's still a mystery. And the Hollands—they're collateral. Leave them be, for now."

With one final glance at the case files, he felt the familiar blend of exhaustion and urgency. The night pressed in, but the pieces aligned—even if the full picture remained frustratingly elusive. The three men sat together in the humming light, maps and case files between them, as night pressed in around the unit.

EPILOGUE

Special Agent Anderson wrapped up the Palo Alto investigation a week later and took the next red-eye to Washington, DC. The plane's cabin lights dimmed as he spread crime scene photos across his tray table, studying them one last time before landing. Even before his first meeting with IO Division Director Jason Hooper, he sensed the clock ticking; too much paper trail, too many open items. The transfer of the Baker International, Bentz, Koslov, and Mishkin cases to IO went smoothly, at least on the surface.

Then, a week later, IO circled back with an update on Baker International: Mark Jones, plant manager, still missing. No sign. The IO team, along with IRS agents, were also tracking Terry Sanders of Laubner. Sanders had vanished, too. According to State Department cables, Sanders had managed to slip past Russian authorities at Moscow Airport. The Bureau reacted: Sanders' assets in the US real estate and stock totaling $1.2 million—frozen. Worse, someone picked up a large transfer of funds, just days prior to Sanders' departure, to a Swiss account.

Anderson delivered his findings to Assistant Director Mark Brown in a windowless conference room which smelled of stale coffee. Stevenson's report and his own sat side by side. Brown, reading, showed sympathy for the Holland family, but also a contained frustration, the kind which simmered beneath the surface, about the inability to bring the instigators of three agent deaths to justice. His jaw clenched as he closed the folder. The Assistant Director accepted their conclusions: the Bureau would leave the Holland family alone but keep the security detail in place for a few more months. Anderson agreed, relief washing over him.

Three weeks later, Ray and Tessa Holland settled into a quiet routine, both returning to their jobs, cautiously looking forward to family life. Tessa's morning sickness had subsided, and Ray couldn't help but smile at the baby furniture catalogs she left open on the kitchen counter. As he logged two controlled hover tests in the reinforced garage workshop he'd constructed, he pushed himself to acquire the remaining stones from the hazardous storage facility in Washington State. The thought of the GG devices moving toward production filled him with hope, yet he kept this dream to himself, even from Tessa, cherishing the balance they had begun to build together.

Made in the USA
Las Vegas, NV
05 June 2026

47640382R00204